SHOT
TO
DEATH
WITH
PEARLS

R B MARCHANT

The first person to send in the correct answers to the movie quotes and the relevant movie they come from will receive the prize of a vintage mystery movie poster.

Please send entries to :-

R B Marchant
Mail box 306
28A Church Road
STANMORE
Middlesex
HA7 4AW

CLASSIFICATION: Fiction

A CIP catalogue record for this book is available from the British Library.

Printed and bound in Great Britain.

Published in Great Britain by
United Press Limited.
2011
ISBN 978-0-85781-063-2
© R B Marchant 2011

www.unitedpress.co.uk

What would it pleasure me to have my throat cut
With diamonds? Or to be smothered
With Cassia? Or to be shot to death with pearls?

"The Duchess of Malfi"
By John Webster

6

- 1 -

Jack Vettriano's exhibition at the Portland Gallery was packed. People who crowded around Detective Inspector Lancaster barely gave him a chance to view the pictures. Lancaster rarely had time to go to exhibitions. But he made up his mind that this one was on his hit list come what may. For Lancaster, Jack Vettriano painted movies. That's what they were. Moments in the movies. He remembered the moment when Glenn Ford walked into a room and saw Rita Hayworth in "Gilda". A glorious sort of film noir full of sexual excitement and obsession. Things he used to think about when the Jazz singer lived with him. Things he didn't often get time to think about any more. He waited patiently while the two women in front of him endlessly discussed the picture they liked.

He needed to get close up to look at the image that told him so much about himself. The painting showed a man in an evening dress standing behind a film projector. There was a beautiful girl seated in front of him. A girl with thick black hair, wearing a black dress and a white collar round her neck. She was holding a cigarette and watching a film. The smoke was curling up, filtering through the light of the projector. Lancaster imagined it was the jazz singer sitting there. The painting was called "An Imperfect Past".

He tried to work out why. What was imperfect? The two of them sitting there in the dark. Did their relationship rely on imagination and pretence? Had their past been bad? Well, the jazz singer wasn't around now and he was the one sitting in the dark. He stared at the picture for a long time. Then before he could stop himself, he did something stupid. He went over to the girl at the desk, and pointing to the picture said "I'll have it". The only excuse he could make to himself was he didn't buy the original but a silk screen print. Crown would call him an idiot and it would hang about on his credit card for years. But something about the whole idea of the picture made him feel good.

He simply had to have it. He was looking at himself and the jazz singer. He handed over his card and gave the girl his name.

"Detective Inspector Dana Lancaster."

She looked up, "Always thought detectives were out looking for murderers," she smiled.

"Well this one's a sucker for the movies."

****

Just as Lancaster had dropped off in front of "Outlaw Josie Wales" he heard a ringing in his ears. He opened one eye and picked up the phone, said "Damn" and looked at the blue screen.

"Sir, wake up. It's me, Crown."

"What the hell are you phoning me at this hour for? You're supposed to be at a party."

"I've been to the party. I'm home and it's one o'clock in the morning. Look at your watch. You'd better wake up. We have to get down to East Wood right away. There's been a shooting."

Lancaster turned off the television.

"East Wood?" Lancaster roused himself. "Where?"

"A house called *The Badgers*"

Lancaster often wondered who thought up these house names. If it wasn't *Badgers* it was *Squirrels,* or *Crow's Nest.*

"Probably some kind of shot gun accident," Crown continued. "A young woman is definitely dead." He knew if he used one of Lancaster's pet phrases he might get him in the right frame of mind. "Seems her neighbour found her early this morning. The neighbour heard loud noises, so she went next door to have a look.

"Nosy neighbours eh? Who was the neighbour? Man, woman or child? My theory is that everyone is a potential murderer."

Crown hadn't heard that theory before. It was one o'clock in the morning and he didn't want to start thinking about theories. But he wondered. He should have been wondering about murder. Surely at one in the bloody morning Lancaster couldn't be throwing him film quotes. The man had hardly woken up. There was no time now to think about it. Lancaster was mumbling something into the phone.

"Say what you like Crown; they're all too old to murder anyone in East Wood. They couldn't hit a squirrel with a walking stick," he chuckled.

"See you in fifteen minutes," Crown answered. He knew what Lancaster was like when he woke up in front of one of his movies. He only hoped it wasn't Hitchcock; if it was he would suffer for it. He scribbled down 'theories' on a scrap of paper near the phone.

Lancaster grumbled as he got up from the armchair. He closed his eyes for a minute. He had just come back from a week's holiday in Venice and should have stayed there longer if he had any sense.

He looked at his watch. Crown was always on time.

Lancaster shuffled upstairs in his slippers and opened his wardrobe pulling out the first tie he could find. Lancaster was the one who was always late. He went downstairs with the tie in his hand and opened the front door. Crown was standing on the doorstep.

"You're bloody lucky it was Clint Eastwood," Lancaster said.

"Did you go to the Vettriano exhibition?" Crown asked.

"Yea, I popped in, was too crowded to see anything. I'll have to go back."

****

After the party Clare would be gone. She would slip away and meet René in the narrow lane behind the house. He would be waiting in the car. Clare had only been in love once before and that was with Cliff. But Cliff left her after they were engaged and all she had was his ruby engagement ring which she always kept with her.

She heard from a friend that Cliff had married not long afterwards, and she prayed his wife would die and Cliff would come back to her. She imagined him banging on the front door begging to come back. But he never came back, and he was gone forever. That was why she married Trevor. But things like that happened when you were twenty one, and she married Trevor on the re-bound to punish Cliff. But she only punished herself. before she married Trevor she always hoped someone else would come along and she wouldn't have to go through with it. But no one came along. She suffered for years after Cliff deserted her, and even on her wedding day her Father implored her to cancel the wedding. He never liked the Austins.

"They're not your kind of people Clare," her Father said. "Nasty mean lot."

But she married Trevor and the years proved her Father right. She could isolate the moment he told her about the Austins'. Well the hell with Trevor, and the nagging image of Cliff that dogged her all her life. Sometimes she hated Cliff more than she hated Trevor.

But now she was thinking of René. She had been with Trevor for ten long years. Trevor with his never ending meanness, and his constant questioning.

Now she could reverse her life and start counting backwards to number one. And it wouldn't be with Cliff, but with René Valmere. This birthday would be a hell of a lot better than her twenty first.

From the terrace, she could hear a faint sound of the jazz group playing Jobim. Trevor said he couldn't see any point in making a party at home. Why couldn't they go out for dinner? Then he said that no one in their right minds would want to have a jazz trio, when most people liked pop music. And what about the enormous expense of the catering staff? Well he could go to hell now.

This would be one evening when he wouldn't be checking up on her. He had become so possessive over the last few months she sometimes wondered if he might know about René. She had been so careful every time they met. She told him she had evening classes, and girl friends dinners, and shopping trips. One slip up and she was done for. This was something he would never find out about.

She dropped her red satin dress over her head and watched it softly ripple over her full breasts and slim waist. The dress was cut up one side showing a long leg. Then she opened her ribbon drawer and brought out a bright yellow bow attached to a slide. Did she look too over excited? Her eyes were alight. She let her silver bangles slide up her arm, and clipped the yellow bow into her hair.

From her bedroom window she heard the waitresses chattering and laughing as they laid the tables round the pool. Trevor wanted the pool tiled in blue and gold. Even then he was penny pinching, and in the end the pool was tiled in white squares. She never used it, which always irritated him. She said she didn't want to swim in a pantry.

How many times she wanted to see Trevor drown in his own pool. She imagined him going under and little bubbles coming up to the surface. He couldn't swim. A man who built swimming pools and couldn't swim, that was a laugh. She felt pleasantly warm at the thought of him floating on top of the pool, all nice and dead, with a few strands of his hair showing between the bubbles.

She turned away from the mirror, closed the drawer, and decided to change the colour of her lipstick. Bright red would go better with her dress.

Money she supposed was the reason most people stayed together. Wasn't it sometimes love? Still it didn't do to think of that word love.

She watched the waitresses arrange the glasses and serviettes on the bright green and yellow cloths. Speaking to René this morning, she felt close to desperation.

Trevor had invited his family to the party. Well she would carry off this evening if they were here or not.

She looked long and slim, and her silver bangles tinkled as she moved her arm. Then she went to a small drawer in her desk... Tonight she would wear her pearls. The pearls René had given her. They were becoming more daring. She managed to get away last week saying she had theatre tickets to celebrate her friend Elena's birthday. They met at a hotel for dinner.

"You are like champagne," he said to her. "All bubbly."

"You make me sound like an advert," she laughed softly.

"Come on give me your glass," he laughed in response.

She watched him as he opened a box he was holding. She didn't care what was in the box ... as long as he was there in front of her where she could look at him.

What an idiot she had become since she met him, foolish and reckless. She was like a school girl.

She watched him as he pulled the ribbon off the box, opened it and lay the box on her dinner plate. Clare could see little white beads shimmering in tissue paper. Then he picked up the string of pearls in his slim fingers and before she could stop him, he dropped the string of pearls into the glass of champagne. That was what she liked about him, everything he did was so unexpected. Sometimes in full view of everyone, he would kiss her. She became fascinated with the pearls in the champagne. Who had ever seen a glass of pearls? It was crazy. Then he handed her the ice cold glass, with its sticky, sugared edges.

"I dare you to put them on," he laughed again.

Sometimes she wondered if they were in some sort of valley and there was no one else but them, and the only way out was to climb even higher up over the mountains. His voice always made her loose her footing.

Her fingers felt icy as she lifted the pearly out of the glass.

"You are something I never thought I would have," she said earnestly looking at him, trying to tell him how she felt.

She clasped the pearls to her neck just as she was holding them now.

"To hell with the dinner," he had said to her. "Let's go and drink the champagne off the pearls."

It was all so easy being with René, that it seemed to be the only thing in her life that came to her without effort.

She met him through the newspaper. She couldn't remember when she started putting advertisements in the paper. She used to read 'Love Lines' every week with no interest. Then one week end one of the names caught her eye. It was signed Cliff. Surely it couldn't be the Cliff she knew all those years ago. Out of sheer curiosity she answered it leaving her mobile number. They arranged to meet in the local hotel. But it wasn't Cliff, it was just another man. The man was quite taken with her and they went for dinner. It became a habit. She was becoming an expert on men who hated their wives, men who had left their wives, men who wanted to take her away to Cuba, and men who's idea of a walk was a quick trip to the bedroom. She knew she was hooked and could keep on doing it. She never thought she would find anyone worthwhile and she knew it might eventually lead to disaster, but she had learned to be very careful. Then there was the night she met René.

She phoned the number he put in the paper and listened to his voice. He had an accent, and she thought he sounded French. His voice captivated her. She left him a message asking him to meet for a drink out of town at a small Inn she knew about called 'The Stag'. She would be wearing pastel blue, with a large black bow clipped at the back of her hair. He phoned her mobile leaving a brief message saying 'yes'.

She knew of course, as soon as she met him. It was like striking a match, and making a yellow flame.

****

After the party when everyone had left, Rod Stewart was still singing Sinatra's numbers.

Even Mrs Bolton who lived next door loved Rod Stewart. She had been to Clare's party and was already tucked up in bed when she got up to close the window. Though she loved Rod Stewart she couldn't sleep with all that racket. Surely by now it was late enough for the music to stop. It just went on and on, and seemed to get louder and louder. Mrs Bolton opened the window wider and leaned out. She could see Clare's house in darkness, and she could hear the music droning on.

Just then there was a sudden loud noise that made her jump. It sounded like a fire cracker. And following swiftly came another two loud cracks. My God she thought, whatever was that. Had a car back fired? But there were no cars outside at all. If she wasn't careful she would turn into one of those nosy neighbours she read about in the papers.

And yet they were not ordinary noises, they were louder than the noises she was used to, and more frightening.

Still, maybe she ought to go round there and see what it was. It could be anything. She would never sleep.

She went into the bathroom, taking her warm dressing gown and wrapped it around her. Then she put on her flat shoes. She found Clare's keys in her dressing table drawer, and stuffed them into her dressing gown pocket. She went downstairs and out of the house, crossing the front lawn.

The music was still playing. As she got nearer to the house it seemed to be much louder. Now she was here she felt a little apprehensive. You're an idiot Ada she told herself again, going out into the night like this all on your own. Why anybody could be in there. The French windows were still open and the curtains were pulled back.

She should have phoned first to speak to Clare, not taken things into her own hands like this...

She moved towards the house and went inside through the French windows. Reaching across the curtains she turned on the lights. Her heart stopped beating.

Clare was lying on the living room floor. Oh my God. She was naked, and just lying there all hunched up. Ada Bolton moved a little closer.

"Oh no," she screamed out loud. "Oh no," Clare Austin was in a pool of blood.

Ada put her hand to her mouth. There was blood all over the floor. Clare was bleeding. Had Clare shot herself?
That must have been what she heard. A scream began to come up from Ada's chest and lodged itself in her windpipe.

The string of pearls that had been round Clare's neck had been neatly sliced in two, leaving two halves of the necklace balancing oddly across her naked body. Very slowly some of the pearls fell off the string and dropped onto the floor sticking in Clare's bright red blood.

Ada Bolton ran screaming from the house.

- 2 -

An invitation was propped up on the mantlepiece between a pair of porcelain cases and a photograph of a crowd of people with their arms round each other. Crown recognised Clare Austin in the photograph. It was almost Monday morning, and the room still smelt of smoke and drink, and there was a dead woman lying on the living room floor. She was what Inspector Dana Lancaster liked to call, 'definitely dead'.

"Definitely dead, Crown," he mused to his sergeant, tapping his finger on a nearby table, lifting up and looking at some of the ash trays.

"I'd say so sir," Crown answered taking out a notebook and pencil. He didn't know what to make of it. A dead woman lying in a pool of blood with a string of pearls round her neck, only the string of pearls had been cut in two. Some of the pearls had fallen off the string, and were lodging in the small pools of blood that drained out of the woman.

Lancaster walked over to the window looking into the garden, then turned to survey the room. Outside the sky was just turning from black to a pale grey.

"Why don't people murder each other at a decent hour, Crown?"

Crown gave a massive yawned answer.

Lancaster bent down, picking up an empty bottle from the floor, idly turning it round and round... 'Lanson Black Label' Champagne. He dropped the bottle back on the floor.

"Glasses all over the tables, and cigarette ends. That will keep them busy at the lab," he said.

"We'd better speak to the woman next door sir, the Constable says she's terribly agitated."

"Is that the woman who phoned the police?"

"That's right. She also said she knew there was going to be a party here because she was invited. She went to the party at about 8 o'clock, she stayed until about twelve o'clock then left. She said when she left all the lights were still on and she could still hear the music. Damn loud it was too."

"And?" Lancaster said, taking the invitation from Crown's fingers.

"I think we'll have to get her quietened down a bit so we can get some more out of her. The constable has sent for her daughter."

"So Crown," Lancaster read the invitation. "It seems that Clare and Trevor Austin invited their friends to a cocktail party at seven thirty in the evening. Did you happen to ask the woman next door if she knew if anyone left the party late? Maybe she likes looking out of windows. If she does we're in luck."

"She didn't know what time the party was over. Or who was the last to leave."

Lancaster looked decidedly puzzled. "Open the windows wider Crown for God's sake."

Crown pushed open the windows as far as he could. There were windows on both sides of the room. The French windows led to the front lawn.

"Well sir, she knew everyone was invited to the party for 7.30 because she received an invitation from the couple herself. Name of Austin."

"I can see that Crown, I can see that."

Crown watched the expression on the Inspector's face. He often wondered why Lancaster never found anyone else to live with after the jazz singer left.

Lancaster was a handsome man, but far too pale, he needed a bit of colour in his face, his blonde hair made him look like one of those old time film stars he was always rattling on about. Crown thought he looked like that fellow in 'Gone With The Wind'. The one Scarlet was in love with. How she could love that wishy-washy Ashley instead of Clark Gable God knows. Still he never could work out things about love. Half the time he didn't know why he put up with Eric. But Eric cooked and cleaned the place up. He was out with the bloody hoover from morn till night. He wondered why Lancaster never threw him a quote from 'Gone With the Wind'.

Anyway that Howard fellow was a weed next to Lancaster. Heaven help the fool who might try to tackle him, he'd be pinned to the wall before you could say definitely dead. Power should be Lancaster's middle name. Lancaster was difficult to fathom. His thought process was totally filmic. Some days he worked in black and white, and others in colour. Lancaster always told Crown 'I stick my neck out for nobody', and didn't Crown know it.

Sometimes he was in a Bogart vein; other times he was in Hitchcock or Eastwood. Crown reckoned Lancaster mostly stuck to Warner Bros, MGM or Paramount. If ever he was lent out to another station he would never be able to work with anyone else.

He saw every case now in black and white or colour. Sometimes there was a double feature with two murders. Eric was always telling him to ask for a transfer. Get away, work with someone normal, sort himself out; make life easier for himself. But he couldn't do that now. He just went from day to day with his sharp eyes looking for clues, working like bloody MGM with early morning calls, listening to Lancaster's mad quotes. Still he could always be an extra in a film, if he really decided to chuck it all up.

Crown often reckoned he should be a bit more like Lancaster. He'd made a few mistakes with suspects before, under rating them. He watched as Lancaster went for his cigarettes. Crown carried on, "The woman's name is Ada Bolton. The one who lived next door. She says she wasn't the first to arrive at the party. There were a few already there when she arrived ... she told the PC she always feels embarrassed if she arrives too early." He closed his notebook.

"Ah!" Lancaster murmured. "Let's look at the body," Lancaster said bending down over the dead woman. He bent over her red lips and sniffed her mouth.

"Looks like a kind of old fashioned murder, eh?" Lancaster frowned.

Strangely Crown never through of murder as old fashioned. He wondered if that holiday in Italy did his boss any good at all. Lancaster looked down at the naked woman.

"Propped up on a pillow. Must have done that with her arm damn quickly. Then she's lying sideways on a blanket. Almost as if she's looking at us. Was she on a blanket when she was shot? Or was she rolled onto it afterwards? Her eyes are wide open."

"There's only a bit of blood on the blanket sir, the rest is on the floor with the pearls."

"Beautiful woman Crown. What a waste. Eyes like a baby's. She looks so innocent like this, as if she didn't know what hit her. She's lovely enough to be a model. Look at those cheekbones," he put his fingers to her lips. "Lip gloss," he said. "Who do you suppose she's kissed Crown?"

Crown turned towards the Inspector. "Be nice if we could cover her up with the blanket sir. You know."

Lancaster remarked, "When a dame gets killed she doesn't worry about how she looks. Shot. Three bullet holes. Shot to death unless we find out otherwise."

Crown thought maybe he was getting too old these days to work out two puzzles at once. The murder on, and Lancaster's habit of drifting off into film quotes whenever the fancy took him.

"What's the bet this time Guv?"

"Lunch at wherever you want?"

"Right."

Not only did Crown have to figure out why dead bodies were lying around, he had to work out what film the quotes came from. It was like a game with them. Two years ago Crown got all the quotes and they went to lunch at Oslo Court. That was his favourite place really... Lancaster would ask him sooner or later if he had any answers.

"Thought of that line yet Crown?" It was like a quiz show with no money involved. Crown was continually folding the papers in his pad in half. Half for the murder, and half for the film quotes. He used up more notebooks than anyone in the station.

"Selling these on the side Crown?" They asked him. He sighed as he folded his yellow paper in half. If only he could think about it for a second or two. Where had he heard it before? Something about a dame? Most black and white movies had dames and broads in them. It must be a black and white. But there was a dame in 'Bullets over Broadway'. To hell with it.

Lancaster gave him a gleeful look. Then his expression changed as he looked down at the victim.

"Naked, with a string of pearls round her neck. Look at the ends of the string Crown. Just hanging there round her throat. Some of the pearls are on the floor. Looks like the string was pulled apart by force."

"Maybe they were cut."

"That's possible." He carefully lifted up the end of the string.

"You're right Crown, You're right. Sliced in two. Now why would anyone want to put a string of pearls round a dead woman's throat?"

"Maybe they were cut before."

"I don't think so Crown. I don't think so. She couldn't have staggered around shot, with a string of pearls in two pieces. There's a wound in her head, and chest, and one in her arm. Look at those bangles. Almost up to her elbow. The wound in her arm almost missed its mark but didn't quite. She must have lifted her arm to ward off the bullet. Why the hell were the pearls cut?

Can't see anything left around. The killer must have cut the pearls and taken the knife with him. Or the scissors. We'll check and see if anything has been left behind by mistake, though I doubt it. Have you checked the doors and windows?"

"Yes sir. All open. Some of the upstairs windows were open too. She must have been waiting for her husband to come home, so she didn't bother to lock up. The back door was definitely unlocked."

"So where did the killer hide himself?"

"Hide sir?"

"Well," exclaimed Lancaster. "Doors open, or should I say unlocked. Windows unlocked, easy for a killer. So where did he enter the room? Get the boys to look round the house and see if anything has been disturbed or turned over. Was the killer looking for something and did she try to stop him? To me it doesn't look like it. Maybe the killer was at the party himself Crown, *or* did he arrive later and come in by the French windows."

Lancaster knew that women's beads always broke when they least expected it. But it wasn't so easy to pull them apart so they had to be cut. With what?

"Sir," Crown said. "Whoever did it didn't mind the sight of her stripped naked did he? There must be a reason for that. Maybe deliberately, to humiliate her. But where was the husband or even a boyfriend? The husband wasn't her when Mrs Bolton found her."

"So where is he now?"

He'd seen enough cases to know it could be either jealous husband who finds his wife with her lover. Or jealous lover who can't bear his loved one to be with her husband. The computations were never ending.

"Where indeed. There seems to be a husband according to the invitation. Where the hell did he get to. He's certainly not here where he should be at this time of night. Or should I say morning."

"Seems strange there's no one around," Crown said. "It's three o'clock in the morning. We'd better check and see just where this Trevor is, or if there's a boyfriend. I wonder if she arranged to meet anyone after the party?"

"Yes, good idea, maybe she got her old man out of the way on some ruse," Lancaster answered wearily. "But I'm not satisfied, it's too obvious."

"Maybe she was naked before she was killed sir."

"What, running around the house naked with all the doors and windows open, I don't think so. But there could have been a reason. Let's look around and see if we can spot any clothes. Dressing gown, dress, shoes, underwear. Anything."

They moved into the kitchen. There were dishes of food covered in cling film. Left on the table were a few bowls of salad. Lancaster opened the fridge. He took out a few of the foil parcels and opened them. Fresh salmon, cold meat, sausages, and turkey. He wondered what time the help left. Maybe they heard something unusual. Was she in her dressing gown before the help arrived? She must have been dressed when the killer arrived.

They moved upstairs to the bedrooms. Lancaster opened the first door he came to. It was obviously the master bedroom. Next to the bed lay a pile of clothes. He stooped over and picked up a red dress. He could see some lacy black underwear left on the bed.

Searching about he found a pair of backless evening shoes on the bathroom floor.

Picking one up he exclaimed, "Gold heel. Unusual."

A dressing gown was thrown over the bath. Lancaster picked it up. "No blood on this," He put it to his nose. "Lovely perfume. Wonder what it is."

The jazz singer never wore gold heels. Only black ones. Sometimes they had diamante on them, so her heels glittered in the spotlight when she went on stage. She always glittered. And she always wore the same perfume. Chanel.

"Looking at it from here Crown it adds up to crazy. The murderer must have either undressed her downstairs then rushed up here and put the clothes where we found them. Or undressed her when he arrived and then forced her downstairs, pushed her to the floor, then shot her. Or she was undressed before the murderer arrived," he felt weary.

Crowns face creased up in a bewildered look.

"Doesn't make any sense at all sir."

Lancaster hated early morning murders. It was never his best time. It was morning blackness as far as he was concerned, he was never any good early in the morning.

"It never does," was all he said.

Crown held up the red dress. Lovely thing it was. All beaded with pearls and sequins. Nice quality. Must have cost a packet. He dropped it back onto the white lace bed cover.

"Lets get downstairs," Lancaster said. His mind was racing. It was all so vague. He took out his cigarettes. As soon as he got to the bottom of the stairs he found his jacket pocket and brought out his matches.

Clare Austin was like a naked model in one of those nonsensical virtual reality displays at the Tate Modern. The difference was the polished wood floor had globules of red on it.

"I suppose you could say," he said, as he got onto his knees to pick up a pearl., "Shot to death with pearls."

"Well sir she couldn't have been shot to death with pearls. Bullets you mean."

"Don't be so bloody practical Crown. Let's have a bit of imagination with this. What do you think?" The last time he saw someone so beautiful was when the jazz singer stayed the week end. Then he was always out investigating murder.

Crown thought Venice definitely had an odd effect on

Lancaster.

"I know it's crazy, but I just remembered that line from somewhere. You know Crown, 'Shot to Death with Pearls.'"

Lancaster wondered why he remembered pearls.

Crown bent down. "Funny the way she's lying sir. Her left hand is holding her face and her right arm is a little way out almost holding the blanket. She's on her left side too. Why should a corpse be placed on it's left side? Looks like a pose doesn't it? I've never seen a corpse twisted up like that. It's eerie. Naked with a yellow ribbon in her hair."

Lancaster looked at the body again. Crown was right. She was on her side almost in a pose.

"I think we'd better leave all this to the lab boys," Lancaster shook his head and said. "Then we'll find out where the husband or boyfriend is, and why he's missing more to the point. It's after three in the morning and there's a dead woman on the floor and no one about except the bloody woman next door to talk to. Get her in here Crown. Or better still we'll go in there. I wonder if she'll still be up. We don't want to frighten her to death."

"Sir. Let's leave it 'till the morning. I'm all in."

"You're right. Cover her with her dressing gown, and leave the pearls where they are. In the blood."

- 3 -

Dana Lancaster was thinking about his holiday in Venice. He certainly never through about murder when he was there. But there must have been murder in plenty when Venice was a republic. Apart from the murders committed when lovers fought duels, and dressed in masks and capes, and pretended to be someone else. He thought that was a marvellous idea, most of the villains he knew wore masks, till you managed to rip them off.

Usually his holidays were spent under glass shelters in some ghastly sea side town, waiting for the rain to stop. Then there were those package holidays where everyone was grumpy or drunk, and they spent all day in a coach looking at Churches.
But Venice was different. He dreamed he was back in Murano having lunch under a blue striped awning at 'Veechia Furnace'.

He could taste the grapes in the wine. And no one made risotto like that. After lunch he went a few doors down and bought a pink glass vase for his sister, and a coloured mille fiore paper weight for Crown. He wished he could have bought that beautiful string of beads he saw on Rialto, he would have given them to the jazz singer. She loved bright colours. But maybe if they were together she would have gone with him to Venice and she would have chosen the beads for herself. It was a long time ago since they parted. But in Venice he wished it wasn't.

Inspector Lancaster put his feet on the desk.

"Bomber" they called him in the force. If you were bombed by a Lancaster Bomber in the last war you were in for it. That was the way it was with Lancaster. His father piloted a Lancaster in the war and took Lancaster flying with him as soon as he was out of short pants. Lancaster took his first solo flight when he turned eighteen, and he never forgot it. He still loved to go out to the small airdrome in Hertfordshire on a Sunday and take up a light aircraft. Most women called him sexy. His made more than one or two women try their best to get to know him better. Not many succeeded. That is except the jazz singer. She was the one who tripped him up.

He couldn't afford to get out of shape because Crown would say something if he did. He thought about Clare. Her picture was in front of him on his desk. Her picture before she was shot. Every thing about Clare had been listed, cross filed, and checked, and all on paper. He liked his notes. The computer made his eyes tired. When someone was done away with on his patch, he opened his folders and put out all the photos across his desk in a straight line. Then he would copy all of them and they would go up on the board. He trusted nobody.

"I like to look at the bastards Crown, don't shove them in a computer. Leave them on my desk so I don't forget them."

His desk was a mess. There were photos and files and lists. He would list every personal trait, likes and dislikes, hates and quirks, marriages and divorces. He used to look at them and smoke. But since that scare he had a year of two back he was told to give it up. Still where was the harm in lighting one or two every now and then?

Crown appeared in the doorway. How long had Crown been here? Five or six years? Time flashed by so quickly Lancaster seemed to be old and Crown had stayed young.

Crown was sharper than he was. He liked Crown. he hoped he would stay with Eric, and not drift off to someone else like Roger. That was a disaster. Come to think of it Eric and Crown had been together a good few years now. Crown's mother had left him a nice house near Brighton. Most of Eric's friends ended up living there rent free. There was a piano in the sitting room, and sometimes Crown played on a Sunday.

Crown never found difficulty in settling down with anyone. It was Lancaster who did.

Crown was dressed in a navy blazer, tan trousers, and a navy and tan striped tie. His black hair was combed back very carefully. It was cut into a V in the back of his neck. He only went to the best hairdressers. You couldn't call them barbers these days. A haircut like that must have set him back a few bob.

Crown looked good in clothes because he was tall. He carried his clothes like a bloody model. Maybe he should have been a model. He reminded Lancaster of that film star Robert Ryan. He must have had to take his shoes off when they filmed him with Mitchum.

Crown came attached to a peculiar family name: Kilvert. Kilvert Crown, Detective Sergeant. Someone said Crown was born near Hay-on-Wye, that was where the Reverend Francis Kilvert came from. Others said Crown's father was a Kilvert. Still no one had a name like Lancaster's. Dana Lancaster. Lancaster's mother had a passion for Dana Andrews. That was why he dragged Crown to see 'Laura' whenever it was playing.

Lancaster didn't trouble with Kilvert, as far as he was concerned Crown would do nicely. He didn't want to lose Crown to some other idiot on the force. He was too sharp for any of those fools. None of them dared mention Eric to Crown; they would have been thrown over backwards if they even hinted anything. Crown could mind his back, and Lancaster's as well while he was at it.

"Why do you bother taking out a cigarette?" Crown was asking him. "You're supposed to have given it up."

"Makes me think Crown, makes me think."

"Looks a bit odd sir if you ask me, walking round all day with an unlit cigarette hanging out of your mouth. Doesn't anyone try to light it for you?"

"Wouldn't dare," smiled Lancaster. "Besides, I don't do it all day do I? I think we'll get ourselves down to that nosy neighbour in East Wood. Time we did a bit of digging."

"Sir. I've found out where the husband was. He was visiting his step sister Joan Ross."

"Was he now? I presume he's decided to go back home. Let's leave him for today Crown. We'd better get over to the neighbour's place."

"Apparently Steven Ross phoned to let us know he was there."

"Who was where Crown?"

"Sir. Trevor Austin."

"Affectionate lot these Austins aren't they? Seem to like each other a lot. Get the car our Crown and don't forget your notepad."

The weather had turned warm for the time of year. April was always a dodgy month for Inspector Lancaster. It was an April day when the jazz singer left him. Sunshine one minute, and the bitter cold wind of her leaving the next. Spring always stepped out with sadness to Dana Lancaster, not with dancing feet, but feet of lead. Crown drove the car down the main road to East Wood.

The blossom was beginning to show on the trees, despite the cold. It would all be white and pink soon, like a Spring wedding. Crown took off his jacket and wiped the back of his neck. "Getting warm.

There it is sir. Number fifteen. Couldn't tell what it looked like last night in the dark, like one of those cottages you see in magazines. I bet the porch has Wellingtons left in it. You won't believe what it's called," Lancaster stared out at the house.

"Let me guess, not Hornbeams, or Clover Cottage."

"Good Lord no. Primrose Cottage."

"Jesus," sighed Lancaster. "What will they think of next."

Crown steered the car into the driveway. There were daffodils peeping up all round the trees.

"Look at that Crown. Spring is here. Don't run over the daffs," Lancaster left the car and walked across the path into the porch. Wellington boots lie scattered here and there, coated with thick mud. There were some old shoes and slippers. Umbrellas were standing in an old bucket. He put his hand around the heavy black lion's head knocker.

"Makes the place sound hollow," he said.

"Taking their time about it," Crown was feeling anxious today. He didn't like seeing that naked woman laid out on the blanket with her string of pearls sliced in two. It was sinister. The door was finally opened by a slight grey haired lady holding a small garden trowel. She dropped it into a corner of the porch when she saw them. Dressed in a pair of grubby black trousers and a sweater that was decidedly shabby looking, her eyes were alert but her face showed signs of strain. She looked up at Crown.

"I'm pleased you're here," she whispered.

"Detective Inspector Lancaster and Detective Sergeant Crown," Crown waved his ID.

"They told me you were on your way. I hoped you might come last night. You'd better come in," she glanced round quickly towards the road.

"This business has terrified me," she said. "I'm very careful, I can tell you. Can't tell who's about," she led the way into the sitting room.

"Would you like a cup of tea?" she asked, moving towards the kitchen without waiting for a response.

"Please," said Lancaster as he took out a cigarette. She soon appeared with a tray of tea things, a large teapot and some biscuits.

As she poured the tea Lancaster spoke. "Have you lived here long Mrs Bolton? That is your name isn't it, Ada Bolton?" He saw an elderly grey-haired lady, with a round pretty face. She must have been quite a beauty when she was younger. Her eyes were sparkling blue, and she was wearing a faint smudge of lipstick.
She handed them each a cup of tea.

"Please excuse my appearance. Yes I'm Ada Bolton. I thought I'd do a bit of gardening as it's a pleasant day. With Spring coming on I needed to do a bit of tidying up."

She poured some tea for herself. "I've lived here ten years now. Albert's been gone that long. It's hard to believe it. If I'd had any sense I would have remarried long ago, but you can't remarry if no one asks you, can you?"

"I suppose you can't," said Crown. "Might be a bit difficult."

He wondered if he and Eric would stay together. He didn't think so. Eric would eventually leave, like all the others. It was this damn police work that did it. He was always called out and never home in time for meals. He pondered if perhaps it was easier for women to be on their own. They could cook and do all the house-hold chores. All the washing and ironing he loathed. Why share all that? But then again a lot of his friends shared all that even if they lived with someone. They had fancy names for all that stuff these days: Caring and Sharing. Everyone shared everything. Crown hated tidying the place or bother with meals. He was happy if Eric made dinner, and he was happy when Roger came over and they had dinner together, and he was happy when Roger shared and did the washing up. Was that a reason to live with someone? Because he didn't want to share?

"You'd think," went on Mrs Bolton. "That with all the people one meets you might find the right person, what with bridge and the Institute, and the charities and all."

Lancaster was thinking of the days he lived with the jazz singer. Then he always came home to the sound of piano playing. She wasn't much on cooking. But she was exciting to be with and she was always so damn desirable in those black dresses and ankle strap shoes. He tried to remember why it all ended. Or how it ended. She used to play 'You and the Night and the Music'.

He shrugged and drew his attention back to Mrs Bolton. Lancaster was certain she knew all the gossip round here. Women's Institutes' seemed to know more than the Internet.

"Ever met any of your neighbours family Mrs Bolton?" He asked.

"Oh yes. And what a lot they are too. High and mighty. Not like the people on the other side."

"The other side, you must mean the Austins."

"Of course I do. One's on one side, the other's on the other," she set her chin.

"What were they like, those on the other side to the Austins?" Lancaster felt this was going to be a most difficult case. Neighbours, and their comings and goings. The one on one side, the other on the other. Oh Christ.

Crown leaned forward and poured himself another cup of tea. Nice to have a teapot. Made a change from tea bags at the station.

"Well the other side are very pleasant. Always have a Good Morning or a Good Evening. Not that I'd pry mind you. I never saw them much. They travel a lot. You know, business and all that sort of things. They've been all over the place. But they're no bother when they're here. Keep themselves to themselves."

"Tell me about the Austins, the ones we're officially investigat-ing. What about them?"

Lancaster helped himself to another tea biscuit.

"No children. They've been here as long as I have. They have a large family, brothers, sisters, step brother and sisters and heaven knows who else, and cousins that sometimes come from abroad."

Mrs Bolton was beginning to enjoy herself. She seemed to have recovered from her ordeal, and she loved tittle-tattle.

Lancaster liked gossip too. It could be more informative than any of his lists of facts.

"Were they popular around these parts? As a couple I mean," Crown asked.

"Well they didn't mix really. Might have had the odd game of bridge with some of the locals. Asked me in for a cup of tea once or twice. Smashing place they've got there. We shared a daily you know. She came in to me on a Monday and went to them on a Tuesday. Aggie told me Clare spends a fortune on clothes. Loved to gad about. Used to give her some of her cast-offs. Would you believe that Aggie came in here one day in an outfit from Gucci to do the dusting? Who do you think you're working for I asked her. The Queen?

"Clare worked in a book shop a few days a week. I'll say that for her she did have a job. She once told me she couldn't bear to stay at home all day. Aggie said the place was always spic and span, and she never understood why they really needed her there. But she did a bit of shopping for them."

Here Mrs Bolton drew a deep breath. "Told me they used to have rare arguments every time Mr. Austin's brother came over. Trevor never got on with his brother."

"And which brother would that be Mrs Bolton?" asked the Inspector beginning to perk up a bit.

"Trevor, next door, is a swimming pool builder, and the other one is a pharmacist. I never saw the third brother much."

Crown wrote in his notebook, 'Swimming pool fellow'.

"So you told us there was a party last night. And the reason you phoned the police was because late in the evening you thought you heard some noises. You decided to go into the house next door, and see what happened. You found Clare Austin lying on the floor near the French windows. Dead."

"Yes. Well I wondered what that noise was. I suppose I shouldn't have gone there on my own. We all keep guns round these parts you know. Some people here have large tracts of land. They like to keep the rabbits under control. And the foxes. I didn't know what to think. I went across the lawn with a torch. The window was open so I went inside. I turned the light on and then I saw Clare. It was awful. It was horrifying. Naked on the floor she was, poor thing.

And it looked as if she'd been shot. There was an awful lot of blood, to tell the truth I was frightened to death."

"I can understand that Mrs Bolton. What time did you open your bedroom window?"

"I was in bed, when I got up to close the window and heard a bang. I thought it was a firework or a car back firing at about 12:30. But there was no one about. By that time there was another bang. I thought it sounded like a shot. My nerves had got the better of me, so I decided to go round to Clare's place. I can't have been home that long. You know I'd been invited to her party." She wiped her lips with a handkerchief.

She carried on, "When you live alone sometimes you think you're hearing all sorts of noises. After I found that poor soul I came home and phoned the police. I never saw anyone around to help me, and I was terrified. I wished I'd never gone there. I thought I might be murdered too."

"Well thank you Mrs Bolton. You've been very helpful. Did you receive an invitation to the party?"

"There was a proper invitation. Very fancy too. Called it a 'cocktail party'. But it wasn't really."

"May we see it?" Crown asked.

"Of course. I'll get it for you," she went into the kitchen and came back with the invitation in her hand. Lancaster read:

**CLARE AND TREVOR INVITE YOU TO A COCKTAIL
PARTY
ON SUNDAY APRIL 14th**

**COCKTAILS AT 7.30
DINNER AT 8.30
LADIES DRESS ABSOLUTELY FABULOUS
GENTLEMEN SMART AND STYLISH**

**R.S.V.P.
THE BADGERS
EAST WOOD**

"Nice party it was too," Mrs Bolton said. "All catered. Plenty of champagne. Smoked salmon and roast beef, just about anything you could fancy. All set up by the pool."

"I wouldn't have thought it warm enough to sit outside this time of year."

He gave her back the invitation.

"Well Mrs Bolton," he sought to reassure her. "Whatever you tell us will be treated with confidentiality."

Crown turned to her.

"Oh we all put our wraps on. They had heaters placed all around. I'll tell you something else too, they didn't always mix with people in the village. Kept themselves to themselves," mused Mrs Bolton who was getting well into her stride now. "The last time she spoke to anyone, Clare I mean, was to ask if there was a daily help in the village she could use. Someone to give a hand occasionally."

Lancaster plucked a cigarette from a pack inside his trouser pocket. Crown cast a questioning look at Lancaster. Mrs Bolton carried on.

"Someone told Clare about my Aggie, and she asked me if I could spare her one morning a week. Of course I said yes. Aggie didn't mind earning a bit extra. She told me that Trevor was hardly ever at home in the evenings. Clare was always complaining about him. Aggie said he was as mean as muck. She told me she heard the owner of the bookshop fancied Clare like mad. There were even rumours, well you know, about men I mean."

With this she sat back in her chair shaking her head.

"Well thank you," Crown said. "What time exactly did you leave the party?"

"Oh I was the first to leave. It must have been around twelve. I'd had enough by then. They were all dancing and drinking, so I said goodbye and left."

"And did you see anyone hanging around outside? I don't mean a party guest, I mean a stranger. Someone you hadn't seen before. Someone looking the place over?"

"No one Inspector. When I got to my front door, there was no one about."

They got up to leave. Crown went to the front door and opened it. "Mrs Bolton, did anything strange happen at the party. Any arguments, or any problems between any of the guests?"

"Oh no. Nothing like that. Nothing strange at all."

"Well thank you again Mrs Bolton. Here's our number," he handed her a card. "Perhaps something might come back to you."

Mrs Bolton was delighted to be involved in a murder, and her eyes were gleaming. Her fear had vanished.

"Thank you, very much Mrs Bolton," Lancaster went on. "We'll be in touch."

The door slammed behind them.

"It must be nice to work in the garden Crown. Relaxes your brain, all you think about is when the next flowers will be out," he gave one of his rare laughs. His garden needed a weeks work in it God knows. Maybe he would put in a few daffodil bulbs himself this year.

"Right. We'd better file all this. Get cracking Crown. Then we owe Trevor Austin a visit, the husband who wasn't there."

"Apparently he stayed over at his step sister's place. Joan and Steven Ross'. He told the police he didn't want to get home until the next day."

"Why was that. Did he say?"

"Said he didn't want a divorce."

"What's that got to do with going home?"

"Sir, I wish I knew."

"That's the craziest excuse for not going home to the wife I've ever heard."

"I'll put it on the list, in case we come across it again."

- 4 -

"Found out anything about the family, Crown? Did you pop over to old Prince?"

"Yes sir. It's all here," he handed Lancaster a file of papers. Lancaster scrutinised it. "All seems pretty straight forwards. Money left to the rightful family."

"What about the Mother's children?"

"Nothing, maybe they had a row."

"Mmm," Lancaster pursed his lips. "That's usually a good reason. Seems unusual for a mother not to leave her children anything. There must be more to it."

"You're right. I think we should go and speak to Edward Austin before we get round to Trevor. I think he'll keep for a while. He's got plenty to think about."

"Right," Lancaster took his feet off the desk. "Get your hat, and your car Crown."

"Are you leaving those photos all over the desk like that?"

"For the time being yes. Also, put Clare up all round the room so I can think."

"You're not getting into 'Laura' are you sir?"

"Laura wasn't dead Crown."

"Yea, but Dana Andrews thought she was."

It was a fine day when they arrived at the house. "Must have a few bob sir. A big place like this."

Edward Austin lived in a large house along one of the lanes near a farm. The area was considered exclusive and Edward's house backed onto The Green Golf Club. He liked to think it gave the house a type of cachet. What it did was put the market price up every year. There was nothing that pleased Edward more than the estate agent asking him if he wanted to move to one of the new developments going up around the area. Edward would never move. He was happy with his dark oak front door with its country church knocker, and his beamed ceilings and his old English furniture.

Lancaster lifted the heavy knocker and gave it a few bangs...
A woman appeared with a duster in her hand. Must be the help, Crown thought.

"Yes," the woman asked. "What can I do for you?" Her voice had a hint of impatience in it.

"I'd like to see Mr or Mrs Austin please," Lancaster said. "This is Detective Sergeant Crown and I'm Detective Inspector Lancaster."

He held his identification out. She peered at it for a moment. She was a plain woman. Dressed in trousers and a shirt. Her hair was chopped short and had a few grey streaks in it, her nose sat at wrong angles on her face. She had large dark eyes hidden by round horn rimmed glasses. Even her lips were untouched with lipstick.

She beckoned them into a long hallway which led to a small study. As she led them through the hall Lancaster noted her slight build.

"I'm Mrs Austin," she said in an irritated voice. "Sit down please."

"Well Mrs Austin," Lancaster answered, trying to be as civil as he could, as her manner grated on him. He would get to the point briefly. "I'm afraid I have some bad news for your husband."
He shifted in his chair. He always hated breaking bad news, even to someone as antagonistic as this woman. "Do you happen to know what time he'll be home?"

"Well, I think you'd better tell me about it," Mrs Austin answered. "I'm not sure when my husband will be home. He runs the pharmacy in Chiddingly. It doesn't close 'til eight tonight. It's always open late on a Thursday."

She was dismissive.

Inspector Lancaster studied her face. He always found features important when he thought about murder. Her nose was bulb shaped, funny that he was just thinking of daffodil bulbs. To Lancaster she was a plain woman, with no redeeming features.

Mrs Austin placed the duster she was holding on to the sideboard. She looked at him expectantly.

She didn't seem too taken aback by the heralding of bad news from this man. In fact she seemed very cool and distant. Lancaster pounced on her.

"Like your sister-in-law do you?"

"Which one would that be," she answered in a cold voice. He fancied his question had taken her off guard, her lips quivered for a moment. She spoke slowly, her large eyes expressionless. He hadn't managed to disturb her as much as he would like.

"Why yes, of course, if you mean Clare, not particularly if you mean Belinda."

She seemed very sure in her answers. All cut and dried like an like an actress in a play.

"But I manage to get on with Belinda," she added as an afterthought. "Why?"

"When did you last see the family, Mrs Austin? By the way may I have your full name please. The Detective Sergeant here will write it down."

She shifted in her chair. That always seemed to take them by surprise. Particularly the innocent ones. The idea of a policeman writing their names down seemed abhorrent to most of the population.

"My name is Penny Austin," she answered him. "I saw Belinda and Clare at Belinda's house. She made dinner for a few people, it must be two weeks ago. Unless of course you mean the party."

She hesitated and looked at him shrewdly. It didn't do to answer too many questions. She'd learned that from Edward.

"Anyone else there? At the dinner party?" Crown asked. He was beginning to feel her discomfort as well. He held his pad open and turned a page so she could watch him move his pencil.

He moved about the room looking at paintings, touching the photographs, looking at the books. It was always better to do a little wandering about when Bomber got to the second question.

Maybe he'd better fold his page in half.

"Were you and your husband at the party Mrs Austin?"

"Party?" She realised he had jumped from one question to the other. What had he come to tell Edward?

"Why, why, yes of course we were going to the party. I mean we went to the party. What has this got to do with us? Why can't you tell me what's happened? What have you come to see my husband for?"

Her lips began to feel dry. What could happened? Was it about Edward?

Lancaster always moved in slowly for the kill. Crown watched him closely. There was no one better at firing out questions.

"You know, I've been to so many wonderful parties here, Mrs Austin. Now I'm going to find out how they all ended. I suppose you're wondering how this one ended. Or do you know already?"

"How it ended? Why we left. That's how it ended. We said goodbye and left," she was flustered. "Has something happened to Edward?"

"Oh no it's nothing to do with Edward I assure you. You see we found her at about 1:30 this morning. It was 1:30 wasn't it Crown?"

He looked deep into Crown's eyes. That made her jump. Who had he found? Her hands felt wet. She must ask him.

"Found" she whispered. "What do you mean found? Found who?" Penny knew something serious must have brought this policeman to her home.

Crown knew there was something Lancaster had poked into that conversation. Since when had Lancaster been to any wonderful parties? He hated parties. He always refused invitations to parties. Crown bent his yellow page in half and wrote 'Parties' down one side. Actually he wrote down 'Wonderful Parties'.

"Let's say Mrs Austin that Clare's neighbour rang the police. You see as she tried to settle down, she realised there was music coming from next door. She had only been home half an hour at the most, and she heard some strange noises. Noises like fireworks. She got up and looked out of the window only to see the house next door was in darkness. Maybe she heard a car backfire. It seems this neighbour, name of Mrs Bolton, also went to the party at your sister-in-law's place. Now let's see what was the date? Ah, April the fourteenth according to Mrs Bolton. Mrs Bolton was one of the first to leave the party, as she was beginning to feel a little tired, it was twelve thirty according to her watch."

Lancaster looked the woman directly in the eye.

"Were you introduced to the neighbour by any chance?"

"Oh, you're talking about Clare's party ... I really don't remember," Mrs Austin answered. "There were so many people, and so much noise, it's possible I met her but I can't recall."

Lancaster leaned across to her. He took out a cigarette and placed it between his lips. Penny Austin looked alarmed now. Lancaster knew she was hiding something.

"You don't seem to recall much at all do you Mrs Austin? You know just what I'm talking about. The local police found your sister-in-law dead. Shot to death. It was your sister-in-law all right. She's been officially identified as Clare Austin."

Penny Austin passed a hand over her face. "My God," she uttered.

Lancaster brought his lighter out, and lit his cigarette, taking a few quick puffs, the put it out in the glass ashtray on the coffee table.

"Identified her by photographs. We looked through all the family photos."

He spoke as quietly as he could watching her face. Penny Austin uttered a cry. Her mouth fell open.

"Crown," he said. "A glass of water please."

She was shocked all right, he'd seen enough people who pretended to be shocked to know the difference. But was she shocked because she already knew about Clare, or was it because there were two policemen asking her questions?

Crown went to find the kitchen. Lancaster bent down to Mrs Austin.

"Head down between your knees," he said. She looked as if she would pass out. Just then Crown came in with a glass of water. Crown held out the glass and she lifted her hand to hold it but couldn't control her shaking.

"Take it slowly Mrs Austin," the Bomber said just completing his mission.

She shook as she put the glass to her lips. The water trickled down her throat. She tried to drink more but it was impossible.

"I don't believe it," she winced. "It can't be true."

"Ah but it is, Mrs Austin, believe me," Lancaster's face told her it was so. "Definitely dead."

He noticed her opening and clenching her fingers, the pale blue veins becoming more apparent with every movement.

"And I shall ask you again Mrs Austin, can you tell me approximately what time you and your husband left the party? And how did Clare seem to you while you were there. What was her husband's behaviour like? Please think hard, I need to know what went on that evening."

She was startled. Hands opening and closing again. She began to answer Inspector Lancaster more eagerly. As if she wanted to spurt out all that happened at the party. But what did happen? It was just a party. There was food, and music. Nothing went on. Her short sharp description of the party became more hurried. Fingers lacing together again. She held her head slightly lower as if she didn't want Lancaster to see her eyes.

"It," she hesitated. "It was a nice party. Clare wore her new dress, a red satin one. I remember her telling me about it. Edward and I must have arrived there at eight thirty. She had a group playing music. I remember the music because it was a lot of old stuff. You know the Beatles, Sinatra, Ellington, the music I like. The food was buffet style so we helped ourselves. We sat at a table in the garden. It was a surprisingly warm evening. Of course they had heaters on round the pool. Trevor put them in. He was very fussy about his swimming pools."

She suddenly stopped. Was she remembering something important. She tried to recall the few strangers that were there. In her mind's eye she was at the party sitting at one of the tables, and someone asked if they could join her. But she just couldn't remember who it was. Perhaps it was best if she didn't mention it.

"Please go on Mrs Austin," Lancaster spoke quietly.

"Well, later on we danced. Of course Edward told me he had to get to the pharmacy early in the morning, but he always says that if we go out for dinner. He behaved the same as he always does."

It was rather like being told there was school in the morning she thought. He always dictated the terms.

"Did Clare seem happy to you?" Lancaster asked her.

"Oh yes, she brought me over a glass of Champagne herself. Then she said it was lucky she could get hold of the musicians because they were booked up for a year ahead. It was a jazz group. I remember she said to me how glad she was to see us, and she was enjoying her party."

"And tell me. How did she look?"

What would this almost ordinary looking woman say about Clare? She might have been jealous of Clare. But the side of Penny she was a beauty.

"Oh she looked lovely. She wore the red dress, I remember her showing it to me. I mean before the party. Clare asked me to meet her for lunch in town because she wanted to discuss the food and show me what she bought to wear. She said she found this enormous bow for her hair in Portobello Road, and she was going to sew sequins on it to match her dress. Then she lifted the dress out of some tissue and held it up. It was quite stunning. Of course I could never wear anything like that. It's my complexion you see, I'm very pale. We must have spent an hour or so, then she said she had to leave for an appointment. Said she was meeting someone important. Come to think of it she looked quite excited about it."

Crown moved from the corner. "Did she say who she was meeting by any chance?"

He knew the answer would be no. Where did Clare get to that afternoon?

"No. She just said she had an appointment to meet someone at four thirty. I remember that because I had to get back because the traffic would be hellish going back to the village. Clare just picked up her shopping bags and left," Penny felt tired now. This questioning was a strain.

"No one picked her up then?" Lancaster asked, glancing at Crown.

"Oh no. Not that I noticed. I suppose it's possible. She just paid the bill and left. I think she said she would get a taxi."

"And you Mrs Austin? Where did you go then?"

"I walked to the garage to get my car and drove home of course."

"By the way Mrs Austin, you never mentioned where were you having lunch?"

"Oh Harrods. We often go there. They have a garage, which makes it easy for us to park. Otherwise we have to look for meters. And you know that's impossible. Anyway we like the pizza there.

They have real coal fire ovens. The pizza tastes like it does in Italy."

Lancaster sat back and closed his eyes. He remembered the taste all right. In Venice the pizzas seemed to be set on fire. They had a crispy burnt toast taste, and the tomatoes were sweet as honey.

"Right," he said. "So you met Clare for lunch and a week or so afterwards you went to her party. Did she tell you who she decided to invite to the party?"

A sudden unexpected question brought Penny back to thinking about murder. She shivered.

"Yes. It was a week or so later when she made the party. And she didn't tell me who she invited to the party. I mean apart from the family being invited, why should she? She never mentioned the invitations either. I thought she might want to, but she never did. She, well it seemed as if she didn't care who came."

"Do you?" Crown asked her. "Do you make parties?"

"No," she answered. "I don't."

"So she wasn't asking your opinion on the guest list?"

"No."

"Did she say what made her buy the dress?" Lancaster recalled holding the dress and examining it. Red was his favourite colour. She must have looked very lovely. Had she bought it on a whim, or for someone in particular? Women did that. The dress had a long slit up the side. As he held the dress in the light of the lamp in the bedroom, he remembered how the sequins glittered.

He changed the subject to try and trip her up on something.

Somewhere in this enquiry she had misled him. Or else she had forgotten something. Whatever it was she was holding something back.

"So how were you invited to the party Mrs Austin? Phone call, invitation?" Did Clare invite you when you met her for lunch?"

"Oh yes, of course she did. But she said she was sending invitations out."

"So all the family received invitations?"

"Why, yes, they must have. I mean I can't be sure, can I? They never showed them to me."

"No, Mrs Austin you can't be sure. You can't be sure of anything."

Her face changed colour. "There," she whispered to him. "on the mantlepiece. Our invitation."

Lancaster got up and went towards the mantlepiece. He picked up the invitation.

```
┌─────────────────────────────────────────────┐
│                                               │
│   CLARE AND TREVOR INVITE YOU TO A COCKTAIL   │
│                    PARTY                      │
│            ON SUNDAY APRIL 14th               │
│                                               │
│              COCKTAILS AT 7.30                │
│                DINNER AT 8.30                 │
│       LADIES DRESS ABSOLUTELY FABULOUS        │
│         GENTLEMEN SMART AND STYLISH           │
│                                               │
│                  R.S.V.P.                     │
│                 THE BADGERS                   │
│                  EAST WOOD                    │
│                                               │
└─────────────────────────────────────────────┘
```

"Same as before," Lancaster went on. Crown joined him at the mantlepiece.

"No note, Crown, no note."

"Note sir?" Crown scratched his head. "What note? It's an invitation, that's all."

"No note of brotherly love. Nothing scribbled on it like 'hoping to see you'."

"Well not everyone writes notes on invitations sir. Maybe he didn't hope to see them. Maybe they didn't want to see him. Maybe he only invited them because he had to."

"You're right," said Lancaster. "I'm just thinking aloud. Not everyone wants to see their family. Sort of a duty most times isn't it?"

Lancaster knew most of his family only met at funerals or the occasional wedding.

"With my lot sir, just a duty," Crown smiled. "It's something to get over with."

It occurred to Crown that it would be a bit awkward if he turned up with Eric. What would his provincial relations say if they met Eric? Why would he visit his relations with Eric anyway? That lot from Lancashire, Eric called them. And if he turned up to weddings by himself, one of his Aunts always asked him if he has a girlfriend and why didn't he bring her along? They didn't want to acknowledge the fact that he'd lived on his own for years now.

And maybe it was best if they didn't know about Eric. Too

many questions that he didn't want to answer. Certainly Eric would never dream of going to any of those family things with him. He had enough of his own family to deal with.

Lancaster put the invitation back on the mantlepiece between two Royal Blue Porcelain vases.

"I think I'd like an Aspirin please," Penny Austin asked.

For the moment her voice interrupted Crowns thoughts.

"Of course," he said. He closed the buttons on his blazer and answered. "Certainly. And where are the aspirins?"

She looked at him with an almost pleading look. What hadn't she told them? Or was it simply fear?

"The aspirins are here in my bag," she said simply. Crown bent down and picked up her bag. He saw her hands were still shaking. She took the bag from him and opened it taking out a small bottle. She shook two aspirins into her hand and quickly swallowed them.

Crown spoke, "Pretty woman, this Clare, wasn't she?"

He had picked up a photograph from the small table nearby. He brought the picture over to where Penny Austin was sitting.

"Yes, yes she was," she answered quickly.

"And who would the others be in this photograph?"

"Oh that was at a dinner. The family were together, the brothers and their wives. All of us."

"I thought there were only six Austins'," Lancaster said. "There are ten people in this picture."

"Oh, the others are our step brothers and sisters, Joan and Steven, and Betty and Frank," she took another sip of water.

"But," she insisted. "We're all family. We're very close. One of those roving photographers took the photo. They posted this picture to us."

"No other family?"

She hesitated. "No, no other family."

"Can you point out your husband Mrs Austin?" The question from Lancaster was sudden and sharp."

"There," she pointed. "There, that's Edward," her hands dropped into her lap.

"And please point the others out to me," Crown asked.

"There's Belinda and Charles, and Clare and Trevor."

"And?"

"Frank and Betty, and Joan and Steven."

"And you are sure there is no one else missing from this party?" Lancaster quizzed her. "You haven't by chance cut anyone out of the picture?" They could soon tell by opening the frame. He wanted to test her.

"Of course not. Why would I do that for? There are no other family," she was insistent.

"Whose birthday was it?" Lancaster asked lowering his tone. Were they really that friendly? Most blood families always hid their disagreements at parties, even the ones who had fallen out for years. They just stay at separate tables. He knew his Aunts did. His two Aunts hadn't spoken for so many years it was hard to remember when they did speak. Half the families he knew didn't speak to the other half. Sometimes the hatred was buried deep for the sake of appearances, and people cam together for weddings or funerals as Crown said. Was there something he was missing?

"It was Belinda's Birthday," Penny volunteered. "She didn't want a party so we all went out for dinner," she explained.

Lancaster got up and touched the keys of the piano.

"Play do you?" he said.

"No," she answered. "No, I used to but I don't anymore. Edward still plays."

"I see he likes Chopin," Lancaster said as he leafed through the music on the piano. "I'm a Jazz man myself. Prefer a bit of passion and crescendo from Billie Holiday or Stan Getz."

Lancaster put the music back on the piano and glanced around the room again. There didn't seem to be any decent paintings here. A few antique vases. Old furniture, but nothing special. No nice Regency desks or tables. He's seen enough of those in his time to know the difference. No, either they weren't interested in those kind of things, or perhaps their money didn't run to it. Or they didn't have the taste for good things. Strange they didn't have the cash to buy a nice print. He didn't notice any silver tea pots about either. Most of the families round here kept their silver tea sets on the sideboard. He would check to see if they had any debts when he got back to the station. Money always had a lot to do with murder.

"So according to this photo it seems the whole family gets along."

"Yes."

"Any of you have children?" Crown asked. Penny shifted in the chair.

"Yes. Yes we do. A boy and a girl," it was an unemotional reply.

"So you see each other often, and invite each other to parties. Most step children hate the sight of one another. You don't seem to live too far away from them."

She sat quietly staring into space.

"Of course you shared the goods and chattels?"

"The what?"

"The property of your Mother and their Father?"

"Well my Father had the rights to it all. Their Mother died before him you see."

"Any problems after that? I suppose your solicitor dealt with the estate," he was staring at her now. Willing her to answer.

"Well it was left to us," she sounded adamant. She nodded her head.

"Ah! Well I trust they got personal items eh? Jewellery perhaps? Not worn too much these days, the real stuff I mean."

"They got some money."

"Money and not souvenirs."

"Souvenirs? Oh I don't know Inspector. I really don't remember. I thought you were here about Clare. My husband saw to all that. I'm sure he did the right thing. We're all friends so whatever he did things seemed to work out," her face reddened. Crown wondered if it was a lie.

"And of course you never queried anything? Or said a word about the will?"

"It was a long time ago," Penny Austin replied.

"Well, I think that will be all for now Mrs Austin. Thanks for your help. Does Mr Austin happen to be at the pharmacy now?"

"I really can't say. He has a meeting this afternoon."

"Thanks Mrs Austin. I am sure we can catch him before his meeting."

He glanced at his watch.

"They have meetings everywhere these days don't they Crown? Years ago no one was at a meeting. They were seeing someone about business. Or out of the office. Or they were round the corner having a drink. Every time I phone my accountant he's always at a meeting. By the way Mrs Austin, I'd appreciate it if you would let us break the bad news," Lancaster smiled at her.

"I'm sure you understand. Police work is very difficult sometimes, and I would rather be the one to tell your husband about his sister-in-law."

She didn't answer him.

Crown picked up his jacket, and turned to leave.

"By the way, Mrs Austin, I shouldn't bother your head about the will. I made a few enquiries from old Prince, before I came. Or should I say young Prince as the father has shuffled off. I like to get all my facts straight."

"Yes?" her voice was hardly audible now. "Is there anything else Inspector?"

"Never mind," said Lancaster pausing. He always liked to leave them wondering what he was going to ask. Made it easier to question them next time. They usually slipped up somewhere.

Hard nosed woman this one, untruthful too.

Lancaster reached into his pocket to phone the station.

"Where's my mobile Crown?" he demanded.

"Sir, you must have left it in the house. Why do you always take it out your pocket?"

"Can't stand the damn thing Crown. Why can't we use a phone box like we used to?"

"Because we're not in a black and white movie, that's why."

"People always got shot in phone booths in the forties, didn't they Crown? Bang, bang, bang, the telephone receiver fell dangling on its wire, the victim crumpled up on the bottom of the phone booth. Then some unsuspecting fool gets up to make a phone call, opens the door and there's the inevitable scream. I loved that. The old dangling wire."

"Lucky there are not phone booths round here," Crown observed.

"They were usually in a drug store," Lancaster answered. "And the barman was always wiping the bar down."

"Good night, Mrs Austin," Crown said.

Penny could not utter a word. Two mad policemen had been in her house discussing phone booths and drug stores. It was the worst day she could remember. Who was at that party? She tried to ease herself out of the armchair, but found she couldn't move. she must get to bed where she could rest and think. Think about the party. Why did Inspector Lancaster's questions make her feel so frightened? She must try and remember what happened that evening. Clare was dead. Murdered. It was all she could do to stop herself passing out.

- 5 -

After they left Penny realised she had been rude, and her answers were evasive. How did she appear to them? She knew they would compare her to Clare, and they would say she was dowdy, dull, and plain. Perhaps she should have kept calm when she answered their questions. Looking at her they may think she murdered Clare out of spite. People killed for all sorts of reasons and they may say she was jealous of Clare.

She met Clare for lunch because Clare always had something exciting to tell her. She lived in a different world to Penny. Clare was invited to dinners and parties because she brought life to the evening. Men looked at her when she walked into a room. And women envied her. And maybe Clare had love affairs. She read somewhere that love affairs could make you look beautiful. Clare loved life. She didn't love Trevor much, any fool could see that. He didn't deserve Clare.

Why were the police bothered about their lunch date? Clare wanted to show Penny her dress, and tell her about the party. That was all. Then Clare left to meet a friend. Clare was always meeting friends, why should it matter?

She remembered how lovely Clare looked that afternoon, and Penny had worn a suit she'd had for at least five years. That was the difference between them, she was always worried about saving money, and Clare always spent it. Well at least Clare enjoyed it, which was more than she did. And now Clare was gone.

Penny was thinking back to when she had first met Clare and Trevor. She had just become engaged to Edward. When they were introduced Clare had looked at her with amazement. Edward so good looking and such a catch and Penny was boring and dull. But she was clever enough to have worked as a secretary at the Nations Centre for Science in Four Bridges. She also worked in the local Library when they needed her helping to arrange exhibitions.

In his young days of course, Edward Austin was sought after by legions of women who came into his pharmacy where he was working. And especially by women who had time on their hands. Penny could never get over her good fortune in her conquest of Edward. She met him when he came into the Library one evening. He was looking for a book on a particular drug. She was working late because the head librarian had gone home with a migraine.

She knew the stock well so she was able to help him. He wenter in such beautiful surroundings, happily married. After they bought the house, he sold the flat and deposited the money in his account.

Even she was surprised that it had all moved so fast, but because she was so much in love with him she didn't stop to think about him living in her flat. Why didn't he have a home of his own? If she objected he might leave her and she wanted to marry him desperately.

Probably her friends told her not to be in such a hurry because they were jealous.

But she never quite laughed off the day he said he was going to a meeting with Dr Grant to discuss a new drug. He told her not to wait up as he wouldn't be home 'till late.

On the night he asked her not to wait up for dinner but just leave him something cold, at nine thirty she decided she was feeling a little lonely so she decided to go down to meet him at the hospital. She parked outside the hospital exit. He surely wouldn't be later than ten o'clock. She knew Dr Grant had family, and would want to get home after their meeting.

She waited outside the Hospital until half past ten, and she felt chilly and tired from sitting in the car. She decided to go in to the receptionist and find out what time Dr Grant would be leaving.

The receptionist, who wouldn't have minded a dinner or two with Mr Austin herself, told Penny with a hint of glee, that Eddy had just left with Dr Grant and his nurse. Horrified she drove home trying to understand why he hadn't told her he was going out to dinner with a nurse and Dr Grant. What was it about? When she got in, there was a message from Edward's assistant on her answer phone.

"Mrs Austin, Mr Austin said to tell you he won't be home till late. He has an urgent appointment after his meeting."

Then she knew.

She was used to it all now, he was hardly ever at home when the children came along. But what good would it do to stir things up. One evening he told her that they might be better off living in London. But they couldn't sell the shop could they? After all the children had their schools here, and she knew her neighbours. But he was so determined and driven he never changed his mind about anything.

If he decided to go to London, nothing would stop him even if she implored him to stay in East Wood. She reminded him how much his customers relied on him. He could suggest medication, and always looked at children's injuries. They had a nice home and a fairly pleasant social life. Even if he wasn't there when she needed him she had to put up with it. Lots of women brought up their children alone, and the children loved him. She knew the sex had cooled between them, or he had deliberately made it that way. He could be as ice cold with her as he was when he made up his prescriptions. On some days she hated him. Those detectives had unsettled her. She must have been sitting here for hours. It was hair raising talking to them about Clare. She got up from the armchair and reached for the telephone. She spoke into it for two or three minutes.

Lancaster made a point of getting Crown to linger about after he left. "See when the husband gets in Crown. Find out if she waits up from him."

As the darkness closed in, Crown waited quietly by the tall hedges in the back garden. He knew he should have worn his warm coat. It was still chilly in the evenings.

Just as Crown decided to go home Mrs Austin get out of her chair and go to the telephone. He tried to get as near to the window as he could without being noticed. He could just hear her say, "Hello Edward, I must ... " and that was all.

He could hear the far off rumble of thunder. That's all he needed now, to be soaked by a storm, he was cold enough already. He felt a smatter of rain on his jacket. He didn't intend to hang around here any longer. Lancaster had the most stupid ideas about suspects. What difference did it make if the husband was home late or not, or if she made a few phone calls?

He walked up the driveway and crossed the road to where he left his car. He spoke into his mobile ... "Sir? No husband yet, she phoned him though. I couldn't hear much."

"Okay. You'd better get off home. Are you sure she called her husband?"

"Of course I'm sure. Who else would she call?"

"Well fancy that," Lancaster tapped his fingers on the sides of his armchair. "Just when I asked her not to. So the husband and wife exchange confidences after all. I wonder if we'll find it's the same with the rest of the family. Pity you couldn't hear what else she said." Crown sighed.

"She just said Edward."

"Pity. You don't think it was Edward G, do you?" asked Lancaster.

- 6 -

"Jazz, Crown, jazz."

Crown knew that whatever Lancaster was saying now, he was thinking of something else. He was bound to mention Ronnie Scott's.

"He should never have died Crown. All those marvellous jokes. Remember the one about the Pygmies?" On the button Crown was thinking.

"How could I forget."

"And the one about the small rooms he stayed in, when he turned the door knob he rearranged the furniture." Here it comes thought Crown.

"Harry James, Stan Getz, Ella. I fancy a nip down there this evening, just to see if there's anyone worth listening to. Most of the best ones are dead."

"Paul McCartney isn't."

"I'm not talking pop Crown, I'm talking jazz. Anyway a bit of music makes me think things over."

"You mean things like why Clare Austin was so perfectly arranged on the floor? With a cushion behind her. The whole thing's bizarre. Who would do that? There must be some screwy reason. She was propped up like a bloody doll."

"Let's get some tea. People don't kill reasonably. They kill unreasonably, passionately. Go and ask Harry for some tea Crown," Lancaster considered Clare Austin. He picked up her photograph.

Crown stopped in his tracks. Why was Lancaster meandering on about passion. That wasn't one of his usual descriptions of murder. Passionately. The word ran round in his head.

"We'll know more when forensic are through with the body," he muttered. "But I wonder...now you've mentioned it. The cushion I mean."

He heard Harry coming along the corridor.

Lancaster said, "What was the point of it. Arranging her like that. What for? Someone hated her enough to murder her, so they murdered her. It can't be for money, the husband probably inherits. They don't have any kids. So why go to all that trouble. And they know a bit about rigor," Lancaster meditated.

The door opened and Harry appeared with the tea tray.

"Saw the photo on the board Guv," he said to Lancaster.

"Must be some nutter. Done deliberately if you ask me. All that posing."

"Perhaps Harry. Perhaps. Thanks for the tea," Lancaster waited until the door closed. Even Harry thought it was a pose.

"He's right Crown. we'd better get down there and see the other brothers as soon as we can. See what they've got to say."

Crown picked up the mug. Where had he had seen the pose? He was damn sure he had seen it somewhere.

"Funny that sir. Now you've mentioned it again. It sounds crazy I know but I've seen it somewhere. It reminds me of something, but it's not logical."

"What's not logical. Since when did logic have anything to do with murder?"

"Well it reminds me of a painting."

"Painting?"

"You know sir, the one where there's just a woman lying on the ground staring into space. Balancing on her elbow and holding her face on her hand."

Lancaster looked eagerly at Crown. "What woman staring into space?" he asked.

"I can't think of the name of it. Or the artist. But I've definitely seen it."

"Come on Crown. Don't tell me you're going to be trolling through books on art! For God's sake, most corpses stare into space, until their eyes are closed," Inspector Lancaster sighed.

He was baffled.

"It's not the staring sir, it's the pose. They don't lie on their elbows."

"You mean someone put her in a special pose. That's crazy. But why?"

"Blowed if I know," Crown answered. "Maybe I'm wrong and it's just my imagination."

"Maybe it is," Lancaster answered. "But I wonder what made you think of it just the same. You know what Crown. I think I'll forget Ronnie's tonight. I need to think about murder. Right now I'll nip off to the films. I read somewhere in the paper they've re-coloured that Hitchcock film. Sharpen us up. Give us a few ideas."

Crown's face dropped. Us. That meant he had to go and see 'Vertigo' again for the umpteenth time. No one in the station had seen 'Vertigo', what was he a screen-writer?

"Get the car out Crown, and put on the siren." Crown turned to leave the office.

"By the way, what film is it sir?" as if he didn't know already.

"Come on Crown. You know me by now, what film do you think

it is?"

A slow smile creased Lancaster's face. He took out his cigarettes.

"Bloody 'Vertigo'," Crown answered.

"No Crown. Not this time. It's 'Catch Me If You Can' ."

"What?"

"You heard me."

"You're not Tom Hanks, for God's sake."

"No, but Spielberg knows a hell of a lot about murder."

"But it's not murder," Crown said.

"It is in a way, Crown. Conning is murder in a way."

Crown shrugged, "Whatever you say Boss."

- 7 -

Simon whispered to her as they held each other in the four poster bed at the Old Barn Hotel. This was one of their special days. She called him Simon but that wasn't the name he put in the newspaper. In the paper he called himself 'The Saint'. Well Simon Templar was 'The Saint' wasn't he?

"I like your smile, besides which you're brainy."

"I'm pleased," she smiled. "I thought men didn't like brainy women. Preferred them pretty and dim."

He's always in her thoughts. Why didn't she leave Charles? She wanted to live on her own, so did Clare. What kept them here playing games? Neither of them had a family, so there were no children to worry about.

She studied Simon, wondering why he put a 'Love Line' in the paper in the first place. She knew about men like that; married ones. They did it all the time to get away from their wives.

Simon seemed too attractive a man to have to resort to a newspaper ad. Surely there were enough women in the office, or wherever he worked, to give him plenty of scope. Still perhaps it was best not to think of that. He was with her, that was what mattered.

She tried to imagine what it would be like to live with Simon. She looked into his eyes. They were dark, dreamy eyes, he used glasses to read. Unmanageable hair, a little grey in places, his body was young and slim. More than likely he was younger than she was. She picked up his hand noticing the gold band on his third finger. Why hadn't she seen it before? Maybe he wasn't wearing it when they first met. She would like to bet he was meeting his wife later and she might wonder where the ring was.

"You never said you were married," a slight pang of jealousy struck her.

"God," he laughed. "I thought you'd never ask."

She knew she ought to sound more brittle, more off hand.

"You're young, and good looking. What's your wife like? You can't have been married that long."

He lay back comfortably on the pillows.

"Are you? Married I mean?"

It had certainly taken them both a few months to get round to that subject Belinda thought to herself. Funny how they had both taken it as read. Both answered the advertisement in the local paper, and both assumed the other single. Not that it mattered terribly. He would never know her name in any case. And she would probably never know his. That was part of the arrangement. Charles would never find out, and Simon's wife, if he had a wife, would be none the wiser. She lay back filling her head with suppositions and recriminations.

"Yes," she finally answered trying to be casual and diffident as possible. Suddenly she started to laugh.

"Let's not continue this. Just let's talk about something else," she looked at her watch.

"I have to go soon," she managed to get her legs out of the tangled bedclothes. She remembered the first day she met him. When they got to the hotel bedroom and she took off her shoes, she had to walk over the carpet in bare feet. It gave her the shivers.

"What does your husband do?"

"Do? What does it matter?"

"Well we can compare. My wife works with children." She went towards the bathroom, and picked up a large towel ... She turned to him. "He's a manager."

She dropped the bath mat on the floor, and ran the water.

This all started out as just a bit of fun. Something to do that was wildly different. At least that was what she tried to tell herself, but now she found it hard to think of giving him up. The whole thing was getting out of hand. Sooner or later one of them would slip up and then where would she be? She handled all the others well, why couldn't she handle this one?

She decided to answer his question with a few embellished details.

"He sells furniture. Has a job in a big store and he earns a lot of money." He didn't need to know the exact truth, and what she had told him sounded feasible.

"Well I hope he's busy selling his furniture today," Simon laughed. "Because you're my wonderful bit of luck. My peaches. Even though it's not your name, I'm not that foolish, but who cares. 'Peaches'." He shook his head. "What made you think that one up?"

She lowered herself into the warm scented water..

"For the same reason you called yourself 'The Saint', it was the most stupid name I could think of at the time." He slipped out of bed and came into the bathroom. He bent down and kissed her.

"All right then, you can be my Peaches," he said to her. "My Peaches and cream."

"Fool," she said. "Give me the towel."

He held one of the towels out.

"I'd like to stay longer," he said looking thoughtful.

"Impossible. I have to go. By the way I've got a party tomorrow night at my sister-in-law's. I won't be able to meet you until it's over. Unless I slip away of course."

"Slip away then, I must see you tomorrow. Even if it's only for half an hour. I'll call you in the morning on the mobile," he sounded determined.

"And come to think of it Simon, what's your real name?"

"Oh no names, definitely no names. We had a bargain remember? You can call me Simon if you like. As long as I'm with you it doesn't matter."

"Ah," she smiled.

He turned to her and held her, and pulled off the towel.

"We have to end this," was the last thing she said as he held her.

"Let's stay together," he whispered. "Don't let go."

****

When Inspector Lancaster got back from the interview there was a note on his desk from Forensics.

"Bomber," it read. "This one is definitely dead from the three bullet holes. Or should I say two. One just caught the corner of her arm. A good old fashioned case of shooting."

Lancaster sat back in his chair. This case was like a ball of wool tangled up by the cat. He wondered what was going on before the party.

He heard Sergeant Hilarie Carson tapping something into her computer. Bloody computers. No one took notes any more, only Crown did when were on a case.

"Carson, where's Crown?"

"He's not here sir."

"Of course he's not here. I can see that," Lancaster was moody this afternoon. He hadn't slept well, and thinking of Clare's murder had kept him up. He thought of the red dress all the time.

"Said to tell you he couldn't find the book, so he's gone off to the Royal Academy. He said something about Paris. Said to tell you he'll be back soon."

He can't be going to bloody Paris, Lancaster told himself. He shuffled the papers on his desk. He took out a cigarette. Next he would go to meet Trevor Austin. Damn lot of family in this case. He looked down at his list.

He picked up the phone and called the lab. "Any news on the bullets yet Peter?"

"Sorry sir, the report will be finished this afternoon, I'll get it sent up when it's ready."

"I'm off to see the husband. Let Sergeant Carson here know as soon as it comes in."

He stood up, and put on his scarf.

"Of course sir. I'll call you on your mobile," she smiled.

Lancaster thought mobiles and computers were a pain in the ass.

- 8 -

The chemist shop had been going at full trot. As soon as a summer shook its blossoms and grew its roses and lavender, everyone had hay fever. One of the local consultants phoned asking for a special hay fever drug from Switzerland for hay fever. Did he by any chance have it in? Would he be able to get it as soon as possible? Edward Austin stood at the back of the pharmacy, keeping the overhead light trained on his fingers. Covering the back of his head were the few dark hairs he had left. He studied the next prescription. He wasn't feeling too well today. It must be that damn party they went to last night. Trust Clare to serve something that upset his stomach.

Day in and out he had prescriptions to be filled for his customers. It was remarkable how many drugs human beings managed to put inside themselves. Since natives had scratched the bark of a tree, and man had picked leaves and eaten them, it had been going on forever. At least, some days it seemed like forever. Every day seemed to be the same, year in and year out. He hardly seemed to have time to keep up with it. There were so many new drugs poured out by the drug companies. He would read late into the night, sleeping in the spare room, so as not to disturb Penny.
He was glad to be in another room when she starting to ask him questions. It was best to be out of the way as much as possible. She was becoming a nag. Last week he had to go to Oxford to collect some special papers on a new drug for asthma ...

He stayed overnight, and there were some pretty nurses at a lecture there, which helped pass the time. Never the less it was a treadmill. But when someone asked for his advice it made him feel indispensable. How Penny envied that. Well there was nothing stopping her taking a job, or going back to study at the local college. Lots of women did that when the children were in school.

He turned to Margaret Carter. "Margaret give me some of those indigestion tablets, will you?"

Margaret handed him some tablets, and a glass of water. Then went back to counting out the pills for the prescription he was making up. The phone rang at his elbow.

"Answer that Miss Carter will you please?" He hoped it wasn't Penny. Margaret Carter knew how to put her off.

"Of course Mr Austin," her hand went to the receiver.

"Hello, Austin's Chemist."

"Oh hello Dr Grant," she said. "How nice to hear from you," she turned to Edward and signalled with her hands. Did he want to speak? Margaret Carter knew Edward's moods very well. She never took it for granted that he would speak on the phone, and she knew never to ask him what time he would be arriving at the pharmacy. She had learned to carry on without him when he went to some of his meetings. She and Pam could deal with emergencies. She also knew when not to put his wife on the phone.

And he paid her well.

Edward put the pills down and picked up the phone.

"Hello Eddy. It's me," Grant always seemed to be cheerful and optimistic. Whatever he had to face, he kept himself calm.

"Have you got some time early this evening? I'd like to chat with you. Haven't seen you in ages. It's getting like school days eh? Always studying for exams weren't we? I'll be at the hospital all day, I'm operating early this evening. Maybe we can meet in the canteen for a cup of tea say around six."

Edward was happy. He was fond of his old school friend, and he respected him. Grant carried on speaking.

"Fine," Edward answered. "I'll see you then. Six o'clock should do nicely. And by the way let's arrange for dinner one evening with the girls. How's Evie?"

"Oh she's in top form. Keeps them on their toes in the ward, I can tell you."

Evie always had interesting stories to tell them. Penny could always tell them about the library. Alan was a link with his childhood. He must be the only friend he had, as he found most people difficult.

Edward glanced out of the window at the High Street. People were rushing along with umbrellas up to keep off the driving rain. This summer was starting out wet and chilly. No wonder he always felt cold. He'd better check and see if he had an umbrella in the back of the shop.

Edward felt tired, but if Alan Grant wanted a chat, he would be glad to meet him.

Margaret could lock up the shop for him. He decided not to waste time doing that any more. He could get home a little earlier and miss the worst of the traffic.

"Margaret, here's the list of the new drugs we need to order. Will you deal with it? I'll be leaving at about five o'clock. I'm meeting Dr Grant. If Penny phones tell her I won't be in for dinner."

He went back to counting out the tiny yellow tablets.

"They're holding him in Emergency," he commented to her.

"Who's that sir?" Margaret enquired.

"Dr Grant told me some fellow who fell down a mountain. Bloody fools. Cause everyone trouble. Trouble for their rescuers, trouble for the emergency doctors, and trouble for their families."

Unsympathetic bastard, Margaret thought. She wondered how Alan Grant could be friendly with a man like Edward.

Idly Edward wondered if there were ever any awards for this kind of work. Some sort of lifetime achievement for running the best pharmacy in the village High Street. He smiled to himself. If only that could be possible it would just about kill his brothers. They would die of envy. He was pipe dreaming again.

The phone rang. Margaret picked up the receiver.

"It's your wife Mr Austin. She says she has something terribly important to tell you."

Edward picked up the phone.

"My God," was all that Margaret could hear him say. "You're absolutely positive?"

She thought it best not to ask what the trouble was. Edward could be upset over the most trivial things.

****

Just as Belinda was driving her car into London Road her husband was picking up the morning post. He was used to the post arriving early, that way he could deal with household bills and sort out any problems. But these days the post was arriving later and later. He glanced through the envelopes on his way to the kitchen.

He opened the first letter that came to hand. Suddenly he remembered the date. It was that blasted party tonight. He went over to the mantlepiece to look at the invitation.

```
┌─────────────────────────────────────────────────┐
│  CLARE AND TREVOR INVITE YOU TO A COCKTAIL PARTY  │
│             ON SUNDAY APRIL 14th                  │
│                                                   │
│                COCKTAILS AT 7.30                  │
│                 DINNER AT 8.30                    │
│          LADIES DRESS ABSOLUTELY FABULOUS         │
│            GENTLEMEN SMART AND STYLISH            │
│                                                   │
│                   R.S.V.P.                        │
│                 THE BADGERS                       │
│                 EAST WOOD                         │
└─────────────────────────────────────────────────┘
```

Trust his sister-in-law to write, "Gentlemen smart and stylish." Thinking about the party he went into the kitchen to make himself a cup of coffee. He could hear Belinda's car pull up outside the garage.

"Charles," she called out.

"Yes, I haven't left yet," He answered. What was she doing shopping this early?

Belinda felt disturbed. She hadn't expected to see him at home at nine o'clock in the morning. She thought he would have gone straight to the office from his Mother's place. He was staying at his Mother's place last night wasn't he?

"I thought you were staying at your Mother's?" she said, dropping the shopping bag onto the kitchen table.

"I was, but I had to get back for the post. She's well now, the doctor says she can be left on her own. I'm expecting a letter about the insurance. I'm changing the company over. The damn post is always late."

He reached over the table for the sugar and added more to his coffee.

"Where the devil have you been so early?"

Belinda had to think quickly. She hadn't expected him to be at home. It was a stupid mistake. She should have been prepared. Why did she expect it all to go perfectly?

"I had to get up at seven. Remember Denise Martin? Well she's had a few problems with her husband. Crying over the phone. You know the kind of things. She woke me up early, so I went over to see if I could calm her down. Apparently he went away for a week and stayed away for two. Doesn't want to come back," she emphasised this. "And that's the problem."

Where did she get these stories from? They popped into her head like writing a novel. It was better than some of the novels she had to read at the boring literary group she belonged to down at the Church Hall. But Charles didn't seem very concerned. She breathed a sigh of relief.

"Funny thing Belinda," he ran his hand over his chin. "We received another invitation to the party."

"Party, "Belinda asked. "Oh the party. I'd forgotten."

"Yes the party. I suppose we'll have to go."

She sat down, feeling slightly out of breath with her story, and slightly tired from being out all night and having to rush back on the motorway.

"But we've already got an invitation. You remember. It came last week. It's on the mantelpiece in the dining room."

"Of course I've seen it. So why the hell have they sent another one. They must be getting a little cracked. I always knew they were," he shrugged his shoulders.

Belinda started unpacking the groceries. She felt she had to be occupied.

"Why would they send us two invitations? Probably a mistake. We haven't replied yet, and they haven't even bothered to phone us. Maybe we'll give it a miss."

She would be glad if they could stay in tonight. She was tired. It was anxiety, feat that perhaps someone had seen her arrive home at nine o'clock this morning. That would complicate things.

"I really don't care if we go or not," he was saying. "Their parties are boring and so are their friends. And their food is rotten," he took his glasses off and put them on the table.

"Why can't Trevor accept I've fallen out with him. Bloody families. Why would he send a second invitation. It's crazy."

"Maybe that's his way of saying he'd like to see you," it was all Belinda could think of to answer him.

"Perhaps you're right. Then we'll have to go. I suppose it's better to try and make some sort of peace," he put the cup and saucer in the sink. "I'll try and be back as soon as I can. I've got a few appointments. Someone in Hampstead wants me to put a bookcase in. Where did I leave my briefcase?"

"I'll look for it," Belinda said. "Personally I'd rather we didn't go," she opened a cupboard next to the kitchen dresser. "But I suppose it would be easier to go than start looking for excuses. Anyway it's too late to phone them now. Do you think you left your briefcase in the bedroom?" Without waiting for an answer she fled upstairs.

She would decide what to wear after he left. His voice broke her thoughts. He shouted from downstairs.

"I've found my briefcase, it was in the dinning room. I'll see you later. And make sure you get the plumber for the upstairs bathroom, the tap's been tight for ages."

That was all he could think of. Bathroom taps. At last he was gone, she watched as he opened the car door and threw his briefcase on the back seat.

She needed to relax and forget about Charles. Now Simon had given her something different to think about. Love. She looked forward to having a hot bath before she dressed, so she could lay her head back and think about him. If she was lucky they would snatch a few minutes together after Clare's party. That was the reason she asked Clare to send two invitations. So she could persuade Charles to kiss and make up with Trevor and she could meet Simon. Her only concern about last night was that someone might have seen her with Simon. They should be more cautious. They were taking too many chances and becoming too devil may care. She went upstairs to undress, ran the bath and opened a bottle filled with her favourite aromatic lavender oil. Sprinkling it into the water, she dropped her robe and slowly lowered herself into the soothing lavender scented water. She lay back and closed her eyes. She had never experienced the passion she shared with Simon and she would rather lose Charles and the house than give him up. None of that mattered now. She dried her hands and reached for her mobile.

- 9 -

Edward Austin walked the last few steps in the corridor before reaching the hospital cafe. He could see Alan Grant seated at a table.

"Hello Austin," he called out. "Come on sit down," he waved towards a chair.

"The operation isn't going to be a long job. Go and get yourself a cup of their watery tea. You'd better ask them for two tea bags."

Edward went towards the snack bar. What awful choices they had. No wonder people complained about hospital food. Even if you were waiting for an opinion from a doctor, the usual miserable biscuits and chocolate bars stared up at you. He picked up the cup of tea and went to sit with Alan Grant.

"How are you? Penny well? Why do they change the names on all these drugs Eddy?" He laughed. "They're always re-marketing something or other."

"You're right. Changes, changes. Everyone has to look up the drug book. But I'm keeping on track," Edward smiled.

"You're right, even the specialists have to look up the names," Grant took a piece of paper out of his pocket and scribbled down the few names of drugs he was using for the next patient.

"I don't know why they do this all the time. Take a look at his. It's got a new name now."

Edward looked at Alan. Alan was the only one he could discuss his business with. He had given up talking to Penny about it. Edward always asked Alan's advice about the pharmacy, and whether he should change the frontage of the shop. He was thinking of adding a new window. Alan spoke of his busy schedule. He was glad to snatch a few minutes with Edward.

"I must ask Evie when we'll be free. We can go out to that new place near the river. They serve drinks outside. Well thanks for coming in Eddy," he smiled. "I have a date to patch up the bloody mountain climber I mentioned. Why do they do it I ask myself? Climb up these mountains then come down again. I suppose it's like everything else. Just to do it. Anyway I'm sure we'll pull him through."

"It probably gives them some sort of thrill. Reaching the top."

Looking at the clock, Edward realised they had been speaking longer than he anticipated. It wouldn't be the first time he'd been late for dinner.

"Did they tell you, Alan, about Clare, my sister in law?"

"What about Clare? Pretty woman."

"She's dead Alan. I was at her party last night."

"Good Lord. That's dreadful. How did it happen?"

"She's been murdered."

Alan Grant leaned over to Edward.

"That's utterly unbelievable. Murdered. Here?"

"She was murdered in her house."

"Was it a break in?"

"I don't know yet. Penny's in a dreadful state. We were only at her party last night."

Dr Grant could see the theatre nurses he worked with leaving the canteen.

"I'll see you soon Eddie. I must go now. Regards to Penny. I'm so sorry, about Clare I mean. Maybe it was suicide. If you've got nothing else going on, you can wait for me and we can grab a bite together," with that he was gone.

Edward finished his tea, and decided to linger for a little while. He was feeling extraordinary tired, and sat down on one of the few armchairs dotted about the canteen. He had been tired all day. He had felt so well when he got up this morning. Perhaps he was coming down with the flu. Or perhaps the news of Clare's death made him feel wretched. He must get over to see Trevor. It was a ghastly business. And only last night they were all together.

So many people came into the pharmacy with mysterious viruses and flu symptoms, he felt sure he had picked up a bug. The change of season always brought on different kinds of illnesses. As he sat there he could see into the long corridor. He watched as a patient was being wheeled towards the lift. He wondered if it was the mountain climber going down to the operating theatre.

The nurse holding up the drip must be the one in love with Dr Fellowes. He heard some women gossiping about is in the pharmacy. How did these people find out about what went on in the hospital? They must know one of the nurses, or someone who worked in the hospital. If Grant found out someone was talking about Fellowes it would be more than their lives were worth. He hated gossip.

How long had he been sitting here? It must be over two hours. He was the only one left in the canteen. He could vaguely see the girl behind the counter of the snack bar making a cup of tea. She looked out of focus. He must be getting a migraine, there were small circles of bright colour jumping about in his eyes.

Drops of perspiration trickled down Edward's glasses. He

forced himself to stand up and walk to the double doors that led to the reception area. The corridor was longer than he thought, or was it his vision that changed the perspective. He took out a handkerchief, and removing his glasses wiped his eyes.

He tried to speak but the words came to him in slow motion like an old movie. Why was he speaking so slowly?

"I ... " he muttered. "I feel sick."

He managed to leave the canteen, and manoeuvre himself into the main reception hall.

"Please, a glass of water," he struggled to get the words out to one of the nurses behind the desk ...

Nurse Evans, who had just come on duty, looked at him questioningly, and rushed to get him a glass of water. They had plastic cups stacked next to the water machines. As she rushed down the hall, she had a strange idea that she had seen this man somewhere before. She knew he was a friend of Alan Grant, and that he had a chemist shop in the district. But why was the idea troubling her?

She held the plastic cup under the water filter, and tried to remember where she had seen his face. When she got back to the desk she could see him sitting on the floor, holding his head in his hands. Now she remembered his name, Austin, that was it. As she handed the cup to him, she remembered where she might have seen him. It was when she visited her cousin Vera in the West End. It certainly looked like him. But she knew it was easy to mistake people for someone else.

There was a definite similarity to this man, and the man in the lift at Vera's. She remembered he asked her if she lived there, and he had pressed the button for the fourth floor. She said no, she didn't live there, and was visiting her cousin. She had left the lift on the second floor.

He had said good night to her when she got out. She vividly recalled that evening. She had some dinner with Vera, and Vera told her later that the man downstairs was very ill, and a doctor was staying with him until he could go to hospital. The porter mentioned it to her again when she left the building.

"Poor old bloke up there. Seems to have some illness or other. You're a nurse. I'll bet you'd know all about it. These days who knows what it can be. Maybe typhoid or TB, or even AIDS. You've got to be so careful. There are all sorts of things you can catch in the street with all these visitors bringing over their germs. Years ago you travelled by ship. The germ was probably dead when it got here."

She was indignant when she answered him. She told him not

to be so silly. There had always been illness and disease, how could anyone tell what was being spread about? He hoped he wouldn't frighten Vera, with talk of the man upstairs. Why Vera would be frightened to come home.

"Don't mention it to Vera George, you know what a nervous person she is."

The porter smiled at her.

"Didn't mean to frighten you miss. Or your cousin come to that. Can I get you a taxi?"

"No thank you," she smiled back at George. "I think I'll walk to the station."

She was very fond of George because he was always helpful to her cousin. Vera had lived there for years and George always carried her shopping in, or let in the plumber, and saw to the post.

And now, here in the hospital corridor, she felt positive it was the same man she had seen that night.

"Oh dear are you ill sir?" she asked as she leaned over Edward. The funny thing was, she was beginning to feel quite queasy herself. It must be her vivid imagination playing tricks again.

What if this man had one of those terrifying diseases, and he contracted it just by being in the building where Vera lived? And what about Vera? She must tell Vera to see a doctor! She was always very careful never to allow herself the luxury of panic. She was supposed to be the person that everyone else could rely on, and especially Sister. She must never fall apart in the face of an emergency. And yet she was absolutely sure that this was an emergency.

"Yes, yes, I feel quite bad. I must lie down. Can't tell what it is," he was stuttering now. He felt the blood draining from his face. His lips were cold.

Nurse Evans called out to the other nurse on reception. She could see her rushing over. They both tried to hold him up to take him over to the couch in the waiting area, but he had slipped down onto the floor, and it was impossible to move him. Edward Austin dropped the cup of water as he fell. Nurse Evans felt as if she could slip down herself. She might even faint. She watched as the cup of water rolled across the floor and left little puddles across the polished wood. The man's temperature must be dropping, as his face had turned quite pale. He looked almost bloodless. Nurse Evans rubbed her eyes. People who had suddenly gathered round her were becoming fuzzy little blurs.

"Quickly, call emergency," a voice shouted.

"Take his pulse and don't move him. Let him stay on the floor now until we get emergency down here," Nurse Evans shouted, gaining command of the situation. She couldn't faint now, even if she did feel sick, what would happen if the hospital found her unreliable? Fainting when a patient passed out. There was no reason to faint. If she did a doctor would examine her and they would find nothing wrong, or they would think she was pregnant, or had fallen apart in an emergency, and then where would she be? Back in accident and emergency if she was lucky.

She might even be accused of incompetence. Who would believe her if she said she had seen this man before, and that he made her feel frightened. Why did he frighten her? And why tell anyone anyway? They would simply laugh at her and say it was her imagination running riot. Just because someone in her cousin's building was sick, what did that mean? People were sick all the time in all sorts of circumstance. She didn't even know what was wrong with this man, he hadn't even been diagnosed.

She had to help get this man onto the couch and see him up to the emergency floor. Would Sister Bates think she was remiss for not reporting she felt ill that morning. But what could she report. She didn't feel sick this morning, she was perfectly well.

Control yourself Evans, she thought. It was all because George had told her that the man upstairs had some dreadful illness, and she had seen this man in the lift that she jumped to conclusions. She had never done that in all her nursing career. What made her panic so?

She reached for the phone to call the emergency team. She knew Dr Grant would want to be told what was happening here as Mr Austin was a friend. She glanced quickly at his schedule.

He should be finished the operation soon. He always came out to the reception when he was finished and asked one of the nurses to join him for a cup of tea if they were changing shifts. Glancing at the clock they would be changing very soon.

A passing doctor had seen Edward fall, and rushed over. He knelt down and took his pulse.

"What the hell's happened here?"

Nurse Harris told him the man had passed out cold. "It happened in a second," she said. "There was nothing we could do. Nurse Evans has called emergency."

"His pulse is very slow," he said. He looked up to see Dr Grant coming down the corridor into reception.

"What happened doctor?" He knelt down and looked at the patient. "Good Lord, it's Eddy. We just met in the canteen."

He spoke briefly with authority. "Have you called emergency?"

"Yes sir."

"Tell the team to get him moved upstairs as soon as possible. We better get him into Sister Bates floor. There'll be a bed there."

He looked puzzled.

"We must get him checked over immediately," the doctor who saw Edward fall, looked up at Dr Grant.

"I've taken his pulse. It's terribly low."

Dr Grant glanced at his watch.

"Why he must have been in the canteen for hours. I must get back to the theatre. I've got the patient in recovery. It took longer than I thought."

He turned to Nurse Evans. "He's an old friend of mine. Make sure he's taken care of. Go up to the ward with him Nurse Evans, and tell Sister Bates what happened. I must say it's very strange."

Nurse Evans looked up to see the emergency team arrive.

"I'll be along to see him as soon as I have time."

What could have happened, Alan Grant wondered, surely Edward should have left for home long ago. He sighed. As if he didn't have enough on his plate already.

He turned to the Nurses at the reception desk.

"Don't let anyone know about this. Carry on with your work and don't speak to your friends. It can be anything. We don't need any panic in this hospital. It's probably a sudden surgical matter. Could be appendix, or something to do with his bowel. It wasn't his heart, I'm sure of that. We'll find out what it is soon enough."

Nurse Evans was holding a handkerchief up to her mouth.

"Anything wrong Nurse Evans," Dr Grant asked. "You look a bit peaky. Get yourself a cup of tea."

Nurse Evans held on tightly to the chair in front of her. She wished he would go so she could rush to the ladies and be sick. Shrugging his shoulders, Dr Grant said, "Good night. I'll be off myself soon. I'll speak to you all tomorrow."

Nurse Evans watched him as he walked down the corridor, then she rushed to the staff toilet. As soon as she got inside she put her head into the basin and threw up her dinner.

It was there Nurse Collins found her, holding her head and crying.

"I must tell Vera," she kept repeating. "I must tell Vera."

- 10 -

A smile creased the face of Frank Gordon when he picked up the local paper. So the bastard had collapsed. Pity it was in the hospital where he would be looked after. His sister would be pleased. This was a bit of good news for her to start the day. What with the Footsie so low and the Dow Jones creaky. It was a good excuse to go out for a drink with the boys later this evening. He wondered if Joan was at home. He hoped so because he wanted her to see the newspaper. He popped it under his arm and went out the kitchen door to get his motorbike.

****

Belinda slept late. She hated every moment of the party because Simon hadn't shown up as they planned. She had told him she would slip out and meet him in his car. No one could possibly know whose car it was, there were so many people at the party. He had never disappointed her before.

She was bending down looking for her slippers when the door bell rang. Who could it be at this time of the afternoon? She must stop thinking about Simon. She was becoming obsessed.

She went downstairs barefoot. Looking through the window she saw a blonde man standing on the doorstep. She didn't recognise him. She slipped the chain on the door, and peered through the opening.

"Who is it," she said. "I'm not expecting anyone."

"Detective Inspector Lancaster."

"Detective Inspector? No, you must have the wrong house," she answered loudly.

"Mrs Austin, Mrs Charles Austin," he called through the door. He held up a card, some sort of identification, thought Belinda. How could you believe what it was. She had never seen a card like that before.

"I assure you I am the police," Lancaster said. "Here's a phone number for you."

It looked genuine. There was a car outside with another man

sitting in it.   She removed the chain from the door and opened it slightly.

"Sorry to trouble you Mrs Austin," he smiled. "But if you have the time I'd like a word with you."

Belinda felt a sudden chill. Charles had only just left. It couldn't be anything to do with him surely. Maybe he had an accident.

But he hadn't been gone long. With a sickening thud, she realised that if anything ever happened to Simon there was no way in the world she would find out.

"Please," she said. "Come in and sit down," she made her way to the morning room.

Lancaster chose a chair near the window. He put a cigarette to his lips. The room looked over the front garden and the road.

"So Mrs Austin. I'm sorry to be the bearer of bad news."

"Bad news?" Belinda was alarmed. Lancaster watched as her face drained of colour.

"What bad news? Please tell me."

"I can discuss this now, or if you prefer I can call back when your husband is here."

Lancaster looked into her eyes. They showed him nothing except apprehension. Pretty woman. A strong face with no weakness there. She was blonde, with a short haircut in jig-jags. Lancaster knew he wasn't up to date with the latest hair fashions. There were tints of different colours of beige and blonde in her hair. Her large green eyes opened wider in anticipation, and her high cheekbones made her face look more rounded, her lips were full and very attractive. She had obviously been in bed. He wondered how she would handle the news of Clare's death. There was a high colour on her cheeks. At that moment she reminded him of Clare. It must have been her youth.

"No, no, I don't want you to come back," she managed to say. "You can tell me what is is now. My husband isn't home yet. I'm not sure when he'll be back."

She sat opposite him on a small padded chair. She was no more than five foot two inches. Lancaster noticed the dressing gown she was wearing. The sleeves were edged with blue satin. Or was it silk. It wasn't the usual gown he'd seen most women wearing. She must have bought it in town. It looked expensive.

"It seems your sister in law, Clare Austin, has met with an accident."

He shifted in the chair. He was furious with Crown. He usually saw to these things. Just when he needed him he'd disappeared. Damn him. Lancaster hated knocking on doors and breaking bad news.

Crown couldn't be down at the "Black Cat", it was far too early. Or did he stay there all night. God knows. Was Crown also in bed. Maybe he'd been to one of his parties last night. They usually went on late. Crown always seemed to be celebrating something with his friends. St George's Day, or V-E Day, or even the Queen's birthday. The last party Lancaster went to at Crown's place, was arranged to celebrate V-E Day. There was a doorman standing outside wearing all his medals. Crown had put sticky plaster criss-crossed over all the windows in the house. That was compulsory in the last war. They did it to stop glass flying about after a bomb falling. And then he closed the black out curtains. There were flags all over the ceiling, and what Crown called bunting. What a lovely word. It was another word that had disappeared from the vocabulary. There were dozens of blue and red balloons all over the floor.

The drinks were served by a young waiter who was doing a show in town. Eric had arranged a large photograph of Churchill and Roosevelt over the fireplace, then he played Vera Lynn on the record player. Every so often Crown put on a special tape recording of the sirens that wailed in the last war. He remembered the wailing as a child, then his parent would pull him out of bed, and rush him to the shelter. After a few minutes of the sirens wailing, Eric put on the all clear. Some of the people there wouldn't even know what the sirens were for, let alone the all clear. Then three smashing-looking drag queens arrived dressed in uniforms like the Andrew Sisters, and they sang "Apple Blossom Time."

Just the same he wished Crown would make another party like that. He seemed to be thinking of parties a lot since Clare's murder.

Lancaster must have parties on his mind. The only ones he ever went to were at Crown's place. No he'd given up going to parties. He often wondered why Crown chose to be a detective.

Lancaster reached inside his pocket and pulled out his mobile. Maybe Crown was at the bar in the local pub. Maybe Crown thought it was still Sunday.

He pressed in the number. He could see Belinda Austin anxiously waiting for him to speak.

"Lancaster here."

The bartender answered. He knew Lancaster was usually chasing after Crown.

"He's not here guv. Hasn't been in since last night."

Then he remembered something Harry had said this morning. Crown had gone to look at paintings. In the middle of a case too.

What was wrong with the man?

He brought himself back to the present.

"Accident? What accident?" she trembled.

Lancaster noted her reaction. He felt sure she had been told nothing.

"Yes, bad news," he continued. "Unfortunately Clare Austin has been found dead. She's been shot. Shot to death."

"Shot to death," Belinda repeated. "Shot to death. Clare? It can't be true," she pulled her robe tighter to stop herself from shivering, but her legs were shaking.

"I'm sorry Inspector. You're wrong. She just invited us to a party. We were there last night. At her house. You've made a mistake. It's the wrong Clare, you've made a mistake."

Lancaster stood up.

"I'm sorry Mrs Austin but I'm afraid it is true. Clare Austin is dead. Found lying naked on her living room floor in a pool of blood. All she had on was a rope of pearls."

He didn't want to terrify Belinda, but it was always best if suspects knew where they stood.

"Pearls," Belinda repeated. "I don't understand. What have pearls got to do with it? Who would do this? I can't believe it. Who would want to hurt Clare?"

"Not hurt, Mrs Austin, not hurt. Murder is the right word. You can use the word murder." He stopped speaking to light a cigarette. "You wouldn't happen to know if anything was wrong between your sister-in-law and her husband would you?"

"What could be wrong? We were at their party last night. Nothing was wrong."

"Mrs Austin," said Lancaster. "I need to ask these questions. And I need some answers right now. So if you don't mind, please think about it."

"I ... " Belinda murmured. "I don't know. They seemed like most married couples. You know, jogging along. No children. Nice home. No I don't know if they were happy or not," she wouldn't dare tell him the confidences about Clare.

She was visibly upset.

"Well," smiled Lancaster. "I'm sure you'll tell your husband the bad news. Or if you prefer I'll get my Sergeant to pop over later," Lancaster stood up. "Ah, I think I heard a car. It must be your husband driving up."

Looking outside he could see it was Crown driving up after all. About bloody time.

Lancaster went to the door.

Crown stepped inside the hallway shaking out his umbrella.

"Sorry sir. I just got finished with the investigation. Couldn't get here sooner. It's pelting out there. I'm soaked," Lancaster was decidedly peeved.

"This is Mrs Belinda Austin," he said. "Mr Charles Austin's wife," Crown took out a handkerchief and wiped his face.

"Good morning Mrs Austin," he said.

"Mrs Clare Austin's sister-in-law," Lancaster added.

"Thunderstorm sir."

"Well you'll dry off in here," He said sarcastically. "Get your notebook out."

Belinda Austin left the chair and went towards the telephone.

"I think I'll phone my husband if you don't mind. Get him to come home now, so I don't have to answer any more questions."

She picked up the phone.

"By the way," Lancaster said. "Just before you do that, I'm sure you won't mind telling my Sergeant your movements before yesterday evening Mrs Austin? I think perhaps it would be best if I wait until your husband arrives home after all. I need to check on him as well."

He watched her eyes, there was a hint of caution there, a marked hesitation.

"I'll be checking on everyone in the family as well. It was a particularly violent crime," he became demanding. "Mrs Austin this is a criminal investigation."

"I went shopping locally," she looked haggard now. "We were at the party of course," she was becoming confused. There were so many questions.

"And you were at home all day, before the party I mean?"

"Of course I was. Who would do this to Clare?" Belinda asked again. She mustn't answer any more of his questions, she would trip herself up if she hadn't done already. She hoped Charles wouldn't remember about Denise.

She was almost imploring him to tell her. Perhaps they would try to kill her. But what would their reason be?

"I don't know Mrs Austin. I just don't know. But I assure you I shall find out."

Lancaster tapped his fingers on his lips.

"Yes," he repeated. "Definitely dead."

Belinda was crying now. No one spoke. Crown opened his notebook.

Nice place they had, Crown decided, it was all yellow and white. Just a few other colours here and there. A green carpet and a paler shade of yellow furniture. No kids here that was for sure. He also wondered if the grieving husband had arrived home yet so they could question him. He was making things look difficult for himself with regards to an alibi. Murderers sometimes went on the run. And sometimes they stayed put to make it look good, as if they had nothing to do with it.

He and Lancaster had seen it all now. Weeping and tearing their hair, telling him they had come home to find their wives dead. More often than not they had done it themselves.

Lancaster was thinking the same thing. All sorts, thought Lancaster. All sorts like bloody liquorice.

From where he was standing he could see an invitation on the mantelpiece. It was next to a silver framed photograph. Lancaster picked up the photo and peered into it. It was the same one he found at Clare's and Penny's. The Austin family all standing together with their arms round each other. Love, love, love he thought, all you need is love.

"Who's in the photo Mrs Austin?" Lancaster asked idly fiddling with the party invitation.

Her voice held surprise. Why was he asking about photographs?

"Oh, oh, all of us, Eddie and Charles and Trevor and their wives. There I am," she pointed to herself. "The other photo is with our step brothers and sisters. All the family."

"Family," repeated Lancaster. The invitation was the same as Mrs Bolton's.

"And what time did you and your husband leave the party? I presume you both went to the party together?" Crown was questioning her now.

"Of course we did. We must have arrived there after 8.30, then we left at, let's see," she paused. "We must have left at about 12.30. I'm not sure."

"So you arrived late for the dinner."

She looked surprised. "Oh no one arrives in time round here. Parties always begin late."

Either she or her husband could have had something to do with the murder, Crown thought. One of them could have slipped back to the house after the party. Or maybe they planned it together? Would they give each other an alibi?

Belinda wiped her eyes. She went into the drinks cabinet and took out a bottle of scotch. Clare dead, out of the blue. Her head was swimming.

The party invitations were staring her in the face. One on top of the other. She lay back on the chair. Suddenly she sat upright.

"Something you remembered Mrs Austin," Lancaster asked gently. He felt she was alarmed about something. Was she frightened of someone?

"No, no," she said. "It's such a shock. I hope Charles gets in early."

"And your husband Mrs Austin. What does he do? In business is he?"

"Yes. Yes he is. He works in London. He has a factory there. He manufactures furniture."

"Of course," Lancaster turned towards her. "I think as my Sergeant has been out all day, we'll have a cup of tea. I'm sure you won't mind obliging us. We'll wait to speak to your husband, he may be able to help us more about times. And suchlike,"

Lancaster was into an old Kojak movie.

Crown was into a migraine.

Brenda felt her heart thumping. She poured out a whisky and drank it down. Thank God Charles would be home soon.

Charles would know what to say.

What frightened her more than the murder was being deceitful. Had she slipped up already? Did she say the wrong thing, or give them a wrong answer? Her head began to throb from the whisky. They couldn't possibly find out where she was the whole night before the party. What would she say if they found out? She had better think something up now, before they got too inquisitive, just in case. A fine perspiration broke out on her forehead.

She would have to warn Simon this was happening, and that Clare was dead. He wouldn't know anything about Clare, only what she had told him, that she was her sister-in-law. It was becoming more urgent for her to speak to him.

Should she make an excuse that she needed to go to the bathroom. Would the Sergeant follow her? She would hide in the bathroom and speak to Simon.

But where would Simon be now? This was all stupid. She didn't know where he lived, and she didn't even know what he did. He wore a gold ring on his third finger. But what did that mean? It might be there as a warning sign. It would be better to leave phoning him 'til tomorrow. She prayed she would get through the night. Secrets always got found out because someone passed on gossip. She must hold on to herself and not fall apart. Her shoulders sagged like an old sweater. She was trying to hold herself up.

"Biscuits with the tea Inspector?" she asked.

- 11 -

As a result of Edward's collapse in the hospital, Sister Bates needed to speak to the Staff urgently. She instructed them to meet her in the staff room at mid-day.

"I suggest," Sister Bates said with her voice of authority. "I suggest you speak to no one in the hospital about this. I don't know where the idea sprang from that this was a contagious case. Whoever spread this rumour will be very sorry I assure you. And don't stand there looking like a lot of headless chickens."

Dr Fellows turned towards her with a grim look.

"Sister, I also suggest we try and find out what happened to Nurse Evans. We have seen enough emergencies on our team. I appreciate the desk nurse got a terrible fright when Austin fell to the floor, and God knows we all felt sick when we thought it could be something contagious. But surely those are things we're trained to deal with."

"I know that Dr Fellows," Sister Bates said. "But these were unusual circumstances. However I shall certainly see Nurse Evans myself, I can't understand why she was so shocked when Mr Austin collapsed. The reputation of this hospital has to be our top priority whatever happens. Now as to Mr Austin, we must wait on the reports Dr Fellows, I expect they will be in as soon as possible. Dr Grant is up there now with Mr Kane Palmer the consultant. I am sure the diagnosis will be absolutely thorough. Mr Palmer has called in Miss Gillian Frampton from the hospital for tropical diseases. We have to find out if he has picked something up abroad.

As to the rest of you I've asked a nurse to bring in some tea," she turned to Nurse Collins. "Just where is Nurse Evans now?" she queried.

Nurse Collins answered crisply. "She's in a room on the second floor. I thought it best to have her taken up there away from any patients."

"Well done Collins," Sister Bates replied re-adjusting her cap.

"Just the same," interrupted Dr Fellows. "I'm not used to hearing that trained nurses are given to passing out. I wonder if there was something else that upset her?"

The nurse sensed a glimmer of tension arising between the Sister and Dr Fellows. They were hoping Dr Grant would come up soon, and calm them all down. "Possibly Dr Fellows," Sister replied to his sharp retort. "It's unfortunate Nurse Evans wasn't off duty when this occurred. You can come with me. Perhaps there was something unusual that upset her. I shall check with Dr Fullerton, the doctor who attended to Mr Austin when he collapsed."

She turned as the door opened.

"Now here's the tea. I urge you all not to gossip to anyone about this. I'm going to see how the patient is. There is a team in there examining him now. Then I shall find out what happened to Nurse Evans."

With this she abruptly left the staff room leaving the rest of the team to their tea and gossip.

****

Charles Austin parked his car close to the front door. He got out his house keys. The rain was still falling heavily. As he looked up briefly, he noticed there was a strange car parked in the drive-way. He could hear the faint rumble of thunder. Nervously he let himself inside.

"Belinda," he called.

"Charles," she called from the dining room. "I'm so glad you're here, there's a family problem."

"Never mind that, who's here Belinda? I saw a car in the drive-way."

He looked across the room. There was a blonde man sitting next to Belinda. And another fellow standing in the corner near the window with a notebook in his hand. Who the devil were they? Belinda was in her bath robe, and looked very edgy. What could this be about? It was only early evening.

"Ah. Mr Austin. We've been waiting for you. I hoped you would be in early, we were just on the point of leaving."

The man gave a sympathetic smile. There was command in the voice, courteous, but at the same time he spoke with forcefulness.

"What are you talking about, and just who are you?" Charles asked, taking off his wet coat and shaking out his umbrella.

"What have you been discussing with my wife and how did you get in here?"

"Quite simply sir. Your wife let us in through the front door. My name is Lancaster, Detective Inspector Lancaster. I shouldn't worry unduly about your wife, she has been most helpful. Oh and this is

Detective Sergeant Crown."

Lancaster had taken an instant dislike to the man. He had a sly face with no expression, a man who kept most things hidden well inside. His long pointed chin with thin cold lips made him look particularly unattractive. His eyes were bloodshot and covered in low hoods. He probably gave his wife aggravation if she didn't jump to his command. Well, Lancaster could be cruel too, he could shoot his questions out like poisoned arrows when he needed to.

Charles threw his raincoat over a chair. He became more concerned, what had all this to do with the family? He hoped it wasn't an accident.

"And just what business of yours is it when I get home? That concerns myself and my wife. If it's a matter of a parking ticket for Belinda just tell me so I can pay it tomorrow."

He knew that the police didn't usually come round about parking tickets these days with all the computers at their disposal. It must be something more serious, he could see Belinda had been crying. Had there been an accident after all?

"Detective Inspector Lancaster," said the man again holding up his card for the second time today.

Charles glanced the card. And what was Belinda doing huddled up like a bundle of washing in the chair?

"What can you possibly want with me?" He was becoming offensive.

"Raining out sir? Your coat is wet, and your umbrella is dripping. I thought I heard thunder," Inspector Lancaster went over to the window and glanced outside, then he pulled the curtains.

What kind of answer was that Charles wondered. Why was he discussing the weather?

"Best that no one looks in," he said. Lancaster definitely didn't like this man's attitude.

Charles Austin's eyes were squinting at him. He wondered if Charles was short sighted, he obviously wore glasses. His hair was plastered down from the rain. Just where had he been this evening Lancaster wondered? Faces meant a lot. They told him more than any investigation. He did not like this face, but that didn't mean he was a murderer. He'd made that mistake with the last case he was on. Man with a face of an angel had done three murders. Brutally too. Charles might be a calculated bastard, and on his guard. It was up to Lancaster to find out why.

"I'd sit down if I were you sir. I have a bit of bad news I'm afraid." Lancaster spoke carefully, and watched the squinting eyes.

Had Belinda smashed her car up? He had better calm down

and be more amicable. She may have run over someone, and killed them.

Inspector Lancaster noticed the expression that crossed Charles Austin's face. It was an expression of anger.

"I'm afraid to have to tell you that your sister-in-law has been found murdered."

He watched Charles Austin closely. Bomber delivered this bomb swiftly on the button. No flying up and down in the clouds. Fly in, straight on target.

Crown liked it too, he liked seeing a suspect with their pants down. He waited for Charles Austin to answer. He carried on writing everything in his notebook.

For once Charles was taken aback.

"Murdered," he echoed. He managed to control himself.

"Then it's nothing to do with Belinda. It's my sister-in-law, but which sister-in-law? I have two you know."

Lancaster was right. Austin had given him a quick snappy reply. No upset there. No caring. This was a chilly, well ordered man he was dealing with. Crown would have to do some digging.

"Oh I'm fully aware of that Mr Austin," came a swift retort from Lancaster.

"Well then, perhaps you'd be kind enough to let me know which one. Which sister-in-law?"

The man was squirming in his chair. He wasn't troubled at all to hear one of his family had been done away with. He even had the audacity to remind Lancaster he had two sister-in-laws and which one was it?

Most people would have reacted differently even if they didn't care a hoot about family. Lancaster sensed Charles Austin's peculiar look of relief. To think they all had their arms around each other in the photograph.

"Ah. Of course you have two sisters-in-law. It's your brother Trevor's wife, Clare."

He gazed at Charles intently.

Charles opened his mouth to speak, but could say nothing. He was shaking his head.

"Impossible," he said.

"Oh yes indeed, I'm sure you wish it was impossible. That is exactly what your wife said," Lancaster agreed. "Unfortunately it's a fact. A fete accompli one might say."

Charles got up.

"Mind if I pour myself a drink Inspector? Perhaps you'd care for one too."

"One's too many and a hundred's not enough" smiled Lancaster.

If Charles could only steady his nerves he would know what to say. He almost knew what was coming next. There would be questions as to why he was home so early, and where had he been. He came home early so as not to confuse Belinda. If he was late she would want to know why. It wouldn't do to let this man know he had been flirting with a lady in Hampstead over a furniture order. He might ask to speak to the lady. Still, he could soon sort that one out. A little flirting wasn't a crime after all. He picked up the whisky decanter and poured himself a large scotch, drinking it down without a pause.

"So," Inspector Lancaster smiled. "I'm sure you won't mind telling me your movements this afternoon. And this morning. What time did you leave the office? Is it usual for your evening appointments to end at this hour? Or did you by chance make another visit? Of course your answers will be treated as confidential," he smiled.

The question hung in the air like a dust mite.

Charles felt the scotch reaching his blood. So the bastard was clever.

"Of course I'll tell you where I've been," he waited another moment. "I've been working all day. I had a contract to finish and I needed to read the fine print. It took me ages, so I went downstairs to get a cup of coffee and took a coffee back to my office. Then as soon as I'd finished I packed up and headed for my afternoon appointment in Hampstead. I work in London. I sell furniture. We do a lot of built in stuff. We make bookcases and dining room furniture. That sort of thing."

He tried to make himself calm down. He was being too uncooperative. He'd read cases in the paper where the police took you in to the station to be questioned if they suspected anything. But what could they suspect?

"Friends of mine asked if I could design a bookcase for them. Something that would fit over a door and down the sides of it. They wanted something ornate and fancy. Long columns, arches, everything but the kitchen sink."

"Oh I know about furniture all right," Lancaster answered him pointedly.

"I once tried to convict a man for selling office furniture out of a company that didn't exist. We got him in the end. Set someone up to buy some of the furniture, and bingo, we had him in the bag. So simple really, it was just a matter of common sense. You can look all around the houses sometimes, and once or twice the answer is easy. To a cop the explanation's always simple. There's no mystery in the street, no arch criminal behind it all. If you find a body and you think his brother did it, you're gonna find out you're right."

He looked towards Crown with a raised eyebrow.

"You can't assume my brother did it, or that I did it. I think I'd better call my solicitor," Charles went to the phone. This man was crazy.

I know it, I know it, Crown thought. But the film has gone out of his head. He had seen it with Eric. What the hell was it? It was a few years ago, they went to the screen on Baker Street. He wrote down 'there's no mystery in the street,' on the opposite side of his creased paper where he had written. 'Furniture. Bookcase. Suspect antagonistic'.

Lancaster opened his packet of cigarettes, pulled one out, and lit it. Little puffs popped out like lost clouds.

"Oh, I shouldn't go as far as to say that Mr Austin. I'm not accusing you of anything. Just an idle comment."

Lancaster narrowed his eyes and shifted his position.

"Crown here will note down anything we say here. Even my idle comments," he gave a lop sided smile.

Charles became wary, he would have to be careful with his answers to this man. Was it Belinda he suspected? It must be. He watched Belinda out of the corner of his eye. Had she been accused of harming Clare? She was still shivering, and kept her face turned away. She seemed withdrawn, and she never uttered a sound. She must be terrified. Why would she harm Clare? What reason could she have?

"Used to do little models of furniture myself once," Lancaster said. "Never get the time these days. Pity. Mind you, I was a lot younger then. You need a lot of patience to make little models. I used to like making chairs. Well, we'll check up with your secretary about your movements this morning, I'm sure she'll confirm everything you said. Used to like swimming too in those days. But it's all the palaver of going to the pool, getting undressed, then having to shower and get dressed all over again."

"Swimming?" Charles was bewildered.

"Yes, that's what your brother does for a living isn't it? Builds pools to swim in."

Charles could only mumble. "Oh, Trevor. Yes that's his business," he found himself trying to say something kindly about Trevor, but couldn't find the words.

"Poor Trevor," he whispered. "He must be heart broken," how

false it sounded.

"I'm sure he is," Lancaster looked his quarry in the eye. "Did Trevor pop in here after the party?"

My God, thought Belinda. Do they suspect Charles of harming Clare? They couldn't. But she didn't know where he was the night before the party. He said he was at his mother's, but suppose it was a lie. If they ask if she was in the house all evening she would have to say she was out at a friends. Which friend should she call?

"Trevor come in here? To see us after the party?" Charles enunciated. "Whatever for? We only met at parties and funerals. I don't get on that well with Trevor."

He coughed and cleared his throat. "In fact I didn't want to go the damn party."

"And why would that be Mr Austin?"

"Oh, nothing much really, we had a row at the last dinner we went to. It never blew over, and we haven't spoken in months. That is until last night."

"And you decided to go to the party despite your row?"

"Of course," he grunted. "Belinda wanted us to make up. When the party was over, I waited for Belinda and then we left."

"And this afternoon Mr Austin?"

"I told you. I was in Hampstead on business. I had a three o'clock appointment. I told my secretary she could leave early as I wouldn't be back."

He began to wonder if anyone could have possibly seen him leave the building just after his secretary left. They would vouch for him. He could see his colleagues going in and out. But why would that matter now if Clare died last night? Could he be a suspect?

"No problem sir, I'm sure we can verify everything. I should look after your wife, she's had a nasty shock. Get her up to bed with a nice cup of tea. We'll leave you in peace now. I'll be in touch."

Lancaster picked up his coat and hat.

Crown went to the umbrella stand and lifted out his umbrella. Little drops of rain that had settled on it dripped across the hallway and out into the street.

"Looks like another storm," he mused out loud. "Dreadful the weather we've been having." He left Belinda and Charles Austin, each for their own reasons, looking frightened to death.

On the way home Lancaster stopped off to pick up a video. There wasn't much to choose from. The old black and whites he loved never seemed to be in the shops. Everyone was switching over to DVD's except him. In his local shop half the stock had already been changed. He might as well choose one he'd seen already.

Looking down the shelves he saw 'The Usual Suspects'. He enjoyed Kevin Spacey. He reached across taking it off the shelf. He wanted a nice quiet evening at home. He knew one of the Austin's had something to hide, but wasn't too sure which one. Charles looked as if he'd been caught smoking in the school playground.

Had he been seeing someone else? Highly possible. He'd put up a bit of a fight over an innocent afternoon in Hampstead. He was aggressive and antagonistic. As for his wife, she was very off hand answering his questions.

He went next door to the fish shop, and bought himself a piece of fried plaice, with a double portion of chips. He used to look forward to going out in the evening when the jazz singer lived with him. Take her out for dinner, then go and listen to some music together. Now he was looking forward to staying in.

- 12 -

The nurse on reception on Wednesday evening made sure Edward Austin was being checked constantly. It would be impossible not to see him, as Sister Bates made sure the door was propped open with a chair. Woe betide anyone who decided to move it. Sister Bates' instructions were carried out to the letter. Nurse Martins had felt the wrath of Sister Bates once before, and she didn't want it to happen again, so she constantly went into the room to check on the drips and the heart monitor. Nurse Martins couldn't remember ever seeing a door kept open with a chair, but if that was Sister Bates request she would make sure every nurse on the floor adhered to it. Sister Bates never left anything to chance.

"Better look in the room every so often Martins," Sister Bates had told her. "And keep all the staff on their toes while he's here. No one is allowed in unless they sign on, gown up, and then report to me. I don't want any mistakes made."

Sister Bates had personally told her, "I think it's far the best thing to barrier nurse him for the time being, until we find out the results. I don't like the look of him and I've seen a few cases like this before."

Sister Bates was being so cautious that it made Nurse Martins feel very apprehensive. What was going on? Nurse Martins had not worked on emergency for all these years not to realise this was a dangerous case. And she had an inkling of what it might be. It was a contagious disease, and it was on her floor, and she would use the utmost caution to see that everything ran smoothly. Surely the patient should be in an isolation unit. But they couldn't move him now, it would be far too dangerous. And they were still waiting for the lab results. Every time the phone rang, she jumped.

And look at what happened to Nurse Evans. Hadn't Nurse Collins found her being sick in the nurses toilet? As soon as Nurse Collins arrived tomorrow she would ask her about it. It wouldn't do to discuss any of this with the other night nurses. She didn't know them that well, and besides, they might spread rumours about and Sister Bates would trace the gossip back to her, and she would be in serious trouble.

Even the Chief Consultant had come down and asked if Mr Austin's bed could be turned towards he corridor. Why was it so important for the nurses to see if he was sleeping? No, this was all very worrying and she didn't like it at all. Rattling around her brain were some of the dreadful diseases she knew about. Fortunately most of them had been done away with by vaccination.

She had better go into the room herself, gowned up of course, to make sure the call bell had been pinned to the patients pillow, if anything was amiss he could press it to gain the attention of one of the nurses. But he was still asleep, and didn't look as if he had the strength to push a bell, or move his head on the pillow.

She was jarred from her reveries by Staff Nurse Forbes asking for a cup of tea, as all the patients were sleeping.

"Wake up Martins, I've called you twice," Staff Nurse Forbes said giving her a frosty look. Just then the phone rang at her elbow. She automatically looked at her watch. She always made a note of what time the phone rang while she was on duty, and who was on the line. Then she wrote it down in her notes. It was important if there was a medical emergency. She noted down that it was 2.30 a.m.

"Yes," she answered. "Nurse Martins speaking. Fourth floor."

"Hello Martins, it's Doctor Cooper from the lab."

Thank God she thought. At last the results must be in.

"Oh, hello Doctor Cooper. What keeps you up so late?" She tried to be as calm as possible.

"Well it's a funny thing Martins. You know I was asked to check up on the Austin case? I didn't think too much of it at the time, thought it was some kind of flu or even a virus. But Doctor Fullerton told me there was a faint tinge of yellow in Austin's eyes. Anyway the blood tests came back half an hour ago. One of the results showed a strange kind of sediment in the blood. So I ran it for Hepatitis. Sure enough it came back Hepatitis B."

"Good God," Nurse Martins drew a breath. At least it wasn't Hepatitis A. He would be done for if it was, and so might they. She had thought of other diseases that had been coming into the country recently. But Hepatitis B on the fourth floor was no joke. It was highly contagious and they would all need jabs.

"I'll have to get the Staff Nurse," Nurse Martins whispered into the phone. "My nurses have all been in and out of that room gowned up of course. He is being barrier nursed. We may have to move him to isolation."

She felt panic stricken.

"I know," Dr Cooper said. "Of course you must tell Sister immediately. But only Sister and staff. I don't want anyone panicking. I can't understand why this wasn't picked up right away. Someone only had to look into his eyes. Still it's easy to be misled. Sometimes it's just a mild case of jaundice. You know Martins, this is highly contagious."

"I'll get Sister immediately," said Nurse Martins, she was thinking about Austin collapsing on the floor in the entrance corridor. Any one of the patients could have been in contact with him in the canteen.

She was running away with herself.

"Do you want me to come up?" Dr Cooper asked. "I'm only in the lab. It won't take 5 minutes. Wait for me at the desk. Don't do anything. Just get hold of Sister Bates. By the way, how's Nurse Evans? I heard she was on the floor in the nurse's toilet being sick. There's always something going around the hospital. Probably a virus. Let me know how she is."

With that the phone was put down.

Staff Nurse Forbes looked at her cup of tea. She pushed it aside. It was cold.

"Staff Nurse," Nurse Martins turned to her. "Doctor Collins is coming down immediately."

She felt as if she was in some kind of trance. How was all this possible? She knew hospitals hardly ever allowed patients with Hepatitis across their doorsteps, unless they were caught unaware like they had been by Austin. She remembered once when she was training a patient had been admitted and isolated on a whole floor, because she was dying.

She could see the lift doors opening and Dr Collins appearing.

"Hello Forbes, have you found Sister Bates, looks like we've got a rotten job on our hands."

- 13 -

Nurse Martins was searching under the desk for her notebook when she looked up to see Sister Bates standing in front of her. She looked none too happy.

"Nurse Martins. How long has Mr Austin been with us?"

"Three days Sister."

"And what have my instructions been?"

Nurse Martins was puzzled. She answered immediately,

"Barrier nurse, constant checking, and sign the list before going in the room, and report to you if there was anything unusual happening to Mr Austin."

"Exactly. And what else?" Sister Bates' voice became louder. More strident in fact. What could she have forgotten? "Martins! And you Staff Nurse. What were my instructions?"

"We've carried out all your instructions to the letter Sister. Mr Austin is very ill, and we are managing to keep him stable," Staff Nurse Forbes answered, her shoulders slumping.

"I know that. Haven't I been here myself every evening?"

"Of course Sister," Nurse Martins swallowed hard. Something must be terribly wrong. What could it be? They had all been so careful.

"Forbes. In that case I've come to ask you why Mr Austin's door is closed. I've just passed it a moment ago on my way to speak to you about the new admissions."

"Closed?" gasped Staff Nurse Forbes.

"I gave strict instructions to my nurses to keep it open at all times," Sister Bates was breathless with anger. Her voice was rising in decibels. "I was going to look in on Mr Austin this evening. But on my way down the corridor I noticed the door was closed."
Staff Nurse Forbes' face went red. She felt hot and sticky.

"Well Forbes you had better come with me and find out who closed that door. I must admit I should have looked inside, but I automatically assumed that one of the nurses was in there changing him. Who has not signed on Forbes?"

Staff Nurse Forbes hurried back to Edward Austin's door and picked up the clipboard from the small table outside the door. My God, she uttered under her breath. There was no new signature. The last nurse to go in there was Nurse Parker at twelve fifteen. No one had signed on since. She glanced at her watch. It was twelve twenty five. Who could be in there? There would be hell to pay. She carried the clipboard back to Sister Bates.

Swallowing and stuttering, she said, "No, Sister Bates. there is no signature. Who could possibly be in there?"

Sister Bates narrowed her eyes and tried to control herself.

"Just wait until I find out who has ignored my instructions and disobeyed me. I'll have their guts for garters. I shall gown up and go in there myself."

She turned on her heel quickly and her feet marched up the corridor towards Edward Austin's room.

Staff Nurse Forbes felt dizzy. She opened her mouth to speak and she couldn't find the words. Who could have closed the door? And why? She looked for the bottle of water she kept under the desk, and hurriedly took a sip. She never realised the door was closed. It must have happened very quickly because no one had seen anything amiss. In fact the door could only have been closed a few minutes. She could hope that Mr Austin was all right.

Maybe it was closed by an unsuspecting nurse, who had just come on duty moments before Sister Bates came down the corridor. Or perhaps it was closed by someone from kitchen staff. Either way her life wasn't worth a candle.

She must find out how many people had been in and out of the room. And she had been in charge. Now she was for it, once Sister Bates was aroused there was no stopping her. Forbes would be accused of being unprofessional, unobservant, and not on top of the job. Sister Bates had a ream of words she used to the staff when she was on one of her rampages. But hadn't she been in and out of Austin's room to check everything herself?

Suddenly realising that Sister Bates was going to Edward Austin's room, she jumped up in terror. She must follow her.

"Sister, Sister Bates," she called. Leaving her post she rushed along the corridor following the determined figure of Sister Bates who was striding towards the nurses equipment room.

"Don't. Don't go into that room," she cried out. "Please Sister, don't go into that room without me, I assure you everything is in perfect order!"

Nurse Martins left her post and fled to the water cooler. She filled a paper cup with water and drank it straight down.

Now they were for it.

****

Lancaster was just getting into bed when the phone rang. He was thinking of the movie. He knew most of the dialogue he had seen it so many times. the plot was as good as Hitchcock. No one knew Keyser Soze, no one. A mysterious man invented to put the fear of God into everyone so they could carry out a robbery. Bloody clever. Even he couldn't work out the ending. Then when that mug of coffee fell to the ground, he should have known. He should have guessed it right away but he had seen the movie twice before it came to light. He was definitely getting too old for mystery men, and robberies. He had enough with families. He picked up the 'Evening News'. Even here in England some of the police were carrying guns. He never thought he would live to see the day when that happened. He put his night time cup of tea on the bedside table with the paper.

The phone rang.

"Sir?"

"Yes Crown," he sighed. "It's me. Only sometimes I wish it wasn't."

"You're usually someone else sir."

"You're right Crown."

"There's trouble at the hospital."

"Hospital? What hospital?"

"Eastern General."

"What's the problem Crown?" Lancaster took a sip of tea.

"Hepatitis."

Lancaster's mind was racing. "Hepatitis? What the hell has that got to do with us Crown? Can't they deal with their own epidemics?"

"It's Edward Austin sir. It appears he's been in hospital for a few days with hepatitis."

"And?"

"We have to get over there as soon as possible."

"Do we really need to deal with another one of their family Crown? But why should we go over there at this time of night? That's a contagious disease isn't it?"

"It looks like it could be sir."

"Lots of people get contagious diseases Crown."

"Well we are dealing with murder sir, not illness."

"Well you'd think someone might have told us."

"Maybe they didn't think it was serious."

"So why do we have to go over to the damn hospital? Call his wife and tell her if he's had a relapse."

"It's worse than that sir, much worse. Austin's dead. They found him dead in his hospital room."

"Dead? Who found him? Well that's sometimes the outcome of a serious illness isn't it? It must have happened after we interviewed Charles Austin. Look up the data crown."

"The problem is sir, when they went into Austin's room, the Staff Nurse and the Sister, and found him dead, all his tubes, blood transfusions and everything else, you know the kind of thing, had been yanked out of him. And with tremendous force. And everything else on the bedside locker had been thrown on the floor."

"And the nurses didn't notice anything? They didn't see a stranger on the floor at that time of night. What the hell is the time Crown?"

"Nearly one o'clock sir."

"Who could have pulled them out? If you're nursing someone, you do look inside the room now and then. Didn't he call out, or press the bell for a nurse?"

"No one heard anything. The door was closed to his room. The bell wasn't where it should have been, on the pillow. It was unpinned. At least that's what they're saying. The Sister is going crazy, and wants us to go there right away."

Lancaster looked at the paper next to the cup of tea and sighed, heaving himself out of bed.

"I'll be there in fifteen minutes. What floor is it?" he asked wearily. Crown hesitated for a moment. How should he put it?

"You can't go directly there sir."

"You're talking in bloody riddles Crown. Why not?"

"Because," he would have to take this one slowly, very slowly indeed. "According to a Dr Collins we have to go to the hospital pharmacy first."

"Whatever for?" asked Lancaster scowling. "Why can't we go straight up to the room? What the hell is going on here Crown?"

"Because sir, we have to have a jab. A jab for Hepatitis."

"Jab? I don't want a jab," responded Lancaster sitting on the edge of the bed feeling quite alarmed thinking about needles.

Murder he could deal with, but not needles.

"This is the worst case I've been on," he grumbled trying to hide his fear.

"Tell you what sir, I'll pick you up in half an hour," Crown said. "That way you'll have time to swig down a whisky."

"Are you sure that's what this Dr Collins said Crown? About the jab I mean. I think you've made a mistake."

"I think we should have seen Trevor Austin by now sir."

"I've got a man there. He hasn't left the house."

Crown wondered again about method. Go figure. Madness and

method sometimes went together.

- 14 -

Sister Bates and Staff Nurse Forbes were anxiously waiting outside the door of Edward Austin's room. Staff Nurse Forbes had turned white as a hospital sheet. One of the night nurses had written a large notice forbidding anyone to enter the room. It was taped on the front of the door.

Inspector Lancaster sat down next to Sister Bates. There was a couch opposite Austin's room. All he wanted to do was lean back and fall asleep. His buttocks were aching from the jab he received at the hands of Dr Collins, and as usual at the sight of a needle, he had been a thorough coward. He asked himself why he could deal with the most abhorrent murders, and yet behave so childishly when it came to a mere injection. He hoped Dr Collins would forget about his behaviour.

It was now two in the morning, and he'd better get on with his investigations or he might doze off. Nurse Forbes stood near them dabbing her handkerchief to her eyes.

"This is Detective Sergeant Crown," he nodded towards Crown. "We'd better start with you Staff Nurse, would you tell us who was on duty this evening?"

"I was," Staff Nurse Forbes answered looking nervously at Sister Bates. "And the night staff of course. There were five other nurses on the floor with me. Nurse Bourne, Nurse Taylor and Nurse Martins. Nurse Parker had been sent up specially to see a very difficult post-op case by Dr Devan, he relies on her for these cases. And of course there was Nurse Harris. She was arranging the drugs cabinet. There were a lot of new medications to set up after the operations. There were two new patients on the floor this evening. It was a very busy night. That's why we had an extra nurse on duty. And Sister Bates of course."

She cast an apprehensive look at Sister Bates, scarcely daring to say more. But Sister Bates was immersed in her own thoughts. "There was a doctor attending to one of the patients, and a surgeon looking at a post-op in another," Staff Nurse Forbes thought it better if she carried on talking. But she couldn't think who else was there that she didn't recognise.

"Now," said Lancaster. "I want you to tell me exactly what happened this evening. My Detective Sergeant will take note of everything."

He took out a cigarette.

"I'm afraid it's no smoking here Inspector," Sister Bates happy to change the subject for a moment.

All this trouble, and on her floor. It had never happened to her before.

"Don't worry Sister," Lancaster went on. "Just a habit of mine, I never light them. Just use them to think with."

"That's just it," Sister Bates said. "I've been thinking, and I know the last time I passed by, that door was definitely left open. Someone must have closed it shortly afterwards. Is that someone still in the hospital, that's what I want to know? I must protect my patients Inspector. And did that someone kill Mr Austin?"

Lancaster sighed, and leaned back into the couch. "That is exactly what I hope to find out. You're quite right Sister. But I doubt they're still in the hospital. They must have disappeared very quickly indeed. Let's see, the door was closed when you passed by the first time Sister. The question is why didn't any of the nurses notice the door was closed? Was the door supposed to be open all the time, or just some of the time?"

"I ordered the door to be open all the time. Day and night. I gave strict instructions to the day staff," Sister Bates replied in an agitated manner. "Nurse Martins helped me prop the door open with a chair. She is a very reliable nurse," she nodded her head. Staff Nurse Forbes dabbed at her eyes.

Sister Bates addressed Staff Nurse Forbes, "Now stop that crying Staff, immediately, and pull yourself together. This is no time to fall apart. I won't have it on this floor."

"I was asked by the Consultant," Sister Bates continued. "To have Mr Austin's bed turned around, so it faced the door. That way all the nurses could keep an eye on him if they were busy, without having to go into the room too often. We wanted the patient to get some sleep. He was sick so much of the time. Of course we never dreamed ... "

"Of course," Lancaster continued. "Austin didn't die of the illness after all. 'I'm not afraid of death, but I'm afraid of murder,' Sister Bates."

A frightened look came over Staff Nurse Forbes face. Murder. Another word that would rattle about her brain together with Hepatitis.

Crown knew Lancaster had slipped something in there. But what? It couldn't be anything about opening or closing doors. He knew it was to do with murder. That was something Lancaster had never said before. He knew most of Lancaster's film quotes, or pretended he did; but to be honest with himself, he didn't. Did

Lancaster expect him to sit in the movies every night? He wrote down 'I'm not afraid of death,' in his second column.

"So you think he's been murdered?" Sister Bates was incredulous.

"Oh I would say so Sister," Lancaster answered thoughtfully. "Quite thoroughly murdered. I would think it was shocking for you Staff Nurse, to find one of your patients so brutally attacked. I can't give any further comments until I have actually seen everything for myself."

He winced as he manoeuvred himself off the couch. Looking over at Crown he wondered if he was feeling the same way. Like a bloody pin cushion.

"You had a very sick patient, yet no one noticed the door of his room was closed."

"I know," Staff Nurse Forbes said, her face turning pale again. She knew this was no time to make excuses. She turned her head away from Sister Bates, unable to face another one of her angry looks.

"I was at my post," she continued. "I had sent one of the nurses to have a quick look into Mr Austin's room," she began to wonder how long it had taken Nurse Bourne to go to the room and return to the desk. Now she started to think about it, Nurse Bourne didn't come straight back because she asked Nurse Parker to go to the drug cabinet with her. She hadn't thought of that before, because it didn't seem important. Perhaps that when the door was closed, while Bourne and Parker were at the drug cabinet.

"They can't have been gone for about four or five minutes, and Nurse Parker pushed the drug trolley down the corridor and Nurse Bourne was standing behind her."

"What makes you remember that Staff Nurse?"

Staff Nurse Forbes took the handkerchief from her eyes.

"Because I wondered when Sister Bates would be coming down the corridor, and they seemed to be a little agitated."

She hung her head. "We run everything here to strict timing. Drugs have to be given at certain times, and we make sure they are."

"Why were they agitated?"

"Because one of the drugs hadn't come up from pharmacy yet. I phoned down to make sure it was on its way."

"Let's get back to Austin. He's been in hospital ever since he collapsed in the ground floor corridor."

"Yes," Staff Nurse Forbes answered timidly.

"Mmm," Lancaster was thoughtful. "I need to know who was going in and out of his room. I want everyone's name and rank. Also

I need to know about the cleaners, what time do they arrive in the morning, and what time they come in during the afternoon? Who delivers meals to the rooms, and do the nurses sometimes take things in and out? I presume you told the catering staff not to deliver anything to his room without permission?"

"Everyone who goes into that room Inspector, has to sign on, and gown up. Those are Sister Bates' instructions. Whether they're kitchen staff or hospital staff, that's what they have to do." She attempted to wipe her tears. "We told the kitchen not to bring anything up for Mr Austin. He couldn't eat yet. He could only drink small amounts of soda water."

"That's enough from you Staff," Bates commanded. "Wipe your eyes and get some control," She turned to Crown. "Most of the nurses on this floor were in his room at one time or another. You must appreciate that. There was a drip to check on, and replace if necessary, and the heart monitoring machine to check. And of course the catheters had to be seen to. He wasn't well at all. Sick all the time and he couldn't leave his bed. He didn't improve, but he remained static. Of course with hepatitis it can take a long time to get well. On occasion it can be fatal. The liver may fail to rejuvenate. But that's usually the A strain, and Austin had the B. But I have known some patients with B become seriously ill just the same. The blood cells change too much. Then unfortunately, there isn't a lot we can do for them."

"Right. If you'll be good enough to write all the names down for me I'll interview everyone later."

"So you had the door propped open with a chair?" Crown commented. "Isn't it usual for some kind of door stop to be used? When I was in hospital there was sort of a leather tie wrapped around the door handles."

"Yes, yes it is, but I was nervous. Dr Grant, who's a friend of Mr Austin, might come up and want the door opened. It was best to be on the safe side, so that's when I got the chair myself. It might seem a ridiculous thing to do, but I knew Dr Grant would want it done. He has funny ways Dr Grant, and I've seen him do that with some of his patients. He doesn't care if some of his patients don't sleep well at night, because they'll drift off during the day. He's not even keen on giving them sleeping pills. And Mr Austin was in a bad way. Perhaps he was right. He wouldn't have had the strength to press the bell on his pillow."

All the doctors who worked here had their own quirks and ideas, and she fell in with them.

"So I instructed Nurse Martins and Staff to make sure all the nurses were told to leave the chair there."

"What else did you do?" Crown asked Sister Bates. "What other tests, I mean, when he was admitted?"

"Every test possible. Blood, urine, temperature, heart, everything. Of course we couldn't move him about. We did what we could for him. He was burning hot so we cooled him down, and then gave him a sleeping draught. He couldn't seem to keep anything down. Once the illness was confirmed, we knew the outcome. In fact it was all he could do to swallow water. With a straw of course. We also left a bowl just near his hand on the bed in case he wanted to be sick."

"How did you know it was exactly eight thirty, when you found the door closed?" Crown asked.

Sister Bates looked askance.

"My dear man," she said. "Everything runs strictly on time on my floor as Staff has just pointed out. I assure you if that door was closed I know the time exactly. In fact I glanced at my watch as I went past. It was eleven thirty six exactly."

She nodded her head to emphasise her words.

Staff Nurse Forbes and Nurse Martins were beginning to feel a little comfort now that Inspector Lancaster was here. Nurse Martins was sure he would leave a policeman on duty to watch the stairs and the lift.

"So," Inspector Lancaster said. "We have to speak to every nurse who dealt with Mr Austin, or even poked their heads into the room to look at him. Then we'll go through the catering staff, and the porters and cleaners. The lot. Then we'll try to find the culprit who closed that door. They may have been in association with the killer."

Nurse Martins gave a slight shiver. Maybe the killer was still here after all.

Lancaster turned to Sister Bates.

"Now Sister," Lancaster said nodding to Crown. "We'll go in and look at what remains of Mr Austin."

****

Frank was getting nervous. With the death of Clare, he knew the police would be round sooner or later. They would surely be interviewing all the family. Then what would he do? Betty would be the first one to tell them everything. She only needed a policeman to look at her and she would be in a blind panic. The trouble was he had absolutely no one to turn to for advice. He couldn't go to the solicitor or to his friend Arthur in the next village. The whole episode was full of complications, and might bring up his past.

No, there was nothing he could do, only sit it out and keep quiet. He couldn't afford to get involved in any questions and answers. He could never mention a word about the accident to anyone at all. Otherwise they were for it. Then God knows where it would end up.

The only person he was worried about was Betty.

- 15 -

Belinda's private world was falling to pieces. Terrified of making phone calls from the house, even on her mobile, she decided to phone Simon from the station. The trouble was at the station there were those damned open telephone booths. She would have to talk quietly so no one would overhear her. It was best if she didn't take the car; her number plate was noticeable. She would catch the bus at the top of their road. She threw on a coat, zipped up her boots, and taking her umbrella, quickly left the house. She had better get a grip on herself quickly or everything would come apart. The one thing on her mind was to let Simon know what was happening.

But why was she so worried about it? She hadn't heard from him. Not a call. But she must tell him that it would be safer not to see each other for a few weeks.

She knew she wasn't capable of a long separation, however dangerous it might turn out to be. Now Clare was dead everything she did would be noticed. If not by the neighbours, it would be noticed by Charles. Even the police might watch her.

She was glad she was wearing her old winter boots. She was being lashed by the rain even with the umbrella.

She held the umbrella in front of her face, and made her way to the bus stop. Standing there in the wet unhappy afternoon, she realised she had forgotten how bad public transport was. It must have taken half an hour before a bus came crawling round the corner from the village. She was a fool to do this, someone might notice her when she got off the bus at the station. She would have been better off taking the car after all.

When the bus finally arrived she made sure she found a seat near the exit, that way she could jump off quickly when the bus came to a stop. The station was a faint watery blob in the distance. Lots of her neighbours got the late train home. She must be on her guard in case she was seen. Charles would want to know why she went to the station at this hour, and in the rain.

It wouldn't be far to walk, even though she would be soaked to the skin. She hurried inside the entrance and found the telephone booth. Even her fingers were wet as she dialled the number. She was so intent that she never noticed a man lingering at the newspaper stand.

Just then the London train disgorged a crowd of people. The station became a hive of activity, with people buying papers, while some stood inside the doorway waiting for their wives or husbands to pick them up.

The man at the news stand kept a short distance away from her, his woollen hat pulled down closely around his head. He was holding a magazine in front of him. Simon wasn't there. It was just his answering service. In desperation she decided to leave him a message. there was no other way. He was probably having dinner with his wife.

The man watched her as she put the phone down and adjusted her head scarf.

Now at last he would find out where she lived. He smiled, feeling very pleased with himself.

****

"Now Sister we'll have a look inside that room," Inspector Lancaster said, as he put his hand out to open the door.

"I think we should wait a moment for Dr Collins," Sister Bates said. "He's bringing up some extra gowns for you and the sergeant."

Crown looked down the corridor where the lift doors were opening and Dr Collins appeared carrying masks, gloves and green aprons.

"Good evening," Dr Collins said. "Please put these on."

"Come, come Staff," Sister Bates addressed Staff Nurse Forbes. "And you too Martins. Get gowned up."

Inspector Lancaster put the apron on and glanced at Nurse Martins.

"Death's at the bottom of everything Martins, leave death to the professionals. You know what Crown," Lancaster said. "I've never worn one of these damn things in my life."

"They must have worn them in 'Panic in the Streets' sir," Crown commented with a superior look.

Crown's retort startled Lancaster.

He smiled for the first time. "Well done," he said to Crown. But even he couldn't remember what they wore in 'Panic in the Streets', he thought Jack Palance was swimming in the Hudson, that was all he could remember about 'Panic'. The only thing he knew was the present, he was gowned up with a mask and apron and his backside was sore, and he must look like a green ghoul from one of the Hammer horror films. He could hardly breathe, he felt like he was going into a war zone.

Then the sharp voice of Sister Bates took command.

"I'll open the door," she said, gripping the handle.

The room was in darkness as they entered. She reached her hand out and clicked on the main light. The sudden brightness caused Inspector Lancaster to put his hands in front of his eyes. No one spoke.

When he took his hands away he looked towards the man in the bed.

"Definitely dead Crown. Definitely dead," Lancaster said as he moved towards the dead body of Edward Austin.

Austin's eyes were closed. his right arm was flung out over the bed, his face turned towards the door. His left hand lay on his chest. His left thigh was carelessly thrown over his right leg. Lancaster noticed the window at the side of the room was slightly open.

A faint breeze was blowing, causing the curtains to flutter. the other thing he noticed was a rusty tin box, it's lid open, standing on the bedside table. The ECG line had been ripped out,and the tube from the saline drip lay on the floor. The transfusion bag was lying beside it, dripping little droplets of blood. Something which had been attached to Austin's arm, he wasn't sure what, had been ripped out, leaving a cruel mark on his arm where the plaster had been. His arm had been bleeding.

"Vicious," Crown uttered, speaking in muffled tones through his mask. "What's a tin box doing on his bedside table? Surely it wasn't here when the man was admitted."

Sister Bates eyes were blazing.

"Of course it wasn't. Who would want to put something like that near a sick patient? Why it's unheard of. I've never seen anything like it."

"A job like this wasn't done in a moment," Lancaster spoke.

"Someone held the door closed for some time, otherwise they were very fast workers. Have you seen this box before Staff Nurse?" he enquired of Staff Nurse Forbes.

The expression in Forbes' eyes was answer enough for Lancaster. She was thoroughly startled.

"Never," she exclaimed.

"So, someone spirited a large rusty tin box into this room?" He shook his head. "What we have to find out is how could anyone do that? And why?"

Lancaster was at the bedside now, holding up his small torch. He played it up and down over the dead man.

"How did he manage to throw his left leg over his right one? If he was that ill it was impossible. Nothing has been taken off the body. He's still in his hospital gown. His long socks are still on. Was he wearing anything else Sister? And why are his long socks still on?"

"As he was so ill, and on the ECG and a saline drip I decided to leave the socks on him. He complained he felt cold. We always keep a blood transfusion unit by in case of an emergency. His blood count was very low."

Sister Bates was clearly distressed.

"But it's all wrong," Lancaster said. "It's all wrong," he opened the bedside drawer and rifled through it. "Where's his watch?"

No one replied.

Staff Nurse Forbes suddenly remembered.

"We got him into the room in such a hurry, whatever he was wearing was taken off and put in the wardrobe. It's probably on one of the shelves."

"Look in the wardrobe Crown," Lancaster ordered.

Crown opened the wardrobe door.

"His clothes seem to be here. Shirt, tie, suit, shoes, socks, no underwear. But I can't see his watch," his hands moved swiftly across the shelves.

"Please tell me everything that happened when he came in," Lancaster said.

"I remember someone putting his things in the wardrobe," Nurse Martins said. "Someone said something about his watch then, and we got him into bed." What was it? And why did she suddenly remember it?

Crown felt he was getting hot. He wished they could get this over with quickly and get out of this damn room, and out of this damn green gown.

Sister Bates spoke, "Get on with it Martins. Think girl. There's a dead man here, before we know it the hospital board will be breathing down our necks. They'll want to know why he died under our care, and on my floor. And you are on it Nurse Martins!"

Staff Nurse Forbes tried to recall everything that happened in this room. There was something said about Austin, something said about his illness and some comments about the watch. What did they say?

The room became silent, the only sound they could hear was the little click of Lancaster's torch as he switched it off.

"That was it, it was a word. A word about the watch," Staff Nurse Forbes blurted out. "One of the nurses held he watch and said 'Cartier'."

"Cartier?" Crown asked. He quickly wrote it down in the left hand column.

"Yes, 'Cartier'. I remember because at the time, while we were getting Mr Austin into bed, and emergency was setting up, one of the nurses held up a watch."

"A watch," echoed Lancaster. "Belonging to whom?"

"Why, to the patient of course. Yes, a watch. One of my nurses took the watch off his wrist and said something like, 'Cartier, we'd better hand this to Sister.' Yes, someone definitely said that. Isn't that odd. I remember the watch now. It's quite clear in my mind. It didn't seem important at the time. One of the nurses took the watch and put in her pocket."

"Which nurse would that be Staff?" Sister Bates was watching her earnestly. "Come along girl try and remember."

"I don't know Sister. I'm afraid I can't remember who it was."

"All right Staff Nurse, we'll leave that for the moment and carry on with the rest of our investigation," Lancaster pondered about the box.

"It looks as if Austin was reaching out for something," Crown spoke in a subdued voice. The room gave him the creeps and the gloves were making his hands perspire.

"The man is dead, probably murdered, and for some crazy reason someone has left an open tin box next to him. Austin's arm is hanging out towards it," he said. "So he may have tried to reach out for it. But why?"

"Maybe he was trying to reach for the bell," Staff Nurse Forbes suggested.

"Bell?" Lancaster queried. "I can't see a bell. There's usually one pinned to the pillow."

"But the bell was pinned onto the pillow. I did that myself," Sister Bates said.

"The bell is unpinned. Look it's hanging down at the side of the bed," Crown observed.

"Unpinned!" Staff Nurse Forbes voice was filled with horror.

"I saw the bell pinned on the pillow," Nurse Martins said. "I checked it."

She was beginning to wonder if she really remembered anything at all. Her life on the hospital floor was always so carefully timed, everything ran like a bloody Cartier watch. She would check the patients, take their temperature, make sure their medication was being correctly administered, and check the levels of the drips and blood transfusions. Now, with everything so horribly wrong, with a dead patient, and a missing bell from his pillow, and a wretched rusty looking box on the bedside table, she felt as if she was drowning in a sea of self doubt and fear. She began to hate Sister Bates and was glad Edward Austin was dead. Her job was at stake, and perhaps everything she said to the Inspector and Sister Bates had been quite wrong.

"His pills look as if they've been thrown all over the floor. His water jug is smashed," Sister Bates was looking round the room in terror. "Whoever did this must be found right away."

They all turned to look at the broken glass which lay in fragments at their feet.

Inspector Lancaster suddenly took command.

"Thank you Sister Bates, Nurse Martins and Staff Nurse. I think Sergeant Crown and I will be able to carry on ourselves now. You've both been very helpful. Please close the door now," he sighed, glad they had left the room.

"I don't know Crown. The man had Hepatitis. I don't know how advanced it was or whether it attacked his liver or any other organ suddenly. We're not doctors Crown, we're policemen. There's a full hospital of doctors who will be glad enough to tell us all about Hepatitis. Meanwhile this man is an Austin, and now we've got two dead Austins on our hands. I don't like it. Is it connected Crown? And if it is, why?"

"It's all bizarre. Maybe we should go outside and take off this bloody uniform," Crown answered. He was so hot now, if he didn't' get these rotten gloves off soon he would die in the room himself.

"But on the other hand, it can all be coincidence. Clare Austin was murdered, and this is an illness, surely the killer wasn't prepared to wait. This man's been murdered in cold blood."

"Sir, you don't think it could possibly be suicide, do you?"

Lancaster looked at the dead man.

"No, I don't. I think if he was so weak he couldn't manage to rip the drip off the stand and on the floor. The water jug has been flung across the room, a long way from the bed. And all the other paraphernalia, pills and bottles and everything else are lying under the chair over there. They were thrown forcibly Crown. No. This man has been deliberately put to death."

"And there's no bell on the pillow. Do you remember having a bell on the pillow when you were in hospital?"

"Don't remind me Crown. I'll be there myself soon, after that bloody injection. I'm beginning to feel a bit sick."

"Well didn't you have a jug of water next to your bed? And a glass?"

"I did."

"Well there isn't a glass."

"Maybe the nurses filled the glass for him and brought it in. He certainly couldn't lift a jug. Maybe the nurses didn't bother with it, they have plastic cups these days."

"Look!" Crown suddenly exclaimed. "There's the pin sir. The pin that held the bell on the pillow. It's lying there under the chair."

"The poor bastard couldn't even stand up. He had to get the nurse to undress and wash him, and change his bed socks. He was plugged into all these gadgets, and was taking medication. He was incapable of doing anything for himself. He certainly didn't throw it over there," Crown moved over to the chair and bent down. His head was beginning to throb now.

"It's open, sir. The pin is open. Someone took it off the pillow and left it open."

"Why the hell did they do that?" Lancaster asked. "Why didn't they take it with them? Why drop it under the chair?"

"God knows sir. They were probably in a hurry to get out of the room and just threw it down. There doesn't have to be reason."

Crown shrugged his shoulders. "Sir when can we go outside and take this stuff off?"

"When I say so Crown," Lancaster felt sweaty himself. How did they perform operations with these bloody gloves and masks on? He must be running a temperature. An open pin left casually under the chair. What was that for? Lancaster could only mutter to himself.

"Crazy."

"And sir," Crown said. "He's just lying there with his arm thrown out like that. Like he tried to get help."

"Or grab at someone. And that tin box. Take it with us and check it out. By the way Crown, who called us to come here tonight? Was it Staff Nurse Forbes?"

"I don't remember," Crown reached inside his pocket and took out his notebook.

"Call was logged in at twelve."

"Who took the call?"

"Sergeant Smith. He just said there was a call from the hospithing at all. Her life on the hospital floor was always so carefully timed, everything ran like a bloody Cartier watch. She would check the patients, take their temperature, make sure their medication was being correctly administered, and check the levels of the drips and blood transfusions. Now, with everything so horribly wrong, with a dead patient, and a missing bell from his pillow, and a wretched rusty looking box on the bedside table, she felt as if she was drowning in a sea of self doubt and fear. She began to hate

Sister Bates and was glad Edward Austin was dead. Her job was at stake, and perhaps everything she said to the Inspector and Sister Bates had been quite wrong.

"His pills look as if they've been thrown all over the floor. His water jug is smashed," Sister Bates was looking round the room in terror. "Whoever did this must be found right away."

They all turned to look at the broken glass which lay in fragments at their feet.

Inspector Lancaster suddenly took command.

"Thank you Sister Bates, Nurse Martins and Staff Nurse. I think Sergeant Crown and I will be able to carry on ourselves now. You've both been very helpful. Please close the door now," he sighed, glad they had left the room.

"I don't know Crown. The man had Hepatitis. I don't know how advanced it was or whether it attacked his liver or any other organ suddenly. We're not doctors Crown, we're policemen. There's a full hospital of doctors who will be glad enough to tell us all about Hepatitis. Meanwhile this man is an Austin, and now we've got two dead Austins on our hands. I don't like it. Is it connected Crown? And if it is, why?"

"It's all bizarre. Maybe we should go outside and take off this bloody uniform," Crown answered. He was so hot now, if he didn't' get these rotten gloves off soon he would die in the room himself.

"But on the other hand, it can all be coincidence. Clare Austin was murdered, and this is an illness, surely the killer wasn't prepared to wait. This man's been murdered in cold blood."

"Sir, you don't think it could possibly be suicide, do you?"

Lancaster looked at the dead man.

"No, I don't. I think if he was so weak he couldn't manage to rip the drip off the stand and on the floor. The water jug has been flung across the room, a long way from the bed. And all the other paraphernalia, pills and bottles and everything else are lying under the chair over there. They were thrown forcibly Crown. No. This man has been deliberately put to death."

"And there's no bell on the pillow. Do you remember having a bell on the pillow when you were in hospital?"

"Don't remind me Crown. I'll be there myself soon, after that bloody injection. I'm beginning to feel a bit sick."

"Well didn't you have a jug of water next to your bed? And a glass?"

"I did."

"Well there isn't a glass."

"Maybe the nurses filled the glass for him and brought it in. He certainly couldn't lift a jug. Maybe the nurses didn't bother with it, they have plastic cups these days."

"Look!" Crown suddenly exclaimed. "There's the pin sir. The pin that held the bell on the pillow. It's lying there under the chair."

"The poor bastard couldn't even stand up. He had to get the nurse to undress and wash him, and change his bed socks. He was plugged into all these gadgets, and was taking medication. He was incapable of doing anything for himself. He certainly didn't throw it over there," Crown moved over to the chair and bent down. His head was beginning to throb now.

"It's open, sir. The pin is open. Someone took it off the pillow and left it open."

"Why the hell did they do that?" Lancaster asked. "Why didn't they take it with them? Why drop it under the chair?"

"God knows sir. They were probably in a hurry to get out of the room and just threw it down. There doesn't have to be reason."

Crown shrugged his shoulders. "Sir when can we go outside and take this stuff off?"

"When I say so Crown," Lancaster felt sweaty himself. How did they perform operations with these bloody gloves and masks on? He must be running a temperature. An open pin left casually under the chair. What was that for? Lancaster could only mutter to himself.

"Crazy."

"And sir," Crown said. "He's just lying there with his arm thrown out like that. Like he tried to get help."

"Or grab at someone. And that tin box. Take it with us and check it out. By the way Crown, who called us to come here tonight? Was it Staff Nurse Forbes?"

"I don't remember," Crown reached inside his pocket and took out his notebook.

"Call was logged in at twelve."

"Who took the call?"

"Sergeant Smith. He just said there was a call from the hospital and would we go round at once."

"But no one knew Edward had died then, did they? At two thirty no one knew a solitary thing. It was only when Sister Bates came down the corridor and noticed that Austin's door was closed, that anyone knew a damn thing about Austin being dead."

"And if no one knew he was dead, or if no one knew he was dying, who the hell called us?"

"Someone wanted us here Crown. Someone called in for some cockamamie reason, and we'd better find out damn quickly who that someone was. And why they want the police here? Most people steer clear of the cops, unless it's an absolute necessity. No, it's curious all right. Hospitals in the middle of the night, and a member of the Austin family dead. Furthermore, everything that seems to be used by modern man to keep you alive, is ripped out of him and tossed onto the floor of his room. He didn't die of Hepatitis, someone wanted to make sure he never recovered.This wasn't surgery. It was murder.'"

"I think we'd better interview the nurses, as soon as we can," Crown said. Crown wished he hadn't given up smoking. Smoking was what you had to do to work with this man. Drinking too. You needed to be on the booze. You needed to sit and drink and look at your notebook, you needed to look at murder, and then you needed to look at the movies. You could actually go to the movies every night if you wanted to. Crown didn't want to. He reckoned he wasn't worked to death really, just puzzled to death.

Let Lancaster have his fun. But he never seemed to get the answers as quickly as he used to. He would sweat over them for weeks.

Suddenly while he was thinking of surgery and murder in the stillness of that awful room, a knock came at the door. Thank God. He could take off these damn gloves and masks and get some air in the corridor. He hurried outside the room, dropping the plastic gloves on the floor as he went.

It was Nurse Martins.

"Sir, I thought I'd better tell you. You've left your mobile at my desk."

"Yes. Thank you Nurse Martins, of course. I must have forgotten."

"Let's get out of here and ring the station Crown, see if the wandering husband is at home," he dialled the station and waited. "Harry, it's Lancaster, find out if Trevor Austin is still being watched, I'll hold on," he tapped his fingers on the desk.

"Right," he said. "I'll let him know."

So the disappearing husband had turned up. He turned and spoke to Crown.

"He's home."

Lancaster scratched his head and put a cigarette to his lips. Crown could see on the side of the desk, the remains of one of Lancaster's cigarettes propped on the cigarette packet.

"I think we'd better speak to him before we interview the nurses," he said. "Then we'll get back to the hospital as soon as we can."

"You'd better take that ashtray with you sir."

"The husband has had time to cook up a good story about

where he was and wasn't that night. We've let him hang about too long. The funeral's over. Then we'll visit the rest of the loving family. The non-blood relations."

"I don't think he's been anywhere sir. Probably scared to death if he did it, and scared to death if he didn't. You know what? Maybe our killer is thinking of bumping off Trevor Austin."

"An interesting thought Crown. You sound like a James Cagney movie. Congratulations."

It was only four weeks since Clare's death, and now they had another victim who was related to the family.

"You know what I think Crown? This case is like a virus. One is powerless to stop it sometimes, until you learn more about how you catch it. And murder seems to be running riot in the family. And our problem is who is going to catch it next."

- 16 -

Lancaster looked at things the wrong way round, leaving the main suspect till last. He felt it gave him an edge.

When they arrived at Clare's house, the missing husband was standing on the spot where they found Clare.

"Ah, Mr Austin," said Inspector Lancaster. "I believe you've been staying at the Ross home."

"Yes, I have," the reply came in a whisper. "She's gone. Forever I mean."

Lancaster saw a slim man dressed in a blue shirt and navy jeans. His face was round as a bagel, with tiny little brown eyes that looked as if they'd been crying. The few hairs he had left were combed down over his forehead. He had taken off his glasses and was holding them in his hand.

Crown thought he looked a mess.

"I'm terribly sorry about your wife Mr Austin, this is all very difficult and it must be very hard for you. But it's hard for anyone to get to grips with murder. It's a dreadful business," Inspector Lancaster spoke sincerely. He slipped his mobile out of his pocket and put it on the coffee table next to him.

"Mr Austin," he would soon get what he needed from this man. He'd just needed a little prodding. Lancaster waited, looking at him for a long time.

"I believe you were asked to stay at the Ross' place for a few days eh? "

"Yes, they were kind enough to offer to put me up after the funeral. I need time to get used to living here again after ... " his voice trailed off. "I've been here two days now."

"A few days is a long time after murder. Are you a good house guest?"

"Yes. We're friends."

"I knew you'd have to come back eventually. No one stays away forever, only Lord Lucan."

"Lucan?"

"Of course we knew where you were. My Sergeant is very good at keeping tabs on things like that. Apparently you went missing after the party. We were told you left in rather a hurry after the party, and you didn't return until some ungodly hour the next morning. Of course Sergeant Crown and I had left the scene by then. You must have been shocked to find police cars all over the driveway, and your wife dead in your living room."

"Of course I was shocked. I was grief stricken. I thought Clare would be there waiting for me."

"I would have thought you might have stayed at home after the party. Seems the usual thing to do. Help your wife clear up, tell her what a lovely evening it was. Unless you didn't think it was lovely," here he gave a chuckle. "My Sergeant and I call you 'the missing husband'. Dangerous title that."

"You don't think ... "

"I don't think anything Mr Austin. I like a man who can run faster than I can. Either I know or I don't know. You were missing after the party and I intend to find out why."

He saw Austin hesitate. Lancaster waited for the excuse.

"Get it all down Crown," he called over his shoulder. That always made them more amenable to questioning.

The answer from Trevor sounded feasible. There was no way to confirm his alibi now Clare was dead. Lancaster waited in anticipation.

"I decided to leave the house after the party because I didn't want to hear what Clare was going to say. She wanted to discuss something. Something important."

"And what might that be Mr Austin?"

Trevor began to stammer. "She wanted a separation."

"Ah. A separation from you. Is that what she meant?"

"Of course. What other separation could there be?"

"Oh I don't know. From business associates, from your family, who can tell?"

He was being deliberately flippant.

"I knew Clare wanted to leave me. And I wanted to get as far away as I could to think things over. I didn't want to stay at home and have a row. I hoped she might change her mind. She was so off hand with me lately. We hardly ever spoke to each other. I wondered if she was seeing someone else. Another man. I couldn't understand her attitude, I loved her. I wanted to stay with her. That's the reason I stayed away. I knew she would corner me as soon as the party was over. So I decided to go to Joan's and stayed for breakfast."

"You say you went to Joan's. Why not Betty and Frank?"

"Of course I wouldn't go there. I wanted to talk to someone who knew how I felt about Clare. Anyway, after breakfast I came home. I had to find out what Clare wanted to do. Of course when I got back it was all too late." He grimaced and lowered his head. Tears welled up in his eyes.

"Mr Austin, you say you were nervous about your wife leaving you. I say you did have a discussion with your wife after the party, and the discussion turned into an argument, which turned into a blazing row. In your fury you went upstairs, found your gun, and shot her. You left her to die on the floor, and seeing what you'd done, you panicked. You didn't dare wait to call an ambulance or the police, because you knew you'd be definitely be taken into custody. So you stayed at Joan Ross' place as late as you could to give yourself an alibi.. Anyway we will find believers as long as it's fantastic enough."

Trevor Austin looked ashen. "No, no, that's not true! I couldn't have killed Clare. I don't even have a gun. I wasn't missing, I was at Joan's. I wish to God I had been here. Maybe then I could have done something to stop Clare being killed."

He suddenly broke down in tears.

"Please Mr Austin. I know this is terrible time for you."

Inspector Lancaster adjusted his tie. He patted Austin's shoulder. He's seen men cry before. Especially when they'd just murdered their wives.

Crown had seen it too. He had seen husbands weep and pull their hair. Like a Greek tragedy he'd been forced to sit through with Eric. Why was he sitting through Greek tragedies and movies all the time?

"Mr Austin I will ask you again. Will you explain your absence from this house immediately after the party?" Trevor Austin took out a handkerchief and blew his nose.

"I've told you the truth. I went to see Joan and Steven. They're my step-brother and sister. My mother married again. I get on well with them. I hadn't seen them in a long time so I thought it would be a good opportunity to pop round after the party and discuss the position I was in with Clare. Tell them Clare and I weren't getting on. I wanted to ask them what I should do."

"Seems a strange thing to do Mr Austin. Make a visit at that time of night. The party was over at about twelve thirty I believe. Why didn't you leave with Joan and Steven?"

"Because I waited to tell Clare I was going over there for a few hours, and maybe we could discuss our problems when I got back. Clare didn't mind, she said she was tired, and we would talk about it in the morning. I think she was glad to see me go. She was in a different frame of mind by then. She told me to think over what she asked me about the divorce."

That was the flimsiest excuse Lancaster had heard in a long time. He rubbed his hands together. The bomb would come now.

Crown waited for it.

"Obviously there was something else troubling you Mr Austin, there must have been another reason you decided to stay away. By the way, where were you on the morning of the party?"

A hint of a smile crossed Bomber Lancaster's face.

"Mr Austin, we usually find out in the end. It may take a long time I'll grant you, but eventually we get there. There are a lot of gossips in East Wood."

"I've told you everything. There was no other reason. On the morning of the party I had to pop into my office. My business is called 'Swim In'. I build and design swimming pools. You'd be surprised how many people have pools these days. I get a lot of orders and I had a lot of paperwork to see to. And I had to arrange some meetings for the week."

Lancaster thought to himself how much the word 'meeting' had changed. If he phoned his accountant he was always at a meeting. When he phoned his brother, which wasn't often, the secretary would say, "Sorry sir, he's at a meeting." Where was everybody years ago when they were busy? He tried to remember. Dictating a letter? Out of town? Gone for a hair cut? He visualised large meetings of people. But now he realised only two people made a meeting. Like one pair, two pair, three of a kind in poker.

"Right Mr Austin. Can you remember Clare's last words to you? It might help."

There was a slight hesitation in Trevor's voice.

"Her last words? Well she said more or less of course, that she had something important to say to me. About us. About how we were getting on together. Or weren't getting on together. She didn't want to give it another try. She wanted a divorce."

"And your answer Mr Austin?"

"Oh I was angry. I said that we got on well and that I loved her. But I didn't want to discuss it then. I wanted to talk to her about it later, after the party, when I could think straight."

"And what did she say to that?" Crown interjected.

"Oh she said if I wouldn't give her a divorce she wanted a trial separation."

"I see."

"So that's the reason I stayed out late, and didn't get back until the next morning," Austin's eyes filled with tears again.

"She also said I was being stupid."

"And this obviously didn't make you too pleased?"

"No. No it didn't please me. Of course it didn't."

"Mr Austin, Crown and I arrived here about one thirty in the morning and by the time we left, according to my time piece, it was well after two. You are definitely on our hit list."

According to my time piece? Crown had never heard Lancaster mention a time piece. He was growing archaic. What film had a time piece in it? Was it 'Under the Clock?' Jesus.

Trevor Austin looked uneasy and slightly desperate. The inspector was crackers.

The question hung in the air for a moment or two like a party balloon.

Crown was thinking 'hit list'.

Trevor spoke loudly now, "I have nothing else to say. I need a solicitor."

"Yes, as you said. May I suggest Mr Austin, you were possibly out with another woman. Perhaps you murdered your wife so you could be with this other woman. Or on the other hand, perhaps you found your wife with another man and you didn't like what you saw. So when this other man left, you killed her. There are any number of reconstructions I could give you. You see all these ideas spring to mind when I find a dead body on the floor," and here he emphasised his words. "In the house of the absent husband, and the dead body on the floor, well it turns out to be that of the absent husband's wife."

Lancaster put his face as close as he could to Trevor Austin's.

"Do you have any yellow cushions in the house?"

It was the kind of question that Lancaster liked to fire out staccato.

"Cushions?" Trevor sat down in the nearest chair.

Crown watched Lancaster's eye flicker.

"Mr Austin, we follow every line of enquiry we can. We were called round to find your wife's body on the floor of your sitting room or patio room, or garden room, or whatever you call it. She was brutally murdered. Our intention Mr Austin, is to find out who murdered her, and why."

Trevor Austin slumped forward. His face became a mask of fear. Lancaster had seen masks like that in Venice. Not quite so fearful, but startling just the same.

"Yellow cushions?" Trevor Austin asked.

"Oh don't worry yourself now, we'll be leaving shortly sir. I think we've asked enough questions for the time being. I'm sure you will want a little time to yourself. Just for the record, what was your wife wearing on the night of the party?"

"Wearing?"

"Yes. Clothing. You see she was naked when we found her.

Nothing on at all. Just a string of pearls. It would help if you could tell me."

Trevor swallowed hard. He could barely whisper.

"She was wearing a red dress."

"Ah yes, we found it on the floor in the bedroom. Anything else? Please think!"

"A bracelet. No lots of bangles, that was it. Bangles. You know the kind."

"I don't actually. What colour were these bangles?"

"I don't remember. I'm sorry."

"What about her hair?"

"I think she had one of her ribbons in her hair. Clare loves ribbons. If she doesn't wear ribbons, she wears large bows that she clips into her hair. But I can't remember the colour."

His eyes were red and swollen now.

"You can't remember the colour? Most unusual. Thank you for the trouble sir. We'll be in touch," Lancaster stood up. He motioned to Crown. Crown was happy to hear it. There was something strange about this man. Either he was a fool, or intensely shrewd. Was this all a show he was putting on? If it was, the tears were real enough.

"If you can think of anything else, Mr Austin. I'd appreciate it if you would let me know."

Lancaster handed him a card.

Trevor looked up at him without expression, tears trickling down his cheeks. "Who would want to kill Clare?" he asked. "Who would kill Clare?"

"Did you get all that down?" Lancaster asked.

"Of course."

"And?"

"I don't know sir, I ... "

"I tell you what Crown. Let's get a coffee somewhere and we can talk. For someone who loves his wife, he hasn't got much of a memory has he? Couldn't remember about her hair bow, or her bangles."

"Sir, it's nearly time to get up."

"You're right. I'm not interviewing nurses at this time of night. Get on to Sister Bates and tell her we'll be round there tomorrow evening. Tell her to make sure the same staff are on duty that were there when Edward died. We'll go through them with a fine tooth comb. Funny that Crown, I haven't seen any fine tooth combs about lately."

"You don't go to many shops sir."

"One of them must have seen something. Or maybe one of them is hiding something. Not deliberately, but out of fear. Find out anything. Who was operating late at night, did any other emergency cases go up there at the same time, and like that."

"Okay sir, I think we had better get home and get a bit of shut eye. Then we can think clearly in the morning."

Lancaster looked out at the rain. It was always raining. Where were they now, in June? It would soon be Wimbledon fortnight. Then it would rain every bloody day, that was one thing you could bank on.

"Take me home Crown," he said.

Kojak, that's who it was, Kojak. 'And like that'. Tonight Lancaster was Kojak.

- 17 -

Overnight Lancaster suddenly had an idea. He couldn't be sure if it came to him in his sleep. He had fallen onto the bed when he got in, and didn't wake until past nine. The evening paper was scattered all over the floor. He looked at the clock.

Crown must be as tired as he was as he hadn't phoned yet. He got up and slipped on his dressing gown, then went into the kitchen to make coffee. He found the percolator he'd bought in Venice and filled it with water, and Italian coffee. The jazz singer liked Italian coffee. They used to enjoy it with a muffin at breakfast. Those were easy years, the days were never empty, and nothing was difficult, as long as she was there. Now she was gone, everything made him feel he was like hiking up a mountain. Maybe after all he would put a small advert in 'The Stage'. See if he could find her again.

Then he thought about Paul. He had been with Paul at university. He would go and see Paul just for weekend break. Get some advice.

There would be no murder in two days time. He would put off Betty and Frank Gordon until Monday.

He started the letter. "Dear Paul," he typed. Then he sat back. He wanted to ask about the body of Clare Austin and how anyone could prop her up like that. Oh he knew about all the hours and seconds before rigor set in, but Paul always had brilliant ideas. Paul should have been the detective. He ran his hand over his chin ...

He met the jazz singer when he was out one night with Paul. They went to a jazz club in town, and she was singing with a group. He remembered sitting down and being startled at how beautiful she was. She was singing, "You're mine you," he would never forget that song.

Lancaster and Paul were always together from when they were kids. Always trying to work out why frogs swam this way, how birds camouflaged themselves. They had a special switch in their brain, when it was on they wondered about all kinds of crazy things. How did cats get thin to go through cat-flaps. Paul even bought a toy cat and pushed it through it through the cat flap and couldn't get it out. They had to cut it to bits with the scissors.

Paul went on to be a Professor of Science at Oxford in one of the research laboratories, and Lancaster had gone on to study psychology. He was offered a place at university, teaching. But it was puzzles that attracted him. He wanted to work at something where he could use his powers of reason.

It all started with films because he loved trying to figure out the plots. In those days he went to a film nearly every evening. The black and whites and the thrillers. And those plots. Dead women coming alive, sisters going out in a boat together and one kills the other, all over a man. Women mesmerising men to kill their husbands. They were packed with drama.

Dramas that had real kisses in them. Not the open mouthed kisses on the screen today. Real kisses, kisses that he used to kiss the jazz singer. And the women, they were glorious women. There was no one to touch Lana Turner or Ava Gardner. How many times had he sat through *Casablanca* or *Vertigo* or *North By Northwest* and later on *Dirty Harry*.

His first job as a young man was with a movie distributors in Wardour Street. His father didn't want him to travel so far, but Dana didn't mind the journey. He realised after he saw *Laura* why his mother had named him Dana. After Dana Andrews in *Laura*. His mother had a thing about Dana Andrews. Even his father liked the name. Dana Lancaster sounded very Hollywood. But on his first day at work to start him off they put him on filing.

He slaved over files for years. Filing was what they did in those days. They filed every mortal thing in large drawers with labels on them. Now you didn't find a bloody thing. Every damn letter or caseload was on the computer. What a crazy world.

He was always naming lists of films and asking in everyone in the office if they had seen *The Lavender Hill Mob*. Did they enjoy that darling skinny landlady in the film who had always addressed Alec Guiness and Alistair Sim as naughty boys? What film did they like? Did they prefer American films to British, did they see *Passport To Pimlico*? His friend in filing said his wife liked a good cry at the movies. There weren't many good cries about. Most of them liked the 'Carry On' films. John Wayne was the favourite of men and Robert Redford for the women.

One evening when he got home from work, his father told him one of his old school friends had gone missing. My God that happened years ago, whatever made him think of that? He was seventeen at the time, He had put his case on the table and sat down near his father.

"Bad business son. Seems she took off and never told her parents anything. Must have gone off with a bloke I reckon. So does your mother."

Lancaster remembered taking out his pen and saying, "Dad, I could find that girl if they let me."

His father put down the paper.

"What? What makes you think you could find her?"

"I'd do a list."

"List?" His father looked faintly interested.

"Yep. First thing Dad, what time did she leave college? What did she do this time last week? Is she allowed out on a Wednesday evening? Where does she usually go? Does she have money on her? Does she have an allowance? Does she drive her father's car?"

"Hold on son. Don't you think the police are asking the same questions?" his father asked.

"No," he answered. "I suppose they'll ask some of them. But I'll bet they won't ask how far her house is from the bus stop. And how long it would take to get to Shelbourne Village."

"I suppose you get all this from the movies," his father stood up. "What makes you think of Shelbourne Village Dana? That's miles from here."

"Well she could take off from there. Go to The Shelbourne Arms for the night and then get the London train the next morning. No one would think of that."

"Well you could be right, it seems simple enough to me."

Lancaster could actually see in his mind's eye where they were sitting in the kitchen. He always sat himself next to the old black boiler in the kitchen. It was warm and comforting there. They kept that old boiler for years. If he closed his eyes he could imagine himself physically there. He could even smell the aroma of the dinner his mother had left in the oven. He opened his eyes and looked up expecting to see his mother and father and his heart gave a turn. All he could see was his typewriter and a desk full of books and cups that needed washing up. It was like the saddest poem he knew.

Then he recalled the day an old friend of his father came to visit. He couldn't even remember the man's name, but he worked for the police.

He was a sergeant in one of the local stations. He was fond of Dana and always discussed movie plots with him.

"Now what was the plot in that film *The Lady Vanishes*? What was it now, Dana?"

He leaned forward and looked in Dana's eyes, waiting to hear. He knew Dana would remember it. "Did she really vanish, or was she spirited away?" he asked.

He told him, no, but she was nearly spirited away by Paul Lukas.

Dana got carried away talking about the film and the two

men who wanted to get back to see the cricket.

"Dana, you're so excited, you're mixing it all up," his mother said. "Jack won't understand a word of it."

He suddenly recalled the friend's name. Jack laughed too, and said since he knew so much about plots he should be a policeman. They all laughed heartily about that.

And now he thought about it, maybe he'd get out that Harrison Ford thing, *Air Force One*. He liked his style. There was little worth watching on the television as it was summer and full of kids' programmes.

Dana Lancaster sighed and pushing the typewriter aside he picked up the phone. He would go down to Oxford next weekend and see Paul. He had become a policeman because of the movies and especially because of Ethel Lena White and Hitchcock, and *The Lady Vanishes*.

And now he wanted to see the jazz singer. Where was she? He wasn't clever enough to find her. She'd vanished into thin air, like that film. He could find murderers but not the one woman he loved.

-18-

Simon watched as Peaches (why did she call herself such a stupid name?) walked over to the station phone kiosk. At last he'd struck lucky. There she was, holding up an umbrella against the driving rain, wearing a head scarf and her high-heeled winter boots. She kept her head down and only looked up when she crossed the busy main road.

He remembered what she said one night, that she often got the bus to Lewis Station when she wanted to go up to town. She had let the information slip out by mistake.

It was the first time she had ever mentioned anything to do with where she lived. He was quite surprised really. She had been so secretive before. It was probably forgetfulness on her part. He had hung around the station for weeks now since she mentioned Lewis Station. He mostly waited during the day time because that must be the time she would leave to go to London.

Occasionally he would wait in the early evening just in case he might see her coming off the London train.

He had been here so many times he knew every person's face, and who got on and off the bus. He decided to give himself another few days of waiting then he would forget about it.

This particular week he told his secretary he had to go up north. He only hoped his business wouldn't suffer. His secretary might become suspicious with all his excuses and he would lose the few clients he had.

He usually sat at the station buffet once he found out the times of the trains, and ordered a coffee between their arrival and departure.

He asked himself why he was willing to neglect his business to find out where this woman lived. Wasn't it enough that he was meeting her all the time? He wanted more of her and he wanted her to leave her husband.

His plans, which were so cleverly organised originally, were beginning to fall apart. He was becoming obsessed with her and could be in danger if he was seen anywhere near the area. He was a stranger and the police would want to know what he was doing there. He knew it was cruel of him not to phone her, but if they they traced his call he would be in deep trouble. He had to rearrange everything now, and al because of Peaches. He would have to find out where she lived so he could just appear suddenly and take her away with him. He knew she would do it. He couldn't take any more chances with phone calls or meetings.

He decided to give it one last shot this week, starting on Monday, in the hope that she might turn up. He had quizzed her the last time they met as to what day she usually went shopping in town but she didn't commit herself. She just laughed and told him it could be any day she fancied.

He couldn't risk being seen by anyone who might know him and he had often bumped into people a along way from home and sometimes in the oddest places. Now at last he had found her after all the weeks of waiting. It was five o'clock in the evening when he saw her walking into the station and going towards the phone booth. The sky was black and the rain was becoming more intense. Even thought he was standing against the wall of the newspaper shop he was soaking wet. He would probably get a chill and be confined to the house if he wasn't careful.

Suddenly she reappeared in the crowd of returning commuters. So she wasn't going to town after all. There was on one with her. She went into the phone booth and slipped some money into the phone box. He could see her dialling the number. His mobile rang. He knew she would call him.

"Simon ... I'm desperate."

He had to move round the edge of the station so she wouldn't notice him.

"What is it?"

Why had she come here to phone? She spoke into the receiver in whispers.

"Oh Simon, I must warn you. Something has happened to Clare."

"Clare?"

"Yes, my sister-in-law. I told you about her."

"What about her?"

"She's been killed Simon, killed."

"God! How awful. Who killed her?"

"They don't know Simon, they don't know. I'm terrified.They're questioning everyone. Simon, we'd better not meet this week. I'm frightened."

"Right darling. Where are you?"

He could see her clearly. She was bending her head down over the phone.

"It doesn't matter. I'll call you again when I can. I miss you. I'm frightened they'll follow me and find out about us."

Tears were welling up in her eyes.

"Look. Just be careful. Don't worry. Call me again when you

get a chance. Go shopping, go anywhere, and call me. I love you. I must see you."

"I'd better go. I'm outside the station and I may be recognised. I don't want to be seen on the phone."

"I know. But be careful. I'll call you tomorrow. I love you. I want you to come away with me."

"Goodbye darling."

He was shocked at the news. My God, her sister-in-law murdered. His blood ran cold with fear. If only she'd told him before he would never have followed here here. If she was so frightened she would never answer his calls. Maybe she was not only frightened of the police, she may be frightened of her husband.

Now he started this he would have to go through with it as he may never find her again. Once murder was involved people kept away from each other for God knows how long. He was just as deep in it.

He waited until she crossed the road again and made her way to the bus stop. Why hadn't she brought her car in this miserable rotten weather? Surely she realised she'd end up soaked.

He would see which bus she took and then he would follow behind. He mustn't push his luck. The rain helped him as she had her head bent down under her umbrella.

After ten minutes a bus came along. It was a number five. It was obviously her bus because she clambered up the steps hastily, her umbrella dripping as she folded it down. All he had to do now was to follow the bus.

He turned round and quickly got into his car. The bad weather must have driven all the wardens away as there was no parking ticket on his window. He slowly followed the number five bus in what was rapidly becoming a thunder storm.

Belinda was also trying to make a plan. She should have taken the car. The bus was already ten minutes late and she was soaked to the skin. But then she would have to tell Charles she had been to town. She didn't want to do that. It meant inventing another excuse. Having to find excuses to give to Charles was becoming more and more difficult. Last week she said it was a hen party with the girls, the week before it was the cinema.

The other problem was taking her car to meet Simon. It was always easier to meet in a car park and not near the hotel. Maybe it was time to make a final break with Simon. She would tell Charles she was going to her cousins for a few days. That way she could think things through. Her feet were wet in these damn fashion boots. What would it matter who saw her in the station. It was no one's business.

She held the umbrella lower. Then there was Clare. Her death had altered everything. It was eating into her. The more she thought about Clare, the more terrified she became. Was someone trying to kill her too? But that was a crazy idea. Charles was often late getting home and maybe she shouldn't be left alone in the house. Anyone could have killed Clare, even Charles. She didn't trust anyone. Thank God she had managed to speak to Simon to tell him what happened.

 She didn't know what to think any more. Who was Simon? She had only met him through an advertisement and she didn't know who he really was. Where did he live and how could she find out? Now she had Simon she wanted to keep him. She felt ashamed of herself thinking Simon had anything to do with Clare's murder. He didn't even know Clare. Just the same, it was lucky he didn't know anything about her, let alone where she lived. She desperately wanted to be with him, but now it was dangerous. When she was ready she would ask Simon to meet her and leave this rotten place.

There was no one on the bus who knew her and there was just the one car following them on the main road, but her nerves got the better of her and she was was beginning to mistrust everyone she met.

At last the bus arrived at her turning and screeched to a stop. Sick with nerves, she glanced at her watch. It was already eight o'clock. The bus had been crawling along. She hoped Charles was still with his client. It wouldn't do for him to see her in this state. But she never knew what time he would be home. she couldn't pone Simon from the house and Charles would want to know why she'd been out in this weather and why she didn't take the car.

The need she had for Simon was overwhelming and she was frightened of her own obsession.

Once off the bus, she walked as quickly as she could down the small crescent. Soon she would be home running a hot bath.

The house stood in darkness and she hesitated before she took out her key. Why didn't she leave all the lights on instead of just the tiny porch light and the hall lamp? What kind of life was it when she was nervous to go into her own house? Why hadn't the police got the murderer by now? Where was he?

Belinda let herself in, sat down on the nearest chair and pulled off her boots.

Sitting in the house alone she suddenly had a panic attack. She couldn't catch her breath. Someone wanted to murder her, she was sure of it. She must get hold of the Inspector. She would-n't stay here another minute and Charles could go to hell.

But where was Charles? It was late and he hadn't called, why? Had he seen her at the station? Should she phone Simon to come and get her?

Panicking, she locked the front door and picked up the phone.

- 19 -

The nurses waited in a line. Sister Bates had made sure that the agency sent in temporary staff for the day. The hospital would just have to pay for it. There were enough problems for her to deal with right now. After all, it was the hospital's reputation at stake. Something like this, which she hesitated to say was murder, was impossible to conceive. All the staff must know about it by now. It was all over the newspapers. How could they miss it?

Her face was stern and her resolve rock-hard this morning. Her questions would be fierce. She would personally see to it that everyone on the floor was questioned until they begged for mercy.

This was just as important to her as it was to the police. She had to know if any of her nurses were incompetent or, and she dreaded the thought, untrustworthy. Who put that wretched tin box in Austin's room? Then there was the revelation about a missing Cartier watch. What a frightful business this had turned out to be.

"Now," Sister Bates said, glancing at the time on her watch, "Inspector Lancaster will be here soon and he will see you one at a time in my office."

She turned as the lift doors opened and Lancaster and Crown stepped out.

"Sister Bates," Crown said smiling, "are they all here?"

"Absolutely," she replied. "The sooner we get this over with, the better. I have patients to see to."

"Thank you, Sister," said Lancaster, "send in the first nurse."

He sighed. There must be fifteen or more people to interview. As well as the nurses there were two porters and the kitchen staff. What a task. Well they had better get started.

As they passed the room where Edward Austin had died, a sudden thought crossed his mind. The more he thought about the room and Edward Austin lying across the bed, the more he tried to remember something. There was something embedded in his memory, something niggling which he could not quite grasp.

"Sir," Crown said, "shall we ask Nurse Parker to come in? She's the first on the list. Sister Bates says she relies heavily on her for common sense as well as being a first rate nurse. She was on duty when Austin died."

120

"Send her in then, Crown. We could do with a bit of common sense on this case. And ask her not to mention anything to do with needles, please."

"Sit down Nurse Parker," Lancaster smiled across at the nervous figure.

"I hear Sister Bates thinks of you as an excellent nurse." That broke the ice and a smile lit up Nurse Parker's face.

He knew what these girls had to put up with; difficult patients and watching over their shoulder for Sister Bates all the time. And all for a pittance.

"Don't mind Sergeant Crown here, he's taking notes of everything. Names, dates, times, you know the kind of thing. Perhaps we can discuss what happened on the night of Edward Austin's death. I would like your opinion on a few matters."

Lancaster used the word 'opinion' to make her feel more at ease so that she might confide in him.

"Firstly, to start the ball rolling, how many nurses are on the round with you in the evening?"

She seemed eager to help. Leaning forward she answered.

"Well sir, there must be at least six of us."

"Really."

Lancaster picked up a pencil. He doodled the number six on his pad.

"Yes. And I can vouch for them all. I've worked with them ever since I came to the hospital."

"And how long would that be, Nurse Parker?" She looked very young.

"Oh, at least five years."

"Five years eh? Worked your way up?"

"Oh yes. I started in Accident and Emergency as a student while I studied."

"It must have been hard going," Lancaster commented. He knew all about working your way up.

"Oh yes, I worked on all the floors after that. Then I decided I wanted to work in post operative care. Of course that took a year or two of hard work, but it was worth it." Nurse Parker ventured a little smile.

"And in all that time, I mean the two years you worked here, has anything ever gone wrong on this floor?"

"Gone wrong, sir?"

"Yes. Wrong. Things missing. Mistakes made by a nurse perhaps? Patients dying suddenly and unexpectedly for no reason.

Think carefully Nurse Parker. Think about what happened on this floor to Mr Austin."

He watched Nurse Parker lift her head in disbelief.

"Under Sister Bates no one would dare do anything stupid or careless." Nurse Parker was certainly forthright in her answer.

Lancaster was sure Sister Bates was mentally standing on everyone's shoulder. If anything went wrong it must have been human error, and Sister Bates wouldn't care for mistakes. But all they needed was one small incident. Something that went unreported. Something the nurses kept under their nurses' caps.

"This is the first time anything like this has ever happened," Nurse Parker continued. "It casts doubt on all the nurses. And on Sister Bates."

Lancaster thought that was a straight enough answer. And a protective one. She obviously thought a lot of Sister Bates and didn't want to cast any doubts on her character.

"Where were all the nurses that evening Nurse Parker? I mean how were they placed?"

"Well, it's hard to say where they were exactly. So much happens on this floor. Things tend to happen quickly. Nurse Bourne and Nurse Martins were on duty and so was Staff Nurse Forbes. Nurse Thompson and Nurse Harris were on the drugs cabinet. They each had keys for the drugs cabinet. They measure out the doses and take them into each patient's room. It's a job they may have to do every half hour in some cases. And they have to be extremely careful to check and record everything they do."

"Who else had keys to the drug cabinet?" Crown asked.

"The two nurses in charge of drugs and Staff Nurse Forbes."

"I see, and who actually takes the drugs into the patients' rooms?"

"Well, any of the nurses involved. The patient's name and room number are listed and the copy is lodged at the nurses desk. There's also a copy locked in the drugs cabinet. We are very careful on this floor, I assure you."

"I'm sure you are," Lancaster broke in. He remembered his last stay in hospital and how he dreaded seeing that damn chrome bowl bringing another injection. He was still aching from the hepatitis jab he'd had.

"And you Nurse Parker. Do you have any particular duties?"

"Oh, I do absolutely everything. Answering the calls from patients; taking bed pans or taking patients to the toilet if they can't walk without help; making them a cup of tea ... absolutely everything."

Yes, thought Lancaster ... underpaid and overworked. Who would do a job like that? They were rare human beings. He usually came across just the opposite in his line of work. People who didn't give a damn for anyone except themselves.

"Is there anything else I should know Nurse?"

"Nothing in particular that I can think of. It was just the usual routine evening. Nurse Martins and Staff Nurse were at the desk. And Nurse Martins always helps with anything that's needed. She helped Mr Rafferty that evening. He had just done a major operation and the patient was quite ill. If there's an emergency and there's a shortage of staff, sometimes they help the night porter push the patient up to the ward after theatre.

Of course you have to account for patients calling us with their buzzers, and the time dressing wounds. It's hard to say exactly."

Lancaster bit the end of his pencil and looked directly at Nurse Parker.

"So, if everything was going smoothly, at its usual pace, with nurses running up and down the corridor, why did no one notice the door to Mr Austin's room was closed?" He shot a small bomb, not too powerful. It seemed cruel to be unkind to Nurse Parker.

Her face dropped and she bit her lip.

"I just don't know sir. The only thing I can think of is that the nurses must have thought there was a doctor in there with him. You can't imagine how hectic it is sometimes, especially if there's an emergency. But of course I have no idea who would dare to disobey Sister Bates, or Staff, if they gave an order."

"I'll be brutally honest with you Nurse Parker. I think that someone slipped inside that room, closed the door and killed Edward Austin. It would have only taken them a short time to remove all the tubes and paraphernalia. I think they opened the pin which held the bell then threw it under the chair because they were in a hell of a hurry, then managed to slip out again, without anyone noticing."

He hesitated for a brief second.

"We want to know who went into that room, Nurse Parker."

"I really can't think of anyone that would do such a wicked thing, I wish I could."

The more she tried to think back to the evening in question the more her memory became blurred.

"Oh God, this is terrible," she cried. "Why would anyone want to murder Mr Austin?"

"You are quite right of course. It is indeed terrible. It casts doubt on you and all your colleagues. But I intend to find out who it was, believe me. This happened under your very noses and that suggests it was someone you would never suspect."

Nurse Parker adjusted her cap and tried to compose herself. He would mention the tin box now, even though they hadn't had time to test it for hairs or blood. He stood up and went across to the window.

"By the way, whoever entered that room placed a large tin box on the bedside locker. Sister Bates no doubt discussed this with you. It was probably placed there before the murder. Then they must have thrown the pin under the chair, heavens knows why." He was thinking out loud now.

"Nurse Parker, do you think any of the nurses could have done that? Taken a tin box into the room?"

She was mortified.

"Of course not!" she answered. "Why should they? No one had a tin box that evening. I would have noticed it. If they wanted to give something to Mr Austin they would have to ask Sister. And why on earth would any of the nurses want to give Mr Austin a tin box?"

Why indeed. There was no reason for any of the nurses to leave such an object in Austin's room. Unless they were told to do so. They were all hardworking, dedicated people.

"Could anyone," asked Lancaster looking severe, "anyone at all, be asked to do that, perhaps for a friend. As a favour, I mean?"

Without flinching, she looked into the Inspector Lancaster's eyes. She answered him, emphasising every word.

"Inspector, I assure you that no nurse on this floor would possibly leave anything untoward in a patient's room. Even if they were begged to. No one is allowed to take any item into the room other than medication. It would be more than their job is worth. Sister would discipline us to within an inch of our lives. We may even be dismissed."

"Ah," smiled Lancaster, "that's what I wanted to hear."

However, it was still a mystery why or how the box came to be there. If a stranger had been here at that time of night then surely the nurses would have been aware of it. Nothing seemed to fit. Even if one of the nurses had put it there it didn't necessarily mean that they murdered Austin. He would let Crown interview the rest of the nurses tomorrow.

"You've been extremely helpful. It's good to know that Sister Bates runs such a tight ship. You can go now. And thank you."

She got up to leave. Her delicate features had become haggard.

"You don't think," she uttered with a faint cry, "you don't think the person who went into Mr Austin's room is still hanging about the hospital grounds, do you sir?"

She was jumpy, and looked around as if she could see the murderer in the room.

"I mean, you read about nurses being attacked in hospital grounds. Sometimes killed. I must say, it makes me frightened to go to the nurses building. I have a room there you see." She twisted her fingers together and looked at Lancaster and Crown for reassurance.

"It's very unlikely the murderer is still around." said Lancaster. "Of course," he paused, "it's best to be vigilant."

He was thinking of how Austin had been stretching out towards the tin box when he was killed, and trying to picture what exactly had happened. What had he learned? Had anyone in the lift that night seen somebody carrying a parcel? There were certainly no visitors allowed at that hour. He had better check the emergency patients who came in that evening. Perhaps the murderer was disguised as a patient. Maybe in a wheelchair with an accomplice pushing them. It was a crazy idea.

"I'll make sure one of our men sees you all back to your quarters, Nurse Parker, and we'll keep an officer on watch for the rest of the week."

Nurse Parker's relief was apparent. She smiled as she relaxed.

"Oh, I'm so thankful," she sighed.

Lancaster turned to Crown.

"This case is more difficult than Bogart trying to find the Maltese Falcon."

"You exaggerate, sir." He closed his eyes and touched Lancaster on the shoulder.

"Let's talk about the blackbird," he said.

Nurse Parker opened her mouth to speak but decided not to take the risk. They could report her to Sister. Why, these two men were crazy. They were actually talking about blackbirds and falcons. For God's sake, there was a murderer on the loose. Why weren't they out there looking for him ... or her?

She must tell Sister. She would suggest to her that they get a different investigator sent to the hospital. What had falcons to do with the murder?

She sped out of the door without a backward glance and collided with the figure of Sister Bates who was waiting outside.

"Sister Bates!" she cried out, "They're in there talking about blackbirds and falcons!"

"Who are? Lancaster and his sergeant? Blackbirds?" echoed Sister Bates. "Falcons?"

"Yes, but they'd never allow birds in the hospital, would they Sister?"

Nurse Parker seemed a little delirious and Sister Bates thought that she might need to see a therapist. Shock could affect people in different ways. She would make an appointment for her right away.

- 20 -

Dana Lancaster booked his train ticket to Oxford then threw a few things into an overnight bag. Crown would take him to the station. Only this morning a letter had arrived from the Chief Constable of the area. The powers that be were thinking of closing down the police station and amalgamating it with another station further out.

He and Crown had been there for years, what a blow. He knew so many of the locals and had helped them with all sorts of things, from neighbourhood squabbles and burglaries to disappearing cats. Now they were thinking of closing down the only contact the public had with the police in that area. It was ridiculous. They could find a bloody traffic warden soon enough. Lancaster crumpled up the letter and threw it into the waste paper basket.

He left his office and went to the front desk.

"Harry, I'm leaving early this evening if anyone wants me."

"Sergeant Harry Harris looked up from his paper.

"OK Guv," he said. "Someone phoned for you a moment ago. Said they would call you on your mobile."

"What do you mean, Harris? Who called and how the hell would they know my mobile number?"

Lancaster hated anything complicated and mobiles were complicated things as far as he was concerned. Answering mobiles in the middle of traffic was a pain in the ass.

"Do you know who called, Harris?" He thrust himself under Harris' nose.

"No sir, I don't and who would give anyone your mobile number?"

"Who indeed," he growled, "That's what I'd like to know ... Was it a man or a woman?"

"Woman sir, and she spoke so slowly, like she couldn't get her words out. Sounded like a Mrs Weedon."

Lancaster shook his head and turned away.

"I don't know a Mrs Weedon." He thought for a moment. "Are you sure it wasn't a Mrs Austin?"

"I can't be sure sir."

"That's all I need. Another loony. As if I haven't got enough aggravation on this case already. Did she say where she was calling from?"

"No sir."

Harris watched him go towards his office, and opened his newspaper again. As he turned the pages over to the sports page he noticed a mobile on his desk. It certainly wasn't his. It must be Lancaster's.

He put the down the newspaper.

"Sir!" he called, "you've left your phone behind." Why couldn't Lancaster leave the damn thing in his pocket like everyone else.

He heard Lancaster's office door slam.

Only last week he had found the phone in the gents. Grumbling to himself, he pocketed it and made his way to Lancaster's office.

" Are you sure Paul is meeting the train?" Crown asked.

"Of course.Listen Crown, I want one of you to get over to the hospital and find out if anyone has discovered my mobile number."

Crown knew only the Chief Inspector and the desk sergeant had Lancaster's number. He was certain Harry wouldn't give it to anyone. He tapped his fingers on the wheel. It was a fact that no one else knew any of their personal mobile numbers. The trouble was that Lancaster was always taking his mobile out of his pocket and leaving it all over the place.

"Then get forensic to look over Austin's body again." Lancaster carried on talking. "Yes, and make sure you get a full report on everything about him, even the size if his toes. I can't believe that man didn't show any sign of illness before yesterday. There must have been some tell-tale sign. Surely his wife would have noticed if he had the 'flu or a cold. Men always make a fuss." He knew that he always made a fuss when the jazz singer lived with him.

"For Christ's sake, it's bizarre.The man went to visit his old school friend in the hospital. He has a cup of tea in the canteen with him. His friend leaves to operate. He sits there for an hour or so. Then before you can say knife, he leaves the canteen and is falling on all-fours and collapses in a heap.So find out what happened to Austin before that evening. Where he went, what he did, who he mixed with and what drugs he was dispensing. Everything. Find out if he was on drugs. With all that stuff going through his hands, you never know. Go through all his things and get a search warrant. Then go round to his house and empty it, Crown. And find out where all that Austin lot were before that . party. Was Austin in the pharmacy the whole week?

Did he go away somewhere? Up north,down south? Then report back to me. You've got my number there."

He took out his handkerchief and wiped his brow. He was feeling warm. Was it possible he could have caught the wretched illness himself? He was always frightened of being ill since he had whooping cough as a child. He remembered trying to catch his breath and holding onto his father's hand.

"Here we are sir, the station." He pulled up as near to the entrance door as he could.

" Before you go sir," Crown leaned over and handed a file to Lancaster, "It's a report on the gun that killed Clare Austin."

"Shoot, Crown."

"Very funny, but you won't laugh at this.The bullets were fired from a Colt 45."

"A Colt 45? What is this, a Hollywood cowboy movie?"

"Could be from a U.S.Army issue from way back. The lab can't swear to it yet."

"A Colt 45 eh? It could have been lying around for years.Although you can get hold of anything on the streets these days, unfortunately."

"Our killer either borrowed it, found it or bought it. Then picked it up and used it with a vengeance. Pretty powerful those things. One shot and wham, you're gone."

"And the killer fired three.Plenty of hate there."

There was a pause before Crown decided to speak.

"The first shot to the chest killed her stone-dead anyway."

"Well, you know what they say about guns, Crown."

"What do they say about guns?"

"My, my, my! Such a lot of guns around town and so few brains"

Lancaster alighted and the car door slammed.

"Let me know when you get back sir."

"Get that, what's her name, Sergeant Hilarie to check out the Colt. You know, the new girl who looks like she should be wearing a gym slip."

"Bye sir."

Crown wondered what other guns there might be around town.

- 21 -

Lancaster had been writing his lists immediately he got back from Oxford.Gradually the lights began to go out in the police station.He jerked himself up suddenly. He must have dozed off for a moment or two.

Someone was knocking on the door.

He managed to rise and shake himself awake.

It was the Superintendent.

"Hello Lancaster, I'm back."

He could see the tall envious frame of Superintendent Barker standing in front of him. He was getting much slighter these days. The only difference was his full face. He had two double chins added to it. But his eyes hadn't changed. They were alert and penetrating as an eagle when it swoops on its prey, and he was after Lancaster.

"Oh yes, I heard you were back sir." There was nothing else to say. He tried to look unconcerned.

Barker had been very secretive about his holiday this year.

"I've been to Venice. Crown told me how much you enjoyed it. So I thought I'd check it out for myself."

Lancaster never knew the Chief went anywhere other than Bournemouth. What made Crown tell him about Venice?

He'd better talk about Venice or this little meeting would end up with questions about this damn case.

The Chief took a chair, slowly easing himself into it.

"So Dana, what's happening with this case?"

"It's progressing, but so are the murders. They're particularly vicious. And they're telling me something that I can't figure."

"Well you'd better figure it out soon Dana because the Top Brass is in this weekend. What shall I tell him?"

"Tell him it's a double plot."

"What the hell are you talking about Dana?"

Lancaster realised he was being too flippant. He couldn't afford to be. He'd put in too much work to be dismissed.

But his salvation came in the figure of Harry standing inside the doorway."Yes what is it Harry?" Lancaster tried to look irritated by the interruption, but he could only look at Harry with glee.

"I didn't like to disturb you both sir."

"Well, what is it?"

"Belinda Austin on the phone, she says it's important.You told me not to put any calls through. Remember?"

Now why the hell did Harry have to say that? He could only hope that Barker would leave soon. What was she doing phoning him at the station? How did she manage to catch him so late? He was damn sure she was lying about something. She was too eager to speak to the police. In her eagerness to please, there must be something she was hiding. With a shrug to Barker, Lancaster picked up the phone.

"Inspector," he could hear her crying. "Inspector, Charles isn't home yet and it's past ten thirty."

Lancaster briefly took his eyes off the phone and looked up at the large wall clock. What was he doing here so late at night? Why wasn't he at home with the paper and tv? He never got overtime pay for hanging around like this.

Belinda Austin was trying to get her words out in between tearful breaths.

"Inspector, are you there?" she cried. "Charles isn't home yet and I'm worried."

"Why phone me Mrs Austin. I can't control married couples' comings and goings. I'm in the middle of a murder investigation."

"I know that, I know that. But we were going out for dinner and Charles told me to book the local restaurant."

"So?"

"Well I can't understand where he is."

"Mrs Austin, did he say if he was going anywhere? Maybe he had an appointment and didn't let you know. People do forget things. Surely he's been home late before. He was late when I interviewed you."

His voice had a different intonation now. He was tired losing his patience.

"It's late Mrs Austin, I'm going home, you can get me in the morning."

"He's disappeared Inspector. Why would he do this to me?"

Belinda wondered if Charles knew about Simon and this was his way of paying her back. She was so obsessed with Simon that she would give the whole thing away if she didn't control herself.

Superintendent Barker was listening to the conversation

intently.

"What time did he leave the house this morning?"

Lancaster wondered why she was suddenly so concerned about her husband. She didn't appear to be last week.

"Tell me Mrs Austin, what makes you so bothered tonight? I mean all husbands are late home sometimes."

"I'm frightened Inspector. I fell asleep. Then I woke and looked at the clock and Charles wasn't there."

"Look Mrs Austin, I'm tired. It's late and I'm going home now." Would Charles Austin stay away from home?

"Mrs Austin, please ring the station when he gets in."

This did not put her off.

"Inspector" She was still breathless. "I fell asleep you see. Then when I got up I thought I'd make a cup of tea. So I put on my dressing gown and started to go down to the kitchen. I think I heard noises."

"Noises, what noises?"

I don't like any of this, he thought to himself. This woman is chopping up a jig-saw puzzle for us and leaving out some pieces.

"Mrs Austin, I'll get a constable down there if he doesn't show up."

"I can't be alone here, I can't." She was shouting into the phone now. "Can't you understand, I'm uneasy? I can't stay here. I'm going to my sister."

Her plan was working well. She could get to her sister's place and maybe if she could arrange it properly, she would ask Simon If they could meet before she left.

"You'd better get over there right now Dana." Barker suddenly interrupted.

"Very well." Lancaster sighed.She had him pinned down "Give me your sister's address and I'll be in touch."

But the phone had gone dead and she was already gone.

"By the way," Barker said, standing up, then reaching into his pocket and bringing out a small parcel. "I brought you something back from Venice."

Good God, a gift from Barker? There must be some reason for it, he was sure. He couldn't figure out what it could possibly be.

Barker was holding out the present.

"Thank you sir." Lancaster said. It was beautifully wrapped. "It's very kind of you, very thoughtful."

Lancaster opened it slowly, removing the gold ribbon,

then pulling the tissue paper aside. It was a small tortoise.

"Yes," smiled Barker, "I wanted to thank you for telling me about Venice. And don't be as bloody slow with this case as that piece of glass."

Lancaster had to admit it. The old bugger had a sense of humour.

"I'll keep it on my desk sir, to remind me."

"Good night Dana." With that he was gone.

Lancaster picked up the glass tortoise. He thought of Venice. He placed the tortoise on his desk near the phone. Was he really as slow as that? He tried to think if Belinda had another reason for not wanting to stay at home and why she was in such a hurry to leave the house. She could always get her sister or a neighbour to stay with her. She must have a friend she was close to. Someone who could make a cup of tea and sit with her or take her out to share a meal.

With less than goodwill, he decided to phone Crown.

"Listen Crown. Maybe we should see Belinda Austin tomorrow, some nonsense about her being frightened to stay at home on her own. Her husband hasn't appeared from work, probably gone out with the boys."

"They all seem to disappear off and on, don't they sir?"

"You're right Crown. She needs someone to hold her hand. My Mother's favourite expression was "I'll hire you a brass band". If I'm in late tomorrow, find out about the sister and a bit of family history while you're at it. Bloody funny time to want to go visiting her sister if you ask me. Where does the sister live anyhow? She's not on my list. And get on the phone and see if you can find out the name of the lawyer who dealt with the estate when Joan and Frank's father died, and when the mother died. There's more to this than meets the eye."

Crown yawned. "Right sir, I'll do it tomorrow. Are you over your long weekend?"

"Of course I am. I've forgotten it. I'll ring her back. She can't go prancing off somewhere without permission. Make sure the others stay put. They're all suspects."

But he hadn't forgotten his weekend. On his way home he recalled his meeting with Paul. Lancaster wondered if everyone else felt their school friends never changed, except for the grey hair and the extra lines on the face. Sometimes their characters were different. The jazz singer always warned him about that.

"Nobody stays the same Dana," she always said, "Not me, not you, nobody."

Well, she changed too. She left. That was the bad part.

But Paul was the same.It was stepping back into the old days. Jovial, a bit older, but as interested in everything as when they were boys. He had the same trusting look and he was still what women would call handsome. There must be plenty of girls around here who would fancy him, with his seaside-blue eyes and his cheerful face. How did he manage to keep so optimistic? That was it. Optimism. It was Dana that had changed, not Paul.

They spent he weekend in Paul's old cottage in Oxford.

Paul had poured generous amounts of whisky over the days they spent together. That made them both loosen up and feel easier.

"I'm glad to see you Dana." Paul said.

Lancaster felt good. It was good t know someone was happy to see him.

Paul Summers always held his glass of whisky, and still had his old leather chair from his time as a student.

"Playing golf Dana?" That was one of the things he asked him.

"Golf? I'd like to. But to tell the truth I had to get away from this damned case. I need an outsider's point of view, Paul." Lancaster said. He had drunk a bit too much whisky that week-end.

"That's serious," Paul laughed. "I know the feeling It's happened to me so many times I can't count. Would you do it all again? Be a policeman I mean." Paul asked him.

"Nope" Lancaster gave a great guffaw when Paul asked him that.

"Neither would I, be a science man. I'd be a bloody politician. Or a policeman."

"Don't kid me, Paul, I know you. What's happened to Mrs Paul?"

Paul grimaced. "Gone the way of the other Mrs Paul."

"ah"

"Couldn't stand the life," Paul shrugged. "Come on, let's talk over a good meal and a fine and rare wine."

They spoke over good meals from Friday to Saturday.

Paul enjoyed having his old friend visiting. It was a welcome break. Someone he knew from another life really. Another life when they were both young.

"By the way," he asked, lifting his glass on the Sunday evening before Dana left, "Whatever happened to that jazz singer?"

- 22 -

"So you can force a definitely dead person into a different position Crown. Early on I mean. You can twist their limbs. Sounds terrible."

"It does.But it's odd sir. We've seen everything else, God knows. But no one I've ever seen has been moved about like Clare Austin. Usually when they're dead, they're dead, and left where they are. Not pulled about. What else did Paul say?"

Lancaster didn't answer directly. He just picked up a pen and scribbled something onto a piece of paper.

"O f course I could have gotten all this from the lab boys here. Hunter's brilliant at that kind of thing. I'll speak to him later. I suppose it was an excuse to get away for the weekend and it did me a bit of good. Cleared my head. Made me think. It's always good to spend time with Paul. He's got a scientific approach to things. Makes me think on different lines."

Crown was hoping Lancaster might have mentioned what Crown had said. About paintings.

"Yes," Lancaster said, "A body doesn't actually set in rigor till at least thee or four hours after death. So whoever did this knew what they were doing. But there's more to it. Paul asked me about the pillow. She was propped up with a pillow. He asked me if she had anything else on apart from the broken pearls. I couldn't answer him. There was nothing."

"Nothing sir?"

"Nothing, except Paul agreed with you, Crown. Maybe they're all nuts. Paul said to me if he didn't know better it reminded him of a painting."

Good, thought Crown. His idea wasn't so crazy after all. Incredible of course, but it was possible. He'd bought one of the catalogues from the Royal Academy when he first went to check it out and kept it at home in case he made a fool of himself. But he had it with him today. He knew Lancaster would be more receptive after a visit to Paul. And Crown knew he was a good detective. He was always cautious.He had helped Lancaster put a few villains away over the years. Just because this was such an impossible idea, it wouldn't stop him. When he had a wild idea in his head it wouldn't go away easily, and this was wild alright. And now he heard that Paul had the same thoughts, he went to his desk , opened the top drawer and lifted the book out.

"Unless you call a ribbon nothing. I suppose a ribbon isn't really an article of clothing. Remember, it had fallen over her ear. Reminded you of those paintings where girls wore flowers in their hair. Nude girls, lying around in the sunshine." "Nude ones. You're right Crown. There was a ribbon. The one on the floor by the pearls. It must have been pulled off her hair. Or else it came away in the struggle. While she was fighting for her life the yellow ribbon came adrift. She must have fought hard Crown. But there was nothing under her nails. Nothing when I looked. The intruder must have worn gloves and might have some scratches. Or some hair pulled out. This whole thing is a maze, a maze that adds up to murder."

"I know what it is sir. It's here. I've found the painting."

He put the book down on Lancaster's desk. There was a piece of Crown's yellow paper poking out of the book. Flipping it open he said "Look at this sir. There it is. It's Gaugin's painting."

Lancaster looked down at the page.

"Christ, you're right. It's the same pose. But this girl was in the South Seas somewhere. Must be crazy Crown, we're imagining things."

"I know but let's examine it. There's a yellow ribbon in the painting, so why not just accept the colour yellow as the ribbon? No time to look for a yellow cushion when you've just killed someone. Clare's body was on a blanket, this girl is on a blanket." He scratched his head.

"Where did the yellow cushion come from? I think we're barmy Crown. Don't tell the Superintendent about this mad idea. I mean, there's no point to it. I mean, all we're doing is looking at a painting!"

"Maybe it's not such a mad idea. Maybe the painting is telling us something."

"Telling us something? Something the killer wants us to know? How did the killer know we would look at the bloody painting Crown? I mean..."

Crown was peering down at the painting.

"He gave us a hell of a lot of credit sir. He might have thought we were pretty bright." He smiled up at Lancaster.

Crown bent over the book. "Look at this. There's something written at the top of the painting."

Lancaster put on his reading glasses.

"You're right, there's some sort of title. "Nevermore"."

"I wish I'd never started this," Crown said, pulling his tie open and loosening his collar. "It's a bloody riddle. It reminds me of the words lunatics cut out of the newspapers and send in Poison Pen letters. *You're next on the list. I know what you've been up to.*"

"Maybe it's some kind of clue."

"Why bother with a clue if you can just shoot someone? It's straightforward with no hassle. Bang bang and that's it."

"The killer wants us to know he's done it for a reason and I think he wants us to find out why." Lancaster sighed. "Write it down Crown. Write down "Nevermore" so we can look at it. Nevermore."

Crown folded his notepad in half and wrote "Nevermore".

"Maybe I'm wrong sir but there are other paintings that might look like Clare."

"You've got a lot to learn about homicide. Why morons have committed murder so shrewdly that it's taken a hundred trained police minds to catch them."

Crown knew he had folded the paper at the right time. Now he felt happy because he had his usual two clues. He was becoming masochistic.

"Surely they can't all be morons. I mean, look at Professor Moriarty."

"You're right. It's a clever kind of madness, that's all."

"So what do we have?"

"We have two people in the same family murdered, so that's no coincidence." Lancaster carried on. ""Tricky thing, murder. If you intend doing someone in, you have to make sure you keep it to yourself. Make sure you do it when no one's about. No witnesses. You have to make sure no one knows your where-abouts on the day you decide to commit the murder. You can't keep to a regular pattern. I'm talking premeditated of course. Sudden impulse is a different matter. This whole thing is tricky because Clare was murdered after a party. There were people all over he place before that."

"Absolutely. Someone must have seen something. There must have been a few strangers invited as well. Maybe from Trevor's business. Strangers to East Wood I mean. We better get a list of the people Clare invited to the party."

Lancaster took out a cigarette and a match. He held the match up till it burnt to its end.Crown took out his lighter and held it to Lancaster's cigarette. He felt like a Mafia hard man who was always on hand to light the boss' cigarette.

"Then there's Edward Austin. That was planned with precision. It was planned like a robbery. How do you get into a room in a hospital so you're not seen? I'm not talking about drilling holes in the wall or hanging upside down from the ceiling like Tom Hanks in that Spielberg movie. The killer got in and out of that hospital with no problem. How did he do it? More to the point, why bother to go in an out of a hospital? Why not bump him off before he goes to the hospital? Give him the bloody tin box and then kill him. And how did the murderer know Austin was in the hospital?"

"Because he or she knew him well? Knew his movements?" Crown asked.

"So our murderer knew Austin intimately. He must have seen him during the week in the pharmacy. But he wasn't sick then. Maybe someone in the family told him. But then the family didn't know it was hepatitis and Penny only found out a few days later when the tests came back. The murderer found out Austin was ill and also knew he was in hospital, and also which hospital."

"But you can't make a list of everyone that went in and out of the hospital."

"Better than that. I've got hold of the film from the CCTV cameras. There's one at every entrance and every exit. I've got doctors, nurses, laundry maids, porters, Indian chiefs, every soul that went in and out of that hospital. Lucky there was film in the cameras. They've usually run out when I get hold of them."

"Anyone different bring the food up?" Crown mused.

"Could be. That's what we have to find out. Who delivered the food up to the fourth floor."

"But surely one of the nurses would have noticed a different face. They all wear name tags now. Everyone on that floor had their name tags on when we got there."

"And what a wonderful way," Lancaster drew on the cigarette and reflected "To hide that tin box. He could put it on the trolley with the food."

"So the breakfast, dinner or tea comes up from the hospital kitchen." He grimaced, "When I was in hospital, the food, as they mistakenly call it, came into the room on a trolley. On some days a nurse brought it in and on others a maid brought it in. You would think the food was catered by that fellow on television. There was a round metal cover over the dish, probably made to hide the stuff, and bingo, off comes the cover and it's as cold as Christmas."

"Did you eat it?" asked Crown.

"Eat it? I lost weight in there." Lancaster suddenly burst out with a laugh. His hair flew across his forehead.

"So the food comes up from the kitchen on a trolley, then gets brought into the patient's room," Crown said "Well, we knew all that before, didn't we?"

Lancaster drew heavily on his cigarette, "But we have to figure out if there's space under the trolley to hide a large tin box with all the food on it."

"Well, the nurses wouldn't have to know everyone on the floor." Crown suddenly said. "They would accept a porter or a cleaner. Probably never even bothered to give it a thought. What does a busy nurse care who brings in the food? Maybe we should go back there now." Crown said.

"We should." Lancaster said, "We'll nose around the hospital kitchens. But first we'll go and meet the other two. What are their names?"

"Joan and Steven Ross. Joan was one of the step sisters."

"And the others?"

"Betty and Frank Gordon. Frank is Joan's brother."

"Would they know Austin was in hospital? Would they know if he was ill?"

"Well, if the photographs of them are anything to go by, they're all a pretty pally lot. Maybe one of the family told them."

"But surely," Lancaster's puzzled face looked downcast "One of them somewhere along the line must have noticed something odd that happened at Clare's party."

"Don't bank on it sir. They're a self-centred lot. If it's not happening to them they're not interested."

"I think enough has happened to make them interested Crown. Very interested."

Lancaster and Crown drove towards Joan and Steven Ross' home in silence,

"Where did you say it was Crown? They're at least half an hour away from the others. A sensible move I'd call it."

Crown let him go rambling on. It made the drive easier.He was thinking about the painting. Lancaster was thinking about Spitfires and Lancaster bombers. Didn't need all that these days. Now they had fighters that looked like bats' wings and they had smart bombs that could bomb inside your bread bin.

"You know what sir, let's stop off at the Beeches and have a coffee. We're too wound up."

"Pity they haven't got a cinema, we could have popped in."

Crown realised long ago he was working for a four star meshugana. But murder was a rotten job, so what the hell, he could always retire and become a film critic.

"You're right Crown. I could do with a movie."

It was like a fix.

It was easy to see the house was brand new.The estate agents called it mock Tudor. They had names for every bloody thing these days. There were black beams across the frontage. A sweeping driveway lead them up to a garden which was filled with bushes in six or seven colours. Obviously it was arranged by a garden design firm. one small night time bird was splashing about in a bird bath which was standing on the front lawn. That was another thing Crown had never seen before.

"What's wrong with that bird boss?" he pondered.

"Likes a bath, that's all. So do I if I get in at a decent hour." Lancaster glanced around the garden. "Smart place."

"Wouldn't mind a place like this of myself." Crown said.

"Pull up away from the plants Crown."

Lancaster peered out.

"Night must fall, Crown," he said, "Night must fall."

"Well, it is eight thirty sir." He decided not to comment on "Night must fall". He would only get a list of the cast, the directors and the camera crew. looking up at the house he noticed the front door was open. A small child was standing on the doorstep. Lancaster got out of the car and walked across the driveway.

"Hello there. And who are you?" He bent down and gave the child one of the peppermints he kept in his top pocket to stop him smoking. He hoped they weren't too stale.

"Tom."

"Tom, eh?"

"Yes. My Mummy is coming home soon. I'm waiting for her."

"Who is your Mummy Tom?"

"Who is she? My Mum, of course."

"What's her name, son?"

"Mum? Dad calls her Joan." The child nodded.

Then a figure rushed to the doorway.

"You naughty boy Tom. I told you not to open the front door without me. Especially at night. It's past seven thirty.

"I'm waiting for Mummy," said the boy, beginning to cry.

A woman reached out and took the boy's hand.

"Sorry to trouble you." Lancaster took out his I.D., "Didn't mean to upset the boy. We're police officers. Wondered if Mrs Ross was at home."

"Oh." She was visibly shaken.

"Well then," She seemed unsure. "You'd better come in.Sit down in the study while I take Tom upstairs. It's time he went to bed. I'm not sure what time Mrs Ross will be back. Perhaps it would be better if you called to see her in the morning. That way she won't be too tired to speak to you, I mean. She's always tired when she gets in. She goes to one of her art groups on Thursdays after work."

"Thanks, we'll wait. I'm afraid tomorrow is out of the question." Crown said.

The woman led them across a large hall covered in black and white marble tiles.

"I'm Tom's Nanny." the woman said.

"And your name?" enquired Crown.

"Oh, Elizabeth Carpenter."

"I want to see the policemen," Tommy said, pulling away.

"I really think it's time to go up for our bath Tommy," Elizabeth said.

It was definitely bath time around here Crown thought.

Lancaster searched Elizabeth Carpenter's face. She was young, with dark hair covered with an Alice band. She wore rimless glasses, which highlighted her dark eyes. Her lips were pale and herface plain and unemotional. Lancaster noticed she wore no lipstick. She was dressed simply in a long dark skirt with a white shirt. She seemed to be the epitome of the ideal nanny, at least as far as her clothing was concerned. But no ideal nanny would let a small child run to the front door at this hour of the night. He would have to ask to see her references. It was best to find out who recommended her, and where she came from. Everyone in this house needed a reference as far as he was concerned. She had a very upper-class English accent.

"I'll show you into the study." She said.

They followed her to an open door which led off the marble hallway.

"Well, thank you Miss Carpenter. You can leave us here now."

She was still holding tightly onto Tommy's hand as they walked towards the staircase.

Lancaster looked around the study. A computer was tucked into the corner and there was a large desk covered with papers. An antique bookcase stood on one wall and there were books stacked on the floor next to it. He leant down and picked one up. "Vogue Covers." He flipped through it.

Crown was looking at the silver-framed photographs on the window ledge. More happy families, Betty and Frank, Joan and Steven. Tucked behind was a larger photograph of all the Austins. They were all in evening dress.

"My, my. It's the first family I've met that are so fond of each other," said Crown shaking his head.

"Well, Frank is Joan's brother. I suppose they have a few pictures of each other," Lancaster said icily.

"Frank is Joan's brother, I'll give you that. But what does that mean? I've seen brothers murder each other."

They both turned at the sound of a woman's high-heeled shoes clicking across the tiles in the hall.

The woman who entered had grey hair cut into a fringe. Her face was long and angular. Her large dark eyes were heavily made up with green eye shadow and heavily thickened lashes. Her lips were outlined in bright red and filled in with pale coral. On her it looked good. She wore tight black jeans and a cream sweater. Her shoes were black and extremely high and pointed. She was a tall woman and the shoes made her look even taller. Usually Inspector Lancaster didn't think much of grey hair. It made people look older. But it suited this woman.

"Well," she said in a firm voice. "I don't know what you're doing here or what you want. Please come inside to the lounge. I must get my shoes off."

They followed her into a large room which was an antique dealer's heaven. A round bowl of flowers stood on an antique sofa table. There were armchairs with carved mahogany arms and in the corner was a Georgian bookcase. Lancaster would have liked one of those tables himself. There were two brilliant coral settees. The room was decorated with yellow wallpaper. On the fireplace was an antique marble clock with a bronze figure of a nude draped across it. There were two side pieces in marble with the same type of figures standing upright. She proceeded to one of the armchairs where she sat down abruptly and slipped her shoes off.

"They're hell," she said. "But when you're in the fashion business you have to be up-to-the-minute, even up-to-the-second. Bad enough I forgot to put on my Versace belt today because one of my clients wanted to buy one. It looks good if the owner is wearing one. Versace's very vogue this winter. Big exhibition in London at the V & A coming up."

Crown lifted his eyebrows. She certainly looked smart and well groomed. But he always hated black leather jeans.

"So you're in the fashion business, eh Mrs Ross?" Lancaster nodded, taking a seat on the couch. there were multi-coloured cushions scattered all over it. Some of them were beaded with coral beads. Lancaster fingered them.

Crown took out his notepad

"Yes," she replied. "Have been for twenty years. Shop in town."

"And which town would that be Mrs Ross?"

"Why the West End of course. Well, I mean the Portobello Road end, before you get to the market. Lots of nice shops there. Very busy on the weekends. Hugh Grant did it for us. Prices have rocketed. My shop rent's gone up."

"Ah," Lancaster said,frowning. "Notting Hill. Good film, I like that Hugh Grant."

Joan Ross looked tired and she appeared irritable. Pushing her shoes out of the way she spoke. "Just why are you here Inspector?"

"Why would you imagine Mrs Ross? I'm investigating the murder of your sister-in-law, Clare Austin."
Joan Ross suddenly became guarded.

"What could that awful murder have to do with me? Or my family?"

"I'm afraid it has a lot to do with you. You, your husband, your brother Frank and all the merry Austins were at Clare's party not so long ago. My Sergeant and I were called to her home by her neighbour who found Clare in her living room, shot to death. That's why I'm here. And I intend to find out who murdered her and why.

So maybe it does have something to do with you after all. I'm told that you, Mrs Ross, are extremely friendly with your step brother Trevor Austin, the grieving husband. Does he have an interest in your fashion business?"

Joan's face dropped.

"Why do you mention him? My God, no. I couldn't think of anyone worse to be in business with. I wouldn't have an Austin anywhere near my business."

"Well, what family doesn't have its up and downs?"

"It's not a matter of that Inspector. Trevor is a rotten businessman."

"Trevor Austin told me he came round here after the party. Naturally you know the party to which I'm referring. Came round quite late, according to our notes, eh Crown?"

Crown leafed through his notebook.

"He came here at two o'clock and didn't leave till about four in the morning." Crown read from his notes.

"Stayed a long time." Lancaster said, looking at Joan Ross intently. "I trust your husband didn't mind." He raised an eyebrow. "Austin coming over here so late and celebrating with you both after a pleasant evening, puts a different reflection on things." He smiled and put his hands together. "Did he have something special he wanted to discuss with you Mrs Ross? I might have thought he would have needed some sleep. Or a cuddle with his wife." Lancaster used that line often, a cuddle with wife. He often got a few good results when he mentioned wives, or husbands, that needed a cuddle. For one thing he could tell immediately if there was anything going on between the suspect and someone else's partner. He carefully watched her expression. He knew the fires of jealousy and how they flared up in people's eyes. There was no jealousy registered on Joan's face or in her eyes. Joan found it difficult to give an immediate response. She sat back and amicably agreed with Lancaster.

"Right on," she answered. "You would have thought so. He came round after the party. We had a few drinks, you know how it is. All feeling merry. Stayed for a chat. Then I made a big breakfast. Bacon and eggs and a few tomatoes. Nothing like breakfast after a party. And he really didn't stay that long. He must have left around three or four. But I can't remember exactly."

"You're pretty sure about that Mrs Ross?" Lancaster screwed his eyes up.

"You mean the breakfast? Oh yes, we enjoyed it. Plenty of good food and champagne then a good breakfast." Joan answered, unperturbed by his questioning.

Strong-minded, thought Lancaster, hard to trip her up. He would have to do more digging.

"All the same, four in the morning is a bit late. One would have thought your step-brother would have wanted to get back to his wife before that. Seeing she'd entertained everyone royally."

Crown held his breath as he watched Joan Ross' eyes. They closed tight for just a second. Was she remembering something, or just trying to give herself a small space to think?

"Oh I don't know," she said. "One doesn't always think over every damn decision you make in life. It was only a visit after the party thing. I can't understand what all the fuss is about."

She was right of course. Everything you did in life didn't have to have a particular reason. You couldn't plan every moment. Crown certainly didn't. He liked taking things hour by hour, even before he dreamed of thinking day by day.

"No fuss, Mrs Ross, no fuss. Just pondering why a man like Trevor Austin would not stay at home after a party. Most people would."

Joan Ross did not answer.

"I fancy a drink Inspector. Care for one?" she asked brusquely, suddenly standing up.

"Well thank you Mrs Ross." Inspector Lancaster rose from the settee. "I don't mind if I do. I'm off duty now." He looked at his watch. "And one for the Sergeant here please."

She went over to the sideboard and picked up a decanter of whisky.

"Say when," she said.

"Funny thing that expression, when. I'm always asking people 'when'."

He handed a glass to Crown.

"When is your husband in?" Crown thought.

"By the way Mrs Ross, have you heard anything of your step-brother Charles Austin? His wife let us know he didn't arrive home last night. In fact he hasn't arrived home at all. Coming on the heels of Clare's death and Edward Austin dying in hospital, it's a bit of a coincidence. The coincidence being that all these problems seem to be affecting the same family." He smiled. "You could say he's disappeared into thin air. Been gone for two days. Case of the missing Austin if you ask me. My Sergeant and I thought he might be having breakfast around here. That seems to be the thing to do," Lancaster paused, "after a murder."

He took a swallow of the whisky. "Well, no time for breakfast now is there Crown? I should ring your husband and let him know I'll be interviewing him." He put the glass down on the antique table. "If you want me Mrs Ross, here's my card. *Just Dial M for murder* Mrs Ross."

He loved using that whenever he could and Crown always enjoyed it.

"It's gone half past nine. It seems we've been here rather a long time. We won't keep you any longer. Thank you for the drinks. You must be feeling tired. Your son seemed worried about you. He was waiting on the doorstep when we arrived."

"Tom always waits for me to come home." She paused. "Surely nothing's happened to Charles?"

It was easy from where Crown was sitting to see that Joan Ross was startled. Her lips were open but after mentioning Charles she never spoke. She tried to stand but felt unsteady.

"Oh he's missing, but as yet we don't know why," smiled Lancaster. "If by some chance he should contact you, do let us know. Oh and by the way, please be kind enough to tell your husband that we'll be around in the morning. Late morning that is."

He left the room with Crown following. They walked back the way they came, across the marble floor.

"Nice place, Crown," Lancaster observed as they arrived at the front door. "That's what I like, everything done in contrasting shades of money.

Money? Crown was thinking. What's money got to do with it?

Lancaster turned back to Joan Ross.

"So that makes four little Austins all in a row. One shot, one for breakfast, one has vanished and, I'm certain you must know, one very dead one in hospital. Or didn't you know?"

Her face went white. "Yes. Penny told me. How awful, I never realised he was so ill."

"I'm sure you didn't," Crown said.

"Good evening," she answered. Slamming the door on them, she click-clacked her way back up the marble hallway.

- **24** -

Betty Gordon was glad dinner was over so she could go upstairs to her sitting room. The house was really too big for them now. But East Wood was such a pretty area and not too far from the Green where the shops were. The best part of the house for Betty was the garden.

Betty had her own room upstairs facing the garden. Her problems vanished when she was watering the flowers or cutting off the dead heads of the geraniums and daisies. The daisies were her favourite. That was because there were Michaelmas daisies in the garden when she was a little girl. She remembered how the great masses of blue daisies smothered the sides of the garden in the summer.

Soon it would be time to plant tomatoes and put in some more seedlings. If the days became wet, she would go into town and buy wool; then she would pass the time knitting her daughter a scarf or a waistcoat. Knitting kept her occupied when the weather turned for the worse. When Arlene went up to university Betty was very proud. But she missed Arlene more than ever now. That was why she looked forward to the weekends when her daughter was free and they could spend time together. Sometimes Frank found excuses to stay at home, so she would go to Oxford by train. He would probably rather fiddle about with his motorbike, though what a man of that age wanted with a bike she couldn't understand. Still it kept him out of the way and she was grateful for that. He was so morose these days. He had changed from a kind man into a bully. And it was all because they had driven to Oxford by a different route and now she began to think about it, she wondered why. They usually went the other way, through the side roads and country lanes. What had she said to him? Oh yes, she remembered now. "Frank, why are we going this way? Let's go on the country roads. It's so pretty this time of year." Yes, that was what she had said. Her mind was going round and round in circles. She would make herself a cup of tea and think about it again. She left her knitting on the arm of the chair and got up to plug in the kettle. She might as well not go downstairs at all, now that she had started knitting every evening again to occupy her hands. It was high summer when the accident happened and she wished she could turn the clock back.

Her worries revolved around that wretched evening. She poured her tea and put the cup on the small table next to her chair, then tried to recall everything that happened. They had made a late start because Frank was a watchman at thee local market and when he got home she made him a light supper before they left. After supper she went upstairs to fetch her knitting bag and wrap the waistcoat for Arlene in a piece of tissue. After they left and were on the main road, she asked Frank why he wasn't going the other way. He didn't answer and she thought it was best not to start an argument while he was driving. The next thing she remembered was waking up just past the Cat and Canary pub. She must have dropped off to sleep with the motion of the car. She remembered their car had screeched to a halt and she woke with a start. Her knitting bag and book had tumbled off the back seat and she was thrown forward. She heard Frank shouting.

"Bloody fool didn't get out of the way. Oh my God Betty. I've hit someone."

It all happened so quickly that in her terror she tried to leave the car.

"Stay where you are Betty.I'll go and see what's happened."

Frank had run across the road. In the distance she could see a man getting out of the car opposite bending over a figure in the road.

"Help me," the man was crying, "help me."

My God! What had happened? She couldn't hear the next few words but she could see Frank bending down over the body in the road.

Why had it taken her so long to remember what happened that night? She'd read lots of articles about memory loss and how people pushed things to the back of their minds so as not to re-live them. The weather had been warm and she had worn her new beige trouser suit. She had wanted Arlene to see it.

Now her recollections were tormenting her and she felt a headache coming on. She got up and went into the bathroom to get the aspirins. It must be all this thinking that was making her ill.

She remembered winding down the car window when Frank was bending over the figure in the road.

"What's going on Frank?" she called out..

"Nothing's bloody going on," Frank shouted at her.

She heard the man from the other car, again shouting.

"Look what you've done, you bastard, look." He was raising his fist to Frank. "You've nearly killed her."

She wished all this had stayed hidden. Hidden from herself so she could carry on living a normal life. Frank could never have killed anyone. He was a careful driver. He always took the wheel if they were driving on the back roads at night.

Then she heard Frank, The wind was whistling and a few words came back to her.

"We were nowhere near her."

It was then that Betty realised their car was facing the way they had come. It must have hit something to skid round in the road like that. She didn't dare move. After all, she had been asleep and maybe it was true. The man was gesturing to Frank.

"Help me get her into the car. I'll get her to the nearest hospital."

"But you can't move her," Frank was shouting, "she may die. I'll call an ambulance on my mobile."

Then she watched as Frank helped to lift the body into the man's car. It was all a bad dream. That was the reason she couldn't remember it. Then Frank stepped back across the road and climbed into the car beside Betty. How could she have forgotten his ashen face and his scratched and shaking hands? Then the other car sped away in seconds. It was truly a nightmare.

"Why didn't you help take the girl to hospital Frank? You should have called an ambulance and the police."

"Sit still Betty. We'll go home and call the police."

"But Frank, we must call now. We're running a risk. We can't leave like this. The police should be here. We may be needed as witnesses."

She remembered weeping uncontrollably.

"We'll have to leave it to the other driver Betty. Now please don't be difficult. If we don't do as that man said he'll tell the hospital we deliberately ran the girl over. He threatened to call the police if I didn't agree."

"But what would that matter? He can't tell them that, it's not true. There's no evidence. Unless the bumper is damaged or the headlights are broken."

She knew she had better say no more. She had already been too persistent.

"I'll look when we get home," Frank said. "If there is anything I'll be held for dangerous driving and possibly manslaughter. We're driving home."

She hunched herself up in the car, trying to be invisible. He had a look of uncertainty about him, coupled with a look of fear.

"I'll phone the police as soon as we get in. You get into bed with a hot water bottle and a cup of tea. I'll deal with this. I can't afford to be accused of manslaughter. I'm just earning enough to pay the bloody mortgage. You wanted the house. I'll be thrown out of my job before you know it. And what with that other trouble...." His voice trailed off. "what will happen to you then?"

He was right of course. A husband in prison and the neighbours talking, she would be forced to move. She remembered the last time Frank had been in trouble. They had to sell up and move to get away from the gossips. They were lucky to find a house they could afford.

She put the kettle on again, remembering all this had made her feel sick and giddy. And she had behaved like a mad woman that night. She had phoned Arlene with an excuse that she wasn't well and Dad had thought it best to bring her home.

Now, tonight, sitting in her upstairs room with her new knitting pattern and a bottle of aspirin, she felt she would never get warm again.

Had Frank called the police? He never discussed it when he came to bed that night. He was so restless that he told her he would sleep in the spare room. Then he said it was better for both of them if he slept in there from now on.

She was too frightened to ask him if he had found dents on the car or smashed headlights. She had scanned the local newspapers and listened to the radio. But there was no report of the accident. Perhaps if anyone saw broken glass on the road they wouldn't consider it unusual. There was always broken glass on the roads near the shops, and the car seemed fine.

It was then she heard the sound of something smashing, just at the moment when she was thinking of glass. She looked down. The tea cup had fallen from her hands and dropped onto the coffee table, leaving sharp slivers of china scattered across the carpet. A sudden unearthly feeling came over her, a feeling that she herself could be in terrible danger. And she wasn't sure where the danger was coming from. Perhaps it was from the man they met on the road that night. The man who drove away with the body of the girl in his car. The body of the girl they had run over. And the awful part of it was that they never heard anything about it again.

- 25 -

"I don't know, Crown," Lancaster said as they got into the car. "We've got one dead woman, one dead man, a disappearing husband and a step-brother who stayed at his step-sister's house having breakfast after the party. I think we'd better get hold of a bit of family history. Let's speak to Frank Gordon and his wife. Frank is Joan's brother so he'll be careful not to say too much about her. She's got her old man under her thumb tack."

He dug in his pocket and, taking out his handkerchief, gave a loud sneeze.

"You're not getting a cold are you?" Crown was perturbed. If he caught a cold from Lancaster, Eric would lock himself away. He was so damn prima donnish. "No colds allowed in the box office, dear." That's what he said last time. "Can't afford to sneeze over the tickets."

He wondered if the jazz singer was like that when she lived with Lancaster. After all, she had to "go on" at her gig. If she had a cold she couldn't sing. He just couldn't figure out relationships. That's what they had in this case, relationships.

"You don't think he's gone abroad do you?" Crown ventured.

"Abroad? Who?"

"Charles Austin. I mean the abroad kind of place you go when you have to get out of town."

"My, my, Crown," Lancaster lit a cigarette and blew a puff of smoke into the air. "You're beginning to sound like a screen writer."

"Maybe Belinda's killed him. Why is she so frightened? No one's threatened her as far as we know. As for Trevor, Joan Ross verifies that he was at her place after the party. Now why would she do that, I ask myself, if it wasn't true? Was her husband Steven there to substantiate Trevor's alibi?"

"Husbands round here are in short supply. He's on my list."

"Frank Gordon lives quite near here sir. He's only fifteen minutes away on the other side of the hill."

"Yes, I imagine that makes it quite cosy all round. We may be on the sharp end if we don't speak to Penny about her husband."

"Then we shall speak to her, as soon as we can. Meanwhile now her old man is dead she may give something away. And that would be very handy."

"This family were so lovey-dovey, with all their arms around each other. Something must have happened to change it. But times change, that's reasonable. Most families end up not speaking."

"Time is never reasonable. Time is our enemy Crown."

"I get the feeling sir, they're not exactly loving brothers."

Crown was more concerned with *Nevermore* than time.

Betty was raking over the lawn when she saw the car in the distance. Who could it be at this time of day? She looked at her watch. It was half past three. They hardly had any visitors these day and it was her fault. She didn't invite any of her old friends round like she used to. She had always played Bridge with her friends on Tuesdays but had made so many excuses not to play that she had been left out.

But somehow since that terrible day when Clare was murdered (she shivered at that word murder) she felt sure the girls wouldn't want to come over. You couldn't tell what people were thinking, and she was part of Clare's family, wasn't she? Maybe they would think she had something to do with it. It was better to wait until it all blew over and the culprit was found. But it didn't stop her worrying that there was a lunatic running around and the police hadn't even caught up with him yet. It was nerve-wracking. She put down the rake as two men got out of the car. No wonder she had headaches all the time.

"Mrs Gordon?" The one in the hat was speaking.

"Yes, that's me. Who are you? My husband is upstairs."

"That's fine Mrs Gordon. If we could step inside for a moment, we'd like a word."

The one with the hat spoke.

"I'm Detective Inspector Lancaster and this is Detective Sergeant Crown."

He held out a wallet which she squinted at. There was a photograph of him.

"Yes, well please come in."

She wiped her boots on the mat before taking them off. Then she showed them into the small room at the front of the cottage.

"How can I help?" she asked.Maybe they had found the murderer. That's what they had come to tell her. Or had they come to ask about the accident?

"Just a few routine questions Mrs Gordon," Lancaster said as he tried to find a comfortable place to sit. The chairs were so small it was impossible to make himself comfortable. He stood up and went towards the dining room table where he found a chair.

"Perhaps your husband would like to come down?" He smiled.

She hung her head.

"He's not here," she blurted, "I said that in case you thought I was on my own. You never know who can turn up since Clare..." She stopped speaking.

"Fond of Clare were you, Mrs Gordon?" Lancaster asked, tapping a cigarette on his hand. She was taken aback. She thought he would ask something else.

"Well, yes, of course.We were very fond of her." She sat down.It was better to sit than stand wringing her hands and hoping Frank wouldn't suddenly arrive home. He would contradict everything she said.

"So I assume you went to her party?" Crown watched her expression at the question..

"No, we didn't go to the party." What else could she say? It was the truth.

"Why would that be? All the other family members seemed to be there."

She watched as the Sergeant opened his notepad. He was going to write down everything she said. Frank would be furious if she said something stupid.

"Frank didn't want to go."

"And why would that be?" She was bewildered as the questions were coming so quickly.

"Oh, old family squabbles. All over nothing."

"So you didn't want to bury the hatchet?"

She cringed. Why did he mention the word hatchet just when Clare had been murdered?

"No. Well, I wanted to go and Frank didn't."

"And you wouldn't go on you own? Why not? Seems an ordinary thing to do. Leave him at home and go yourself. Not too far away is it?"

"No, no it's not. I wouldn't leave Frank on his own."

She was whispering now, afraid of what she was saying.

Crown was glad he wasn't married. All this business about leaving each other on their own as if they were school children. He would never stop Eric from going out. He might not like it. It would seem far too possessive and he would be furious if Eric stopped him doing anything.

Lancaster thought about nights the jazz singer had gigs and he had to stop at home. He could tell this woman was frightened of her husband. He'd seen enough women like Betty. Subdued and diminished, usually by a bully. How do things deteriorate like this? What happened to love?

"So neither of you went to Clare's party?"

"No, no. Neither of us. We stayed at home, as usual." A melancholy look spread over her face.

"And no one bothered to find out why you didn't go? You must have received an invitation. Everyone else did."

She darted over to a small desk that was in the corner near the window. She opened a drawer and removed a piece of paper. She brought it over to him and he saw she was holding the invitation. Now why would she keep the invitation, if they didn't go?

"Frank phoned them. He said he had to work late. He works at night sometimes." She didn't know what else to say. Better to say nothing.

"And you kept the invitation. Why?"

Why was he asking her all these silly questions? Why shouldn't she keep the invitation?

"I...I kept it because it was pretty. And I visualised getting dressed up for a change and trying to look fabulous, like it said in the invitation."

Lancaster sighed. He had asked her enough questions for now. He motioned to Crown.

"Thank you Mrs Gordon. We'll be back to speak to your husband."

He turned his head away as a rush of tears began to trickle down her face. She hoped she had given the right answers to the Inspector's questions. But he never mentioned Frank's accident, so perhaps she shouldn't worry about it. She hoped she wouldn't be in if those two came back again. Holding her head she went into the kitchen and swallowed down one of the valium she kept hidden. She had another one of her headaches coming on and a fit of nerves.

****

"Bastard," Joan Ross intoned bitterly.

Her husband looked up from his dinner. He shuffled his feet under the table. He didn't want an argument and tried to be as off-hand as he could.

"Who?" he asked. His long thin face, topped with wispy dry

grey hair, seemed to droop over the dinner table. To Joan even his eyes seemed to be drooping, like a sad old spaniel.

"That bloody Detective Inspector, what was his name? I can't remember."

Steven put down his knife and fork. She had been out of sorts all morning. What Inspector was she talking about? A faint perspiration suddenly broke out on his forehead.

"What are you talking about Joan? What Detective Inspector? Why didn't you tell me when I got home? Why wait till I'm eating dinner?" His manner became strained.

"Came round here and started asking all sorts of questions."

Steven found it hard to swallow another mouthful. He pushed away his plate. What are the police doing coming around here? They had nothing to do with Clare's death. Why should a bloody detective speak to Joan?

"I don't remember anyone phoning. Are you sure he was genuine? Not a burglar sussing the place out was he?"

"Don't be ridiculous Steven. Sometimes you ask such stupid questions. He showed me his warrant card. He came round with a sergeant, asking about Clare and that wretched party."

Steven got up and moved away from the table. He went to the sideboard and poured himself a large brandy.

"Brandy, Steven? At this time of day? My, my you are getting adventurous."

"Day? It's night time. Since when did you alter the clocks?"

There he went again, falling into her trap.

"That party again. It was weeks ago. Don't tell me they haven't found out who killed Clare. Must be a bloody lunatic wandering the streets round here."

"Wanted to know if Trevor had come round after the party. Of course he did I told him."

Steven gulped down some more of the brandy.

"We had breakfast together for God's sake." Steven emphasised.

"It probably looked fishy. I mean fishy that Trevor was here for such a long time, especially after the party. The Inspector wanted to know why Trevor wasn't at home with his dear little wifey after the celebrations and why was he here until three in the morning."

"Yes, it would seem odd.After all we are entitled to go where we bloody well like and stay as long as we like. Or is there a new law in this country?"

He went over to the armchair and, taking off his slippers,

sat on the arm of the chair.

"Well, you don't look too happy about it, do you Steven?"

"No, I'm not. Why did Trevor come round here in the first place? He never told me. All that flannel about relaxing after the party, as if he made it himself. Clare organised it all. Let's see, we didn't get back till at least one o'clock. He should have stayed at home. Why did he come over anyway?"

Joan ran her finger round the rim of her glass.

"Stop that. You know I can't stand it. Just why did he come here for breakfast? It doesn't make sense."

Thinking back, after that damned party, Steven remembered coming home feeling tired and needing a cup of tea. He had gone to the kitchen and put the kettle on. No one was in the house when he arrived home. He was sure of that. He always felt how difficult it must be for someone to be asked in a murder trial "Where were you on the night of December 3rd?" They always asked that question in those detective movies and on television. Surely no one remembered where they were half the time? Most things people did were mundane and dull except for the odd highlight. You could remember if you were at a wedding or a party. But where did he go that was so memorable? He knew that after sharing breakfast with Joan and Trevor he went upstairs with a cup of tea and the paper and then went to bed. Weeks had passed and they still hadn't found the killer.

Joan was silent. Then after a lull in the conversation she began to tell Steven what the Inspector had told her about Charles.

"Then he asked me about Charles."

"Who asked you about Charles?" Steven tried to be civil.

"That damn Inspector"

"Charles? What about Charles?" What did Charles have to do with it? Steven wondered.

"Seems he's disappeared."

"What are you talking about Joan? How could Charles disappear?" He got up and began to tinker with things on the sideboard. He moved a sugar bowl onto a tray. Charles disappeared?

"He's been gone for two days. Or was it three?"

"What? Where's he gone to, for God's sake?"

"That is exactly what the Inspector wanted to know. Belinda's a nervous wreck. But Charles? He always seems so cold and level-headed."

"I know. Have you spoken to Belinda?"

Belinda was bound to have been on the phone telling Joan all about it.

"She rang me of course to tell me. Asked if he was here or did I know where he was. Of course not I told her. Why should I? I don't speak to them all the time, do I? I certainly never speak to Charles. Why would I speak to Charles?"

Steven was decidedly puzzled. He looked at her intently, trying to prise some more out of her.

"It's a storm in a tea cup," he told her. "He's probably gone away on some errand or gone to a meeting somewhere. Probably forgot to let her know," he said, tightening his grip on the glass. They'd been given those glasses by his aunt for a wedding present. He always thought of her when he had a drink. He missed talking to her, asking her advice.

"It's preposterous. Charles wold have called Belinda if he was going out of town." He got up and poured himself some more brandy.

"Well, he didn't." She was clearly irritated by the Inspector's visit.

"By the way Joan, I'd like to ask you a question."

He decided to plunge in and to hell with it. If it meant another row, then he would put on his coat and go for a walk.

"Just why did your dear step-brother decide to come round here after the party? I think you owe me an explanation and it had better be a good one. What were you two discussing? After all dearest, I did go to bed and left you both sitting down here. Just what the hell is going on?"

"I always tell you Steven, you ask the most bloody stupid questions."

"I need an explanation Joan."

"Do you? So does the Inspector. Just as he was leaving he mentioned a movie. He said if I wanted to phone him I just had to *Dial M for Murder.*" She flashed a smile at him. "Dear Steven." Joan said, her voice crispy as burnt toast. "As I said, one day your questions will get you into trouble."

As Steven stood up to answer her the glass he was holding dropped to the carpet. He mustn't let his temper get the better of him. But it was too late. The glass had smashed into pieces on the parquet floor. He wasn't thinking of Clare now. He was thinking of Joan and all her phone calls and disappearances

Joan tip-toed across the small carpet, missing the glass shards. Then blowing him a kiss, she began to leave the room without a word, leaving him on his own, looking down at the broken pieces of his aunt's wedding gift.

For the first time Steven felt no inclination to reply. He

never really felt married. He thought being married meant thinking the same things. That was another of his mistakes. They were too different.

She called to him as she left the room.

"By the way, remember me telling you my my dear step-brother Edward was in hospital with hepatitis? The hospital hoped he would pull round. It doesn't appear so. The Inspector told he just died."

- 26 -

On Saturday evening, Inspector Lancaster sat in the cinema watching the freshly-minted copy of *Vertigo*. He watched intently his favourite part of the film. There was James Stewart waiting for Kim Novak to come out of the bathroom transformed into another woman, a transformation that James Stewart had forced on her. He'd asked her to tint her hair. He'd bought her the clothes his lover wore. He had done everything that was possible to change her into his lost love. Hitchcock had the audience waiting with Stewart, waiting in the hotel bedroom while the scene was bathed in a sickening green. Hitchcock held the audience in his hand. He made the cameras spin in a dizzy whirl, round and round the room. Everyone copied that these days. Then, after an eternity, Kim Novak emerged, in a pale grey suit, surrounded by the sickening grey-green light. How did Hitchcock keep up the suspense? James Stewart was suspended in an inexplicable place where time had no meaning. Waiting, waiting to make love to a woman transformed. If you wanted to comment you could call it sick. But obsession, love and desire were all desperate. He should know. The more he saw this film, the more he became intrigued. What a joy to be cut off from everything like this, sitting in the dark with just the silver screen and no blasted mobiles ringing. He compared sitting in the dark with the Austin murder. That's what he'd been doing really since Clare was murdered, sitting in the dark. He sat back. When the film was over and the audience left the cinema he was the last to depart. Hitchcock was a genius, yet he never won an award. These days every film was Oscar, Golden Globe or Palm d'Or nominated and God knows what else. Lancaster sighed. As soon as he left the cinema he phoned Crown to see if there was any news. He hadn't noticed a slim figure in the audience watching him. The figure followed shortly after him and, after waiting for him to finish his phone call, vanished into the grey-green mist which had just filtered across the river and over the dimly-lit street.

Crown always knew when a case had got the better of Lancaster by his grumpy attitude and how many evenings he went to the cinema. He knew for a fact Lancaster had seen at least three films this week. He shuffled the files on his desk and tried to go over them again. Glancing up at the office clock he realised it was after ten in the morning. The door opened and a large figure appeared, looking tired and depressed.

"Well Crown, what news?" Lancaster said, smoothing his hair with his fingers.

"Nothing sir. Charles Austin's not back. Christ knows where he is. Maybe he's guilty of the murder."

"Not necessarily Crown. Man doesn't come home. How long is it now?"

"About six days"

"Crown, I've been thinking about *Nevermore.*"

Crown had been thinking too much about *Nevermore.*

"Let's go over everything again. Let's talk about the blackbird that's flown. There could be any number of reasons for his disappearance. Think of all our cases. Man leaves the house to go off with a girlfriend. He has a dozen excuses for being away from home. Business is number one. Then more business is number two. He may be in a hotel somewhere on the coast. But why not phone the wife with some cock-and-bull story? Has he suddenly decided he's madly in love with his girlfriend and is leaving his wife? No, no, that won't wash. If he leaves his wife for the girl, the wife will sell the house and get the money. Has he suddenly realised he's chosen a bad time to see his girl because the newspapers are asking where he is and did he murder Clare. So fear keeps him away, fear of being suspected of murder."

He picked up the files Crown had been looking through.

"But sir, no one has spotted him yet, that's the odd thing."

"It's not odd Crown. It's us. We're missing something."

Crown took his feet off the desk. He was getting too much like a detective in a precinct in the movies. They always kept their feet on the desk. Then they grabbed their jackets off the back of the chair when the phone rang.

"Yes." Lancaster puffed at his cigarette, gave a look of distaste and put it out in a nearby ashtray as he answered absently.

Crown looked at him. He could see an untidy tired man who looked as if he hadn't slept last night.

"All clever, Crown, all too clever. Can't get to the bottom of it. Went to see *Vertigo* last night."

"Ah." Crown mused. How many times had Lancaster seen *Vertigo*? Four, five, eight, ten times, who could remember?

"Yes, Kim Novak becomes two people." He took another cigarette out of the packet.

"Oh I know sir, I know." He too had seen it with Lancaster one evening when they were working on a case in Bournemouth. What was that case they were on? And yet there was a connection to Clare with Edward Austin. He was lying across that hospital bed with his body in a very peculiar position. No one crossed their legs to call a nurse. Or to reach out for that bloody tin box. Why was he lying like that?

"Well we can't hang about. Get your feet off the desk and grab your jacket. As for Charles, he may die and if he does, it'll be murder." He smiled to himself.

"The Postman always rings twice."

"Well done Crown, absolutely." Lancaster said. "Absolutely, I'll buy lunch today!"

His telephone gave a sharp ring. Crown reached over and picked up the receiver.

"Sir, there's been an accident reported. Some woman phoned in and said there had been a hit and run near the cross-roads at Polegate. Better get down there now."

They arrived at Polegate crossroads late. The traffic was heavy that Friday night and there had been an accident on the same road. A journey which should have taken less than half an hour had dragged out to an hour and a half, with Crown grumbling all the way. When they finally arrived, the squad car with forensics had beaten them to it. The road was pitch black. Crown left the car beside a large bush. There was no lighting but the local police had put up some standing lights at the junction.

"Well, what is it?" Lancaster asked the team, as he opened the car door and got out into the cold night air.

"Hit and run eh? Well, who's been hit and who's run? I can't see a damn thing. Do you really need us?"

"Bloody miserable night for all this," old Hunter said, rubbing his hands together. It was always best never to answer Lancaster when it was a cold night. Hunter enjoyed Lancaster's quotations and his odd asides even more than watching Crown fold his yellow notepaper in half. He knew why, even if no one else did. Lancaster had an unusual turn of mind, found out things by going to the movies. Oh well, it took all sorts and it made him turn in his fair share of killers whereas he,the forensic expert, had to solve his cases with clinical expertise and a scalpel more often than not.

Lancaster was examining the roadside.

"Well man, where's the body?"

All he could see were tall trees blowing in the wind and casting shadows across a pitch black slippery road.

"Isn't one." Hunter laughed, packing his case.

"What the hell are you talking about Hunter?"

"Someone is playing silly buggers. There's no one here."

Hunter pulled off his white gloves and picked up his black bag. He'd wrapped a scarf around his white outfit. It made him look quite odd to Crown. A white outfit with a mask hanging down and a bright red scarf. It could be cashmere. Eric bought him a cashmere scarf last Christmas. He should have worn it. It was bloody freezing out here. Lancaster turned to the constable who was just fixing up a road block.

"Have you looked around?"

"Yes sir. My men are in there now." He pointed to the trees and bushes that lined the road.

"Nothing here ," he heard one of them call out.

"Keep on looking," Crown shouted to them. "And on both sides of the road. Jesus, what the hell are we doing out here in the middle of the night? I should have put on a warm sweater."

"Can't say sir," the constable said. "Got the call and came out. There's nothing to be seen. My men are still checking. If you want to get back we'll phone in and let you know if we find anything. But the strange thing is that there are definitely tyre marks crossing each other over this part of the road."

"Crown," called Lancaster. "Get over there and look at those marks. The way it's raining they'll be washed away by morning. And get them photographed."

Crown came nearer and taking his torch, looked along the road. Bending down, he scraped away at a few pieces of glass and dropped them into an envelope.

"Tyre marks," he said, "and pieces of glass. The glass could have come from shattered headlights, or tail lights. Can't see anything else. Even with the lights it's darker than hell out here."

"Cordon off all this part of the road Constable. The traffic will have to go on the by-pass. And keep someone out here in a car for a while. We'll be back at first light to check this all out."

Back at first light. Crown would have to remember that. It sounded perfect. If he was out late he would say to Eric "Back at first light." Must be from a bloody film.

"Let's go," Lancaster said. "I'm beat." He turned to Hunter. "I'm ready for my bed. What do you make of it?" he asked Hunter.

How long had he and Hunter gone to cases together? Years and years of examining how one human being killed another. Same as in all the wars only in a minor way. But the victim's families didn't think it was minor. And neither did Lancaster.

"I'll be jiggered if I know," Hunter replied using an old-fashioned expression. He looked old-fashioned with his tiny moustache and short hair. He reminded Lancaster of this Inspector in *Dial M for Murder.* He knew Hunter was born in Singapore and was an old British colonial. That was Lancaster's description of Hunter, tall and colonial.

Hunter spoke. "Someone is having us on, dragging us out here on a Friday night or...."

"Or what?"

"Or maybe this mysterious caller did see an accident. Perhaps the victim wasn't injured or only slightly hurt and decided not to make a fuss. So he got himself up off the road and went home to recover."

"Possibly," Lancaster muttered. "We'd better check out the hospitals near here. Unless he went to his own doctor."

Just then his mobile rang. There was a muffled voice on the line.

"Hello," Lancaster answered. "Who is this?"

"Sir, it's Harry. Someone, a woman, called for you. Why can't you hear me?"

"Because the wind is blowing like bloody mad, I'm standing in the middle of the road and it's raining. Who called me?"

"Can't say Guv. But whoever it was quickly cut herself off. She just said she would ring again. She mentioned the word sisters."

"Sisters?"

"Yep. Sisters. 'Night Guv."

Lancaster turned off the phone and slipped it into his pocket.

"It's insane Crown. It's all insane. Some bloody loony just called and said something decidedly odd. She just said the word sisters."

Crown yawned. He shook his head.

"This makes no sense either. Why drag us out here by the light of the moon?"

"As for me ," Hunter interjected, "I'm ready for a night's kip. New day tomorrow. I'm off home. Tally Ho and yoiks!"

" 'night Hunter. Thanks for coming out," Lancaster said.

Hunter amused him. He was from the old school, usually cheerful with swift observations and good diagnoses. Lancaster liked working with him. It made a change from the usual cut-and-dried miserable sods he sometimes had to deal with if Hunter was away. But there was nothing to observe on this windy jolly night.

"Someone's bouncing me around town," Lancaster said.

Crown closed his eyes, and his notebook. He would think about it tomorrow. Lately he was always thinking about things tomorrow. He giggled to himself. This wasn't only detective work. This was like working for Barry Norman or Woody Allen. He took out his yellow pad and, folding a page in half, wrote "bounce around town". He wanted to bounce, right into bed.

"Crown, where's our list? And what are you laughing about?"

Crown looked at his notes.

"Here it is, sir, Belinda' sister. The list gives her as Ellen Redman. She died years ago. And there's another sister. She went abroad and hasn't been seen since. I can't find out much because I've checked her out under Belinda's maiden name, with no luck. Anyway Ellen Redman lived at Orange Tree Cottage, Bridge Street, Hailsham. It's about half an hour from here."

"Let's get there first thing after breakfast. By the way you're becoming quite poetic. By the light of the moon eh?"

- **27** -

How odd, thought Inspector Lancaster as he pulled on an old cardigan and wrapped his scarf around his neck. How odd that Belinda's sister lived so close to where they were last night. Was it coincidence he wondered? He should have interviewed everyone related in this damn case. Now that they knew Belinda's sister lived in the country it wouldn't help them much. Everyone lived in the country. Now Lancaster only had himself to blame for not going visiting in the first place. He should never let sleeping dogs lie. He looked over the list of the family again. Only Belinda had two sisters. Penny had a brother who lived in Australia and Clare was an only child. He should have been more careful.

As he finished his coffee he opened the front door. Wet leaves covered the path and where there had been pretty colours, all the flowers were wet and sad. He should have planted a few marigolds around the back door. This weekend he would rake over the grass. Clare had been killed in the spring. Why was he always thinking of Clare and not Edward? Was it because he knew she was so lovely, even in death, and that her life could have been filled with laughter? Yet she had lain there like a sleeping wooden doll. He was thinking of Laura.

A car was slowly coming up the road. It must be Crown. It was nine o'clock. He kept thinking that they were missing something.

"Morning sir, hop in." Crown shouted out. "It's a funny thing but , according to this address, we couldn't have been five minutes from this place last night."

Crown looked fresh and tidy and was wearing a cream cashmere scarf. That must be a Christmas present from Eric. Eric liked Crown to look smart.

"I was just thinking that myself," Lancaster said as he got into the car. "You look wide awake. Personally I never slept."

"I was thinking about the case last night."

"Ah! Any conclusions?"

"None," he answered simply. "Just a few ideas I've been mulling around. *Nevermore* and that kind of thing, the kind of thing like poet or even forger."

Lancaster thought it best not to pursue the matter as they approached Orange Tree Cottage but he mumbled forger under his breath. Crown could be right. They would have a two word message if he was. *Nevermore, forger.*

"You don't think, Crown, Belinda's sister gave us that message do you?"

"Message?"

"Yes, on the mobile."

"I don't know sir. It was deliberate alright.. Either she or Belinda wanted us to come here for some reason. Or someone else did."

"But surely she she would have realised we would get here sometime or other once Charles turned up."

"Did they trace the call on the mobile?"

"Yes, to a mobile phone shop. Whoever it was used a mobile in the shop, maybe on the pretence of buying one."

"Well, whoever called us might have been trying to incriminate someone else."

"The vanishing husband?" Lancaster nodded.

"Could be," Crown answered as he got out of the car. "Or someone she confided in."

"Will you look at this Crown, Lancaster said with surprise as he gazed at the house. It looks as if we've arrived at a run-down shack. I bet it has a name too. They should have called it *Psycho.*

"I wonder how she deals with having a rich sister like Belinda."

"With the usual happy family feeling I suppose. Envy mixed in the pot with a bit of hatred."

"We are in a jolly way today, sir."

"This place looks like it hasn't been touched in years. It's not possible that Belinda would have stayed here even if it was where her sister lived. It's falling apart. Belinda must be in an hotel somewhere.. Would you believe it? There's a name on the door, Orange Tree Cottage." Lancaster grimaced.

"Where the hell do they think them up, Bluebell cottages, Orange Tree cottages."

Crown was standing on what once had been a path but was now no more than a few broken slabs of concrete. Lancaster joined him at the door and thumped on it lightly. Crown shivered.

"Bloody cold out here," he said. "Must be the early morning air. I could do with a hot drink."

He began to stamp his feet.

"Next year I get boots," he grumbled. "What month is it?"
"It's supposed to be the end of June. Don't you look at the date on your paper? Who cares Crown, when you're dealing with murder?"

They stood looking up at the windows, waiting for a reply. Lancaster jerked his head towards the door.

"OK," said Crown. "I'll look around the back. Maybe Belinda came here, spoke to her sister and decided to leave. What a place. She should have told us."

Lancaster knew he should have come here before this. Spring had suddenly become the end of June and they were no nearer finding the killer. They had asked the wrong questions. they had circulated the pictures of the two corpses to every station nearby and to Scotland Yard. They had better send pictures of Charles to the ports, train stations and airports. After all he was a suspect. Lancaster wrapped his scarf closer round his neck and turned his coat collar up.

"Maybe they went out for dinner," he said to himself, rubbing his hands together. "Belinda and her sister"

That's what he wanted to do, go out to dinner and relax, have a glass of wine or two, just think about nothing. He was thinking of the mobile call. He could hear Crown moving about in the back.

"No one in, as far as I can see." Crown called out.

"Is the back door open?"

"No, but I can open it. It's so rusted it's a wonder anyone can turn the handle."

"Well put your gloves on, get in and let me in the front door."

In a few moments Crown had managed to prise open the back door. Then he went through the hall which was dark as hell. He stumbled across a table and brought it crashing to the ground. He took out his torch and turned it on.

"Come on Crown," he heard Lancaster calling him. The stench inside the house made him feel sick. He covered his nose. He knew what it was. He had smelt it before.

"Coming"

He opened the door to Lancaster, saying "Bad smell here sir. I think we've been here before."

Lancaster frowned.

"This place gives me the creeps. Makes you wonder where Mother is."

"Mother?"

"*Psycho,* Crown, *Psycho*"

"I've never known you to be nervous sir."

"Not nervous," Lancaster frowned. "Agitated, anxious, apprehensive, it's this place. The sooner we check it out, the sooner we get back. It doesn't seem right .... "

They crept slowly along the hallway seeing some battered hats hanging on a wicker hat stand. Canes and muddy shoes were littered beneath it. The mud had hardened into white rock. Someone had cooked something years ago. there was a sickening smell of burnt sausages. And something else.

"God!" Lancaster screwed his face up. "Find the light switch for God's sake Crown. We'll be lucky if there's any electricity here."

The table and chair in the hallway were stacked with fraying papers, magazines and books. The smaller table into which Crown had stumbled had scattered its contents across the threadbare carpet. They moved towards what must have been the sitting room. It was filled with broken furniture, some of it leaning against the blackened fireplace. A coal scuttle was still filled with coal and a pair of fire tongs were standing next to it. The floor was covered with papers and cheap rugs.

"There isn't," Crown said.

"Isn't what?"

"Any electricity"

"Well hold your torch up. Bloody place hasn't been lived in for years.

Crown ran his finger over the mantlepiece.

"Filth and dirt, no wonder she died living in a place like this."

"Maybe she was the eccentric in the family. Maybe it isn't even her sister. That could be a lie too. Look at this paper, over a year old Crown," Lancaster gestured, picking up a piece of newspaper. "Let's go into the kitchen.That must be it over there," he said, motioning with his chin. He realised he must have left his own torch in the car.

They picked their way through the litter. The kitchen table was full of grimy knives and forks and stained plates. Dirty glasses lay in a washing-up bowl in the sink. There were frying pans, thick with grease, and remnants of meals that were cooked a long time ago. A pair of kitchen gloves had been left on top of the frying pans.

"That's funny. Who'd use gloves to wash up when the rest of the place looks like a tip? You'd need gloves just to dust the place."

Lancaster sat on the nearest chair. It creaked under his weight. He considered the scene.

"It looks more and more like my kitchen," he laughed, despite his unease.

"We've been fools Crown, or I've been a fool. We should

have come here before. I was so hell-bent on finding Charles and the killer that I never stopped to visiting any of the other family. Why didn't someone say anything?"

But he knew it was his fault. He had allowed a prime suspect like Belinda off the hook and now she was terrified of staying in her house without Charles. He had missed the obvious. Maybe she never had a sister. There was no one in this damned place. And he was sure belinda would never come to a hole-in-the wall like this. Who had deliberately lied to him? There was no sister. Had they both murdered Clare?

"I think whoever it was that phoned is playing games with us. Sent us on a wild goose chase. That's two wild geese in one week. Let's get upstairs."

As Crown placed his foot on the stairs the stair rod loosened and the carpet moved. He slipped and shouted out "Damn".

"Grab hold of the banister, for Christ's sake Crown."

"It's a danger trap," Crown shouted to Lancaster. "Be careful." He held the torch beam over Lancaster's feet. Lancaster sneezed an answer.

Crown opened the door nearest the stairs. He thought of Eric and how he was always going round with the bloody hoover, dusting the sideboard, then the table. Then he cleaned the sink with bleach. That must be better than this.

"Bathroom sir," he said looking into a small room with a grubby sink. There were rock-hard sponges and filthy pieces of old soap on the window ledge. Medicine bottles were lying at the side of the sink and the bath. A broken clock sat on the linen box. There were tins of powders and make-up scattered everywhere, eye shadows and lipsticks without tops. He opened the medicine cabinet to find the usual aspirin and cough medicine containers, almost empty. Someone must have spilt something because bits of cotton wool were sticking to the shelves. Lancaster closed the medicine cabinet feeling distinctly uneasy.

"Let's look in the other rooms. It's chaos in here."

He drew himself up. He couldn't ever remember being in a house like this. The next room was a small bedroom.

"Bed's not been touched. Just look at it. Just a miserable old duvet thrown over it."

He bent down and looked under the bed. He found a pair of slippers which were worn and shabby, a pair of men's slippers. Thrown over the back of the bed was a fringed shawl which had seen better days. He opened the wardrobe and moving the few clothes aside, he peeked inside.

"Nothing," he said. He could smell the dust.

"OK sir, we'll get to the other rooms."

Lancaster was glad Crown was with him. He wouldn't have wanted to come here on his own. For a man who had seen plenty of terrible scenes he was puzzled as to why he should feel so badly over a dirty house. But the rank odour told him why he was fearful.

"Unless, unless he or she was trying to tell us something," he mused.

"Who?"

"The woman who called us," Lancaster answered gruffly.

"I don't know sir, this is barmy. A filthy house with no one in it and Belinda Austin and her sister are nowhere in sight."

"Reminds you of a movie set Crown."

"Another two rooms here sir." It was best not to get into movie sets.

They went back onto the landing. Crown tried the next door.

"I don't like it."

"Christ," said Crown in fear. His stomach churned.

"The dark at the top of the stairs, Crown." Lancaster said in a whisper. "The dark at the top of the stairs... use your torch and get inside."

- 28 -

Simon looked ahead, trying to keep the bus in view through the pouring rain as it turned onto the main road.He tried to drive cautiously as the splashing of the bus tyres came up and muddied his windscreen. He must maintain a good distance or the bus driver would get irritated and may get out and stop him. A woman was trying to cross the road and his wheels forced a torrent of water onto her legs. He could hear her shouting after him but he wasn't interested. Why was she so carelessly trying to cross the road, in this weather and in front of his car? She had nearly stopped him following the bus.

The bus turned right at the next corner into a narrow turning lined with large trees.Then they came to a small crossroads with traffic lights. The bus stopped and he pulled up behind it, keeping his eyes on its rear lights. There was a great snort from the bus' engine as it pulled away again and went slowly onwards. Then it stopped. He pulled his car to halt, the tyres screeching, remaining as far back as he could. A man got off the bus, opening his umbrella. The bus started again and so did he.

How far away could she live from the station? They had been driving for fifteen minutes at least. Although one had to make allowances for all the stops it seemed to be a long journey. Then again the bus came to a halt and he watched Belinda coming down the steps, her umbrella in her left hand. She tried to put the umbrella up but it seemed to be stuck so she tied her scarf round her hair. She held her head down to ward off the rain and struggled again with the umbrella. She finally managed to put it up. Then she walked swiftly down a side turning and vanished. It would be foolish to follow her down there, she was bound to notice a car on an evening like this. There were only a few houses on the lane. He watched her go into the last house on the lane. At last he finally knew where she lived. If he drove slowly past once she was inside he would know where she was. He moved ahead slowly looking at the numbers. It was the last house, with a small porch light giving out a dim gleam. Under the porch light he glimpsed a name. It must be the name of the house. It was the kind of place where houses would have names. He had to put on his glasses to read it.

Charlinda it read.

"*Charlinda*" he said to himself. He certainly wouldn't forget that. Deep in thought, he reversed the car and drove back the way he came. No one could possibly have seen him in this downpour. There only seemed to be two other houses nearby. Taking a flask out of the glove compartment he took a swig of whisky. At last he knew. He knew where she lived. He knew where he could find her. It was as if he had come alive again.

But what could *Charlinda* mean? Was it Charles and Linda? Was she Linda?

****

As Inspector Lancaster pushed open the bedroom door in a house in Polegate, Belinda Austin was in Selfridges in London buying herself a wig. She was caught up the crowds of shoppers. She had to wait to see a salesgirl. Why were so many women buying wigs? A blonde woman was holding up three long dark wigs.

This was the best thing she could think of at a moments notice. She needed some sort of disguise to throw off her pursuer. She could always rely on her intuition in tight corners. Sometimes she could tell what people were thinking. That was why she knew instinctively someone was following her. For the last few days someone or something had been hovering around her and that was why she had a room at the Selfridge Hotel. It was near the shops and no one would dream of looking for her there.

She felt as if her space was being invaded. That's what they call it these days, your space. Whoever it was, it felt dangerous and she knew she had to avoid it. She didn't care where Charles was or what he was doing. When he got back he would have to carry on without her. Right now her main concern was herself and getting out of the country as soon as she could. She realised every move she made was being watched. She tried to think of all the places she could possibly go.

Who was following her? Simon loved her, he wouldn't follow her, would he? He would just phone her on her mobile like he always did. But she had told him they couldn't meet for the time being. Would he leave her?

Looking at the wig in her hand she thought how lovely it would look at a fancy dress party, instead of a disguise. Fancy dress made her think of Venice and how wonderful it was at Carnival time. She stood up, pushing aside the chair. She would go to her younger sister in Venice and try to stay on for the Carnival. Charles knew she had a younger sister. She had visited her years ago for a cousin's wedding. He knew she lived in Venice. But he never asked about her now. The wedding was so many years ago he probably never thought about it anymore. Venice would be an escape hatch when she needed it. Her sister had a flat on the Zattere. That was the place for her to go, and quickly. She heard a voice

"I'm free now Madam. Can I help you?"

She jumped with shock. She was becoming a bundle of nerves. It was the salesgirl. She turned and sat down in the nearest chair.

"Yes, yes," she answered. "I want a black wig, long. And if it's possible, may I have a glass of water. I'm feeling faint. It's terribly warm in here."

"PLease rest Madam. Of course it's possible, shall I call for a doctor?"

"No, no, I'm just a little overcome. It must be the crowds and the heat. I'm not used to shopping on a weekend. I just need a few moments moments to get myself together."

The girl hurried away to the cloakroom. She soon came back with a plastic cup of water. Belinda gulped it down.

"There," she said. "Thank you, I feel much better now."

The girl smiled and went over to a stand. There were dozens of wigs displayed there. Underneath the stand were various drawers. The salesgirl reached into one and searched for the appropriate size. She came over with some wigs in her hands.

"There" She took out a fresh dark wig from a plastic bag. "This should suit you. It's a new model."

She pulled Belinda's blonde hair back and fitted the wig. Belinda hadn't seen her hair dark for years. She liked being a blonde, even if it meant hours at the hairdresser having a tint. She looked into the mirror. No one could possibly recognise the face that stared back at her. She looked a different woman.

"I like it," she said. "I'll take it."

The salesgirl, unused to such a quick purchase, said "Are you sure Madam, you haven't tried on the others?"

"No," Belinda said, almost breathlessly. "This will do perfectly. I have a party to go to." Best to say that in case anyone had traced her here. But how could they? No one knew where she was.

"I'll wrap it up then. Charge card or cash?"

"Oh" It wouldn't do to pay on a card.

"Cash," she answered. "And is there a travel bureau here?"

"Oh yes, on the first floor Madam."

Belinda paid for the wig, looked around her and hurried

over to the escalators. She slipped the bag containing the wig over her wrist and made her way to the travel bureau through the crowd.

"Jesus," said Crown. "whoever locked this bedroom door did a bloody good job of it."

His shoulder ached and there was perspiration on his face. Lancaster wondered again why he wasn't a film director. He could have done this scene a million times in black and white. He would have had Mitchum in it. Film noir style with camera panning to the door handle, then to the door opening, then to Mitchum's dark shadow on the opposite wall. It was all wishful thinking. He would have to confuse Crown with another of one of his quotes but for the moment he was speechless

The door suddenly gave way and he almost lost his balance. There was nothing there. It must have been locked for months. They rummaged through the drawers - empty!

"That's it sir. We've looked up here. I think we should get back downstairs."

"Right and be bloody careful on that staircase."

It was like going down a mountain.

"Where the hell is that smell coming from Crown?"

As they returned along the hallway they saw a previously unnoticed alcove, probably a coat storage area. The smell was strong now. Crown shone his torch into the pitch black of the alcove.

The dead body was lying against the rear wall. Crown tied his scarf around his nose and mouth. The body had its mouth taped open with wide sticking plaster.

"It's no good taking the tape off sir. He's dead."

"All the way," Lancaster answered, suddenly.

"With his mouth taped open, wide open"

"And his hands lifted up and taped to his ears"

"We can't open this tape sir. Let's get the techs in. Let them deal with it."

Lancaster got down on his knees to examine what he could of the body.

"This case is sick Crown. Not only has he been murdered but the killer deliberately trussed him up like a turkey."

"That's a turkey and two geese sir." Crown raised his eyes to the ceiling. Dana Lancaster swiftly rose to his feet. His face was white.

"What is it sir?"

"Good God Crown. Don't you recognise him? I think I know who he is."

"How could you know who he is, with all that stuff all over his face? Can't tell him from an orangutan."

"It's Charles Austin."

"But what's he doing here?"

"Crown, I think you're a very stupid person. You look stupid. You're in a stupid business. And you're on a stupid case."

Crown got up and opened his pad, then folded his yellow paper in half. At least it took his mind off the smell for a moment. This time he knew. It was one of Lancaster's favourite stars who said it. One of the stars he would never have cast if he'd been a director instead of a detective. He wrote *I think you're a very stupid person* and put a tick next to it like a school teacher. Maybe he was a stupid person to work with this lunatic. Then he sighed and looked at the corpse.

"Oh, he's here for treatment, like a health farm. Crown, sometimes I despair of you. You met him, I met him. And I don't forget a face. You should know it's Austin. I'll stake my life on it. Doesn't look a lot like he used to of course.Look at him, rolled up like a ball of string and pushed almost into a circle, ghastly."

Crown was angry with himself. He should have recognised Austin.

"Anyway, you mean who put him here and why Crown. Someone must have managed to entice him here. And from the look of it, whoever dragged him inside must have needed help to do it."

"Maybe he wasn't even killed here."

Lancaster threw the newspapers off the nearest chair and sat down.

"Let's think," he said.

He looked along the hallway. Upstairs there was a room that was clean and the rest of the place was a pigsty. Nothing touched up there. No one's used the bed and even the window is closed. It's as if someone laid the place out. Maybe wanted to put him on the bed but decided against it, so they left him where he was. You couldn't even get yourself up those stairs, let alone a dead body. That room is clean as a whistle and the rest of the house is like Miss Haversham's.

"I think he was brought here after he died."

"You mean they killed him somewhere else?"

"We'll have to find out how long he's been dead. He's all trussed up like a Christmas dinner."

"Couldn't be one person's job doing that, you'd still need two people to drag him down the hallway."

Lancaster had a sudden thought. "Get his overcoat off Crown."

"I'll have to cut it off."

"Never mind, do it. I'll explain it away later."

Crown slipped a penknife out of his back pocket. He carefully began to cut down the seams at the back of the coat. When he had managed to cut away as much as he could he slipped the back of the coat away from the body.

"Hold him on his side Crown."

Crown bent on his knees and gripped the body.

"Well, well, well, look at that," Lancaster said. "Just as I thought."

Crown looked across the dead man's back.

"He's been killed by an impact, a heavy impact.. Been pushed up against something. Lift up his shirt."

Crown lifted the shirt. There was dried blood on it which was turning black. His back was covered in bruises and cuts. He was nearly bent in half. Lancaster whistled.

"His chest has been crushed. I'd say he died instantly. Quickly, help me turn him over."

They moved him again.

"Shouldn't be doing this."

"I know. It's against the rule book, badly against it.."

"He's been in some sort of accident. Let's look at the coat. You hold him while I slip it from under him."

Lancaster managed to get the coat away from the body.

"Hunter will have something to say about this sir!"

Lancaster moved the coat slightly.

"Minute particles of something, could be metal, can't tell until we get everything to the lab. But it looks to me like he's been run over. He's been crushed to death."

"You don't think...."

"It's possible Crown. The hit-and-run wasn't far from here. And I'm thinking of the someone who told us about it. And there was an empty road with no victim. How the hell did he get here?

"Did he crawl away from the car after he was knocked down, make some super-human effort to get himself noticed, lay in the middle of the road or try to use his mobile for help? That's if he was knocked down. But I'd say he was killed in a road accident, deliberately. Why did the killers who ran him over bring him here? Why Crown, why, why,why? And how did they know where to run him over and kill him? They must have been following him."

""Or else they knew where he was going and at what time. We'd better phone the station sir and get the team over here."

"This is the third death in, how long is it Crown?"

Crown could only answer with a shrug. "Soon be Christmas"

"Come on, let's get out of here."

"Sir, the daffodils were out when we started."

"We could have used them to make a wreath."

"There are plenty of winter pansies."

****

Belinda left Selfridges with her ticket to Venice in her bag. Only one more night and she would leave all these problems behind her. She was thankful she had had the wits to bring her passport with her, otherwise it would have meant going back to the house to find it and that would have been disastrous. She left there at breaking point and her valium tablets had nearly run out. She opened her bag and quickly swallowed one of the few remaining 10mg tablets. Her doctor told her it was the best thing to take for the time being. She told him she was going away. She wondered if she was losing her mind. Doctor Kane wanted her to see someone as soon as possible, so she could talk over her worries. He didn't like the look of her and she needed help. But she had no time for that now.

Walking back from Selfridges she wondered if she should tell Lancaster where she was staying. But it was done now and she mustn't look back. She arrived at the reception and asked for her key. The concierge interrupted her thoughts.

"Madam, someone has been asking for you," he said.

She looked at him searchingly.

"That's not possible," she answered with a look of astonishment. "No one knows I am here."

She had signed the register in the name of Mrs Henderson. She hadn't confided in anyone, not even her sister. She had only told her what time the plane was due to arrive at the airport.

"Who was it?" she asked, panicking. "A man or woman? Did they leave a name?"

"Oh, it was a young lady. She just came into the hotel and said she had been asked to deliver a message to you. I put it in your box."

Belinda prayed it would be Simon. He would come and help her.

"Let me see," continued the concierge. Turning to the compartment where herr key had been hanging, he removed a letter. Handing it to her with a smile, he asked if she would like to order a morning paper.

She tried to catch her breath but could only gasp. The concierge, noticing how ill she suddenly looked, asked if anything was wrong. She could just nod. Seeing her face looked ashen, he thought of calling the hotel doctor. Mrs Henderson looked so ill. She rushed up to her room, not waiting for the lift. Throwing her shopping onto the bed, she sat down holding the letter. My God, who could it possibly be writing to her? She could barely tear the envelope open, her fingers were trembling so much. The writing was a scrawl she could hardly decipher. She turned the lamp on so that she could see it clearly. She had never seen such writing. It seemed to go from right to left, then left to right in a circle. She read

> *You're mine, you,*
> *You belong to me, you,*
> *I will never free you*
> *In every way you're mine*
>
> *Simon*

She dropped it from her hands and went into the bathroom. That was her favourite song, by Sarah Vaughan. She had every recording of Sarah's and knew every lyric. Filling the basin with cold water, she splashed her face. She felt a chill run through her. Was it Simon after all who was following her? Was he following her when she left the house? The water dripped down her neck and onto her sweater. All the time it was him. She had been desperate to see him but fear held her back. But maybe Simon sent the letter and someone else was following her. Oh God, if only he would call. She took her mobile out and rang his number. There was just the answering service asking for a message.

"I must lock the door," she whispered to herself. She got up quickly and turned the lock. She pulled out a pillow and lay back on the bed. A wild thought entered her head. Whoever was following her was behaving like one of those obsessed men she watched on late night movies, the ones that followed women and then, because they couldn't have them, killed them. The meetings she had with Simon were thrilling, erotic and desperate. It was obvious

179

from the note he loved her. She was his. But why didn't he appear? Why torture her so? But if they met that sergeant would follow her. But how could she even imagine that he had anything to do with Clare's death?

Now there were police crawling all over the place looking for Clare's murderer. As far as she was concerned, if you loved someone you wanted to be with them. Not send them stupid notes. She sometimes read about these things in the newspapers. People who just wouldn't let go. Sometimes they killed their girlfriends, or their wives, or even their husbands. On top of it all, someone was following her. Her throat tightened and her breathing became difficult. Did Simon kill Clare? No, that was stupid, he didn't even know Clare. Clare was always playing fast and loose with men's affections. She lay down on the bed and tried to think clearly. Her brain was fuddled, she didn't know how she would get through the night. *You're mine, you.* She always said that to Simon.

She rushed back into the bathroom to be sick. Wiping her face with towel she made a sudden decision. She would phone that Inspector and tell him she was here. There was no other way for her to stay sane. Then at least he may be able to protect her. She felt her life was in danger. She dialled 9 and then the number she found on his card.

"Please put me through to Inspector Lancaster," she whispered into the phone.

"Hello, Lancaster here. Who is this?"

"Quickly Inspector, come quickly. It's Belinda Austin. I'm at the Selfridge Hotel in London and someone is trying to kill me."

- 30 -

Lancaster held the note lightly in his fingers.

"Where were you after the party?"

He had struck home.

"Met him at the party did you?"

Lancaster usually found two and two made three.

"No , I knew him before the party."

"And how did you meet him?" Slowly, he said to himself, take it easy, don't rush her.

"Well I," she hesitated. "PLease don't think I'm some sort of ......" Her voice trailed off. "I met him through the personals, in the newspaper."

How sordid this all began to sound. But it wasn't really sordid she told herself.

Crown looked surprised. He never took her for that..

Lancaster gave Crown a look of reprimand.

"Why shouldn't our friend Mrs Austin meet someone through the love ads or whatever they call them. Married people do it all the time. Lots of men I've arrested are at it. You look surprised that a lady like Mrs Austin might do that. So Mrs Austin, why did you do that? A woman like yourself, with a very nice husband?" He added this as an afterthought, even though he thought the man he had met was a prig. When he was alive that is. He'd seen it enough times. Sex and murder so often went together.

Her face was blotched with tears.

"I met him a few months ago. We enjoyed seeing each other. He was very pleasant."

"Hubby know? See each other in public did you?"

"Oh God, I hope not. I mean I don't know if he found out about us."

"Man have a name?" Crown suddenly interrupted. "Where did you go with him?"

She was at her wits end. She would have to tell these people about what she had done, where she went and what hotels they stayed in. If she was unlucky they may even ask her if there were any others before Simon. They were too clever for her.

"His name? Of course he has a name." There was a slight hesitation. "But I don't know if it's his real name. I never knew his real name. He wouldn't tell me. I mean we never knew our real names at all. It was an agreement, stops any problems afterwards, you know."

"No, I don't know Mrs Austin. What name did he give you? He must have given you some name or other."

Belinda wondered if she would have felt better confessing to a woman police officer. No, it didn't make any difference.

"Yes. Yes of course he did. Give a name I mean." She gave way. "It was Simon."

"And the last name, Mrs Austin?"

"Templar. Simon Templar."

Lancaster often wondered, in some of his most depressing moments, and depressing hours, whether he should place an advert in "love lines" himself to try and contact the jazz singer. But he knew she wouldn't read rubbish like that. Maybe he should put it in "The Stage". Of course he would never do it.

"Yes, that's how he advertised, *The Saint*. He was *The Saint*. So I called him Simon."

"Very clever," Lancaster said, brought back to the present. "I remember George Sanders used to *The Saint* years ago., became a big star. His brother took over the role after he gave it up. What was his name? Ah, yes, Tom Conway, a handsome man. But he never reached the big time like his brother."

Why was this fool talking about George Sanders? Was he trying to catch her out? Lancaster continued.

"And you Mrs Austin, who did you pretend to be?" he asked. "Or should I say what name did you use? Lady Day? The Sweater Girl? The Look?" She wouldn't even know who The Sweater Girl was, or Lady Day come to that.

She whispered a name under her breath, her face turning bright red.

"What was that Mrs Austin. I didn't catch what you said." He leaned forward, listening intently.

"Peaches," she answered, tears falling again. Oh God, it all sounded so stupid and common and shameless.

These two had to be the best Lancaster had heard. They had turned the affair into a movie script. Pity they didn't work for Paramount, or Dreamworks.

"Peaches," he repeated. "Simon and Peaches"

Crown thought it sounded like a bloody champagne cocktail, Simon and Peaches. He wondered what to do about Belinda now. In her condition they couldn't leave her here on her own. She would have to leave the hotel immediately for her own sanity. Otherwise he would have to leave a man at her door, which wasn't possible. They were too short-staffed.

"Crown?" Lancaster asked, turning his head.

"Sir?" Crown knew what was coming. How could he tell Eric? Eric would hate having anyone staying at their place. How many nights would she have to stay?

"Get Mrs Austin something to eat. You can nip down to the restaurant or go over the road. I leave it to you. Then take her back to your place. Put her in the spare room. Then you and I will go out and talk this over. Find a table at that place I like in town. I'm tired of snatched meals. And bring your notes. We're going over this case with a fine tooth comb.I'll have to drive it around the block a couple of times, as they say."

He could see signs of relief spread over Belinda Austin's tear-stained face. He lifted up the net curtain and peered into the street. There were buses and taxis racing down Baker Street. It was difficult to look at the pavement, they were too high up.

"So Mrs Austin, who do you think might be following you?"

Her head fell. "I don't know. I really don't know," she said in despair. She noticed his deep blue eyes. Did he have a wife or a girlfriend? Did they listen to music together? She decided to answer his question.

"I felt sure a car was following me. I noticed it when I got on the bus. It followed all the way from the station. It stayed behind us all the time. I had been shopping in town. Then I caught the bus and went home." Did that sound possible? Of course it did, it was true wasn't it?

"Bus? I thought you had a car?"

"Of course I have a car." Why was he asking her all these damn questions about her car? Supposing she needed a lawyer? She was in deep trouble.

"So you fancied a ride on the bus eh? Why didn't you take your car to the station? Most people leave it there all day."

"What day was this?" Crown asked her.

"It must have been a Tuesday." That was the day she always phoned Simon.

"There was a downpour on Tuesday," Crown said, scribbling in his notebook.

"This isn't your husband's writing, is it?"

"It must be your lover's."

"No more fooling around Mrs Austin. This isn't a game of ring-a-rosy, it's murder."

"It's Simon's. It's the song we always played."

"Oh, I know that Mrs Austin. It's the divine Sarah."

He read it out.

"You belong to me,you. I will never free you. In every way you're mine."

"Then you know it?" she asked him.

"Yes, I like a bit of music. I'm a jazz fan myself."

He abruptly broke off, best not to speak of jazz.

"Right Mrs Austin. Crown here will pop out and get you something to eat. When he gets back you can leave with him."

He picked his coat up off the bed.

"I think you've told us everything for now. I'll see you tomorrow at the Sergeant's place. Try and eat something. Drink a glass of wine. And by the way, lock the door until my Sergeant gets back," he smiled towards her.

She rose. As soon as the door was closed she picked up the phone.

"Get me Al Italia, please."

Her hands felt so sticky she could hardly hold the receiver.

"Al Italia? Yes, my name is Belinda Austin. I want to charge my ticket for the first plane out to Venice. First thing in the morning? That's perfect. Thank you."

Now she would have to use her credit card.

She would be gone after breakfast.

- 31 -

"Mr Austin," said Sister Bates, her professional attitude even more pronounced since she was dealing with the police, "Mr Austin contracted hepatitis some weeks ago."

Lancaster had been called to the hospital early that morning. He'd sent a man to stay outside Belinda's hotel first thing this morning and was waiting to hear from him. He didn't like going back and forth to hospitals. He hated hospitals and needles and operations and everything to do with them. He should have let Crown come here on his own.

"Perhaps we should go into your private room , Sister," he suggested.

"Of course," she said. "It's far better that none of the nurses hear this."

Crown looked dishevelled and tired, not at all professional. He felt ashamed in front of Sister Bates who was so starched and white and utterly efficient. He and Lancaster had had a late night, and maybe a few glasses of wine too many. He would have preferred to go to a night club, but then Eric wouldn't have liked that. They could even have split up over it.

Eric and his constant dusting, and hoovering when he wasn't working in the box office, bordered on obsession. how Crown wished Eric had seen the house where they found Charles. He would have run out screaming. Crown asked himself, yet again, if he was comfortable with Eric. They liked the same films, liked the same books, so why wasn't it working? Or was it working for Eric but not for him? Crown was a fairly nice looking man, in a Robson Green kind of way.Always buying smart clothes, so they showed off his dark hair. Blue shirts, cornflower blue ties. In fact he spent most of his money on clothes. Right now he had Clare Austin niggling at him from beyond her grave. He would wake dreaming of her looking up at him, propped up like a doll and bleeding from her wounds, her ribbon trailing down from her hair into the blood, a dead model. It reminded him of that book Lancaster told him about that was turned into a movie, *I Wake Up Screaming*. What a title, how did the author think of it? He woke up screaming quietly every day. He always read a thriller at night, even in the bath. He was a bookshop freak. Publishers must dance when they saw him coming. His shelves were crammed with criminal psychology books. He spent far too much money on books. His card was mounting up with his books and his clothes.

His aunt wanted him to settle down, get married. Well, soon you could marry the same sex. And leave them all your money, if you had any. And they could leave their money to you, if they had any. But he wasn't going to leave any money to anybody. It would break his aunt's heart. So why was he feeling the relationship wasn't working? He turned to Sister Bates.

Lancaster used a very kindly tone when he spoke to Sister Bates.

"Thank you for calling me Sister Bates. What was it you had to tell me?"

Sister Bates held her head up as stiffly as her starched cap.

"It was Mrs Austin!"

"Mrs Austin?"

"Yes, she phoned me late last night, just as I was going to dinner in the hospital canteen. I never had time to go out for something as I was very busy with the patients, as you might imagine. And a poor dinner it was too. The food here is getting worse and worse. I don't know how they expect good results with bad food. My nurses work very hard indeed."

Crown brought her back to the subject.

"You were saying Mrs Austin spoke to you."

"Yes, it was after I phoned and asked her to come here. I broke the news about her husband's death, just as you told me to. I think she had been expecting it for some time. She said it was like living in limbo until she knew. Of course I never told her all the details."

She raised an eyebrow.

"Yes, Mrs Austin said she wanted to speak to me because she had remembered something. She said it had slipped her memory. She just couldn't work out where her husband contracted the disease, but then again her specialist had said you could contract hepatitis by sitting next to someone on a bus. Then when he passed away, there was something nagging her."

Lancaster felt tired and anxious. What could Austin's wife possibly remember?

"She told me she couldn't sleep after her husband died, which is only natural. Then one evening she was at home watching the television, trying to relax, when a film came on.She couldn't remember the name of the film but one of the characters had a loss of memory. And in the film the memory loss was connected to a phone call. The man lost his memory when someone phoned him, someone from his past."

Sister Bates cleared her throat with a slight cough.

"Yes?" Lancaster muttered.

Crown tried to remember films where people lost their memory. Lancaster would know what that film was. There were hundreds of films where people lost their memory. Most people wanted to lose their memory. He'd seen enough of loss of memory films with Lancaster. They had been to some of the worst flea pits it was possible to imagine in some towns. He opened his notebook and began to fold a yellow page in half. If he ever wrote a book it would be called *Quotes and Murder*. But that wouldn't sell as many as *I Wake Up Screaming*. He heard Sister Bates speaking.

"Mrs Austin told me she suddenly remembered that her husband had been asked to visit a Doctor Allbright in London somewhere. At least she thought that was the name. And the reason she remembered was the film. She'd been feeling depressed and couldn't seem to remember anything. It sometimes happens when there's a death. She was very confused Inspector. Mr Austin received a call from someone who wanted to place an order with him. It happened at dinner time and Mr Austin left the table to take the call. Afterwards he told her he had to leave. The doctor wanted to meet Mr Austin that very evening. She said medical people were always recommending each other, but not at dinner time. Of course she was speaking in riddles. Apparently he left his dinner uneaten and rushed off to meet the man. She grumbled to her husband that surely it could wait until tomorrow."

"Had he met this Doctor Allbright before?"

"She didn't say. I had the feeling he was a complete stranger. But her husband had said the doctor worked in the blood coagulation unit of a big hospital in London. Then Mrs Austin said he rushed off. She also said her husband was always rushing about looking for business and was hardly ever home for dinner. I think she just wanted to talk. People usually do when they've had a shock. She also asked me when Mr Austin's body would be released for the funeral. I don't think it occurred to her to speak to you Inspector."

"Did she say where her husband went?"

"As I said, she was extremely confused. She was really looking for reasons why her husband should have died so suddenly. She said her husband must have been gone for hours because she never spoke to him until the next morning."

Crown and Lancaster listened intently.

"Apparently he went to the West End, Seymour Street actually. He told her he went to Burberry Mansions. She said she remembered that because she had an old Burberry raincoat. Strange how we remember names, isn't it Inspector?"

"Most strange, it's association I suppose."

He was fascinated with the story and wondered what on earth could have happened in Seymour Street. He thought about *The Man in Half Moon Street*. But that had nothing to do with it. Sister Bates continued.

"Doctor Allbright gave him the address and told him to be there at nine o'clock. When he arrived at the flat, after ringing the bell, a maid answered the door."

"A maid?" asked Crown.

"Yes, apparently a maid let him in. When he asked the maid where the doctor was, she said he'd been called away unexpectedly. Mr Austin had been told to go to number 14 Burberry Mansions at nine o'clock and now the doctor wasn't there to meet him. He asked the maid if there was anyone else in the flat and she said there was a patient of Doctor Allbright's there. Mr Austin wanted to speak to the patient to ask him if he knew when the doctor would be back. So he asked the maid to show him the patient's room. He went into a bedroom darkened by heavy curtains which only let in a crack of light from the street. A man was lying on the bed asleep. There was a small lamp on the bedside table. Mr Austin switched it on and saw there were various medicines on the side table together with a jug of water."

Sister Bates hesitated for a moment, then carried on.

"Mrs Austin said that the reason her husband had told her about this was because it seemed like a mystery story. He wasn't in the habit of discussing his pharmacy with her, let alone anything to do with his customers."

"Indeed," Crown murmured, growing more and more intrigued.

"Then Mr Austin began to wonder who the patient was and why the doctor hadn't left a note. Perhaps in his haste Doctor Allbright had forgotten. Just the same he thought he would try to ask the man if he knew where the doctor was but the man was sleeping so soundly. So Mr Austin left. If the doctor wanted him he could phone again. Mrs Austin said he was furious for days afterwards. I got the impression he was a difficult man."

Crown closed his notepad.

"Thank you Sister Bates, it was good of you to let us know about Mr Austin and his nocturnal visits."

"Well I thought it might be important. Only Mrs Austin was telling me all manner of things that night. You understand."

"Of course, I'm sure you're very busy. Thank you for taking time out to call us."

Lancaster grimaced as he stood up. That bloody injection was giving him hell. He couldn't wait to get out of that God-damned hospital.

- 32 -

They found out that the flat in Burberry Mansions was owned by a young lady who worked in the City. Her name was Anne Shelby and she was often sent abroad as a loss adjuster on insurance cases, so she rented out her flat for a month at a time. She told them that tourists booked it a few months in advance and she was happy to receive the rent.

The flat had been cleaned out and treated by the lab boys.

"So Miss Shelby, how did this Mr Brittain approach you?"

"Oh, he came from the agency. There's one in Baker Street. They find me the tenants and I pay a fee. It's simple really."

She was a pleasant young woman, dressed for the office in a skirt and jacket, and looked every inch the executive. She expressed her anger in no uncertain terms.

"I'm really upset Inspector," she grumbled. "How could they allow a man like that to come into my home? And then I come back from abroad to find the police swarming all over the place is more than uncomfortable."

"Well we're not sure who the man was. He could have sent anyone into the agency to book the flat."

"You're right, of course," she said shrugging her shoulders. "I suppose I'm lucky I wasn't here. Heaven only know what would have happened if I'd come home early."

"That's a point. Do you always use the spare room for tenants?"

"Of course, I lock my bedroom door when I go away and my bathroom is en suite. There's a guest bathroom off the second bedroom. I don't mind if they use the kitchen, provided they clean it up afterwards."

They looked inside the spare room. The bed had been stripped of linen and the curtains had been taken down. Miss Shelby told them she wouldn't be renting the room again. She was selling the flat and moving. After this she couldn't stay here.

"By the way Miss Shelby, before we go, do you know anyone who works in a hospital?"

She looked puzzled. "Absolutely not," came the swift reply.

Then they enquired of the ambulance service if a patient had been picked up from Burberry Mansions on the night of the fourth. So far they had had no response.

"The patient definitely had an illness," Lancaster said. "I'm bloody sure of it. But how did they get him over there?"

"I'd say they shoved him into a car from either a hospital or clinic."

"Whoever it was worked in the hospital or clinic. The man was brought in, and somehow or other they found out about it. Maybe they worked as a porter or cleaner, kept their ear to the ground and this turned up. What a way to get rid of Austin."

"You can't rely on it though, can you sir? I mean not everyone catches an illness. Some of us are immune."

"Not according to my backside Crown. They didn't take any chances with me."

"Moved by car I'd say, just like *The Lady Vanishes*. Wrapped in bandages and taken to Anne Shelby's flat in Seymour Street."

"So we don't know the patient's name and we don't know the man who made the phone call."

"By the way I checked the local paper out. Love Lines comes out twice a week. The girl on reception said every morning she finds envelopes left with a written advert and cash to go with it. But mostly the adverts are paid for by card."

"A great many mistakes are made in the name of loneliness. Our man could be married and fancied a bit of a lark."

Lancaster frowned.

"Let's get over to Belinda's place and strip it. There could be a letter there or a photograph. Women always keep everything. I've got a feeling, Crown, Belinda is on the night train to the big adios."

Crown couldn't even think about it.

They were lucky with one thing though, Belinda's house was surrounded by large trees. And that meant lots of cover from prying neighbours. The house opposite was in darkness. Closing the car doors quietly they walked across the lawn and round the back of the house. Crown took out his large ring of keys. The lock clicked open but the door wouldn't budge.

"Bloody bolts are on sir."

"Then there's nothing for it but to smash the window."

Bending down Lancaster picked up a milk bottle from the doorstep. He raised his arm and shattered the glass. He looked across the road but there was no response from the house opposite. He put his hand inside and raised the window. Heaving himself up, he got over the sill and eased himself inside. He'd done a lot of breaking and entering in this case. No one seemed to have their doors open.

"No alarm on, if she was so nervous why didn't she leave the alarm on?"

"She wanted to get out and get out quickly."

As Crown got inside he knocked over a lamp. It fell to the floor with a noisy crash. Lancaster sighed and shook his head at Crown.

"You're slipping," he said.

"Well at least we're in. Where shall we start?"

"Close the curtains and put on the other lamp. The one you didn't smash."

Crown clicked the switch and light illuminated the corner of the room. Lancaster looked round and saw a small desk.

"Start here Crown."

Crown rifled through the papers.

"Nothing here, get over to the small table. There's a drawer in it."

"It's locked," said Crown irritably.

"Since when did that stop you?"

Crown took out his penknife and eased the lock open.

"Just a collection of small photographs in this drawer."

He handed them to Lancaster.

"Anything else?"

"Old letters,some of them from the fifties." He peered at the dates.

Lancaster sat down and began looking through the photos. Some of them were old sepia pictures.

"There are some names on the back of these photos," he muttered. Look at this one, Grandmother and Grandfather. And this looks like a family wedding. Nice old photos, I've got some at home myself. They must go back a while too. A few black and whites, and what's this?" He turned the picture over. "Aunt Polly's wedding". He held it closely. Damn glasses, he must get his eyes tested. "lots of bridesmaids and pageboys here Crown."

"Nice frocks too," Crown said.

"Now why lock away photos? No one locks away photos unless there's a reason. Most people's photos are in a shoe box if they're not in an album. Take these with you and we'll check out the rest of the place. I'm sure we missed something."

There was nothing in the other drawers they opened. They turned and went upstairs to the bedrooms.

The first bedroom was painted in a pale shade of lavender with curtains printed with lavender flowers. Lancaster went to the dressing table and moved the bottles of perfume around. Then he moved the clothes in the wardrobe. He decided to check through the pockets of Belinda's clothes, starting with the dressing gowns.

"What have we here?" Lancaster's fingers felt a small piece of paper in one of the pockets.

"Probably a shopping list."

"Not this time Crown." He held the paper under the light.

"Will you look at this, a piece of newspaper. It's an advert. We've hit the jackpot. She must have stuffed it in her pocket and forgotten about it. Let's see." Lancaster started reading.

LOVE LINES

THE SAINT   YOUNG EXCITING AND INTERESTING   LIKES TO DINE AT CLARIDGES   ONLY THE BEST WILL DO   FINE WINES AND GOURMET FOOD   SOUTH OF FRANCE AT CHRISTMAS   IF YOU ARE THE RIGHT ONE WE CAN TRAVEL THE WORLD   LOOKING FOR THE LOVE OF MY LIFE BRUNETTE   ATTRACTIVE AND STYLISH   TO SUIT BOND STREET AND PEARLS   IS THERE A SINNER INTERESTED IN A SAINT WHO CAN GIVE HER EVERYTHING?   PLEASE PHONE MY MOBILE   35454747

Lancaster imagined Clare alive, dancing in her red dress and her string of pearls, swaying to the music. Did Simon give Clare the pearls she died in?

"What did I tell you Crown? They're all looking for the love of their lives. And you couldn't beat this guy for extravagant language, could you?"

"No wonder she answered it. Simon Templar does exist. And there's none of your usual nonsense for him, none of that tall, young and a bubbly blonde stuff. This fellow laid it on with a trowel. I wonder how many women answered his ad."

"Hundreds, I shouldn't wonder. Claridge's, Asprey's, I'd answer it myself."

"That's enough from you Crown. But you're right. Come on. I think we've found what we're looking for. And bring those photos with you. Now we're getting somewhere. We've established the fact that Belinda told the truth. There was a Saint and he must have used the same ad every time."

"Why would he stick to the same ad sir"

"Wouldn't you if you'd discovered a gold mine?"

"What about the breaking and entering?"

"What breaking, what entering?" Lancaster sighed. "You're

a bit of a puzzlement to me these days Crown. You don't seem to be your old cruel self any more. And I had such great plans for your future."

Lancaster studied the photos. He squinted his eyes and tried to see the faces. Crown was right about his glasses. Was it last year since he had his eyes tested, or the year before? Holding the photos close he could see that the people in them were Belinda's family. Why hide them away? Who would want to look at old photographs? A family picture was usually on the mantlepiece or in one of those plastic things you hung on the wall filled with dozens of black and white photos all cut up and stuck together like a jigsaw. In the wedding picture older relatives were standing in the background and sitting on the floor were five pretty girls next to a pageboy. He wondered which one was Belinda.Children changed so much over the years, especially girls, who might tint their hair blonde. On the other hand, was she in the picture at all?

"I think we'd better speak to Belinda, and soon. Maybe she has a few secrets apart from her boyfriend, *The Saint.*"

Crown agreed. "I've got a funny feeling Belinda is going to vanish,"

"Where to Crown? She's a suspect, for Christ's sake. She doesn't know we've got these photos and unless she decides to go home and get them, with some of her other trinkets, we keep them right here in my pocket."

"Why would she worry about a lot of old photos?"

Crown was thinking... trinkets. Was that from a movie?

Lancaster turned one of the photographs over.

"There's a faint name printed on the back of this photo. Maybe it's the studio that took them. Get the photo and the name enlarged right now Crown and hurry yourself. And Crown," Lancaster observed, as Crown was leaving, "It's staring us in the face. Bond Street, jewellery and pearls. Pearls! I don't know why I missed it."

"Sir, I've been telling you for over a year. You need new glasses."

- **33** -

Frank was a different person these days. His attitude towards Betty had changed from casual affection to deep indifference. Since that night he had become mean and spiteful towards her. She thought he would have tried to be more understanding after she had such a fright, but he simply ignored her. If she told him she felt distressed, he answered in muttered syllables. When they sped home in the dark that terrible night, he was totally oblivious to her sheer terror. And now she was paying the penalty. As far as Frank was concerned she was just a burden to him.

Tonight she decided to prepare dinner early. She thought if she followed a recipe for chocolate pudding it would occupy her mind. She cluttered up the kitchen with bowls and spoons and bars of cooking chocolate.

Frank told her he was taking some anti-depressants from Doctor Fielding. Now why would he do that? The police hadn't accused him of any accidents. Powders, why was he taking powders (that was what her mother used to call them)? What reason did he give Doctor Fielding for being depressed? He must have invented a good story.

"What's for dinner Betty?" he asked, turning a page of the newspaper. That was about all he would say to her these days, what's for dinner or where's the paper? And after all those years together. She thought of the meal again and how quickly they would be finished so she could go upstairs to her hideaway.

And then there were the phone calls. He would answer the phone and whisper into it, or go into another room. She could hear him if she put her ear to the door and listened, not that she could make out much. Mostly he would say yes or no. What was she doing prying like that? She had never tried to overhear anyone's conversation in her life.

The calls for Frank were coming more often now and he never told her to whom he was speaking. Sometimes after the calls she would hear him go to the kitchen door and zoom off on his motorbike. He told her he was off to the pub for a drink with the lads.

She was treated as a servant to cook the meals and clear up. If only someone could invent a new dinner. When she was a girl she went to the cinema with her brother every week. She remembered her mother had packed sandwiches for them. They always liked a sandwich in the films. They had gone somewhere in Kilburn High Road to see Laurel and Hardy. And they fell off their seats laughing so much that they could hardly eat their lunch. Instead of food a chemist had invented pills and Laurel and Hardy were taking them at every meal. It was such a crazy idea that it made them howl. Now, in view of what was happening to Betty, it didn't seem such a bad idea, In fact it was brilliant. She sighed. Now she was saddled with a man who didn't want to go anywhere, not to a film or a theatre or even out for dinner to the Horse and Garter. They had a good pub locally where there was a first-class restaurant. Arranging the knives and forks, she stood near the table trying to remember the last time she had laughed.

"Casserole," she suddenly answered under her breath.

Frank grunted.

Someone was knocking at the front door and, in her over-wrought condition, she dropped a soup spoon onto one of her old dinner plates. A large crack appeared on the rim of the burnished gilt on the plate. The knock came again, accompanied by a ringing bell.

Frank threw the paper aside.

"I'll open the door and then I'll be out back if you want me," he said, "Who have you invited round now, you fool?"

"I haven't invited anyone. I don't know who it is," she whimpered, sounding like a kicked dog she thought. She put the chain on the front door and looked out into the night. She heard the voice of Inspector Lancaster.

She ran upstairs. This was all Frank's doing. She hated him.

****

Steven Ross decided the best thing to do was to get out for a bit. His best place for mulling things over was the path by the river. Joan had gone over to see her brother and he had the day to himself. Taking out his winter jacket and his old fishing hat, he picked up his walking stick. That was the joy of living in a place like this. The path by the river wound through beds of wild flowers and often there were primulas. The woodland surrounded his house and he could always see the change of the season by the different

196

coloured leaves and bushes. The winter was his favourite time, all the flowers lying fallow, waiting to burst forth in the spring. Steven wished he had the faculty to do that. The early morning frost was just beginning to cover the ground. He wished he could claw himself back to a new season. Since Clare's murder there was no peace for him or for Joan.

People who lived here called the river the Crooked Path River. But it wasn't that really, it was the River Larch. It trickled itself into a small inlet right past his garden, then rushed off miles beyond. Steven held his favourite walking stick, it was the best one for poking along the river path. He never thought he would see the day when he needed to use a walking stick. He had run through here as a boy and walked with ease as a young man. It was a brisk night and as he strolled along the path he started thinking about Joan and her wretched family.

Ever since the time he overheard the conversation between Joan and Frank he had become uneasy. Why couldn't Joan meet Frank to discuss these things? Why all the phone calls and whispering late at night, or even early in the morning when he was just getting up? What could they be up to? Nothing probably. They always had their little secrets since the very beginning of their marriage. They were always talking about how things were when they lived out in Shropshire. Brothers and sisters often phoned each other all the time. His own brother and sister were always speaking to each other at any time of the day or night. It was perfectly natural. Just the same he had grown apart from his own family. He never found it easy to be intimate with anyone. Joan was the only one he ever seemed to communicate with from the day he met her. They had some good times together then. And now he couldn't discuss anything with her at all. She would brush him off with excuses of business she had to attend to, or fashion shows she was writing about. Anything, come to that, that didn't include him.

Steven poked the undergrowth with his walking stick. He could feel the mist coming in over the river. Things had certainly changed around here. He walked on, still deep in thought.

It was the first time he overheard Joan whispering on the phone that scared him. Joan had taken the phone into the kitchen and closed the door. She had never done that before. Usually he was reading the paper and never listened to a word in any case. But this time she had gone out of the room to speak. He had crept towards the closed door to listen but he didn't hear anything unusual. In courtroom dramas on television if you were in the witness box, a lawyer always asked you what you had heard.

"What did your wife actually say Mr Ross? Word for word, if you please. And do try to remember the exact place where the conversation took place." That's what some clever lawyer would ask. She was in the kitchen and he had definitely heard Lancaster's name mentioned. He was sure of that.

He walked on. Living with the river and woods, he felt sorry for town people who only had pavements to walk on. He owned over three acres of ground backing onto the water. But now he would give anything to be somewhere else, away from Joan and her blasted brother Frank and that pest Betty. Betty had no mind of her own and would believe anything that Frank told her. And she was so edgy these days, he could swear she was frightened of Frank. As for the others in the family, he had always disliked them. Mean, grabby people they were. Well it didn't do them any good, did it, being mean? Clare and Edward were both dead and Charles had disappeared somewhere. He probably had a fancy woman. Steven realised he would have to be more careful from now on if he wanted to learn anything else.

Two boys suddenly sprang out from the bushes on their bicycles. They had found the cycle path and were skirting the edges of the river. It created a diversion for him. He wondered if he should create a diversion of his own. Maybe he would try to follow Joan when she went out. He could always tell her he had to go somewhere.

He had walked in a complete circle all around the river. He could see the house from where he was standing. He found his way back and decided he wouldn't stoop to following Joan. How could he lie about it afterwards? It wasn't the sort of thing Steven was used to doing.

At the house he could see the porch light was on and Joan closing the front door. She was dressed in her Armani coat. It must be another one of her cocktail evenings. Then he remembered the Armani show was on at the Royal Academy. He had seen her invitation to the opening. On an unexplainable impulse, he decided there and then to follow her. He slipped into the garage, opened his car door and was soon driving slowly down the lane. Joan's car was hardly in sight. When he got to the crossroads he realised he'd left his walking stick behind, outside the kitchen door

- 34 -

Lancaster peered through Betty's front window. He could see her bustling about the room gathering up the Sunday papers.

"Busy woman," he muttered to Crown.

"I suppose it's a bit like slave labour," Crown answered, looking into the distance. He thought lots of people liked being slaves if they loved someone. He pulled down the big bell ring. Betty was still holding the papers when she answered the door.

"It's Sunday," she said.

"Oh, murder and mayhem don't look up the calendar Mrs Gordon. I trust your husband's in. More enquiries, you know how it is. I'll sit down while you call him," Lancaster said, pulling out a dining room chair.

Betty went to the kitchen and opened the back door. It was too late to close the door on them. But she couldn't even if she wanted to. You had to let the police in whatever day it was.

"Frank," she called. "It's the Inspector. He'd like a word.."

"So Mrs Gordon, I'm sure you will both be interested to hear the latest on your missing brother Charles."

Betty's eyes opened wide.

"My God, I hope he's alright," she said. "Where was he? And where is Belinda?"

"It depends on what you call alright," Lancaster smiled and watched her face. Had her expression changed? Or was that sheer curiosity? Lancaster could hear movement in the garden.

"What are you doing here again?" It was Frank coming in from the garden through the kitchen door. Crown noticed how muddy and dirty he looked in his old jeans and T-shirt.

"I've got a lot to do out there. Anyway it's Sunday, we're entitled to a bit of peace and quiet. Winter's nearly here and the place needs sweeping."

"Bit early for sweeping isn't it?" Crown asked. "The leaves haven't fallen yet."

"Not round here it isn't," Frank grunted.

"I think you should stay in here sir, if you don't mind," Lancaster said, seeing that the back door was left open. "You see we seem to miss you every time we pop around. This won't take long. Then you can get back to your leaves."

Frank looked as if he had been struck by a fist.

"To continue," Lancaster held his hands together and his face was very calm. "Sergeant Crown here will tell you how we discovered your brother Charles."

Crown opened his mouth to say something but caught Lancaster's eye. He stopped in time.

"Yes, as I was saying," Lancaster was now attempting to re-button his jacket. "We found him by the roadside not too far from here. In a shocking condition of course, one can't expect to look good after being run over. We're hoping he'll live. The doctors say there's a good chance."

"Run over?" asked Frank, biting his lip, his face turning purple. "Run over?" he repeated.

"Yes sir, found in the road about five miles from here. He's in hospital of course. As far as we can discover, he told us he found himself in an empty house that he had never visited before, bound hand and foot and lying on the floor. I'm sure he won't want to visit there again in a hurry. The house isn't far from where he was knocked down. What he was doing there he can't remember. He said the only thing he could recall was crossing the road from the pub and then feeling a tremendous explosion in his head. After that everything went black."

Crown heard Lancaster humming to himself. He closed his eyes. He was sure Lancaster was getting this from one of his film noir movies. He watched as Lancaster took out a cigarette. Crown lit it for him. It was like those mafia movies where the new boy lights the boss' cigarettes and brings the car round to the front of the restaurant. Sometimes he imagined they were actually in a mafia movie. He'd just driven the car round to the front entrance and everyone inside was going to be machine-gunned. "W h e r e was I?" Lancaster continued. "Ah yes, I was talking about Charles. He told us he wanted to call out but his face had some sort of tape over it. It was pitch black in the house, and there wasn't even a lamp on. His next thought was to try and get some of the rope loose. His ankles were tied so tightly they were numb. He felt as if he was bent in half. Sick with fear, he suddenly remembered he had a penknife on his key ring, if only there was some way to get to it. He moved his arms and hands into a certain position and managed to get hold of his key ring, then cut the rope around his ankles."

Was it Harrison Ford who stood in front of a piece of broken glass and slowly sliced the rope off his wrist while his blood slowly drained out of him? He'd seen enough movies where people were tied up and gagged and always managed to fall somewhere near a piece of glass. It intrigued him. Crown scribbled down *bro-*

ken glass. If it was mafia they would all be dead. This was definitely a combination of Harrison Ford and the mafia.

"Where was I?" Lancaster said. "He managed to get himself out of the house and crawled towards the road. By then, of course, he was desperate and losing consciousness. You see the ropes around his ankles had been there for so long that his circulation had almost stopped and he could hardly move his feet. But he had managed to get himself out of the house and into the middle of the road where he hoped someone would see him. A plucky thing to do, he could have been killed outright. But here he was fortunate. A lady who was on her way into the village saw him lying in the road and pulled over. Lucky she wasn't speeding."

Crown didn't dare breath.

"She was with her son and you can imagine the scene. The son said he always carried water in the car, so he jumped out and tried to give Charles a drink, hoping to bring him round. They were terrified of doing the wrong thing so the son immediately called an ambulance and the police. They waited there with Charles until the ambulance arrived. By then he was unconscious of course. We're not sure if he'll survive or not. He's in the big General Hospital down in Brighton if you want to send him a get well card."

Frank Gordon could only gape.

"It's.....it's" Frank stopped. He couldn't utter a sound. He kept pushing his hair back from his forehead, feeling hot and cold at the same time. He took out a handkerchief and began to mop his face.

"Yes, of course it's a terrible shock for you I'm sure. But we'll make sense of it eventually Mr Gordon, I shouldn't worry." Lancaster smiled towards him.

The only sound in the room was was a slight hum from the radio. Radio 4 was broadcasting the news.

"So Mrs Gordon I should have a cup of tea if I were you."

Lancaster lifted his eyes towards Betty.

"You'd better have a cup too Mr Gordon." Crown turned the page in his notebook. He only managed the word "Sir".

"Ah Crown, you'll be wanting to tell them if Charles Austin will recover, won't you? I had clean forgotten."

He beamed up at Crown's face with a dangerous look in his eyes.

Crown became silent , then uttered, "Of course sir."

Why hadn't Lancaster prepared him for this elaborate farce? Perhaps it was better he didn't know. He turned the page. He'd seen enough film noir to add to the script.

"Yes," Crown managed. "I spoke to the emergency team and he's terribly injured. They feel they must perform an operation tonight." There were always emergency operations in the night. "He's lost a lot of blood, internal injuries, dreadful business. We're all hoping they can pull him through but one can't be sure."

There was no response from Frank.

"Yes," Lancaster mused. "You know being a detective, it's like any other business, only here the blood shows."

He thought it would be a good idea to mention a bit of blood. He waited to see Frank's expression. He wondered if Frank and Betty wanted to hear that Charles was safe. Had they something to do with this?

Frank suddenly uttered, "My God".

"Perhaps your good lady will bring in the tea now," Lancaster smiled. "I think you may need something a little stronger, perhaps a drop of brandy.I'm sure it's a dreadful shock to find out one of the family is badly injured. But at least you'll both be glad to know your brother is in good hands and still alive. That at least should bring a bit of colour to your faces.Plenty of sugar Mrs Gordon," he called out to the kitchen.

Crown knew Lancaster wasn't finished with the Gordons. He was over the target and he would press the button. That was the best part, apart from his bloody movie quotes, these sudden explosions. Betty came in with a tray of tea. She suddenly looked very old.

"Well," Lancaster said, getting up , straightening his tie and smoothing back his blonde hair. "I'll leave you now. Just remember," here he spoke very slowly and distinctly, "He might die......and if he dies..... it'll be murder."

"Murder," gasped Betty.

"Oh yes Mrs Gordon, definitely murder. It could all turn out to be a hit and run you know. A dreadful business, imagine that man dragging himself from that house. He must have covered a lot of ground, through the mud and the stones. I don't know how he managed it. It's amazing how human beings can withstand horrendous injuries and still fight like that to save themselves. I'm sure you know it's all in *Capricorn One.* Oh definitely murder."

"*Capricorn One*?" Frank asked. "I really think," Frank Gordon said in a choking voice, "I really think I do need a cup of tea."

"Come on Crown," Lancaster said. "We'll leave them now to have their Sunday dinner. Any news and we'll be in touch immediately."

Picking up his hat he walked across the cottage floor.

"It was this way out, wasn't it?"

But answer came there none.

"Don't say it Crown." Lancaster took Crown's arm. "Let's just get to the car. And look casual about it."

"Why did you say all that sir? The man is dead. You should send that script to Hollywood. It was brilliant. They'll make it into a movie and you can go and see it ten times."

"Crown, when will you learn? Throw coals on the fire. That man had something to do with it. Did you see his expression?"

"Yes, but that could be from shock. Mind you, he did look astounded."

"I'd say more than that Crown. He looked bloody terrified. He thought Charles was dead, I'm sure of it. Either someone told him or he damn well knew it himself. And if he didn't know it himself, who told him? And he could only know it if he'd been to the house himself."

"Sir?"

"Yes"

"You've used that line twice this week. You know, *The Postman Always Rings Twice.*"

Lancaster laughed, "Of course I have. The postman has rung twice. I told you, this is a double plot."

"After your Hollywood screenplay, I don't know why you're in this business."

"You know what Crown. Different people require different types of revenge. One might want you dead, another might want you to lose all your money, another to lose your home or your reputation or even your wife. All different things I'll grant you, but equally damaging. But with murder you are totally blotted out, with murder you're done for. We've got two kinds of revenge in this case, and that's the trouble. There's something in my mind that I can't shake off."

Crown turned the car around.

"By the way, I lost you altogether, didn't I?" Lancaster laughed out loud, his blue eyes twinkling.

"Lost me?"

"There's not much hope for you Crown. I mean for dinner at the *Ivy*. You never see the obvious." Lancaster tried to look disappointed but he couldn't resist a chuckle.

- 35 -

Dana Lancaster slept fitfully. The drink had gone to his head and at three o'clock he had to get up to take an aspirin and open the window.

Against his will his eyes closed.

A window banged in his dream. He woke to see the bedroom window had been forced off the latch by the heavy winds. Rain was teeming down and his curtains were blowing outside the window.

He was not going to sleep tonight. The only time he closed his eyes was this evening when he drifted off in front of the box. He was watching a programme about English painters, and he remembered something from a long time ago at the very moment he had dozed off. He got up and closed the window, pulling the curtains back into the room. He looked out of the window at the street light. Then he remembered. He was watching a painting of a boy lying on a bed, and the boy reminded him of Edward Austin. He reminded him because the boy was in exactly the same position as Edward, with his arm dropping down at the side of the bed and the curtains moving slightly in the breeze. The boy in the painting was wearing blue trousers but they weren't an ordinary blue. They were almost an electric blue, a rich and beautiful colour. Could it be a cornflour blue? And Edward was lying on the bed in that position, with the window slightly open and the curtains blowing in the breeze. But what about the tin box? Was there a tin box in the painting?

He picked up the phone to Crown.

Crown would know where to find it.

****

Belinda and her sister sat on the balcony overlooking the Grand Canal. Sabina still looked beautiful to Belinda. She'd never quite worked out why Sabina looked so Venetian. Was it her dark hair and the dark eyes or the way she wore her clothes? She could never be taken for an English woman. Her Venetian was fluent and so was her Italian.

Sabina picked up her glass.

"To our inheritance, a collection of funeral eulogies. I'm sure the various vicars will send us copies of them for our scrap book."

Sabina looked into Belinda's eyes.

"Why haven't you mentioned Charles? He must be desperate to know where you are."

"Oh, Charles," Belinda answered absently. Could Charles be a murderer? She had been thinking about Simon and what he was up to. Maybe all the time it was Charles who was following her.

"Charles has disappeared Sabina."

"Oh for heaven's sake. Why would Charles disappear? Why didn't you tell me before?"

"What could you do about it? He's simply vanished, been gone for days. Maybe he's back for all I know. It doesn't make any difference now."

"It doesn't make any sense. It's not like Charles. He's so damn predictable. You don't think he ......?"

Sabina thought it better not to say what she was thinking.

"I don't know what to think."

Sabina suddenly felt sick. She had better be strong for Belinda's sake, but everything was becoming too puzzling for her. Had Charles disappeared in order to follow Belinda? It was easy to see that Charles could do things like that. She knew he had a nasty streak in his nature.

"I feel like a hostage Sabina," Belinda said with a sad look in her eyes. "Shall we have another drink, perhaps a grappa? Then you know what? I think we'll go and do some shopping before dinner."

Sabina smiled. "To Canareggio?"

"Of course!"

- 36 -

As Steven followed Joan he felt his stomach churning over. Nothing is forever he told himself. Here he was following someone he loved because he didn't trust her. Just the same he wished he hadn't made such a rash decision. It was unnerving. He kept looking round to make sure no one had noticed his car. He pulled his cap further down on his head. His shoes were uncomfortable and his feet were aching. A slight drizzle was coming down and the sky was darkening. He could see the vague outline of Joan's car. She had driven to the end of East Wood and was now in another part unknown to Steven. Surely she didn't know anyone who lived out here? He certainly didn't. She must be visiting a client. She carried on until her car turned down a small road. Her brake lights flashed red and her car jerked to a halt outside a row of high hedges. Then she left her car and disappeared behind them. It all happened so quickly Steven wasn't too sure where she had gone. There must be a house somewhere behind the dark outline of hedges and trees. He turned off the engine, left his car and followed, trying to keep as near to the trees as he could manage.As he walked he could feel he was moving through thick mud. These outlying places always became muddy after summer. It must be near a farm. Although he could see houses here it was definitely farm land.

He watched and waited. Eventually he saw her emerging from behind the shadowy hedges. Looking at his watch he saw she had only been gone for twenty minutes. It seemed much longer waiting in the shadows like this. Now he saw that she was on her way back. She had a hood on now and was glancing around. He quickly stepped behind a tree. Within seconds she slipped into her car and drove away.

Steven was miserable and damp but he would have to wait here until she was out of sight. Once she had gone he would go home and get himself dry and perhaps come back later on to find out about this house and what she was doing there. But how would he ever remember where it was? He knew something was terribly wrong but he couldn't put his finger on it. Should he tell someone? But. who? That inspector fellow? And what would he tell him? That he had followed his wife into the next village? The inspector would ask if they had had a row. Didn't he trust her? He didn't want to answer all these questions. It would make him look worse than a fool. He may have been noticed and he could be accused of being a prowler.

No, he would have to find out for himself. He couldn't involve Lancaster in his private affairs. He would find out for himself where she was going and discover who lived in that house. He crept cautiously up the lane. Then he saw a gaping hole in the hedge where Joan had disappeared. He moved quickly towards it and could see a rusty garden gate. The place was in darkness, as black as the sky was becoming. He tried to see if there was a number on the gate. He could vaguely make out a name. He bent his head and tried to read it. He put out his hand to finger the lettering, as the the crumbling rust had almost obliterated it. His fingers read the word *Orange.* The other letters must have fallen off over the years. Rain was starting to fall.

He decided to leave and fled quickly back down the lane. His feet were thick with mud. He wiped the bottoms of his shoes with paper tissues. He sat in the car thinking for a moment. Would it be best to look inside the house now as he was here? He may never find the place again. Besides, the rain might be a good cover for him. He reached into the glove compartment and pulled out a torch.

He decided to walk back in his old footprints. His feet squelched in the muddy holes in the grass. Quietly he pushed open the gate and went up to the front door. He flashed his torch quickly to see if there was a side gate. There was just a vast expanse of overgrown shrubs and between them a small pathway. He followed it round to the back of the house. He could smell cows nearby. It must be near a farm. He tried to open the back door but it was locked. He put the torch light close to the window. It was the kitchen. One of the windows had been left slightly open. He wondered how he would get himself up there and in through the window. He found difficulty walking these days and it was a foolhardy thing to attempt. He could fall and no one would find him.

First he would have to get the inside onto the window ledge and then haul himself in somehow. He opened the window and reached inside, placing the torch where he could reach it. Then he dragged himself up, trying to get a foothold on the drainpipe. He scratched his hands and hurt his ankles. Finally his fingers got a grip and, standing on the drainpipe, he managed to prise the window open. Then he pulled himself inside landed face-down in the kitchen sink. His head struck some plates and he gashed his forehead on one of them. It must have smashed when he fell inside. His legs ached and he felt a sharp pain in his side. What an idiot he was to get himself into a state like this. His head was bleeding and the effort to pull himself up was almost too much for him. Levering himself up, he jumped to the floor, knocking some glasses over. They crashed to the ground. Someone must surely hear him. He crouched in the corner by the stove, rubbing his legs and knowing he would suffer for this tomorrow. He held a handkerchief to his bleeding head.

No one had heard the noise. It was as quiet as the grave. What a stench there was here. It was certainly worse than the cows. He was used to their smell, having lived in the country. There were filthy dishes on the table and the draining board and the stink of decayed food made Steven feel sick. Papers and rubbish were scattered all over the floor. The smell was so unbearable he was thankful he had his scarf with him so that he could tie it around his nose and mouth. Who could live in this filthy hole and what could Joan have to do with a place like this?

He flashed his light into the hallway. All the chairs were covered in clothes and dirty shoes and on the floor. He pulled his jacket tighter round him as if to protect himself from the dirt. He crept towards another room and saw the paint peeling off in great chunks. On the floor lay broken furniture, with empty drawers scattered here and there. It was all crazy. The carpets were threadbare and the place was like a rubbish dump.

The faint beam of his torch found the staircase. He should have replaced it with new batteries last week. He was becoming a forgetful idiot. Now it was too dark to go any further. Should he be doing this on his own? The smell was making him feel sick. Wet from the rain and sick from the stench he decided to go back to the kitchen and leave this unspeakable place.

He had no right to be here. He would be accused of burglary if he was spotted. In his frenzied rush to leave he knocked over a chair. Steven let out a fine scream as he clambered over it. Now he didn't care if anyone heard him, he just wanted to get away. The smell in the house was something he'd never forget. In terror he rushed towards the kitchen door and managed to open it. Then he ran out into the cold rainy night.

****

Picking up the phone Inspector Lancaster dialled Crown's number.

"Hello"

"Oh, hello Inspector, it's Eric here."

So those two were still together. He thought he'd heard murmurings of separation last week......

"So how are things in the theatre Eric?" Lancaster asked, hoping not to hear the worst.

"Brilliant, we're madly busy. I'm working at the Donmar this weekend. Their fellow's off sick. Bit of extra cash, got a Jacobean play on. Can't stand them myself but I managed a few tickets. Kilvert likes that dreary stuff. It must be the blood and gore he's used to working on with you. Got some good lines in it. Do you know *The Duchess of Malfi?*"

"*The Duchess of Malfi* eh? Funny, I was just thinking of that play only the other day."

"Shall I get Kilvert for you? I'm just making our lunch."

"Please"

Of course, it was the weekend. He never had lunch at the weekend with the jazz singer. She was always out rehearsing for some gig or other. How he hated weekends.

"Hello Inspector," Crown came on the line. "Nice day"

"Listen Crown, I haven't phoned to discuss the weather. I want you to do something for me. Get down to the library and get out all the Victorian art books you can lay your hands on."

"It will have to wait until tomorrow sir. The library isn't open on a Sunday."

"You're right, but do it first thing in the morning."

"Sir, Eric's got some tickets for the play this evening. I've promised him I'll go. Why don't you come with us? We can talk afterwards."

Lancaster thought maybe. Weekends were worse than New Year.

"Why not come? You know you hate the weekends."

"Right, I'll come. I haven't been to the theatre in a dog's age."

"Good, we'll see you at the Donmar at six thirty and we'll have something to eat first."

Lancaster remembered years ago sitting through that play. It made his murders look tame. Still he had nothing else to do this evening and the play would be a diversion from his usual *Lost Weekend*.

head on one of them. It must have smashed when he fell inside. His legs ached and he felt a sharp pain in his side. What an idiot he was to get himself into a state like this. His head was bleeding and the effort to pull himself up was almost too much for him. Levering himself up, he jumped to the floor, knocking some glasses over. They crashed to the ground. Someone must surely hear him. He crouched in the corner by the stove, rubbing his legs and knowing he would suffer for this tomorrow. He held a handkerchief to his bleeding head.

No one had heard the noise. It was as quiet as the grave. What a stench there was here. It was certainly worse than the cows.He was used to their smell, having lived in the country. There were filthy dishes on the table and the draining board and the stink of decayed food made Steven feel sick. Papers and rubbish were scattered all over the floor. The smell was so unbearable he was thankful he had his scarf with him so that he could tie it around his nose and mouth. Who could live in this filthy hole and what could Joan have to do with a place like this?

He flashed his light into the hallway. All the chairs were covered in clothes and dirty shoes and on the floor. He pulled his jacket tighter round him as if to protect himself from the dirt. He crept towards another room and saw the paint peeling off in great chunks. On the floor lay broken furniture, with empty drawers scattered here and there. It was all crazy. The carpets were thread-bare and the place was like a rubbish dump.

The faint beam of his torch found the staircase. He should have replaced it with new batteries last week. He was becoming a forgetful idiot. Now it was too dark to go any further. Should he be doing this on his own? The smell was making him feel sick. Wet from the rain and sick from the stench he decided to go back to the kitchen and leave this unspeakable place.

He had no right to be here. He would be accused of bur-glary if he was spotted. In his frenzied rush to leave he knocked over a chair. Steven let out a fine scream as he clambered over it. Now he didn't care if anyone heard him, he just wanted to get away. The smell in the house was something he'd never forget. In terror he rushed towards the kitchen door and managed to open it. Then he ran out into the cold rainy night.

****

Picking up the phone Inspector Lancaster dialled Crown's number.

"Hello"

"Oh, hello Inspector, it's Eric here."

So those two were still together. He thought he'd heard

murmurings of separation last week......

"So how are things in the theatre Eric?" Lancaster asked, hoping not to hear the worst.

"Brilliant, we're madly busy. I'm working at the Donmar this weekend. Their fellow's off sick. Bit of extra cash, got a Jacobean play on. Can't stand them myself but I managed a few tickets. Kilvert likes that dreary stuff. It must be the blood and gore he's used to working on with you. Got some good lines in it. Do you know *The Duchess of Malfi?*"

"*The Duchess of Malfi* eh? Funny, I was just thinking of that play only the other day."

"Shall I get Kilvert for you? I'm just making our lunch."

"Please"

Of course, it was the weekend. He never had lunch at the weekend with the jazz singer. She was always out rehearsing for some gig or other. How he hated weekends.

"Hello Inspector," Crown came on the line. "Nice day"

"Listen Crown, I haven't phoned to discuss the weather. I want you to do something for me. Get down to the library and get out all the Victorian art books you can lay your hands on."

"It will have to wait until tomorrow sir. The library isn't open on a Sunday."

"You're right, but do it first thing in the morning."

"Sir, Eric's got some tickets for the play this evening. I've promised him I'll go. Why don't you come with us? We can talk afterwards."

Lancaster thought maybe. Weekends were worse than New Year.

"Why not come? You know you hate the weekends."

"Right, I'll come. I haven't been to the theatre in a dog's age."

"Good, we'll see you at the Donmar at six thirty and we'll have something to eat first."

Lancaster remembered years ago sitting through that play. It made his murders look tame. Still he had nothing else to do this evening and the play would be a diversion from his usual *Lost Weekend.*

****

Lancaster wondered if Crown could have been at one of his night spots last night after *The Duchess of Malfi*. Maybe that was the reason he was so late. He looked up at the clock again when the door opened.

"Good God Crown, where the hell have you been?"

Lancaster looked at the time.

"How long does it take to get a library book out these days?"

He was clearly addled this morning. His hair was uncombed and flying in his face and his suit was crumpled. Crown hadn't seen him look so bad for a long time.

"Anything wrong sir? You look a bit undone."

"Good word Crown. You must be into Jacobean melodrama with a vengeance."

"Sir I've got the books."

Crown looked his usual dapper self to Lancaster. How did he manage to do it? Fresh as a daisy on a Monday morning and on the weekends he always wore his cords with a blazer, and one of those damned Christmas scarfs tucked under his shirt. He reminded Lancaster of David Niven in an airforce film. Was it because he didn't have to do any housework or make himself dinner? Lancaster sometimes ate at the local pub if he was too tired to cook. Come to think of it, why did he live in such a mess? He never really cared if his house was tidy or not, as long as he could lay his hands on a good movie.

"Damn good library in Lewes. Here you are sir. I got a few books to read at the same time. Eric's at the Royal Court this weekend, so I'll have something to pass the time."

Lancaster moved all the files and bits of paper off his desk and then arranged the books in a pile.

"We'll go through them all," he muttered. Opening the first one he began to turn the pages. He looked at *When Did You Last See Your Father?* and *April Love* then he turned to *The Lady of Shalott*. They had to learn that poem in school. He always remembered the words *her blood was frozen slowly,* like Clare's.

"You're not in your *Laura* mood are you sir?"

Certain far away looks from Lancaster always told Crown what kind of reception to expect.

"Of course not"

He wished he was Dana Andrews this morning. There was a large piece of paper sticking out of the next book he picked up.

"Did you put this here Crown? Where's my damn magnifying glass?"

Crown felt around the back of the drawer, bringing out

string, a box of matches and a notepad with some pencils and tape. The glass was tangled up in the tape.

"Remember when we found Clare? I said to you *Shot to Death with Pearls* from *The Duchess of Malfi?* I thought of it again last night. I should never venture into the realm of quotes from plays Crown. They mix me up, turn me screwy."

Crown picked the tape off the magnifying glass. The man was definitely screwy, of that there was no doubt. You had to have a screwy kind of brain to work out the mayhem which he always dealt with.

"Now," Lancaster was saying, "now we have to find something else I remembered, those damned blue trousers."

"It's another word sir, the blue trousers. I've found it for you. The bastard is trying to tell us something."

He opened the page where he had put the piece of paper.

"There it is Crown, you bloody genius. A painting of a boy in blue trousers. A young boy, definitely dead, his arm flung out. Behind him a window, slightly open, with the curtains blowing in the breeze."

"At the same time the killer's laughing. That's his kick, waiting for us to get the word."

Lancaster banged his fist on the desk.

"We'll get the word, don't you worry. Sit down and look."

Crown sat down and they both stared at the picture.

"Maybe we're imagining things," Crown said. He was beginning to feel foolish.

"And will you look at that?"

Lancaster pointed at the painting. There was a tin box on the table near the boy.

"A tin box on the table, what the hell does it all mean? Is there a word painted anywhere?"

Crown peered down at the picture.

"Nothing I can spot sir. It's called *The Death of Chatterton.*"

"Well we'll go and find out about Chatterton. Look at that, a tin box next to him on the table. Jesus, Crown, take the bloody book and we'll go and see Parker at the Wallace. He'll tell us all about it. There's a word here Crown and we'll damn well find it."

Crown didn't feel so sure today. He looked at the picture again. What was it saying?

"Why can't we look on the internet sir?"

"Because as you know I am not an internet person Crown. I am a book person. I am a Wallace person. I am a newspaper person. I want it there in black and white."

"But I can print it out for you in black and white."

"Is that detective work Crown, I ask you? Detectives crawl across cities in traffic jams.Detectives hide in alleyways. Detectives don't use bloody machines. They go out into the night with their raincoats tied with a belt and a hat pulled over their eyes!"

Oh God, Crown told himself, maybe they would retire him soon.

"Now give me the file with those love lines in it. I want to know if anyone else advertised that week, or the week before that or the year before that. Maybe one of these other Austin dames put something in there."

Crown opened the filing cabinet, taking out the bulging file. Dames, he thought. Laura, Dana Andrews. *A dame in Washington Heights got a fox fur out of me,* that was one of Lancaster's last year's quotes. Had Lancaster ever been to Washington heights? Did he know if it even existed?

"What are you thinking about Crown?" Lancaster looked up, scrutinising Crown's face.

"Do you think Simon knew Clare?" he asked Crown, stabbing a finger in the air.

"I've got a strange feeling that Simon knew them all. He may even be living locally."

"But why kill Clare?"

"Who says he killed Clare? Don't suppose things Crown. I'm always telling you that. We don't know if he did. We can't get hold of him for questioning, can we? That means we can't run the rule over him. Just who the hell is Simon? You see our trouble is we don't know! And he's the other half of the story Crown."

Lancaster rose.

"Do you really believe in the perfect murder?"

"No, but then again maybe"

"Maybe isn't good enough. Come on, we'll go down to the newspaper archives in Colindale and then we'll go to the Wallace."

"By the way sir, apropos of nothing, the Superintendent is back from holiday this week."

"Personally, I haven't missed him."

"He wants to speak to you on Friday."

"What? We spoke to him a few weeks ago."

"Well we didn't have much to tell him, did we? And there's not much more now." Crown felt uncomfortable. "I mean except for the paintings."

"He'll tell us we're crackers."

"You mean with the ribbon and all that?"

"And the bloody trousers."

- **37** -

"Cold," said the man in the black knitted pullover sitting at the enquiry desk.

"Blasted heating isn't working again, if you'll excuse the expression. Every winter it's the same story."

"Not really the worst part of winter yet, is it?" Lancaster observed, keeping his coat on. "It's only the end of August."

"What? You want to get yourself a new calendar. What difference what the month is? It's still bloody cold. What are you after?"

He could see they were from the police before they told him. What chance did the general public have if the police didn't know August was the worst month of the winter? No one learned anything these days. Months of the year, how many days in March, they were all idiots.

"Newspapers from the week of, say, February 14th last year."

Best they looked a good few months before Clare was murdered, That would take in the spring and what went on well before that.

"That's a lot of newspapers," the man sniffled.

"Well you know how it is with gunpowder, treason and plot."

The man at the desk sneezed, taking out a grubby handkerchief.

"Right," he said, "wait here while I go in the back. Why don't you look them up on the microfilm?"

"We'd just like the papers please," Lancaster said. "I don't like machines." He gave an artificial smile.

Coppers, the man thought.

Clerks, The coppers thought.

"And the week before too," Lancaster added.

He looked round at the desks and tables piled high with magazines and newspapers. There were a few early morning people, huddled over news sheets. And a few were at the microfilm machines. Must be reporters.

They waited silently in the cold room. Why couldn't they put on an electric heater? How could they expect people to work in the cold? Still, if it happened at the station they would still be waiting for a plumber or an electrician.

It was a good half hour before he came back carrying two bundles of newspapers.

"Thought I'd better get a few papers from the surrounding areas, just in case," he smiled with pleasure at getting one over on them.

"Quite right," answered Lancaster, "I'm a great believer in the police working harder than ever, keeps us on our toes."

The knitted pullover blew his nose again.

"Come on Crown, you can start on these," he said handing him a bundle of papers.

"You can sit over there if you want to," the pullover said. Then losing interest in police work, he went back to some ledgers.

"Come on Crown, let's get busy. Just look up love lines for the murder, please don't look up anyone for yourself."

Crown was going to respond but as the day had only just started he decided what the hell. He would only pay for it later.

They rifled through the pile of papers impatiently, Lancaster scratching his head and tapping his pen on the table. He went to his cigarette packet.

"No smoking here," said the pullover, pointing to a sign.

"Any coffee in this place?" Lancaster asked.

"Cafe round the corner. But I could stretch a point for the police."

Two or three faces looked up with alarm.

Two cracked mugs of coffee appeared on a tray.

"Got a biscuit?" asked Lancaster.

"These are government premises," said the pullover. "No biscuits"

Crown carried on looking through the papers.

"Will you look at this," he said. "*Love Lines March 3rd*"

Lancaster pulled it across the desk.

"It's in another local paper, *The Journal,* East Wood." he remarked.

"Let's see."

He read aloud,

"LONELY LADY   LOVELY LADY   TALL STATELY
ATTRACTIVE   WILL MEET ALL YOUR DEMANDS
FUN AND EXCITEMENT   THRILLING I PROMISE
RING ON MOBILE   778866373748
DON'T WAIT   CAPTIVATING   C"

"Captivating C, Captivating Clare? Get your notes out. Check the number of her mobile."

Crown took out his notebook and turned the pages.

"That's it. It's Clare's alright."

Lancaster leaned back in the chair, making a scratching noise with his pen. The early morning explorers looked up with disgust.

"So it is possible, after all, that Clare could have been involved with someone. What a turn up. I'd say she was dancing on the edge by just writing Captivating C. Now why would she do that? Was it the first time she'd done this? Taking a bit of a chance even giving an initial."

"There are lots of women with the letter C Boss."

"Maybe, just the same I wonder. According to what I know, a lot of men are married and looking for a bit of extra, and some women too. They're taking a hell of a risk. Still it helps the dreary day along."

Lancaster shook his head and bent over the paper again.

"Is that when Clare made her big mistake Crown?"

"The trouble is we may never know the real reason why she did it,"

"We can only guess. But we don't know who answered her ad. It didn't necessarily have to be anyone connected with this case. Was it boredom?" Lancaster asked. Well he should know about nights of boredom.

"Maybe hubby was out of town swimming," Crown laughed.

"Is it possible *The Saint* was around at the time?"

"Then there's Belinda, Simon and Peaches and cream. From her answers she was trying to protect Simon." Crown said.

Was Clare someone's hook? And hooked so well she was never being thrown back into the sea, Crown wondered.

"She was in the deep end, if you'll pardon the pun. Clare was a comfortable woman and if we're comparing money, Crown, she had a hell of a lot more than Belinda. And maybe she answered that ad before Belinda did. I wonder if Belinda knew about Clare advertising in the local rag."

"If she did it doesn't mean she would murder Clare."

"Get your hat Crown."

"You know I don't have a hat."

"You're right. I'm the one with the hat around here, and don't you forget it."

- 38 -

Trevor Austin found no one at home at Joan's on that Tuesday evening. He was sure Joan had said to come for dinner on Tuesday at eight o'clock. It was Tuesday, wasn't it? Every day seemed like a Sunday these days. What with the police hovering about and newspaper reporters hiding in the bushes, life for Trevor was becoming a burden. There were so many articles in the papers about a murdered woman lying naked with a string of pearls around her neck that Trevor stopped taking his daily paper. In fact he didn't go into the newsagent at all. Soon Clare would be forgotten forever, except by him.

He knew that when the police finally discovered the killer that all the revelations and hints of Clare's secret lovers would begin all over again. What did they call it? *Hint journalism.*

People were beginning to pass him by in the street. Not that it mattered to Trevor, most of them anyway, with their petty comments and their dreary lives. Poor Clare's murder must have given them something to talk about. Even his daily help told him the whole village was speculating about who killed Clare and that she wouldn't put it past some of them to sell their story to the gutter press. Well let them talk. Lately the only person to ask him in was his next door neighbour. When he did accept her invitation he thought she looked slightly nervous about it. He could see her wondering if he was the murderer after all. He hoped he hadn't frightened her to death when she poured tea and then there was Edward. Never mind the fact that Trevor had lost his wife and way of life.

Maybe the best thing he could do would be to sell the house and move away, go somewhere further out into the countryside, somewhere he would be a stranger. Then maybe he could start a new life. He sighed, knowing he couldn't go anywhere until the murderer was found. The police wouldn't be too happy if he suddenly upped sticks.

He knocked harder on Joan's door and lifted his head up to look at the landing window. He tried to look through the frosted glass of the porch window but all he could see was a lopsided outline of a figure coming down the stairs. The porch light went on and glimmered faintly. At last one of them had realised he had been waiting on the doorstep for at least ten minutes. Joan must have been upstairs getting dressed and the kitchen, which faced the front, was in darkness.

The door opened and crashed into the opposite wall. That was careless of Steven to let the door go like that, he was usually so welcoming. Perhaps he was in a temper after one of their arguments. Where was Joan? Maybe she'd been delayed in the shop.

Then to his abject horror Steven suddenly fell out of the doorway into Trevor's arms.Trevor was so startled that he lifted his hands to try to hold Steven up, but even in the dimness of the porch light he could see Steven was covered in thick red blood. Oh no, he can't be dead, he can't be.Trevor could see little black spots jumping about in front of his eyes. He was going to black out. What was happening here? He mustn't pass out or there would be no one to help Steven.

Who could have hurt Steven and why was he bleeding so much? Trying to grip Steven's arms, they both staggered about like a pair of dancers unable to let each other go. The effort to hold onto Steven had given way to exhaustion. Tears sprang into his eyes and he found himself crying.

"Joan," he cried out. "Joan, come and help. Something's happened to Steven. He's dying. There's blood everywhere. Oh God!"

Steven's blood was dropping in little rivulets onto the doorstep and it covered Trevor's hands and clothing. He must hold onto him and try and get him inside the house. He tried dragging him past the door but they both fell. Steven was clutching onto him, pulling him over. It must be how a drowning man could pull his rescuer under. Steven's jacket was torn and blood was seeping through it. His only thought was to get Steven inside the house. His hand reached up for the large lion's head door knocker. Pushing Steven aside, he gripped the knocker as hard as he could, then slowly began pulling himself up. A swift pain shot up his arm. He must have twisted it when he reached out to hold Steven. At last he was standing up with Steven in his arms and was able to slowly drag him into the house.

Trevor knew Steven must be dead.

He lay Steven on the floor and sat for a moment on a hall chair. He was out of breath. He had to regain his composure. He could see a trail of blood leading from the front door into the living room. Moving the chair across to the phone he picked up the receiver. Steven's blood came off his hands and smeared the white telephone with a crimson tint.

He bent down to Steven again. "Steven, don't die." He could feel him getting cold. Trevor saw a bottle of gin on the sideboard and, finding a glass, poured a little out. Then he bent down and tried to make Steven swallow it. Steven gagged and the gin tipped over his bloodstained shirt.

He must try to stop Steven bleeding. Looking about him, he pulled a table cloth off the table and pushed it under Steven's chest. But it was no use, the blood was gushing now. He must get the police and an ambulance. He should have done that right away. He cursed himself and picked up the phone again. The police would blame him for Steven's death. No one would believe such a flimsy reason for calling her.

It was then that he heard a slight sound coming from Steven's lips. Thank God he wasn't dead.

"Steven, hang on, " Trevor said as he put his ear to Steven's mouth.

"Jo,Jo," Steven was uttering and Trevor almost shouted with relief.

"Joan will be here soon. Don't give up Steven. PLease hang on, I've called an ambulance."

What would they say when they found him here with a dying man?

"Joan," he cried again, "Oh Joan"

Everything in his vision seemed to be turning from white to red. The churning in his stomach wouldn't stop. He might even be sick. Steven's blood was slowly dripping onto Joan's ice white carpet. Red and white it went, red and white. Her stark white house would soon be bright red. Another time he might have laughed.

- 39 -

Belinda watched the sun play games with the mosaics on the palaces as she sat next to the flag fluttering in the wind at the back of the Vaporetto. She was going on her own to Canareggio. Someone may see her out in the open like this. She wanted to do some shopping before she left Venice. She was thinking she should go back to England and sell the house. But she was afraid, wherever she was.

She wanted to come and live near her sister, in a place she really loved. It would change her life to live near Sabina, she had no one else in the world. It was possible to live out on the Lido in one of those small apartments at the end of the island.

The Vaporetto moved slowly along the Grand Canal. People were being helped on and off when the boat stopped. A child was lifted on in its pushchair. She tried to remember when anyone was helped onto a London bus, That was a long time ago.No one helped anybody any more. But she was in terrible trouble just the same.

As they passed Ca D'Oro she began to feel a little light headed. It must have been the wine she had with her lunch. She mustn't drink so much. Drinking was fast becoming a necessity. She closed her eyes. Perhaps the slight breeze that was blowing across the canal would clear her head. In fact she felt quite faint. All of a sudden things went out of focus. She saw the water coming up over her head. She was drowning. She tried to hold onto the rail but she couldn't help herself, she was sinking down, down into the depths of the Grand Canal. The last thing Belinda remembered was falling across the woman sitting next to her. The boat was upside down and she was going to drown. She tried to call out for help but she was having a crazy kind of dream and she couldn't shout.

She had never fallen off a Vaporetto before, or drowned. What a stupid thing to think.....The woman next to her was calling out now, "Aiuto, per piacere, aiuto."

****

Lancaster and Crown sat in Robin Parker's dimly lit office leafing through some art books.

"Nice one that, love to own it," Parker said looking over

Lancaster's shoulder as he turned the pages of a book on Victorian artists. He was pointing to a Rossetti painting. "Kill for it."

"Really? It would mean that much to you Parker. Funny the things people would kill for. Usually they kill for love, or money. I must say I never expected the reason to be a painting. Parker, we're sure our answer is in another painting."

He noticed how Parker's eyes were sunk deep into his head. They looked like a teddy bear's beady eyes. Must be as a protection against the cigarette smoke. He looked much older than when Lancaster saw him last. Years of looking at pictures and writing catalogues must have done that. The chin was more sunken and you couldn't really see his cheeks, they drooped onto his lips. A cigarette hung there as if by magic. But then Parker was a sort of magician. He could find anything out about art. Anything you asked him, regardless of the period, he would give you chapter and verse.

Lancaster wondered if he looked older than Parker after all the years he had spent looking at dead bodies. He knew his eyes were more watery, and his lips not as full. The blonde hair that was always so golden was fast becoming a pale shade of ivory. He knew his mirror image wouldn't encourage the jazz singer, even if they ever got to meet again.

He understood perfectly why people killed when love affairs ended. He felt like that himself sometimes. On bad days he wanted to murder the jazz singer and on others he felt morose and lonely, and desperately wished she was back again under his roof.

The French understood about crimes of passion. Would he understand if this case turned out to be something to do with passion? He couldn't afford to think that way in his business. He was here to nail murderers, not to sympathise with them.

"You know what," Lancaster paused, "I'd think I could kill for a Hitchcock poster."

"Kill?" Crown looked at him.

"Posters?" asked Parker.

"Old film posters," Lancaster carried on. "Old movies, Rita Hayworth in *Gilda,* Bogart in *Casablanca,* that kind of thing. Can't afford them, that's the trouble. A Clint Eastwood could set you back a couple of grand."

"So show the painting to me," Parker said, going back to his books. He couldn't understand people who didn't want to own paintings. What did they look at? The wallpaper probably, or each other. That would be difficult for him as he lived on his own and had no one to look at except his cat. And the cat was usually out all night after dinner.

He had managed to buy a few paintings over the years. He loved them and was constantly moving them about his little flat. Two of the illustrations he had were now in the bathroom. Cigarette ash fell on his waistcoat as he lifted some more books off the shelf. Posters, what piffle. How could they compare to a painting?

"It's a painting with a young boy. He's lying on a bed and he's definitely dead. Cornflower blue trousers and a window open behind him with curtains blowing. A metal box is in front of him on a table. Curtains, boxes, that's what we're looking for."

"Curtains, boxes? Boy on a bed? Why didn't you say so? I'll bet you a fiver that's *Chatterton.*"

"*Chatterton,* you old weasel, that's the one, *The Death of Chatterton.*"

Now that Parker had confirmed it he felt sure he was right.

"Of course. Wait till I find it." He reached up to the top shelf near his desk. "He was a poet you know."

"A poet? You're sure?"

"Of course I'm sure. Do you think I'm here for my health?" Parker lifted the book down.

"Well you can sleep at nights now, I promise you."

Parker was happy . He rubbed his hands together.

"And there you are," he said with pride, turning over some pages and finding the boy in the blue trousers. "Boy on the bed, young, old fashioned blue trousers, one arm thrown outward, the other across his chest, window open behind him, small curtains, breeze blowing through. And there's the box."

Parker's smoke made him momentarily close his eyes. Lancaster looked down at the boy in the blue trousers. In the painting a small window was open over the dead boy and the curtains blew in a soft breeze.

"Parker, let's hear about it."

"Our blue boy," Crown said.

"Well, Chatterton was a poet.The original painting is in the Tate, the real Tate," said Parker. "Why these damn politicians always have to change the names of things just to make their mark in history I don't know. Got to do something with time on their hands, so they fiddle about naming things.Tate Britain it is now. What a name. Go around and take a good look at the painting."

"But what does it all mean?" Lancaster asked.

"Our boy was murdered," Crown said.

"But Chatterton wasn't murdered," Parker retorted, "he poisoned himself."

"Poisoned himself, well, well." Lancaster frowned.

"But he looks so young."

"He died when he was seventeen. Poisoned himself because he couldn't sell his poems. He used to write his poems on old documents. He collected all the old documents he could lay his hands on, and then he cut off the blank parts. Then he kept the pieces in the box."

"Go on."

"He said they were copies of fifteenth century manuscripts from the Church of St. Mary Redcliffe in Bristol. He tried to sell them everywhere. Then one day he sent some poems to Horace Walpole, but Walpole sent them back because he was told they weren't genuine. You see Chatterton was a brilliant imitator. Anyway, when Walpole sent the poems back his world caved in. So he toddled off to London to try and sell the poems. That was in 1770, you can imagine what it was like in London in those days, beggars on the streets, thieves and vagabonds to contend with. He may have sold one or two but not nearly enough to stop himself from starving. He certainly didn't want to be a beggar, so in despair, he poisoned himself."

"Who would do themselves in at seventeen?" Crown asked. It seemed incredible.

"Funny thing is," Parker continued, "his stuff is very modern. His rhythms were unique and *The Rowley Poems* were adaptations in the fifteenth century style. He really was a poetic genius. You should read *Mynstrelles Songe.*"

"Why are these people recognised after they're dead?"

"Saves paying them royalties," laughed Parker.

"That's just it Crown. Edward wasn't poisoned. It must be something else, something we've missed."

"So the poems weren't forgeries after all. Bloody shame," Crown muttered.

Lancaster's eyes suddenly blazed.

"Forgeries. You don't think someone has been naughty and forged something Crown?"

"Well what can you forge? You can forge a signature or a letter. Documents are being forged all the time, passports, driving licenses, all the stuff we see every other day."

Ideas began to flood into Lancaster's mind.
"Maybe I'm stupid, but is it conceivable that Austin's mother's will was forged? We're looking for something big in this case, not letters or passports, but something worth killing for. And it's usually to do with money."

224

"The wording in the will could have been changed. It's possible. It's all written in lawyer's rigmarole, so no one would trouble to read every word."

"So the murderer knew the will was forged. And he decided to do away with each and every one of them in the cleverest way he could."

"But how can you forge a will if a solicitor has drawn it up?"

"Unless the solicitor has something to do with it."

"But surely it would be more than he dare do?"

"I don't know Crown. We can't be left with *Nevermore Poet,* can we?"

"No"

Lancaster smiled.

"Maybe the murderer wanted us to have a clue with that particular word. Maybe that was all he could think of at the moment."

"He must have a damn good knowledge of paintings. Couldn't think of another painting for Edward on the spur of the moment."

"But the tin box sir. He had to bring the box into the hospital. He must have pre-planned it."

"He could have murdered Edward and then slipped back with the box. The floor was so busy no one noticed him going in and out."

"Let's think about it tomorrow. Unless Edward forged something else and that box was there for another reason."

Lancaster nodded his head, "You're right."

He looked into the distance and sighed.

"Thanks Parker," he said, "keep on smoking."

Parker blew a puffy circle into the air.

"Bye boys"

"I wish I knew what was bothering me Crown."

"It fits together, it fits beautifully," Lancaster said on leaving the Wallace, as he waved his hand in the air. "*Nevermore, Forger.*"

"By the way sir, I got *Blade Runner.*" Crown mentioned this to Lancaster with glee.

"Ah but you didn't get the others my dear man."

Was he Sydney Greenstreet? Or did he always say dear sir?

Crown sat down and looked at his pad. He folded the paper in half and wrote down *Dear Sir.*

A sudden bang on the door startled him.

It was the Chief.

"Ah," the Chief beamed as he walked into the room, "Idly wasting the day are we?"

Lancaster took his feet off the desk.

"We were just going over the notes sir."

The Chief turned to look out of the window.

"And," he continued from the window, "what have you got, since spring I believe it is. Bloody cold in here, why isn't the heating on?"

"Not working sir."

Crown opened his pad.

"We've got Nevermore and we've got Forger. Which says nevermore forger will you forge."

"That's what you've got?"

"Sir, it's important." Lancaster stood up and went over to the Chief. "We think it's a message telling us why the killer has committed the crimes."

"Is that so?"

"Yes"

"And the killer?"

"We're not sure. But I feel the case nearly cracked."

"Well crack this Dana. Steven Ross has been stabbed. They've stuck him in the General Hospital. Bled like a pig from all accounts. You'd better get over to his place. Forensics are there."

"Steven Ross?" Crown asked.

"Isn't this where you're supposed to ask me for 48 hours to crack the case Dana?"

The Chief's face was grave.

Oh God, Crown thought. They're both mad. It must be Venice. The Chief wasn't looking over the Grand Canal, he was looking over the bloody High Street.

"By the way Lancaster, did you ever get to have a Peach Bellini at Florian's?"

"I did sir," Lancaster was worried about the Chief. Peach Bellini?

"Get your hat Crown," said Lancaster, slipping into his jacket, "we'd better get off sir."

The Chief was still looking at Lancaster.

They walked out of the office towards the car park.

"Who the hell would try and murder Steven Ross?"

"I don't know Crown, but we'll get over there as soon as we can. Get the motor."

Crown wondered if he worked in Venice, would he have his own speed boat to go to murder cases. But there couldn't be many murder cases there. Divorces maybe. Was the Chief thinking of working in Venice? Why was he standing at the window so long? Crown needed an aspirin and a Peach Bellini.

They arrived at the house with a winter sun flickering in and out of the trees. The yellow tapes that cordoned off the house were stretched from front to back.

Crown could see Hunter in his white party dress. He looked tired. Since he'd known him Hunter's black hair used to resemble a lion's mane. Now it looked more like straw on the straw man. His pallor matched the straw hair. Maybe seeing so many bodies had made him into an attendant ghoul.

"Morning Hunter," he called, "anything important?"

"Tally ho and yoiks," Hunter said, "jolly lucky he hasn't bought it. Got him off to the General. Plenty of blood. Deep knife wound to the left side, under the heart, just missed the heart but managed to do damage to an artery. Remarkable really, usually these cases mean cashing in your chips. But you man seems to be hanging on to life. Thin little fellow too. Well he's confined to barracks, so he won't be taking off for a long time. The DNA will be done, then you two can work out the rest. We got here right away. That Austin fellow phoned in. The Chief sent us over right away. The attacker must have been smothered in blood. Gone home to wash it off and chuck away his clothing. Definitely an upward thrust Lancaster."

"Upward," Crown said. Tally ho and yoiks. Confined to barracks. Cashed in his chips. He shook his head.

"Yes," Hunter smiled, packing up his ghoul's equipment.

"So the attacker came at him from beneath. Must have been hiding under the stairs, or just slipped out when he saw Steven coming down the stairs."

"You're the detective," Hunter commented. "No one expects that. Maybe he knew the attacker and went to have a cuddle, then wham!" Hunter laughed. "Mind you I'm only surmising. He springs up, chocks away, knife in. Easy really."

"Chocks away?" Crown asked.

"Oh absolutely," Hunter repeated.

"What else?" Lancaster asked.

"Oh yes.Funny thing. There seemed to be a bit of oil around

the wound. Only a trace mind, but it was there. Motor oil, diesel oil, bicycle oil, whatever it is the boys will soon know." He turned and waved."Goodbye you two. The boys are taking pictures   now. I'm off for a bit of kip. Keep 'em flying."

Crown could never figure out who was more cuckoo, Lancaster, Hunter, or, since he'd been to Venice, even the Chief.

"Keep 'em flying," Crown called out. Jesus.

"Come on, we'd better take a gander," Lancaster muttered. He lifted the yellow tape and walked around the back of the house. One of the policewomen greeted him.

"Hello sir, the forensic are in there tearing the place apart," she smiled.

"I know, thank you Sergeant Webb."

They walked down the black and white marble hall. Lancaster remembered how Joan Ross' heels click-clacked across the marble tiles.

"Place looks like a butcher's shop, it's ghastly.," Crown said. So much blood out of a skinny man like Steven.

Lancaster took in the scene. There were red splashes all over the white furniture. The floor was splashed with red, and there were red smears down the table and across the chairs.

"Designer red," he grunted, wiping his glasses. "Where's the lady of the house?"

He turned to one of the forensic boys.

"Sent her off to hospital," he said. "Police car took her."

"Was she here when they took him to the hospital?"

"Nope. They picked her up from somewhere or other. No one was here."

Lancaster went into the kitchen. No cups and saucers out. Everything clean and tidy. He turned to the staircase.

"Can't come up here Guv. Sorry, we're doing the staircase. The guy came down the stairs and it looks like he walked straight into the knife."

"Staggered into the porch," another one said.

"Must have fallen down the bloody stairs," Crown answered him.

"Power of survival Crown," Lancaster told him. "Come on. We've seen enough here.

- 40 -

Trevor Austin was sitting in a chair opposite Inspector Norton.

"Sorry I'm late," spoke Lancaster. "Morning."

"Evening," Norton answered by way of a clever retort. Or he thought it clever. He clicked on the tape recorder.

"Detective Inspector Lancaster has just come into the interview room , with Detective Sergeant Crown."

Lancaster turned to Trevor Austin.

"We meet again Trevor. Seems you have a habit of turning up when someone is dead or on their way out, eh?"

Trevor looked up at Lancaster with a mixture of fear and anguish on his face.

"Don"t worry Lancaster. I've taken a statement," Norton said.

Crown's head turned as Hunter appeared in the doorway.

"Nice day today Lancaster, managed a bit of gardening," Hunter said, "clear for take off."

Jesus thought Crown. We've got morning, noon and night here. Maybe they were all getting too old for murder. But if they pensioned Norton off who would replace him? Some squirt with a big mouth from downstairs?

"So Lancaster," Hunter said as he moved into the interview room. "The patient's not dead yet. Seriously wounded though, we'll have to wait overnight to see how he gets on. I'm going over to the house with the boys later. Big surgical job. Knife entered just under the rib cage. Missed the heart by a thread."

He turned towards Crown.

"No guarantees on his recovery, you understand. He's a bit shell shocked. Can't send him back to the front lines yet."

Norton continued, "It's all on tape. The whole thing sounds like Aesop's Fables to me."

Besides that, Norton hated late enquiries on a Sunday. The only thing that made him happy on a Sunday was the telly.

Crown sighed. Shell shocked, front lines, Jesus they were all mad. Hunter was only slightly more cuckoo than Lancaster. Only slightly.

Norton carried on. "I think we should play the tape."

"Right," Lancaster answered. "Play the tape."

Just then the stout figure of Prince came through the door.

"Evening everyone," Prince said.

It gave Lancaster pleasure to see that Prince must have left his Sunday night poker game. It almost made his own Sunday bearable. He looked at Norton with a smile.

Prince sat down with a thud and looked at the shrivelled up figure of his client.

"We seem to meet at murders and attempted murders, don't we Mr Austin?"

He mopped his brow and raised his eyes to the ceiling. The figure looked defenceless. Then it answered, "It would seem that way."

"Let's make a fresh start," Prince said, taking out his pen.

"I don't think we need a fresh start Prince," said Norton. "I'll play the tape."

"Right, play the tape," Prince echoed.

"I think, after we hear the tape Mr Prince, we shall cover more," Lancaster said. "It's not as straightforward as you may imagine. Your client is in deep trouble." He nodded to Crown. "Let's hear the tape."

Everyone said *play the tape* Crown thought. It was like a nursery rhyme. What was he doing with this bunch of madmen?

"I remember Steven falling into my arms, full of blood. Someone must have tried to kill him." Trevor said.

"Well we'd better hear the tape and discuss it afterwards when I may get a clearer picture of the problems, Mr Austin." Lancaster nodded to Norton. The tape clicked on.

It was Norton speaking.

"And what brought you to the Ross' place this jolly winter's evening?"

Now Norton had an odd turn of phrase.They sounded like they were on stage at the National.

"Dinner"

"Ah, dinner. You were invited to dinner, or were you taking your friends out for dinner?"

"I was expected. Joan invites me to dinner once a week since Clare....." Here Trevor's voice faded away.

"Yes, very good of her I'm sure. So I take it you arrived there for dinner. And what time would that be Mr Austin?"

"I was there at about eight o'clock."

"And then what happened?"

"I rang the bell and then I knocked. The place was dark, I couldn't understand why."

There was a slight pause in the tape.

"So I rang the bell a few more times. I couldn't understand why the place was in darkness. Then an upstairs light went on, followed by a light in the hallway, or was it the porch? I can't quite remember. The door opened and there was Steven. He was covered in blood and clutching himself and crying out. Then he literally fell into my arms. I tried to hold him up but he dragged me down with him."

"Did you notice anyone about, any cars, anything unusual?"

"Nothing, there was no one about. Steven was clinging onto me, poor devil. He was pouring with blood. By this time I could see he was unconscious and we were both in a terrible state. When I finally got him inside, I saw that he had a huge wound in his chest. I thought it was his heart. This couldn't be happening to me again, first Clare and now Steven. I didn't know what to do to stop the bleeding, so found a tablecloth and held it to the wound. Of course it didn't help. I was going crazy. Then I thought of phoning Penny to come over. I don't know why, I must have lost my senses. I needed the police and an ambulance. So I dialled 999 and got an ambulance here. I only pray Steven isn't dead.."

"Thanks Norton," Lancaster said, "you can turn the tape off now. I'll ask a few questions if you don't mind."

Trevor slumped further into his chair.

"How long do you suppose you waited before you phoned the police?"

"Oh, only a matter of minutes."

Did he know Charles was dead?

"You do some pretty erratic things, Mr Austin. You don't think things through, do you?"

Crown waited silently for an answer.

"Sounds like balderdash to me," Hunter said. "Man falling in someone's arms, with a life-threatening wound under his heart. I'd have thought he'd have fallen down the bloody stairs."

"Well, that's as far as we can go Lancaster," Norton said.

"Hunter's right Norton," Lancaster nodded his head. "I think you stabbed him yourself when he came down the stairs."

"No, that's not what happened," Trevor cried out in alarm. "No"

"After all those photographs with your arms round each other I would have thought any of your brothers would help you. I mean the live ones of course."

Lancaster looked pensively at Trevor. Eventually he would probe it out of this sullen man. He stuck to his main point.

"And now Mr Austin I am going to ask you a question. It only needs a simple answer. What did you do with the knife Mr Austin?"

Lancaster searched Trevor's face for an answer.

"Knife?"

"You heard me, the knife. Where did you put it? After you stuck it into Steven, did you throw it away? Did you hide it somewhere?"

Trevor's face went pale.

"Oh my God, you really think I did this?" He looked towards Prince, as if imploring him for help.

"Yes. You told me what you chose to tell me, and I don't believe you."

Norton spoke suddenly.

"I think perhaps we should leave it for a while."

His programme was on soon. He glanced at the time.

"Quite so," Lancaster agreed. "You are absolutely right . It's Sunday after all. Thank you Mr Austin, and you too Mr Prince. You can get off to your cell now Mr Austin. We'll wait until we get a full report from the hospital. I'm sure Hunter has taken all the little samples from you. Someone will take you to the men's room to wash the blood off."

Lancaster gave Trevor a little smile.

"By the way Mr Austin," Lancaster said, as if suddenly remembering something. "I'll be back."

The wily old devil, Crown thought. Lancaster knew he'd seen that movie. Everyone had seen that movie. Even Eric's sister, who was ten years old, had seen that movie. His face opened into a big grin.

"Thought I'd give you a treat," Lancaster said in answer to the grin. "What a load of rubbish it was too."

"Right ," Prince stood up. "That's it for now then. Let me know any further developments." His damn client had given too many answers already. This family was difficult enough without this fool being suspected of two murders. As for Lancaster and Crown and their double Dutch, someone ought to recommend them to a good shrink.

****

"What is it?" asked the doctor on duty in the Ospedale Civile when the nurse came up to him. "You look puzzled."

"I'm not sure. I am puzzled. An English signora has been

brought in by the polizia. She's in emergency. A Venetian signora told me that the English woman suddenly fell across her in a faint while they were travelling on the Vaporetto. The signora was coming home from shopping in St. Marco when it happened. She thought she was being attacked."

"On the Vaporetto?"

"Yes Doctore, Numero uno from St. Marco."

The doctor knew Numero uno was always busy. It didn't matter what time of year, it was always full. Sometimes you couldn't get a finger between passengers.

"So where did you put them?"

"Secondo Piano, Stanza Uno"

"I'll be there as soon as I can."

- 41 -

Lancaster and Crown sat in a far corner of The Anchor. Lancaster was having a bad day. He had a slight chill and was taking aspirins, washing them down with a glass of wine. He hadn't thought about movies and was complaining about the food.

"The food tastes rotten because you have a cold," Crown tried reasoning.

Lancaster pushed the plate away from him.

"Now we have Steven Ross being attacked and stabbed. Why? Why attack Ross?"

Crown shook his head. His blue blazer had been exchanged for a black one. He was wearing a navy spotted scarf tucked in at the neck. He looked like he was taking off in a spitfire.

"Does the Chief know you dress like that Crown?" Lancaster asked irritably.

"I saw the Chief last night," Crown commented.

"I know Crown, I know. You saw the glass tortoise he gave me. I was in his office yesterday. I just stood there and he looked out of the window. Then he asked me if I enjoyed Venice and where did I visit when I was there. Had I been to the Scuole St. Rocco?"

"I don't believe it!"

Lancaster sneezed. "Oh believe it Crown, believe it.I just told him how far we'd gone with the case and that we had a few answers. Like *Nevermore*. He just looked at me as if i'd gone barmy and just said "Get on with it Dana. Get on with it quickly." He wasn't remotely swayed by anything I said to him. He definitely wasn't himself."

"Everyone I know who comes back from Venice is definitely not himself sir. But we've gone over this case a dozen times. And I'm still asking myself one question. Why do this Austin lot all keep so friendly?"

They were sitting next to a blazing fire in a small nook in the pub. The firelight lit up the papers Lancaster was holding.

"This case is full of paintings and love notes."

"I thought it was full of murder." Crown moved his chair away from the heat.

"We've got words Crown, words. Words in a muddle, words in clues, words and pictures. I'm telling them murder and they're telling me wheat."

"We've got *Nevermore Forger*." Crown offered. Wheat?

Wheat? What the hell had wheat got to do with it? Crown couldn't place it. What did wheat have to do with murder? Wheat. *The Grapes of Wrath?* No, they weren't growing wheat, they were growing bloody grapes. *The Corn is Green* maybe. He took out his notepad and folded the yellow paper in half.

"Are you listening Crown?" said Lancaster. "And then there's Chatterton in the same pose as Austin on that blasted hospital bed. But what does that tell us? OK, so we know he was a poet and we know he was a forger, or a so called forger. What else was he for God's sake? He didn't have much time to be anything else because , according to what Parker said, he died at seventeen."

"Maybe he is nothing else. Van Gogh used his paintings to pay his hotel bills."

"What's that got to do with it? We've had enough trouble without Van Gogh Crown."

"So why did they all stay friends?"

"Because the murderer must have made his mind up to get rid of the whole family one by one. Pay them out in the only way he or she could. If he lost touch with them he couldn't get his revenge could he? Families have a funny habit of moving to New Zealand. The killer wanted to make damn sure where they were, so he stuck to them like glue."

"You're right sir," Crown beamed.

"*Nevermore Forger,*" Lancaster said. "That's what we've got Crown. And that makes me think about Charles."

"And the only brother who benefits now is Trevor, because Edward and Charles are both dead. So why kill Clare?"

"I don't know. It's the old story, money. And we don't know if there are a few more people in this family we haven't heard about. It's a double plot Crown. I've known cases where one child in the family is the sole beneficiary."

"Well it is possible we could have the word poet. *Nevermore Poet.*"

"They weren't bloody poets Crown. They were swimming pools and furniture suites and pharmacists. And the other lot dress designers and retired accountants."

His eyes lit up like white sails on a blue ocean.

"*Nevermore Forger*"

"The killer has a gruesome mind thinking all that up. Why not just kill them and have done with it."

"Too simple, far too simple. Make it look like a skein of wool. Get us running around in circles. Enjoy the whole thing like a play. Get it off his chest and tell the world why he did it. Murder is never simple Crown. How many times have I told you that?""

"I can't count sir."

Crown finished off his beer.

"But you're right about *Nevermore* and *Forger*. The killer means that the forger won't be doing any more forgery because he is, to borrow your expression, definitely dead.

"Now we have to deal with the road accident."

Lancaster looked pleased with himself.

"When we arrived at X marks the spot, there was no accident. But we find tyre marks, so we know there were two cars there. And lo and behold there's no victim. Then we find out by chance that Belinda's sister has a house not far from the accident and what do you know we find Charles. And we find him definitely dead."

Maybe the person who called us was scared and drove off, scared they'd be blamed."

"But if it was a hit and run and someone was hit we should have found a body."

"We did. We found Charles, but not in the road."

"Too late for the poor old sod. We should have checked on Belinda's relations long before this."

Lancaster felt chilly. He must be getting a temperature. The fire in the grate was dying down. It was time to put on the heating. Spring seemed a long way off. He recalled driving up Mrs Gordon's path of daffodils.

"You never cease to amaze me boss.This morning we had nothing."

"Yes well sometimes nothing can be a real cool hand."

- **42** -

Crown opened the door with his latch key. He looked outside the house. There was no spy in black, no stalker, no one under a lamp post, plain no one.

"Eric?" he called out. It couldn't be anyone else, could it? Crown dropped into a chair in the dining room.

"I'm tired," he sighed.

He could smell a chicken in the kitchen.

"I'm tired and hungry."

"Oh really Mr Crown?" Eric came into the room with a duster and flicked the table.

"The trouble with you is you're so busy with the films and your mad inspector that you don't see what's under your nose."

"We've got two words Eric. *Nevermore* and *Forger.*"

"I've done the dinner," Eric answered, "So you're a private detective. I didn't know they existed, except in books. Or else they were greasy little men snooping around hotel corridors. My, you're a mess, aren't you?"

Crown let his shoulders drop. He gazed at Eric under his eyelids. "Not you too Brutus."

"Why not? You listen to all that nonsense all day long. I thought it would make you feel at home, as you don't know what home is. I've done the dinner and I've got a nice wine too."

He gave Crown an intimate look.

Crown felt uneasy. Maybe they should go into business together. Eric always knew what was going on in every case he'd been on.

"What did you think of Belinda, Eric?"

"Think of her? From what you told me she's a first class bitch. And she wouldn't care what she did to get her own way."

"You're right, and she's done plenty. She's gone."

"Of course she's gone. Do you think she'd wait around while you two film critics decided to give her a lousy review?"

To Crown everyone sounded like they were in the movies. Even Eric sounded like he was in the movies. Maybe he should work in a box office like Eric and live a simple life. Sell tickets to *On Your Toes* and *Phantom of the Opera,* and let everything else go to hell. Then he would be free of Lancaster's everlasting quizzes, and he would never watch a movie again.

He heard the cork in the wine bottle pop like a pistol..

"Lancaster phoned you just before you got in, Mr Crown."

"What? I've only just arrived home for Christ's sake."

"Have dinner then call him back. You're like his pet slave," Eric said, pouring the wine. He went into the kitchen and brought in the chicken and roast potatoes.

"You know what Eric?"

"What?"

"TI think I'll quit. Become a private eye. Get hit over the head and sink into a deep pool of black like they do in the movies."

He tasted the chicken.

"What did you do to this chicken?"

"Oh, honey and lime."

"How come you're such a bloody good cook?"

"Remember I lived with that French chef two years ago? Well I learned a thing or two."

Eric began to think about the French chef. He wondered where the French chef lived now. Crown was becoming a humourless bastard these days. He should have gone off with that B.T. man instead of hanging around here with Kilvert. Weekends were always taken up with mayhem and movies. He never went near his clubs these days. He was losing his touch.

"I'm damn sure you did." Crown felt a slight pang of jealousy.

"Here's the phone," Eric said.

Crown dialled the number.

"Boss?"

"Yup, it's me. What other bloody fool would be in a police station at this time of night? Who did you think it was?"

"John Garfield? Paul Newman? Sammy Davis? At least that's who I hoped it was."

"Listen Crown, I got onto Interpol. She booked a plane ticket in her own name on Al Italia. We checked all the hotel bills and she phoned Venice at least six or seven times. She must have a relation or a friend there. Anyway it looks like she wanted to get away because there was a call to Al Italia. We showed her picture to all the staff and apparently the stewardess on the early flight remembered her. She jumped out of her seat before they landed and the seat belt sign was on. She was told to sit down. It's her alright, only with black hair."

"She flew to Venice?" Everybody was going to Venice these days.

"We've spoken to the police over there. They're checking on her. I gave them her maiden name as well."

Crown was bewildered. Venice?

"We'll be there in the morning Crown. I've got two tickets on the first flight out."

"Tomorrow morning?"

Eric would definitely leave him for the B.T. man.

****

The call came on the mobile when they reached Venice Airport.

"Buon journo Inspector Lancaster."

"Yes Lancaster speaking.Good morning."

"It is Inspector Rossi here, from the Vigile."

"Ah Inspector Rossi, you spoke to me in London."

"Of course Inspector. I am afraid I have some bad news for you."

"Bad news?" They couldn't trace Belinda, that must be it.

"We have traced the woman you were looking for, Belinda Austin."

"And?"

"She is in the Hospital Civile. The doctors have saved her life. She was poisoned. She collapsed on the Vaporetto and the lady sitting next to her called the police and they got an ambulance to the boat. You can go and see her. I have told them you will be there as soon as possible."

"Thank you Inspector. You are very efficient."

"Oh, we're no backwater here, although you may think so.By the way, welcome to Venice."

"Thank you very much, We'll go to the hospital right away."

"Get a water taxi. You can always put it on expenses Inspector."

The Italians were always ten steps ahead.

****

"Yes, poisoned by Narcissus Psuedo-narcissus." The doctor opened his arms out to emphasise his words.

"And that is?" Lancaster asked Doctore Busetti.

"Oh, daffodil poisoning. I learned about it at medical school. We saw a case once. man poisoned his wife and she died, high temperature and sickness. Even a small amount can cause paralysis. Daffodil bulbs can kill you know."

He spoke with certainty. "Yes, she was poisoned by daffodils."

"Incredible," was all Lancaster could utter.

"Oh absolutely incredible," the doctor agreed.

"May we see her?"

"Of course" He beckoned them towards the lift. "She is on the first floor. We have an excellent ward there."

Crown was impressed when they arrived on the first floor. They walked down a long bright corridor and he saw all the windows were thrown open. It must help the patients to look at the roof tops of Venice.

Belinda was in a room off the corridor.

"We put her in here. Either it was self-inflicted or an attempt has been made on her life," the doctor said.

She was lying asleep. Her blonde hair was spread on the pillow. There was a drip in her arm.

"She looks so still, she could even be dead." Crown uttered.

"Ah no Sergeant. I can assure you she is not dead. Her stomach was pumped out immediately. We were extremely cautious. She had every sign of losing her life but we recognised the symptoms. She's very lucky."

The doctor's expression showed pleasure in his accomplishment. She was alive and he was delighted.

"Still, there's nothing more we can do here," Lancaster said, "I think we'll leave her for now and pop in tomorrow."

Lancaster picked up his coat. Daffodils. They'd seen them when they started this case, driving up to Mrs Gordon's place. He'd never had a case like this before. Next thing you know the winter would be over and they were still in limbo. Had they really put anything together that stuck? The murderer of Clare must be the stalker, or must it? His mind went round and round.

"Thank you Doctor. It's been a pleasure to meet you. Never knew these hospitals ran so well. We've got people lying on trolleys in English hospitals. Can't get to see a doctor and sometimes they lie there for more than twenty four hours. If they do get to see a doctor, they're lucky."

"Gratzia"

The doctor saw them to the lift.

"By the way doctor, if anyone calls or wants to visit, please let me know first. Here is my mobile number. And please try not to let anyone near her. I know it's difficult but someone out there may try this again. Buon giorno."

When they left the hospital Crown spoke.

"I can't understand who did this sir. Could it be the sister?"

"If her sister's scampered we'll soon know. Meanwhile let's have a quick spritz. Where did you say her sister lived?"

"On the Zattere, wherever that is."

They walked sharply round the next corner. He peered into the bars. Beautiful. There was the divine smell of cakes and biscuits he remembered so well.

"I know where it is Crown. I don't think we're in Kansas any more."

Crown didn't bother to take his pencil out. He wanted to take in as much as he could of the Grand Canal.

When Lancaster finally arrived at Belinda's sister's apartment a very attractive tall slim woman wearing a multi-coloured scarf opened the door to them. "Good morning," she said. She was very attractive and extremely stylish.

"I'm Detective Inspector Lancaster and this is Detective Sergeant Crown. And you I presume are Belinda Austin's sister."

"You look surprised Inspector. Please come in."

She ushered them into her apartment. Lancaster saw the dark wood Italian furniture, marble floors and paintings of the Madonna on the walls. There was only one painting of Venice. She asked them to sit down. Lancaster sat near the open shutters overlooking the sweep of the Grand Canal as it turned round St. Georgio.

"Yes," she said, "Belinda and I were never confused. We're totally different and, of course, Belinda is years younger than me. My Mother married again and she is from her second husband."

Lancaster saw how much prettier she was than Belinda. Her face was more rounded and her eyes were a much deeper blue. They were like navy silk. Her nose was tiny and her full mouth was rich with dark red lipstick. Her dress fitted her like a second skin.

"Please tell us your name Signora," Crown said, thinking maybe he had got all this wrong and that wasn't Belinda in the hospital but her sister, and they were here talking to Belinda.

"I'll make some coffee and then we can talk," she said.

She left them looking round the apartment.. Lancaster leaned out of the window and pushed the shutters further back so he could see the sweep of the Grand Canal. What a marvellous place to live. Maybe he could retire here.

Crown was thinking the same thing. Eric would love this place. He could sell tickets at the Fenice.

She returned with coffee and cakes on a silver tray.

"Thank you ," Lancaster said, helping himself to a cup.

"Yes," she said, "I'm Belinda's sister. My name is Sabina Franklin. We've had a very difficult life Inspector. My Father died and my Mother married again. Then not long afterwards she too died young. We had no other family so that made us very close.My second Father worked hard so we could go to college. I went on to run a business and Belinda decided to become a model. Before I went into business, I decided to travel round Europe like the kids do today. First I went Paris, Rome, Madrid, the south of France and then Venice."

Lancaster leaned forward so as not to miss a word.

"Of course I realise you know a little about Belinda's life in England. But please tell me a little more of the background."

Sabina crossed her legs.

Lancaster helped himself to another cake. He knew with certainty what she would tell him. It was his double plot beginning to come to life.

"I was married to an Austin. I met him after my European trip. Yes, it was one of the brothers. His name was Alexander Austin. Two sisters married two brothers, which is not that unusual. You read about it in the papers every day." She paused. "Of course I was very young then, and didn't realise what a terrible mistake I was making. He turned out to be a nasty piece of work. All sorts of behaviour problems. He used to carry on with every woman in sight. I could put up with that to a certain extent because I still loved him. But then he became involved with a certain woman he wanted to live with. He even wanted to marry her. I had no choice Inspector. He would have left anyway. I was broken hearted. Belinda helped me get a divorce. I was married for only four years."

"I'm sorry," Lancaster said.

Sabina Franklin just waved her hand, as if to push the memory away.

"One of those things," she said. "It's easier to bear now because it all happened so long ago. After the divorce I felt depressed and needed a break. I remembered Venice and how beautiful it was. So I came back for a holiday. And here I stayed. I fell in love with Venice, not another man. Venice has never left me."

"I can understand that," Lancaster said quietly. "One can fall in love with Venice. Tell me Miss Franklin, did your sister visit you often?"

"Oh yes. We were friends. She often stayed here. After I was married to Alexander she met his brother Charles when he visited us. She was here at the time."

"And why did you change your name?" Crown asked.

"I didn't want anyone to know where I was. I thought at first I'd use my maiden name. Then I decided to make a new life, la vita nuovo, in a new place. I've been very happy here."

"So you never heard anything about a will when your ex-husband's Father died?"

"A will? Of course not, Belinda never mentioned it."

"You never received anything from a will, nothing at all?"

"Certainly not. Surely they must have informed my ex-husband. He must know because he would inherit something. I don't know where he lives. We're not in touch at all. We had no children so there was no need to contact each other. I heard he re-married not long after we divorced. He married the woman he fell in love with, a French woman."

"So he doesn't know where you are?"

"No"

Lancaster wondered how such a pretty woman like Sabina Franklin hadn't married again.

"Were your husband's parents fond of you?" Lancaster suddenly asked her.

She answered with a lingering smile. "Oh yes. They were very fond of me. And I was of them. They said it would be good for Alexander. I would get him away from the influence of his other brothers. His parents were unhappy about their own children. Amazing isn't it?"

"Not really, most parents know their own children. Your Mother-in-law must have been a good judge of character."

Lancaster glanced over towards the Grand Canal. Boats were skimming past the window in the warm sunlight. Crown knew the bomb was loaded.

"Do you live with anyone?" Lancaster suddenly queried, looking once more around the room. He tried to find a trace of masculinity, a man's coat, a jacket or a photo. There was nothing he could see, in this room at least.

"No," she shrugged her shoulders, "not everyone in the world wants to be married you know."

Lancaster thought about the jazz singer.and why he never married her. She was the one who said it wouldn't work.

"And Belinda, she told you why she left East Wood?"

"Yes, she wasn't happy with Charles. He was never there

when she needed him. But you know how it is. You hope things will improve. Divorce is a pretty messy business and you can end up with nothing, or just enough to get by. People stay together for different reasons and love isn't top of the list. Then one day she surprised me. She phoned to tell me she'd met someone else and had fallen in love with him."

"What did you say to that?"

"What could I say? She was pretty and it wouldn't be hard for a man to fall for her."

Lancaster helped himself to another tiny cake. It was made with a sweet soft pastry and was filled with tiny beads of rice.

"I see you like the cakes Inspector. They are from Rosa Salva. You must buy some to take home."

He found he wasn't concentrating. His mood had altered. He began to feel the way he had when he first came to Venice. It was like slipping into a coma. He pulled himself up.

"Who had she met? Did she tell you his name? It's very important Miss Franklin."

Crown held his pad ready anticipating her answer.

"That's the funny thing. He never gave her a name. That was part of their arrangement. She became besotted with him. She was desperate to find out his real name. I told her to leave it as it was, keep it as an affair. But it got out of hand. She was crazy about him."

"And the name?"

Sabina bit her lips. "Now I remember," she smiled, "I'd almost forgotten. She said it was Simon. She was in a dreadful state when she arrived. She was convinced someone was following her. She was terrified. She was so happy to be here with me, she had so much to tell me. We had gone out to lunch round the corner and after lunch she decided she wanted to do a little shopping so she got the Vaporetto to Canareggio. That was her favourite place for shopping." She hesitated. "Who would do this?" She was imploring him to tell her.

"Oh, I shall find out, you can be sure of that. I'm sure your sister will recover. The doctor seemed convinced of that. Your sister missed dying by a hair's breadth. She's a lucky girl. Tell me, are you at all friendly with Joan and Steven Ross?"

Good firing that, Crown mused.

"Of course not, why do you ask?"

Well she hadn't slipped up on that one.

"As I said, I'm not in contact with any of them. Why would I change my name all those years ago if I wanted to contact anyone in England? No, I cut them out of my life. The Austins were a rotten lot according to Belinda, just as bad as Alexander. She wasn't happy. It seems we were both unlucky."

Lancaster leaned back into the cushions. Why couldn't anyone give him coffee like this in London? He took out his cigarettes and put one to his lips. He got up and started to make his way out.

"We'll revisit Belinda in hospital tomorrow. In the meantime lock your door and don't let anyone in at all."

"But why?" Sabina Franklin asked in fear.

"Because you had better start thinking about why your sister nearly died."

He put on his hat. "Thank you Miss Franklin, we'll be in touch."

Sabina closed the door behind them. She would have to go and see Belinda right away, despite Lancaster's warning. The afternoon was still bright. She went to the wardrobe and brought out a jacket. Her hands were shaking. Would the same person who poisoned Belinda try to kill her?

Perhaps she shouldn't go on her own. She would phone her friend Jada and ask if she would go with her to the hospital. She looked out of the window to the bar. The mass of coloured umbrellas made the piazza look like a cubist painting. People were eating and drinking wine, and waiters were carrying trays of gelati. It was as if a curtain had been pulled down over the piazza and everything had become dark. In the space of half an hour her life had been turned totally upside down.

- 43 -

There was a ringing noise. Crown dreamed he was with Lancaster in Venice and all the church bells were ringing and he was asking Eric if they were actually playing a melody. When they stopped Crown woke and looked at the clock. He jumped out of bed. Jesus, who could be ringing the doorbell at seven in the morning? He must have overslept. He heard ringing again. Grabbing his dressing gown from the chair he wrapped it around him and went downstairs.

The bell was persistent. No one had mentioned they would be visiting at this hour.

"Who the hell?" he uttered, opening the door.

"Buon giorno." Lancaster stood in the doorway. He was dressed in a black bomber jacket and blue jeans. His blue eyes were shining and he was practically gleaning with happiness.

"Of course, I just didn't expect you that's all."

Crown tied his dressing gown tighter.

"Come in, Eric's gone off early to see a friend."

Lancaster looked anxious. He realised it was Saturday. Crown saw he had a book under his arm.

"What's that?" he asked as he motioned Lancaster into the kitchen. Lancaster laid the book on the kitchen table and sat down.

"Do you know what Crown? The last one had me going and yet it was so easy.

"Easy? The last murder?" Crown filled the kettle and took out the milk. There was a note in the fridge from Eric, "Don't forget to buy milk." Eric and his fridge notes would drive him nuts.

"Easy because it was all painted out for us. If it wasn't for you I would never have been thinking about paintings. I couldn't think about it while we were in Venice, I was too concerned about Belinda."

Crown said, "Coffee sir?"

"Yes please. Thinking back it was when Trevor Austin told us that Steven screamed that it came into my mind. But I thought it was crazy."

"Of course he screamed. The man was stabbed, for Christ's sake."

"It was the word *scream*. At that moment I remembered Charles. There was the poor old bastard, trussed up on the floor like a turkey with his mouth taped wide open. He screamed too."

Lancaster waited eagerly for Crown to speak but Crown didn't answer so he went on. "The murderer taped open what must have been a scream."

"He taped Charles' mouth open at a scream? That's sick."

"Of course it's sick. Absolutely, murder is sick. Then it came to me, the mouth taped open, the hands taped over the ears. When have you ever seen anything like that before?"

"We've seen straight shooting, strangling, hanging...."

"Don't let's go into it all so early for God's sake. We've been so stupid."

`"Would you like some toast?"

"Yes, buttered toast with jam. We let the man go to the mortuary taped up like a bloody parcel and didn't bother to think it was another damn painting."

Lancaster looked down at the book on the table and opened it to a page on Munch.

"*The Scream,*" Crown muttered as he looked at it.

"Of course, I've seen it enough times." Lancaster ran his fingers through his hair. "I feel like an idiot. We allowed it to get by us Crown, that's all." Lancaster spoke quietly. "You found the answer Crown but we didn't carry on working on it. I broke my neck with pearls and I drove myself nuts with the blue boy but I couldn't work out a bloody scream."

"So we've got *Nevermore, Forger, Scream.*" Crown said. "The person who did this knew the art world alright."

"He's telling us *Nevermore you forger, nevermore will you forge, but you will scream.*"

"It's sick alright. The message is sick. This killer is boned up on art."

"He knew art. He knew it and spelled out a murder with it and gave us a message for a reason. Nevermore will these bastards forge anything to the killer's detriment. And if they do they'll scream, scream while they're being killed."

"Do you think there'll be another killing?"

"I don't think so Crown, not yet. Short of keeping the family under guard I can't do anything except try to get some answers. I think we have a lot of liars on our hands. And we've also got a man who calls himself *The Saint.* Let's think about Trevor Austin for a minute. "Here you are, toast and jam," Crown said ,leaving the coffee pot on the table.

"I've got a few questions for Penny and I need answers right now."

Right now, everything was right now. Crown knew how that

miserable weasel Prince felt on a weekend. Only Crown wasn't playing golf, he just wanted to stay in bed and read his book on Hitchcock.

****

They arrived at Penny Austin's at a little after ten o'clock. A lone police car was parked in the drive.

"The daffodils will be poking up soon Crown." Lancaster muttered under his breath. He sat there drumming his fingers on his lap. Damn daffodils, he never realised flowers could do so much damage.

"Come on Crown, get your pencil out."

He jumped out of the car and crunched his way up the garden path. More leaves had fallen and they were withered and brown. The trees were nearly bare. Everything looked bleak.

A constable stood in the doorway.

"Morning Constable, any bother?"

The constable shrugged his shoulders. "No sir"

"Good, then we'll go inside."

Penny Austin was walking towards them from the kitchen.She was holding a mug of coffee and Lancaster could see the mug was visibly shaking in her hand.

"Well, well, Mrs Austin, we meet again. And again,.." Lancaster pulled out a chair. "Mind if I sit down?"

Penny Austin put the coffee on the table.

"What's going on Inspector? Why are you here? And what's that police car doing outside? What's happened?" Her lip was quivering. Crown noticed her eyes were swollen.

"Just a few little items we'd like to clear up," Crown said purposefully. "My notes say you had a phone call from Trevor Austin the evening he found Steven Ross." He looked at his notepad. "December 2nd," he said.

"December 2nd? Of course I did." She had better be careful.

"I think you'll find Mrs Austin if you look at the calendar that was a Tuesday evening. We began to wonder where you were before you received the call. Were you at home or out of town? You see it's so difficult to know which way is up with these mobiles. Never use one myself." Lancaster spoke quickly.

Crown could see her trying to decide if she should answer or not. He sighed. She had the `sod you` look. Next thing you know she would ask to speak to her solicitor. "I'm sure you'll remember Mrs Austin, it's only last week after all," Lancaster emphasised. Penny moved toward the telephone.

Right again, Crown thought. I'm having a good day so far. But it's not over yet.

"I'm not answering any more of your questions. I need a solicitor. Will you both leave please?"

She stood up. Was it a Tuesday evening when Trevor had phoned her? It must be because she always did her shopping on a Tuesday morning and she remembered leaving a few bags in the car to bring in later.

Lancaster was impassive. He was staring out of the kitchen window into the garden.

"I have had people walk out on me before, but not when i was being so charming," Lancaster said, taking out a cigarette and putting it to his lips.

Blade Runner, that's bloody it, *Blade Runner.* Why the old devil. Crown felt pleased with himself. It was the first movie he had remembered this whole rotten week.

Penny was extremely agitated now.

"Oh, phone him do," Lancaster answered. His eyes were still staring out into the garden and they looked to Crown like a deep blue lake ready to catch a fish in.

"I'd love to get Prinny off the golf course again." He cleared his throat. "By the way," he said casually, "at the same time ask him if he knows anything about forgery. I mean the time you'll have to serve as an accessory, of course. Once we prove it, that is. And we will."

"Forgery? What the hell are you talking about?" Penny Austin asked. Her hand flew out knocking her coffee mug over. It spilled over the table and onto the floor. Crown listened to the sound of the coffee dripping onto the floor tiles.

"Please do sit down and stop jumping about Mrs Austin. I want to ask you something."

Lancaster cleared his throat. He tried to look his most pleasant.

"You were seen going to Steven Ross' house first thing on that Tuesday morning. Yes Mrs Austin," he blew out a little smoke ring. "Someone happened to see you there."

Her face turned ugly. She blurted out, "I wasn't seen, who could have seen me?" She sighed, letting out a deep breath. It was too late to pretend now.

"Ah let's have the truth now," Crown said. He enjoyed Lancaster's little white lies. They worked every time.

Penny hesitated. She should phone Prince. But forgery, what was this about forgery?

Lancaster was speaking again. His voice had a hard edge.

"I think you went there to see Steven after he phoned you because he had found out something. What did Steven tell you Mrs Austin? Think carefully. You can be accused of murder as well, all in a nice little package, murder and an accessory to forgery." He started to hum. "Not an easy thing to squirm out of."

"My God," she whispered. She felt faint.

"Alright then," she spoke in a strained voice. "I left the house in the morning after Steven phoned me. He said he had something he wanted to talk to me about."

"Couldn't it have waited till another day?"

"I don't know," she raised her voice, "all I know is he wanted to ask me something about Joan."

Crown went over to the stove and pulled a tea towel off the rail. The dripping coffee was irritating him. He couldn't have lived with it at home.

"I went over there and Steven told me he'd found something in one of the drawers. It was a letter and some other things."

"And the other things?" Crown shot at her.

"Old copies of prescriptions."

"Prescriptions? What for?"

She was in tears now. "They were for medication, signed by a doctor. And Edward must have filled them."

Lancaster sighed.

"Who were the drugs for?"

Penny looked at him. "They were for Joan. I don't know what they were for, do I? Steven thought they were for some sort of tranquilliser. I told Steven he shouldn't be nosing around in Joan's things. In her bedroom drawers I mean."

"But why ask you to come?"

"Because Steven wondered if I knew anything about it. Did Joan tell me she was ill? Was she depressed? He was worried about her. She was acting strangely and she had headaches. Then he confessed he had found some prozac in her handbag."

"Were you close to Joan? Close enough for her to tell if she was ill?"

"No, we weren't close. I never knew anything about Joan. She was a business woman. I hardly ever saw her. I think Steven phoned me out of desperation. He was a quiet man and she ruled the roost. He was really asking for advice."

Lancaster rose and put his cigarette in a saucer.

"Thank you Mrs Austin. I'll be back again after I make a few more enquiries. Seems old Prince will be kept busy with all these things goings and comings. I dealt with his father for many years, Prince the elder, a marvellous man. Wasn't a thing he didn't know about forgery."

She stepped back in fear.

Lancaster beckoned to Crown.

"By the way Mrs Austin," he added, "if you're thinking of going anywhere, I shouldn't. You'll never make it to the border."

Her face turned as white as a Venetian mask.

On the way back Lancaster told Crown to meet him at the Gordon's place in the morning.

"It's Sunday tomorrow sir." Crown looked peeved.

"Crown, for a while there I thought you were a detective. How come you can't remember that murder happens on every day of the week? I think I know why this thing is an elaborate rigma-role. Revenge is a powerful motive Crown. Get Penny over to the Gordon's place tomorrow as well. Send Harry with a car to pick her up. They all know a hell of a lot more than they told us. And don't forget Trevor. I want him there as well. And I've decided to arrange a few surprises. Nothing like an entertainer to get a party going."

- **44** -

When Betty Gordon opened the front door Lancaster could see that she hadn't slept. Her eyes were heavy and her hair tangled. She was in her dressing gown.

"Oh Inspector." She was startled. "Whatever are you doing here. I didn't expect anyone today, it's Sunday." She bent down and picked up the Sunday paper from the doorstep.

"I am perfectly aware it is Sunday Mrs Gordon. Murders don't stop because it's a Sunday. My Sergeant here informed me it was Sunday in case it slipped my memory."

"I suppose you want to come inside then," she grumbled.

"You suppose correctly then Madam. You could say we are here on an errand of mercy."

"Mercy," she almost cried out, "What mercy? What are you are talking about?" Why was he talking about an errand of mercy? Why that was what they said in her old school play, something about the quality of mercy.

"I prefer to speak to you inside the house if you don't mind, nosey neighbours and all that."

Lancaster rarely smiled on a Sunday but this time he allowed himself a slight grimace. She dropped her newspaper. The quivering of her hands showed him she was still distressed. He bent down, picked it up and handed it to her.

Betty ushered them into the front room of the cottage, where Lancaster placed himself in front of the fireplace. There was a small blaze from a log fire. He was quite happy to stand while he was waiting for the rest of the family. Sitting in those small cottage armchairs did his back in.

Betty realised she had forgotten her manners. She seemed to be forgetting everything these days. And she never slept for a moment last night. Thinking of Charles made her lie awake in the dark like a dumb animal trying to protect itself from the hunters. Perhaps she should offer them some tea.

Lancaster moved from the fireplace and taking the newspaper from her hands he placed it on the table.

"Now Mrs Gordon I need your attention please. You see I have been trying to work out exactly what has been going on since the murder of Clare. And the more I thought about it the more confused I became. And in my confusion I stupidly looked at the wrong clues."

Betty Gordon opened her eyes wider, "Clues?" She uttered. "What clues?"

"You'll soon be told about that. In order for my Sergeant to make sense of it all I have taken the liberty of asking a few people to drop in on you and Frank this morning. and some of the others won't pop in until the early evening. I'm sure you won't mind if we hang about. We can always sit in deck chairs in the garden. We only want to clear up a few points."

Crown watched Betty put her hands to her mouth. "Deck chairs in the garden?" she asked, "Who is dropping in on me and Frank? Why I'm not ready for company. I'm not dressed properly. I usually get lunch ready for Frank on a Sunday. Who is coming around?"

"Oh, you can go up and get dressed. We're happy to wait. It's just a few of your beloved family coming round on this winter's day. The few that still seem to be left that is."

"I don't understand."

"You will Mrs Gordon. Believe me you will."

A police siren rent the Sunday morning air with its screeching. A car door slammed and a figure walked briskly up the path.

The knock made Betty jump. She opened the door to a constable and Penny Austin.

"Penny, what on earth are you doing here?" Penny was standing on the doorstep looking furious.

Crown knew Lancaster was working up to what Hunter would call a blitzkrieg. He was moving around the room in an agitated manner, crossing from the fire to the windows.

Penny Austin came into the room with her hair covered by a brightly patterned scarf. Ignoring Betty, she went straight over to Lancaster.

"Why are you doing this Inspector? Couldn't you see me in my own home? Are you aware how early it is?"

"Oh I know how early it is Mrs Austin. My sergeant and I have been up since dawn. Please sit down. And please don't tell me it's a Sunday. I'm well aware of it."

He placed his early morning cigarette in his mouth. It tasted foul. He might try to give up.

"By the way, where is your husband Mrs Gordon?"

He turned to Betty raising his eyebrows.

"Why, he's outside in the shed. He always sees to the garden on a Sunday morning. seeing to the flower pots and bringing in some of the bulbs before the worst of the month."

Crown thought about daffodil bulbs. Daffodils were so pretty and yellow, yet their bulbs could be turned into poison. Like a beautiful person, all golden yellow on the outside but you could never be sure what went on inside.

"Of course," Crown answered. "Just tell him we have some important news. No hurry for him to come in, we have a few more people to wait for. May we have some tea please, we haven't had time for breakfast?"

He could see Lancaster was reloading. and his bulk seemed to take over the whole of the small cottage room.

The back door opened to reveal Frank Gordon. His hands were grubby with earth.

"I can't see what you want with me," he complained, wiping his hands on his overalls.

"Oh you may be surprised by what I want Mr Gordon." Lancaster answered him quietly. He moved forward. "Up early in these parts eh?". He looked at Frank intensely.

"I should sit down if I were you, just until the others arrive. Or you can go out and do your pottering about. Some of them won't be here till later."

Frank and Betty were staring at him. They both stood uneasily in the corner of the room.

"I don't know what you're talking about," Frank said.

"No one seems to know what I'm talking about wherever I go. Funny thing that, no one seems to understand the Queen's English any more."

"People, what people?" Frank asked gruffly. "I'm not expecting visitors today. It's Sunday."

"Ah, but I am already aware of that Mr Gordon," Lancaster answered him. He only hoped no one else would tell him it was *Sunday bloody Sunday.*

Crown sat down and waited for Betty to bring in the tea. He hadn't had time for breakfast. Eric always made a cooked breakfast on a Sunday.

Lancaster poured himself a cup of tea. He could hear the loud ticking of the clock on the mantlepiece. An hour must have passed before Trevor Austin appeared. Frank, who had come back inside, sat down and shook his head in disbelief.

"What's Penny doing here? And Trevor?" He turned to Crown. "I don't need them here on a Sunday."

"Oh they're here to help clear up our problems Mr Gordon. I'm sure you're anxious to know about the results of our enquiries."

"About the murders?" Penny asked. "Is that why you've brought us here?"

"Yes, the problem of murder," Lancaster went on. "My sergeant and I have been trying to catch up with murders instead of being in front of them."

The four people sitting in front of him were very still.

"It's a pity we can't have Steven Ross here with us, as part of the family of course."

He watched them fidget in their chairs.

"But," whispered Penny Austin, "isn't he dead?", eyes wide open now.

"Dead? Did I say he was dead? Word does get around doesn't it? Whatever gave you that idea? If I'm not mistaken he'll be here with us quite soon. It's difficult for the hospital to let him out without a doctor to accompany him, so we've had to get a doctor on a Sunday, and you know what that's like I'm sure." He smiled at them. "Steven has only just had a transfusion. Besides that he's been extremely ill as you can imagine. Being knifed isn't exactly a Sunday picnic." He may as well mention Sunday again before someone else did.

Lancaster hummed a little tune to himself. Crown could have sworn it was a jazzy version of *Strangers in the Night*. He opened his pad and folded the page in half. It must be coming soon.

A police constable poked his head round the front door.

"Excuse me please," Lancaster said.

Crown looked at his watch. It was past lunch time now. He would have to exist on the few biscuits Betty had brought in with the tea. He never missed Sunday breakfast.

A gust of wind blew in when the door opened making the room turn cold. And with the wind a slight figure entered, a grey skeletal figure, a man so shadowy that he looked like a branch of a tree broken off by the wind.

"Good grief Steven!" exclaimed Frank, jumping up in shock. They all looked toward the slight figure. A tall man dressed in a grey jacket was helping Steven Ross into the room.

The shadow spoke. "Did I surprise you Frank?"

The shadow moved moved over to the nearest chair and dropped into it. His voice was hollow.

"Now, now, Mr Ross. Just take it slowly." The man in the grey jacket was speaking. He looked up.

"I'm Doctor Berkowitz. I'm looking after Mr Ross for the day. I would never have brought him here but for the insistence of Inspector Lancaster. I believe it's very important for him to be here, so he's been heavily sedated. I hope I can get him back to the hospital as soon as possible."

Doctor Berkowitz was a large well-built man and Crown could see he would be able to lift Steven into his arms with no trouble. He certainly didn't look like a doctor. Anyway, what did a doctor have to look like? He was asking himself far too many stupid questions.

"Of course you will Doctor." Lancaster smiled at the man. "And thank you for all the trouble you've gone to."

"Why, we thought you were dead Steven." Trevor blurted out.

Steven's thin lips opened.

"It seems there's been a mistake," he said, sinking lower into the chair and giving a slight chuckle. "I am alive, as you can see. Of course not as I once was. But then, which of us is? I'm being held together by a remarkable concoction given to me by the good doctor here. He told me it could keep me going for a few hours."

Berkowitz looked down at Steven.

"Quietly, please speak quietly. You need to keep up your strength."

There were dark rings under Steven's eyes and his face was colourless.

"Put a few more logs on the fire Mr Gordon, will you?" Lancaster interrupted. "Don't worry, you'll soon warm up Mr Ross." He patted Steven's shoulder gently. "You won't mind if I continue in a little while. I think it best to wait for our other visitors. They seem to be rather late and I must apologise for them, possibly a delay at the airport."

"Airport?" asked Penny. "Who is coming from an airport?" She twisted her hands in her lap. This was all terrifying. Who was coming from abroad? She couldn't remember any family living abroad. Edward never mentioned it.

As Crown lifted the curtains to peer outside there was a screech of tyres in the driveway. It was a grey winter's day and it would soon be dark. He could make out two figures getting out of a car. Who the devil were they? Lancaster hadn't told him about anyone else coming here today.

"Open the door for the constable please Crown," Lancaster smiled. To his amazement he recognised Belinda Austin and her sister Sabina. They were wearing long olive green coats, and looked as though they had materialised out of a London fog.

"So glad you could make it ladies." Lancaster moved towards them. "I'm sure everyone here will recognise Belinda." He motioned to the two sisters. "Please give your coats to Crown and find yourselves a chair.

He could hear Frank gasp. "Belinda"

"Indeed Mr Gordon, it is Belinda. And may I introduce her sister Sabina Franklin. You've probably never met before as she left England many years ago. I am sure Mrs Gordon here will be happy to make you both a cup of tea, it's a rather chilly afternoon."

Lancaster looked towards Betty with a pleasant expression. She scuttled away.

"And now we are all here I will get on with the business of murder. Get you notebook out Crown."

Crown started to write. Why hadn't Lancaster told him about the sisters coming from Venice?

The little group of people in the room gave each other worried looks.

"Yes." Lancaster drummed his fingers on the mantlepiece. "I have a lot of explaining to do. This case all began with the unfortunate murder of Clare, your sister-in-law." He emphasised her name. "Yes, Clare Austin. And the strange thing is I had all the clues hanging about in my head, but I didn't grab hold of the right ones. I was so busy with what I thought was right that I neglected to see what was wrong. You see I thought the murder was to do with pearls, as indeed it was, but everything eluded me. It was all too clever."

He held his hands in front of the fire.

"You see, the whole of this case has to do with paintings."

"Paintings?" said Betty timidly. "What has it to do with paintings? No one here paints."

"Ah," smiled Lancaster. "That's possible Mrs Gordon. But you can't be too sure, can you? Whoever murdered Clare and Charles and Edward Austin knew about art. they also knew a bit about rigor mortis. Well, that's easy enough to find out about. How many hours it takes before a dead body is quite stiff. That's why they call them stiffs." He laughed at his little joke.

There was a hint of hostility in the air as if these people were silently preparing their lies to protect themselves. No one spoke.

"At first we thought Clare's death was the job of a burglar. An opportunist who saw all the windows and doors open and thought the place was ripe for the picking. But if it was a burglary why was nothing touched? Her jewellry box was still on her dressing table and her rings were still on her fingers. Was she going upstairs for a bath? There was a towelling robe lying on the floor next to her. According to forensics there were no signs of recent sexual relations. Anyway she looked too perfect, apart from the bullet holes, for rape."

Belinda shivered. She was lucky the maniac that was following her hadn't shot her.

Lancaster carried on. "We are presuming Clare Austin was stripped and thrown to the ground with a gun held to her head. There was no mercy here. She was shot three times and left to die. The bullets all entered at right angles and they entered from above. There were three clean bullet holes in her. Still, we don't need to go into all that clinical detail, we have the report here, should anyone wish to see it." He looked round questioningly. No one moved. Lancaster continued.

"She was lying on a blanket with her head on a cushion and her left hand and arm underneath her left cheek. Why was she lying on a blanket? Was it there for a reason? Why the hell would she be lying on a blanket before she was killed? Did the killer force her onto it before shooting her?" Lancaster hesitated. He walked across the room and opened the front door, looked out and then came back to the fireplace.

"Her limbs were bent into a certain position as if she was posing. It must have been enormously difficult to wedge the dead woman's arm under her cheek, but the killer managed it. So here we have, if you can hold the image, a naked woman definitely dead, reclining on a blanket, her cheek resting on her left hand and her right arm thrown forward across her left arm. At first we played around with the idea that it was some quirky kind of crime by a lunatic who came across the open windows, saw Clare, and on the off chance crept into the house and murdered her for the hell of it. There are plenty of madmen about these days who do just that."

Here it comes, thought Crown, folding his yellow paper in half, right on the button.

"But in our business we dislike the use of that word. All people who behave strangely are not insane," Lancaster emphasised.

The women in the room visibly shuddered.

"And now we come to the string of pearls hanging around Clare's throat. The string had been cut, sliced in two."
He waited to see if there was any response. But there was only a fragile silence.

"After weeks of checking to see if there were any mentally disturbed mortals living in the area we couldn't come up with anything. Then my sergeant said that as crazy as the idea seemed, the murder scene reminded him of something he'd seen before. He said it reminded him of a scene in a play, or a painting. Of course I thought he'd had too many late nights working on the case, but the more I thought about it, the more I had a feeling he was right. The murderer of course would have to bone up a bit on anatomy, the library and the internet being easily available. Everything you want to know about murder is available these days unfortunately. Also everything you want to know about medicine. I don't go for the internet myself, personally I prefer the library."

He didn't continue. He let the sentence hang in the air.

Steven sank deeper into his chair. He clenched his fists. The doctor was casting Lancaster anxious looks. He was pondering if he should give Steven another shot of the tranquilliser he had brought with him. He glanced towards his bag.

"You see," continued Lancaster, "the odd thing was the pearls. They were scattered all round her head, all sticky with blood of course, and looking like red beads."

Betty Gordon turned away.

In the stillness Lancaster went to the front door again, opened it and peered outside as if expecting someone. Crown shifted toward the window, giving Lancaster a querulous look.

"It was then," Lancaster nodded, smiling like an actor taking a bow, "that I realised I was looking at the wrong clue. It wasn't the clue the murderer wanted me to find."

"What wrong clue, what wrong clue?" Frank asked, panic stricken.

"Why, the pearls, Mr Gordon, the pearls. You see the pearls reminded me of some lines from a play I'd seen recently with my sergeant here, *The Duchess of Malfi.* I'm sure you all know it."

Old devil, thought Crown. How would they know that play? He'd made the mistake of underestimating suspects before this.

"Now let's see, what was it? Ah yes, a few lines spoken by the Duchess." He lifted his head to speak. Lancaster could always be relied upon to remember a line.

"What would it pleasure me to have my throat cut with diamonds? Or to be smothered with cassia? Or to be shot to death with pearls?"

A cold wind flashed down the chimney making the logs blaze into sparks. He darted towards Steven and suddenly exclaimed, "Mr Ross, do you have any idea where your wife is? I told her exactly what time to be here so as not to keep you up too late."

"Why, I don't know. She never mentioned coming here to me when she visited this morning." Steven breathed deeply, holding his chest.

The doctor became concerned. He opened his bag and

brought out a small phial and a needle for an injection. He proceeded to fill the needle with the liquid.

"Now Mr Ross, I'll ease the pain for you."

Lancaster turned away as the doctor rubbed Steven's skinny arm with cotton wool and spirit and then injected the serum. He busied himself with going back and forth to the front door. There was the faint hum of a car.

"Ah! Here she is at last, if I'm not mistaken." Lancaster said. Everyone looked towards the door. Who could he be waiting for?

Then the door was thrust wide open and Joan Ross strode into the room. She was wearing a long black coat and black boots. Her hair was tied back in a bow and was wet with the rain.

"Ah, Mrs Ross, I knew you wouldn't let us down."

Lancaster gave one of his twisted smiles.

Joan Ross strode across the room. "Hello Steven," she said. "I'll find myself a chair. I didn't expect to see you out of hospital so soon."

Steven looked up at Joan with tired eyes. "Joan you know the doctor said I could come here tonight."

"Of course he did," she replied not looking at him. "I had to leave the fashion group early. It was very difficult." She sat down and crossed her legs, loosening her boots.

"I was speaking about clues Mrs Ross. I was explaining to these people how I came to the right conclusion about Clare but had the wrong clue."

"Ah, the murders. You will no doubt let us know about your conclusions I'm sure." Her cold retort was in keeping with her usual off-hand manner.

"I had some vague misgivings you see." He was looking directly at her. "But you'd be surprised what springs to mind when you see a corpse. Clare shot to death with a string of pearls hanging around her neck. The string had been sliced through. Yes I must admit you can get quite fanciful when you come across a naked body with just a string of pearls hanging round its neck. A beautiful neck, attached to a very beautiful body."

He looked towards Steven to see if he was more comfortable.

"So we have a body which has been set in a pose with a sliced string of pearls round its neck. Indeed the more I thought about it, the more I felt Crown was right. Crown imagined it was a pose from a painting. Of course we both knew the painting but for the life of us we couldn't remember what the painting was. In the back of my mind I could see a figure with a bow in her hair. But it wasn't a bow, it was a flower."

They all held their breath.

"A flower?" someone asked.

"Yes the woman in the painting had a flower in her hair and was lying on a yellow cushion."

He stopped and watched their faces. There was fear on every one of them.

"I have Sergeant Crown to thank for the discovery of the real answer. We found the woman in question, painted in a serene and voluptuous pose, with a flower in her hair and her head on a yellow cushion."

The light in the room began to diminish. It grew darker.

"But what....?" asked Belinda.

"Ah you want to know the answer to the puzzle Mrs Austin?" Belinda blanched. "Simple really. It turned out to be a painting by Gaugin. He painted a native woman lying on her side, with a bow in her hair and her elbow on a cushion. Now who hasn't seen that painting at one time or another? Not many I assure you. Put on another lamp, there's a good man," Lancaster said to Frank Gordon.

The click of the lamp going on made Crown jump. He would never get used to Lancaster's little hesitations, his sudden deviations. He remembered a case when Lancaster closed a pair of curtains with such emphasis that the screech of the curtains going across the curtain pole made the suspect let out a cry. When was that? The year before last maybe.   The light of the lamp lit up the furthest corner of the room. He could see Betty backing away from the others.

"Yes," Lancaster was enjoying this. "Of course the painting had a title."

They were all mesmerised.

"The title of the painting was *Nevermore*," he said quietly. Steven had to lift his head forward to hear him. They appeared to be bewildered.

"*Nevermore?* What does it mean *Nevermore?*" asked Penny.

"I will tell you what it means, because that was the first clue to this whole business," Lancaster said. "The solitary word *Nevermore* was written at the top left hand side of the painting and there was a raven painting in the top centre of the painting. Did Gaugin mean Edgar Allen Poe's *Quoth the Raven, Nevermore* I wonder? Or did he mean he would see England nevermore? But whatever the reason, unfortunately for Clare Austin, she would be seen nevermore. Have you put a cross on your list next to Clare Austin's name Crown? Our first murder."

Crown assented swiftly. Sabina had a stricken look on her face.

"And then of course came the second murder, about three months or so after the first. A member of he same family had been disposed of. Why would anyone possibly want to murder Clare Austin's brother-in-law? Of course the clue for the second murder was utterly brilliant. Couldn't have thought of it myself, considering I've seen a lot of movies. Clever and unscrupulous."

Lancaster took his mobile out of his pocket and placed it on th sideboard.

"The killer turned us inside out with the second murder. We received a frantic call from a Sister Bates in the General Hospital. She was in a dreadful state. It transpired that one of her patients had died. Not an unusual happening in a hospital of course, but when we met Sister Bates she told us that her patient had been interfered with deliberately. All his tubes and blood transfusions and medications had been roughly pulled out of him and he was left to die. Someone had intentionally ripped out all the man's lifelines. The drip that had been hanging on a long metal stand had been dashed to the floor, electrodes on the chest connected to the heart monitoring machine were torn off with the plaster, the catheter for the urine was removed along with anything else they had popped inside him. I don't need to describe the scene. I leave it to your imagination."

He paused and lit a cigarette. He hoped this distraction would have its desired effect. He liked to see a bit of horror and incredulity appear on the faces of his suspects. And he was damn sure in this family they were all his suspects.

"My God," cried Frank. His face had taken on a look of horror.

"Those were the exact words Sergeant Crown and I said when we first saw the patient. It was like a scene from a horror movie, a dead man on a bed minus his life-giving medications. Somehow the murderer had managed to get into a room in a private wing of a hospital which was constantly being monitored by nurses and doctors. And by Sister Bates, who lets nothing past her eyes. And this someone, our killer, managed to murder Mr Edward Austin."

He suddenly turned to Betty Gordon. Her face was twisted with terror.

"Ah Betty, I wonder if you would be so kind as to rustle up

some sandwiches. I'm sure our little family here are hungry. It is getting rather late."

"This looks like it will be a long evening." It was Joan Ross. "I must leave. I have clients tomorrow."

"No one can leave Mrs Ross. Not you, nor anyone else." Crown raised his voice. He could see that Betty had clearly lost control. Maybe it had been wise of Lancaster to give her something else to do. She wasn't the kind of woman who could manage to keep calm while all these descriptions of murder were being bandied about.

"I think," Betty cried out impulsively, "if you don't mind Inspector, that is exactly what I would like to do, make some sandwiches. It is past our dinner time, we eat early on a Sunday and I know you must all be hungry."

She was clearly desperate to leave the room. Crown wondered if there was something else that was making her look so deathly. In the kitchen she hurriedly wet a tissue and placed it over her eyes. Her head was spinning and she felt a sickness in her stomach when she thought of Edward Austin. Gaining a little composure, she found a loaf she had bought yesterday. She couldn't stop her hands from shaking. She must get a grip or else she would cut herself badly with the bread knife. She opened and closed cupboards, finding the tea cups and saucers. Sitting on the kitchen stool she ran her wrists under cold water and then she reached for a bottle of valium which she kept hidden behind the flour bag since the night of the accident. Heaven knows how many she had swallowed since then. Sometimes she thought she would pass out. She could hear Lancaster's voice rising and falling, rising and falling, full of innuendo and accusation. Were they all guilty? Was she living amongst murderers?

"As I'm sure you know Edward Austin was quite an expert on drugs in his little pharmacy. Clever man in his field, instantly dislikeable but you get all sorts. Brainy ones are usually the worst. He was very capable and also up to the minute on every new drug on the market. Quite invaluable to the community I'm sure."

He hesitated and moved once more round the room.

"Edward had to be murdered to fit in with the next clue, and not an easy clue to fit to a murder, quite the other way round. I should have remembered at that point that most murders are totally irrational."

"It's revolting," Penny cried out. "I don't believe a word of it."

Lancaster drew a breath. "But you will Madam, you will,"

he retorted, "I assure you it's all quite believable." He began to think of the film *Les Diaboliques,* what a plan that was. Still this should compare very well. He continued.

"And that clue needed Edward's dead body in yet another pose which would challenge us even further. Edward was much more of a problem than Clare. Edward was either at the pharmacy, with one of his doctor friends or at home with his wife. It would be virtually impossible to get him when he was alone. So the killer had to isolate him. But how? The killer had to get Edward on his own. He couldn't very well lean over the counter in the pharmacy and stab him. He couldn't very well invite him out to lunch without someone noticing and he couldn't push him off a building. But if somehow or other he could get close enough to infect him with something or make him sick enough to be taken to hospital, that would be the answer. If Edward was ill enough to be in hospital, there would certainly be a time during the day when he would be on his own. The killer now had to get a part-time job in a hospital where there is access to drugs and possibly access to something that would put Edward to sleep forever."

He sounded like a bloody medical lecturer thought Crown. A sound of cups and saucers clattering came from the kitchen.

"So the killer found himself a job in the nearest hospital and waited to strike. Either he would steal some drugs and kill Edward or find another way. But luck is now the major part in this murder." Lancaster looked up at the ceiling as if to find inspiration there.

"The killer passes himself off as a cleaner for a few days a week and bides his time. Then one day, by chance, he overhears some doctors discussing a patient. And what does the patient have but hepatitis A. These chance remarks spelt doom for Edward. Here was the killer discovering a unique way to do away with Edward. But how to get Edward in contact with the patient? He now proceeds to find a way of checking the records to find out where the patient lives. It transpires the sick man lives in Chiltern Street, is single and has live in help."

Here he paused as Betty Gordon was bringing in a tray of tea and a plate of sandwiches. His audience was straining to hear him finish the story.

"I shall carry on while you enjoy your sandwiches," he said. "Can't afford to waste time. The murderer now seized his opportunity. He now knows the patient's address and goes up to town to look the place over. The need to murder Edward was so strong, and the reasoning so fierce, that even the threat of being in contact with an illness like that would never stop the him. But the killer was cleverer than that. Why should he take any chances himself? He certainly wouldn't go near the place."

Crown saw the effect of Lancaster's words on the people round him. Only one of them had taken up a sandwich. The others hadn't moved. Crown felt he could touch the warm air that the small group had breathed out. The appearance of Belinda and her sister had truly surprised him and these days nothing much surprised him.

Lancaster took out a cigarette and lit it. The sudden sound of the striking match made Belinda Austin draw back.

"So," Lancaster went on. "We come to the remarkable scene of the planning of the death of Edward Austin. The murderer had to act quickly, for at any moment he knew the patient was going to be moved to an isolation wing in the nearest hospital. It then became necessary to find someone he could trust to continue his plan of action. All he needed was someone to make a phone call, someone to do a little bit of acting. But who? Now here Crown and I had to do a bit of guesswork. We knew it couldn't possibly be a stranger." Lancaster creased his eyes into slits as he stared around him. "So the murderer had to confide in someone very close, very close indeed. He convinced this accomplice that all he needed to do was play a part. And that part would be totally unseen, so the accomplice need have no fear he would be discovered. All that was necessary for the accomplice to do was make a phone call. Of course the accomplice agrees. The accomplice is told exactly what to say on the phone and what time to ring Edward. It all works brilliantly. The phone rings at Edward's house during dinner and Edward's wife Penny answers it. She tells Edward there is a doctor on the line who wishes to speak to him. Of course Edward rushes to speak to the doctor. The accomplice informs Edward that he is a doctor at Eastwood General by the name of Doctor Allbright. He has been recommended to Edward and wishes to meet him. There are numerous items he would like to order from Edward's pharmacy. He is treating a patient at his flat in the West End and may require something special."

Lancaster hesitated and picked up a cheese sandwich. All eyes were on him. Were they still eating cheese sandwiches like this in England? Plain cheddar cheese on white bread? He took a bite but decided to leave it on the plate.

"All accomplished very easily when you come to think of it. As we all know Edward was a bit of an opportunist. All he needed to hear was a doctor's voice telling him he had been recommended

265

to Edward's pharmacy. An opportunity has arrived and he must take it. He quickly scribbles down the address of Doctor Allbright and rushes to tell his wife he has to leave as he's arranged to meet the doctor in two hours time in the West End. And away he goes. And so the trap was sprung. Austin leaves the house, drives up to London with the address and finds Chiltern Street. He looks for Burberry Mansions, parks his car and looks for the bellplate with the name of Doctor M. Allbright. Sure enough there it is at number 14. He presses the bell, gives his name to the maid and is let in. I very much doubt tee maid knew what was wrong with her employer, she probably thought it was influenza or a virus. Once inside the flat he finds Doctor Allbright is absent. He asks where the doctor is, and in response he is handed a note from the doctor saying he has been called away to an urgent case and apologises for his absence. He will phone Edward tomorrow and arrange another meeting. And that is when Edward makes his fatal mistake. His curiosity gets the better of him and he decides to go in and look at the patient. He may have touched him, I dare say he did. I'm told by a specialist in these matters that certain people can be in contact with serious diseases and not necessarily catch them. Unfortunately for Edward he was not immune and he contracted hepatitis. One could call it murder by distance."

Crown wondered if he should scribble that down. Murder by distance.

All that could be heard in the darkening room were the chinks of cups on saucers.

"It's too preposterous," cried Steven Ross. In calling out he had over exerted himself and clutched his side again. His head fell back onto the chair and he grimaced in pain.

"I hope this will soon be over Inspector," Doctor Berkowitz said. "My patient needs to be back in the hospital."

"Oh it won't take much longer Doctor, I assure you." Lancaster confirmed. "As a doctor you'll agree it's amazing what the human mind can dream up. You see when the mind houses two personalities there's always a conflict, a battle. In the murderer's case the battle is over and the dominant personality has won."

Lancaster looked at Crown out of the corner of his eye. Two personalities Crown was thinking? That wasn't Lancaster. He never mumbled on about split personalities. To Lancaster, killers were killers and you nailed them to the wall. Where had he got this business of dominant personalities from? He frowned.It was definitely a movie. Crown wrote down *dominant personality.* Was Doctor Allbright the killer? He scribbled a name in his first column under murder. It had to be Hitchcock.

Lancaster held his audience spellbound.

"So after his remarkable visit, and finding the doctor he was supposed to meet had vanished into the night, Edward begins to wonder just who recommended him to the doctor. After a lot of phone calls to various hospitals and clinics, he finds out that no one has ever heard of a Doctor Allbright, let alone worked with him. It was then he must have decided to visit his friend Doctor Grant to enquire if he knew anything of the vanishing doctor.

He waited for Grant in the hospital canteen and passed the time with a cup of tea while his friend finished an operation. He is next seen staggering along the hospital corridor where he collapses near the nurses' desk. He is immediately examined by medical staff and then taken to a room upstairs in the private wing under the care of Sister Bates."

The family in Betty Gordon's small cottage room sat open mouthed.

"And it was in the private wing of the hospital that Edward was murdered," Lancaster exclaimed. "Of course he probably would have died anyway, but the killer had to get him first. He had to be murdered, and he had to know he was being murdered, and revenge is sweet."

"Why it's evil!" exclaimed Frank.

Lancaster cleared his throat. "Oh I agree, it's all very distasteful. Now the killer had to leave us a clue, and it was a damned clever one. With a hell of a lot of good fortune on the murderer's side, he slipped inside the hospital room, pulled the curtain back, swiftly pulled out every one of the tubes that were inserted into Edward Austin, drips, heart monitoring tubes, urine tube and all the other paraphernalia. He lets Edward get a good look at him, then quickly places a large tin box on the bedside table. He then disconnects Edward's bell to make sure he couldn't call for help."

Lancaster waited, giving the audience time to assemble the scene in their minds.

"I am sure you can see it most clearly. There was Edward Austin, definitely dead, lying on the bed facing the door, one arm thrown out towards us. And the open tin box on the table, the window slightly open and the curtains blowing in a faint breeze. The pin was found later, thrown underneath a chair. Rather careless that, but it was all done in a great hurry. Supposing one of the nurses came in? The killer would have had to rush out pushing the nurse aside. No, it had to be done swiftly so the killer could get away. There was absolutely no way for Edward Austin to call for help. Of course you can imagine Sister Bates' horror when she found Austin's door closed, after she had given strict orders to the nurses to look in as often as possible. In fact she had placed a chair at the door to make sure it was kept open. We should have more of her type on wards these days. Bring back thee Matrons. With the end of the Matron everything in hospital has gone to pot. Being of the same family as Matron, Sister Bates was incensed. How dare anyone disobey her orders and close the door? She would find the culprit and she was for it. Somehow or other the killer managed to get onto the ward without detection and without the knowledge of Sister Bates."

Here Lancaster came over to Crown and took his notebook.

"Cross off Edward Austin, there's a good man," Lancaster said, raising his eyebrows.

"Oh dear, I neglected to tell you the reason the murderer left the open tin box on the bedside table. You see that had us baffled alright."

Sabina Franklin suddenly spoke. "Inspector it's too horrible to imagine."

"You are right Miss Franklin. Life is divided into the horrible and the miserable." He turned to look at her. "Have you ever read many horror stories? In case you're thinking of buying a book, I am sure you will find this more enthralling than any book you could find on the shelves at Hatchard's. It struck us some time afterwards that with Edward Austin's murder we could be looking at another painting."

"Another painting?" Steven cried out.

"But which one? What did it remind me of? What was Edward's death telling us? Crown and I went down to the old-fashioned local library. I can't bear sitting at those damned computers. After we had every single art book off the shelves we finally found it."

Betty Gordon cried out, "I don't believe any of this. Why, you're trying to frighten us with this painting nonsense." She began to cry. "Paintings of dead people, I've never heard of such a thing." She wiped her eyes on her apron.

"Mrs Gordon please, I'm not trying to frighten you. I am telling you the facts in this case."

He stopped speaking and again moved across the room and looked out of the window. Crown felt uneasy. He hated it when Lancaster paced about from place to place. He was reminded of listening to a ghost story as a child. His father read to him every night at bedtime and would never finish a story to keep him in suspense until the next night. If it was a mystery Crown was so frightened he had to keep the light on and the door open all night. In fact he still kept his bedroom door open. And now he was working on murder cases and looking at dead bodies. Life was crazy.

"In the end the trousers did it!" exclaimed Lancaster.

"Trousers?" Trevor whispered. "What trousers?"

"The trousers you see. I remembered the blue trousers."

Crown's voice came from a corner of the room making them all jump.

"It was *The Death of Chatterton* "

It had the desired effect.

The fire crackled.

"*The Death of Chatterton?*" Belinda exclaimed. "Who the hell was Chatterton?"

"I'm just coming to that Mrs Austin. It is a painting I had seen as a boy. Crown and I went to a source of great information, a certain Mr Parker at the Wallace. And what a story we found. You see Chatterton was a poet. He composed some works called *The Rowley Poems*. What he actually did was to compose his own poems, using 15th century vocabulary, on old pieces of manuscript paper which somehow or other he managed to get hold of. He cut the old manuscript paper into pieces and wrote his poems onto them. Then of course he needed to earn some money from his poems, so he sent them to Walpole whom he hoped would have them published. But then Walpole found out they were not genuine poems and returned them. Of course they were genuine poems in their own way, just copied and written in a new and modern style. Now Chatterton is recognised as a genius, like most artists who starved. Particularly Van Gogh."

Lancaster thought this was the right place to pause. They would now be thinking of Clare.

"It appears Chatterton was very unlucky. He couldn't sell his poems to anyone in London, so, nearly starving, he poisoned himself. Dreadful business really. A mere boy of seventeen to kill himself. Yes, God only knows why he resorted to that, it was tragic."

Lancaster stared into the fire. He smiled as he looked at the faces round him and began to hum. He bent over th wood logs and laid one of them across the dying fire. Then he went to the sideboard and picked up his mobile, slipping it back into his pocket.

"Yes we were sure the open tin box was where he kept the pieces of manuscript. But for the life of us we couldn't work out the clue."

He seemed to be asking his rapt audience to help him. No one dared to reply.

"So we went through it all again. First we thought the clue might be *Poet*. But then we realised that didn't tell us anything. *Nevermore Poet*. No poets here tonight? Unless they're good at writing memorials."

Lancaster liked to think of himself as quite inspired on this windy and dreary evening.

Steven gasped, "Memorials! What are you getting at Lancaster?"

"Getting at? Oh we're not getting at anything Mr Ross, we have got there. My partner and I had an inspiration. The clue wasn't *Poet* at all, it was *Forger*. That's what the killer was trying to tell us. He was telling us to take the word *Forger* and put it with *Nevermore*. And then you have *Never more forger,* which to my mind means never more will you do any damage Edward Austin. You are on the night train to the big adios."

Lancaster thought that was a perfect quote to wind up the end of Edward Austin. He could hear Penny's breath gurgling in her throat.

"So now we had *Nevermore* and *Forger*, pretty exciting stuff. That was when we started sniffing around. We found out that in your parents' will not a penny was left to the vanishing brother or the step-children whom everyone seems so fond of. Have I mentioned the brother who has disappeared into the *Lost Horizon?*" He gave another bleak little smile that seemed to crease his face sideways.

"*Lost Horizon,*" Crown repeated. Where the hell did he find that one? He knew he'd never get it. Maybe this time even Eric wouldn't. Crown had to admit it was a perfect Lancaster. He wasn't too sure about horrible and miserable, which was what he was feeling right now.

"Sabina Franklin had mentioned a brother to us during our little visit to Venice, after the attempted poisoning of Belinda." He looked around the room. "We never knew that there was another brother in the family. One that no one ever mentioned and one that we certainly didn't know existed. And that brother happened to have been married to Sabina. Oh it was years ago of course. The marriage was a dismal failure, which sounds much like the other Austin marriages from what I gather. Still marriage isn't my business, murder is. So they divorced and went their separate ways."

There was utter silence.

"So I had to ask myself what if the mysterious brother had

been murdered as well? The will was so cleverly forged that no one except the Austins got a penny. Frank and Betty Gordon, Joan and Steven Ross and the missing brother and his family all got zilch."

"This isn't true," Penny shouted. "It's a lie, all this talk about forgery."

"Oh it is not a lie I assure you. Your Mother-in-law's will was changed over. It was changed in the simplest way imaginable. When she became ill, the brothers, seeing there was plenty of money about, weren't too keen on sharing it with their beloved relatives, the ones they always had their arms around in family snapshots."

He thought of that rotten bastard Prince. He wondered if Prince knew it all along.Could he possibly have gotten something out of it? He doubted even Prince would sink that low. He would think about it tomorrow.

Trevor hadn't spoken at all

"I notice you haven't said anything Trevor." Lancaster cast his eyes on Trevor Austin.

"Yes, an extra few bob for Edward, Charles and Trevor Austin. Of course the wives turned a blind eye. Not so hot at being all girls together, are you girls?

No feminist agenda here. No fair deal for Joan or Frank or the invisible brother. Forgery is against the law but my trouble is that the will wasn't actually forged. It was merely replaced by a different will, probably obtained at Smith's, where you can buy a do-it-yourself will these days. Your Mother Trevor was asked to sign it. Simple."

The Bomber was having a good night.

"What?" came from Trevor.

"Certainly," Crown said. It was all he could manage.

Sabina Franklin took Belinda's hand, fearful of hearing the next words lancaster would say.

"I haven't quite decided if Belinda knew about the will or not. As I said there wasn't much all girls together in this family and Belinda always kept herself to herself from what I gather. The rearrangement of the will Belinda, what have you got to say about it?"

"I had no idea," Belinda whispered, "truly. I couldn't bear Charles but I never thought he would stoop so low."

"But," Penny spoke.

"Oh I shouldn't say anything Penny, if I may call you that." Lancaster smiled. "You could even find yourself in deep water. Believe me I'll think of something to nail you."

"It's some sort of jumbled up nonsense you've invented," Betty cried out. Frank sat still as a statue.

"Come to think of it, perhaps dear old Prince may get you all off and plead diminished responsibility. But we haven't gone down that road yet. As I said my priority is murder. Crown have you crossed off Edward Austin? So then we come to Charles Austin."

"Charles, what about Charles?" Belinda cried.

"Oh but my dear, didn't you know? He's definitely dead."

Lancaster watched her eyes, She was blinking rapidly. She was trying to gain composure.

"But he can't be," she whispered.

"Mrs Austin, you are not listening to what I'm saying. Life moves pretty fast. If you don't stop and look around once in a while, you could miss it."

He peered into her face.

"Your husband Mrs Austin is dead. You have not looked around while you were on the Zattere in Venice. You have not looked around before you were poisoned because you were too busy looking into the eyes of *The Saint.*"

Lancaster thumped his hand on the mantlepiece.

Belinda jumped up. "You're a liar, a madman. Charles can't be dead. You're trying to pin this on me. Why should he be dead? I'm leaving, I need a solicitor."

Crown thought they were all beginning to talk like in the movies. Pin this on me. Who did she think she was? An actress in a B film?

"You'll need a lot more than a solicitor Belinda," Lancaster intimated.

Crown was thinking about life moving pretty fast.

"So now we'll discuss the third murder, that of Charles Austin."

There was a gasp from Steven. "There must be some mistake," he said. "He can't have been murdered."

"Why do you say that Mr Ross? Oh no, no mistake. When Crown and I were called to the road accident, we realised we were informed about it by someone who saw it take place. Someone got hold of my mobile number. Bad habit of mine leaving my mobile lying around. I've just left it on Mrs Gordon's sideboard as you no doubt noticed."

He looked at Betty Gordon.

"A mysterious unnamed stranger wanted me to go to a certain turning where she was absolutely certain she had seen an accident. That mysterious stranger was scared out of her wits and wanted me to know it. That someone was you Betty."

Betty twisted her hands together. "No, no, it wasn't me at

all." she cried.

"You were fortunate to find my number taped on the back of my mobile, never can remember that damn long number. Rather a stupid thing for a policeman to do. But we all have our little foibles."

Frank moved towards Betty, his eyes blazing. His look to Betty made her cringe.

Crown spoke. "I wouldn't try anything Mr Gordon. We've suffered enough of your threatening behaviour. If you touch her you'll be arrested. It's as simple as that." He watched as Betty moved away from Frank in fear. So she was the one who phoned the station.

Inspector Lancaster continued. "You see when Crown and I arrived at the scene there was no victim. Just the boys in blue standing by the roadside on a cold winter's night. Or was it morning Crown? No matter. I've never been to an accident without a victim but still there's a first time for everything. We noticed tyre marks in the road, tyre marks that seemed to indicate two cars had skidded across the centre of the road. Something had happened there, but what? Crown and I were baffled. There wasn't a soul about, no one, dead or alive. It appeared to be a case of my mystery telephone caller's imagination. No one was killed and there was no corpse. So just who skidded across the road? And why drag the police into it? People skid, they manage to turn around and carry on driving without getting help. It had been a wet night after all."

Lancaster still seemed to be thinking. He looked towards Betty Gordon.

"Had the victim been badly injured? Maybe that was what the onlooker saw. But of course there was no one there. So we deduced the onlooker couldn't possibly have been on foot. Not on a cold night like that. No, the onlooker must have been driving himself or travelling with someone else in a car." He mused for a moment. "Only one is a wanderer, two together are always going somewhere."

His eyes moved around the room.Christ, Crown thought, the old bastard. *Vertigo*, he hadn't sat through that film a dozen times for nothing. His head would begin to clear now. He could think more sensibly. He only had two movies to sort out. He watched Betty Gordon with rapt attention. She was holding tightly onto the arms of her chair. He wrote *Vertigo* in the second column.

"I wondered where the mysterious traveller was going. So we had to rethink the whole case. We had to go over every file since Clare Austin was murdered. That took some time I can tell you. We knew we had visited every last one of your family. Every one. So who had we missed out? We realised we had to go further down the family tree, seek out some of the family we had never met and try to find the invisible brother. That was when we discovered we had overlooked an invisible sister. Oh she was dead some twenty or more years but she was your sister Belinda and we hadn't checked it out. You see what puzzled us was the fact that your sister was dead yet some of the family mentioned that you often visited her."

He waited, emphasising his point. He could see Sabina Franklin holding Belinda back.

"That was a bad mistake on our part. It took weeks before we got back on the right track. So we decided to see just where your sister lived Mrs Austin. We found out that when she died her house was never sold. It was left to her husband and the son she adopted, your nephew."

"Oh Sabina," Belinda said, "none of it matters now. Kate died so long ago. No one even knows I had a sister. I used the house as an excuse to get away from Charles. I used to go away for the weekend and say I was at my sister's.I used it as an excuse to meet Simon. I'm ashamed." She pursed her lips. She was mortified to have her life revealed in front of these people.

"Quite so," said Lancaster. "Then Crown suggested out of nowhere that we take a ride out to see Kate's old house. We found out where she lived from records and hoped we could find some identification there that might help us find the missing nephew. It was a whim really. We guessed that whoever lived there wouldn't know a damn thing about a woman who lived there nearly thirty years ago. We had gone up every avenue we could and we were desperate. We drove out there because we had nothing else on our list to check except that we'd found out about a mysterious brother and we wanted to know where he was. Carry on Crown, tell them what we found."

- **45** -

Steven looked terrified. He bent forward so as not to miss a word. "Please no," he croaked.

"We went to the house. It was at River End, not far from here. Apparently it was rented out for years and the rent given to your sister's son. Funny the things you decide to do for no reason whatsoever, as he said it was just a whim. When we arrived we saw the house was dilapidated. The garden was overgrown and the place was derelict. Some of the windows were broken. We couldn't open the front door so we had to get in through a window. There was filth everywhere and the place looked like a building site. The kitchen sink was piled up with dirty dishes, there were old newspapers and magazines lying about, empty milk cartons and dirty clothes on the kitchen chair. You'd think squatters had taken over. Of course we could see no one had lived there for a very long time, We checked on this later and found that bills, like water rates, were regularly paid. Only they didn't use much water. No, this place was for renting out. Why anyone could rent that place out is a mystery I can't solve."

The faint rustle of the page turning in Crown's notebook was the only sound in the room.

"Of course as soon as we were inside we had to hold handkerchiefs over our noses. There was a terrible stench in the place. We investigated the property and eventually located the source of the stench. It was a dead body."

He waited to see what effect that revelation would have on all of them. Steven turned as white as ashes.

"The body was definitely dead." said Lancaster. "But it was trussed up like a turkey dinner. The hands had been taped to the ears, parcel tape as well, hard to remove. And the mouth was taped open into an O. One could say he was bent as round as a human body could be, short of breaking any bones that is. Charles Austin was taped into a circle as near as damn it."

Sabina took a handkerchief from her bag and held it to her mouth.

"Have you crossed Charles Austin off the list Crown?" Lancaster suddenly asked.

"Just about to sir." Another bomb.

"Definitely dead," said Lancaster.

"No, no" It was Steven Ross. "It can't be."

home Joan was upstairs in the bath. She hadn't noticed I was missing."

His narrative was short and to the point Crown decided. He went on scribbling in his notepad.

Joan's expression was furious.

"Why you meddling bastard," she screamed. "How dare you follow me about. What right have you got? I'm a free individual. Just because I married you doesn't give you the right to know where I am all day and night. After this I'm leaving you. I've always found you unbearable and now I don't need a reason. You're on your own Steven."

Inspector Lancaster found Joan's words very forthright. In fact he envied her being able to get to the point without any preamble. She said what needed saying, a remarkable woman. She moved over to the fireplace out of Steven's way.

"Joan please," Steven whimpered like a kicked dog. "I'm sorry. I was concerned for you. I thought there was something wrong. You always used to tell me everything."

"You are detestable," Joan bellowed. "How could you follow me when you're always grumbling if I ask you to go for a walk? Either it's raining or damp or windy. God knows. You always prefer to walk around the woods on your own. Just what do you do on all those long walks Steven, that's what I'd like to know? Maybe you can tell us now we're all together and so cosy. Not only do I run a business to keep you in cigars, but you don't trust me on my own. We're finished Steven. Inspector please give me one of your cigarettes."

"Mrs Ross you amaze me," said Lancaster, laughing. She was the sort of woman he might have been interested in at one time, full of fire and confidence. How did she ever marry Steven Ross? Such a quiet contented sort of man, with no aspirations. Lancaster was always asking himself that same question about most people.People who were so different from each other. Was it because it was time to get married? Did they all fall in love? He'd given up trying to work it out.

"So that is the answer to your little visit to the house in River End, eh Mrs Ross? A client was meeting you?"

She stood back from Crown and lit the cigarette and felt the smoke go to the back of her throat.

"Of course. It's none of Steven's business where I go." She went on, taking a deep drag on her cigarette. "Of course I go to see clients. I'm not to know where these damn people live. I sell clothes for a living. Sometimes people want me to take whole wardrobes to them, film stars, pop stars, those sort of people."

"Fancy that," observed Lancaster. "So you don't mind going out to these places in the dead of night? You're not nervous? Especially when you go into a house that is like a pig sty and the place smells to high heaven and there are no lights on. My sergeant and I couldn't even manage to see our hands in front of our faces without a torch."

He stopped for a moment, wondering how to phrase his next sentence.

"And when we do get in there we find a dead man clutching an order for two navy blue suits. The only trouble was he couldn't tell you what material he wanted. Come on Mrs Ross, what the hell is going on?"

Joan Ross was startled for the moment.

"I can't say," she breathed. "I didn't see anyone. I was given the address and I went there. Someone phoned me back and told me to meet them at nine thirty. No one answered the door so I walked round the back. After waiting a while I decided to go home. Whoever it was could contact me another time."

"And you never mentioned any of this to your husband Mrs Ross?" Crown interrupted. "I would have thought you were slightly disturbed, finding no one about. So disturbed that you might have mentioned something."

"I told you before, I don't tell Steven everything."

She looked at Crown with contempt. Betty's eyes were wide open in disbelief. Whatever was going on here was bad. Terribly bad, so bad that she wanted to run upstairs and hide.

Lancaster was very careful how he approached the next question.

"So you never tell your husband where you go and what you do, eh Mrs Ross? Oh don't worry, my sergeant here has it all written down. Steven did follow you, as we've already learned. A very protective man, your husband, he speaks the truth and nothing but the truth. He'd make a very good defence counsel."

He went over to Steven. "Mr Ross," he continued, "you're not much of a story teller. Of course you went inside, probably by climbing in through a window. You discovered a dead man and you did nothing about it. You'll do anything in your power too protect your wife, won't you? I hope you haven't forgotten that withholding evidence is crime Mr Ross."

"There was no dead man! Just a terrible smell. I went in through the kitchen window, it was left open. I just about managed it. But the smell was so terrible. I left through the back door and rushed away."

He unbuttoned his jacket, loosened his tie and opened the top, placing his hand near his wound.

"And yet Mr Ross, there is something else you will learn which is even more disturbing about this case. It's something as vengeful as murder. It's about the destruction of love. By the way Crown, make sure you have crossed Charles Austin off your list."

- 46 -

"This is what I wish to speak about now." Lancaster waited. "About love."

Lancaster remembered a song the jazz singer used to sing at gigs. What was it now, something about *Love you didn't do right by me*. He took out a cigarette and put it between his lips.

"Where was I? Ah yes, I'm up to love."

"I......" He could hear Belinda's faltering voice.

"Oh I wouldn't say anything Belinda Austin, before I tell you what I imagine happened on the evening of Clare's murder. I know all about your problem with love. And the hurdle for you was that you needed to go to Clare's party and you needed to go there because you were desperate. But your husband, whom I learned later had a fearful argument with Trevor, had refused to go. That was the reason you had two invitations to the party. Usually guests are sent one invitation to a party but in your case there were two. Now why would there be two invitations in your house and everywhere else just one? Because you asked Clare to send another invitation because maybe if Charles was asked twice he would go. That way he would think Trevor really wanted to forget about their quarrel. And if Charles and Trevor made up, you could be at Clare's. And The reason for this was not out of the goodness of your heart, although your heart was involved in another respect. The reason was that was you had begged your lover to meet you a Clare's. And you were going to tell your lover you wanted to leave Charles. You wanted to leave Charles and marry your lover and go off and live happily ever after. Or else you decided to finish the affair. Furtive meetings were not what you wanted any more, you wanted a commitment. So I'm presuming your lover agreed to meet you at Clare's so you could both sort things out."

He pulled on his cuff links

"My lover? How dare you?" Belinda shouted, pulling away from her sister. "You're lying. You're trying to make it look as if I murdered Clare."

"Not at all Mrs Austin. We all know what love is like. It's so easy to become so besotted with someone that you can't think of anything else. Yes I've seen it all before."

The group before him shifted uneasily. They were hearing secrets, intimate ones they never suspected.

"But the irony of it is that these things didn't happen

279

because your lover didn't show up at the party. You must have gone in and out of the house looking for him time and time again. And when it was time to say goodbye he was nowhere in sight. Now you were in trouble. You had to use your mobile to phone him and you had no idea where he could be or why he let you down."

"No," Belinda said.

"You see no one liked anyone in this case. The Austin wives weren't so keen on their husbands, for one reason or another as so much is expected in marriage. You see everybody loves everybody when they're kissin', but when they're not we run into all kinds of problems."

He looked at Crown again. Crown had stopped writing. He was thinking kissin'. Kissin', what did he mean by that? Surely he meant kissing. But Lancaster rarely made grammatical errors.

"I know who your lover is of course Mrs Austin."

Belinda pressed her head against Sabina's chest.

"I found the details in your dressing gown pocket. Or do they call them house coats these days? You were telling the truth. I have the piece of paper here. But more of this love affair later. Right now I have to tell you all about the murder of Charles."

Crown felt stifled in the small room The air smelled smokey and the fire was spluttering.

"Yes," said Lancaster. "When we found Charles definitely dead and we had drawn breath and called in forensics, we knew that Charles Austin's death had to be giving us another of the murderer's clues, another word to go with *Nevermore* and *Forger*. But what could it possibly be?" He was in his stride now.

"And this time the answer came to me unbelievably quickly. I remembered what Trevor Austin had said about finding Steven. He told us Steven fell into his arms and gave a long piercing scream like a terrified animal. I even drew a few pictures of the murder victim tied up with string. And then I had the answer. I knew why the killer had turned Charles into a human ball of wool."

Betty cried, "It's evil."

"Of course it is Mrs Gordon," Lancaster said to her. "Murder is evil. But let us think of the previous victims. They were all laid out as paintings. Ergo Charles too must be a painting, and not a very happy one either."

Crown hoped they had seen the painting. It would give them all nightmares. Lancaster heavily emphasised his next words.

"Charles was *The Scream*, a painting by Munch. I'm sure you may know it. It shows the figure of a man standing alone on a bridge. His head is a skull and he's holding his hands over his ears.

Maybe a bridge to nowhere. It is a frightening psychological painting. I think we all have those feelings sometimes when we don't want to know or hear anymore."

Trevor was holding his head in his hands.. Here Lancaster paused.

"Now the killer has left us with another word and that word is *scream*. So now we have *Nevermore Forger Scream*. And it's not difficult really. It means nevermore will the Austins forge another document or screw people out of their inheritance, or do any of the other nasty little things they like doing. All that is left for them is to do is scream."

He looked into the fire and jabbed at it with the poker that lay on the hearth.

"And they will scream because rapidly the killer was doing his work. An interesting way of punishing Trevor without more ado was to kill Steven and have Trevor there on the night Steven would die. The police would put two and two together, and the two being Clare and Steven. It would be hard for Trevor to get out of that. It was becoming too much of a time consuming job, trying to match the right painting to fit the right murders."

Trevor was horrified. "What are you talking about? I need help. You can't believe I tried to kill Steven."

"I shouldn't worry Mr Austin. You won't need our help. I know who attempted to murder Steven Ross."

Lancaster held his hand to his lips as if he had suddenly forgotten something.

"Of course none of you know that Belinda was nearly murdered in Venice."

"In Venice?" Steven cried out.

"Yes, as I say it was touch and go. She had gone to stay with Sabina. Naturally in Venice one has to use the Vaporetto to go shopping and she took the Number One to go to Canareggio, a shopping area near the station. From what we found from the police, Belinda was found unconscious, having suddenly fainted in the Vaporetto. She fell into the lap of a fellow passenger. The passenger was a shopper who was terrified and tried to move Belinda back into her seat. But she saw Belinda was ill, asked for help and had the sense to call the police on her mobile phone. They were waiting at the next stop with an ambulance to take her to hospital. It was doubly fortunate for Belinda that a very clever doctor was in the hospital that day and, recognising the symptoms, he had her stomach pumped out. He saved her life. Of course Crown and I were informed of this and so in the middle of the case we had to go to Venice, where we met Miss Franklin. We were totally perplexed as to how Belinda could have been poisoned. Was it her sister who did it? Did she really love Belinda? We had to imagine all sorts of scenarios. The doctor thought the poison was in a meat dish of some kind. But how was it possible? When I spoke to Belinda before she left London she kept complaining of stomach cramps. I thought it was from nerves. You see Belinda thought she was being followed by a stalker."

"A stalker?" Joan uttered.

"Oh definitely. Someone was following her alright and we had to find out who it was and why. It became such turmoil for her. But how could she have been poisoned in Venice when she was in the safe hands of her sister. We realised it could take a few days for the poison to work, and somehow or other the poisoning must have taken place just before she left. Then on the day she went shopping it began to take effect. Belinda was poisoned before she went to Venice and very carefully and cleverly. It was done with daffodil bulbs."

"Daffodil bulbs?" The words ebbed and flowed between the opened mouthed people sitting in the cottage room.

"The doctor in Venice didn't take long to find out what it was. He said he remembered something about bulbs from his student days. He even told me the name of the daffodil bulbs in Latin. He was extremely impressive. Apparently it's not difficult to crush up the bulbs, pop them into your dinner, especially into a dish made with onions, and the deed is done. It takes a good few days to take effect. Really you need to dose the victim with a little every day but our murderer didn't have time for that. He had to move quickly if he was to get at Belinda."

Belinda felt she was burning up with a fever.

"Why," she tried to remember, "I'd been to Trevor but we went out for a meal to the Almond Tree. He can't have...." She would choke and die here in front of all of them, she knew she would.

"Where else Mrs Austin?" Crown asked, squinting at her. He made a move to fold his page in half. This time he was ready for Lancaster.

"I can't remember," Belinda was desperately trying to think back."I had a meal with a friend over a week ago, and ....."
She was holding onto herself with all her will power. Oh God, please don't let it be Simon. She had been to dinner with Simon. But she had been to Penny and to Joan and Steven, She had been to them all for dinner.

"In fact Mrs Austin while you were on your own you were invited out for dinner quite a few times, weren't you?"

"Yes,yes," Belinda was holding her throat. "But why would someone try to kill me?"

"Because you were on the list Belinda. You were on the killer's list."

"Yes," Lancaster said, "our killer has been having a busy time. As I said the next one would have been Penny. But he never had the time to try and kill her."

Crown wondered what on earth the pose for Penny would have been if the murderer had to find a painting. Maybe a boxer in a ring? He couldn't recall any painting like that. He looked over towards her. She had fallen back in her chair. She looked as if she was drifting in and out of sleep.

"It tells us that the murderer had to think about killing Penny. But he had an unexpected bonus. After he killed Steven, or thought he'd killed Steven, he waited in the bushes. Suddenly he heard Trevor speaking on the phone asking Penny to come and help him. What an opportunity to do away with another enemy, Penny. So the murderer waited in the bushes. Of course he thought Steven must be dead by now. Who wouldn't be with a knife thrust up at them from an angle where it could slice the heart in two. At last the time had come to get rid of Penny without all the agony of looking for another painting, because by now, there was agony for the killer. He wanted us to know what he was doing, and he wanted us to stop him. This happens often. But Penny never came.

So there was no time for elaborate clues, just a swift dash of undiluted death as quickly as possible. The killer could settle his score with Penny, and Trevor was safely on the hook for Steven's murder. Oh yes, you were next alright.."

Lancaster liked his little celebrations. Crown was expecting quite a quote from Lancaster but was it undiluted death? He wrote it down in his second column. He wasn't too sure. Was it a film Lancaster had seen recently? He wrote down Steven in the other column. He realised there was something else he had missed, something about miserable and horrible.

Lancaster was pacing the room now, back and forth, back and forth.

"So no more murders that evening."

Penny wanted to go to sleep and never wake up.

Lancaster continued. "Of course Crown and I know who carried out these murders. Only one person was capable of planning and executing these killings so meticulously. It took brains, courage and a lot of knowledge."

"Oh no," Steven cried out, thinking of Joan. Why couldn't

he help her now?

"By the way you were telling me where you had eaten before you left for London Belinda."

Lancaster could see Belinda was terrified. She leant forward as if she hadn't quite heard him.

"Why...." She stopped. "One evening at Penny's and at Joan and Steven's." She didn't dare mention Simon.

"Thank you Mrs Austin. Yes, a cunning person, our killer. Someone who would not let an opportunity pass to execute these killings."

"How can you be sure you know who it is?" Belinda asked, fearful of what she may hear. Not Simon, please not Simon.

"Oh I'm not sure, I'm positive," he said with finality. "Yes, she is a very determined woman. Actually one could come to admire her for being so forthright, so sure of herself, so businesslike in everything she does and says." With a small movement he turned his face towards Joan Ross. "An admirable adversary."

Lancaster watched as Betty held her hands up to her face. She was beginning to look like the scream.

"Your planning was immaculate Mrs Ross. I must congratulate you. It's a pity that Hitchcock isn't alive to make this into a marvellous film." He watched as she closed her eyes. The company shifted in their chairs. Belinda accidentally knocked over her tea cup. No one else moved.

"The whole plan was quite ingenious. You wanted revenge, revenge for what the Austins did to you and your brother. They cut you both out of your own mother's will. And what a clever way they did it too. Of course when this happened you were beside yourself. You and Frank left out of your own mother's will. It was too much to bear. So instead of the business of hiring lawyers and going to court, which could have cost you a lot of money, you decided to pay them back. And pay them back you did. You murdered them one by one. And you left me the most remarkable clues I have ever come across, paintings. You knew we wouldn't be able to work out the clues right away so that gave you all the time in the world.

The daffodils were where it all began, funnily enough. And because we were so slow working out the messages, that gave you the perfect opportunity, and all the time in the world after you killed Clare to plan the second murder. If you had shot Clare in cold blood we might have been on to you too quickly. But because you wanted plenty of time to murder the others you devised the brilliant idea of making each murder into a painting. You certainly confused us. We took so long to work out the clues, we used to walk around the park looking at the flowers wondering if we were going crazy. And also we wondered if this would be a case we just couldn't solve.

It was you who waited behind after the party. You who slipped into Clare's house through the garden and into an open door. How could Clare suspect that you were going to kill her? She knew you, you were in the family. You held up the gun, forced her to undress and lie on the floor. All she could do was to raise an arm to ward off yet another bullet. Then you viciously sliced the string of pearls in two. This was not done to confuse us, the pearls were cut with malice. The murder scene looked like some lunatic had been running around on the loose and he suddenly found Clare alone in the house. You placed her in the pose, the pose of the Gaugin painting, and rushed home to meet Trevor. You had cleverly arranged for him to come to breakfast to give you an alibi. Steven was probably on the way to bed and didn't think anything of it.

Everything that you did was to give you more time for the next murder. The clue was there alright but you knew we wouldn't get it. Who on earth could think of a dead woman as a painting? You even made me think of a line in a play and I don't deal with plays, only movies and murder. My sergeant will verify. The line was from a play I had been to see with Sergeant Crown."

He moved across the room towards Crown and looked down at Crown's yellow notebook.

"Yes, *The Duchess of Malfi*, as I mentioned before. You confused us with the clothes, you confused us with the necklace and you confused us with the corpse. After that you had plenty of time. Spring went into summer. It must have amused you immensely. There is one problem I don't seem to be able to work out. Did you have the yellow cushion in the car or was it in the house? Trevor isn't too sure if it was there or not. But men never seem to notice these things."

Joan threw her head up in defiance. "You read too many detective books Inspector. She smiled at Lancaster. "I kept the cushion in my car. You see I was quite prepared."

A muffled sob came from Steven, who held a held a handkerchief to his face.

"Then of course there was Edward," said Lancaster, clearing his throat. He lowered his voice almost to a whisper. "Edward must have presented quite a challenge. You couldn't shoot him because you never knew where he would be and it's quite unwise to run about brandishing a gun. Edward lived a busy life and there was no chance of you cornering him. He didn't give a hoot about any of you so he would never meet you for lunch or a cup of tea. The only time you saw Edward was at a family function. If you wanted to talk to him it would be in the company of his wife. As for killing him in the pharmacy, that was well nigh impossible. So you were left with a problem. And while you waited you needed another painting to fit the sentence you were trying to tell us. And underneath it all you wanted us to know the reason for all these killings, so we could finally stop you."

He glanced at the stunned gathering and looked again into the fire.

"What you did to Edward was particularly menacing. I've never known a killer go to such unusual lengths. Still one does read about them in the newspapers, faulty electric lawn mowers to murder husbands, cars dropping off the edge of cliffs, that kind of thing. At first you might have thought about using the same kind of poison that you gave to Belinda. But this time you didn't want the odd drop of poison or the hired killer did you Mrs Ross? You wanted revenge so diabolical that it would make a Vincent Price movie look like Cinderella."

Would they know who the hell Vincent Price was, Crown wondered. Only he knew about Vincent Price. He was still thinking about kissin'.

"So you abandoned that idea as hospital drugs and medicines are locked up very securely and even on a ward the nurses never let the key out of their sight. I should think you worked as a cleaner in a nearby hospital and got the job with a bundle of false references. You must have worked there for quite some time between the days you were in your shop and delivering suits to dead men."

Joan's face turned white with rage.

"Then out of the blue, one day you overheard something which made you change your mind completely. You would forget the original idea you had about poison as that was impossible. The way I look at it is while you were cleaning the staff room you overheard some doctors speaking about a patient who was seriously ill. So ill in fact that one of the doctors had placed him in quarantine because he thought it might be a case of hepatitis. No one was to be allowed into the patient's flat except his own doctor. The blood tests were being run through that very day. You found out that the sick man lived in a flat in the West End.and that it was intended to send him to an isolation ward. How your ears must have pricked up. Now you really had to move fast. You found out that the man lived alone, except for a daily help who came in every morning and evening to look after the place. It was unfortunate for the help she had been in such close contact with the man. All the doctor could do was give her an injection."

He thought of needles and shivered. He should never have mentioned injections.

"The doctor mentioned that he hoped he could move the patient the very next day. Now you had to find someone to help you with the plan that was fermenting in your brain. The plan was that on some pretext or other, you would get Edward to visit this patient in the hope he would contact the disease. It was a big risk."

Little crackles came from the log fire. Crown dare not even write in his pad.

"But how could you arrange that? It was a preposterous idea in the first place but I'm sure the more you thought about it the more you thought you could pull it off. You could never be sure Edward would be infected with hepatitis because some people are immune to all sorts of diseases, but with a bit of luck it might work. You had gone to a hell of a lot of trouble so far and you weren't a woman to give up. But how on earth could you get Edward over there? After all the patient was being moved on the morrow."

Crown scribbled *on the morrow* in his second column. Surely that was Shakespeare?

"Then all at once," Lancaster continued, "you came up with a breathtaking idea. What if you could get Edward to visit the patient that very night? The one thing you could rely on was Edward's tremendous ego. You knew that if someone were to phone Edward with a large order for drugs he would fill out the order come what may even if he had to work until midnight to do it. It had to be done on that very night. If you could get someone to phone Edward, someone of importance, and that someone were to ask for a delivery of drugs, you were sure Edward would agree to do it whatever time of the day or night, as I said. And who could that person be that Edward would be so happy to please? None other than a doctor. And that doctor could be living at the address you would send Edward to, the flat of the sick patient living in the West End. You would get Edward there by hook or by crook."

Lancaster studied his fingernails and his voice sharpened.

"But who would possibly want to help you in this endeavour? Who could you turn to? Why, no one else but your brother Frank, the only person in the world you could trust."

Frank pushed himself forward. "You just try and prove it," he hissed making the onlookers terrified. They knew he was a bully.

"Frank Gordon," said Lancaster, "you offered to play the

part of the mysterious doctor. Your job was to phone Edward and arrange his appointment with death."

Frank drew in his breath and Betty made a low moaning sound, which turned into a scream.Crown was loathe to go near her. She would soon quieten down. In his haste he scribbled appointment with death next to the word doctor.

"So now we have Frank involved in the plot to lure Edward to Chiltern Street," said Lancaster, ignoring Frank's outburst. "He passes himself off Doctor Allbright and Edward rushes out into the night to meet the doctor. Joan was burning to avenge the loss of her inheritance. She knew her mother would leave her something in her will, her jewellry perhaps, her furniture, or part of her home, something to remember her by, even a a bracelet or a watch to wear. And because she was left nothing she began to wonder. And because she wondered she went to dear old Prince and asked if she could see a copy of the will. And of course the will was impeccable. She couldn't understand how her mother could have done this to her. It made her hate her mother and ruined her life. She had to get revenge. She removed her mother's photographs from her living room and replaced them with the loving family ones. Then she made her first move.

From then on it wasn't too difficult. Clare was easy to dispose of. Trevor was on his way to Joan's at that moment so there was no one to stop her.

The murder of Edward worked remarkably well because he did succumb to the illness and it was easy for her to find a way of getting into his room. She dressed herself as one of the kitchen staff and managed, in front of everyone, to enter Edward's room, murder him and leave the tin box on the bedside table. If Sister Bates had arrived a moment or two before she would have seen the door open.

As for Charles, she knew his every movement from Belinda. He met his friends every Wednesday for a drink and dinner at a nearby pub. As soon as he crossed the road on leaving the pub Joan would drive around the corner and run him down like a rabbit. It was an amazing plan. And here is where Frank came in. He decided to take Betty to visit their daughter in Oxford. Taking a different route, on Joan's instructions he would pass the pub at eleven o'clock. Charles wouldn't dare drive if he'd had a few drinks so he would take the bus home. Frank and Joan simply waited for Charles to leave the pub and as he walked across the road to the bus stop Joan drove round the corner and ran him down.

And here again Joan had her accomplice to help. She knew she would never be able to move Charles from the middle of the road on her own so she suggested to Frank he arrange the visit to Oxford on that Wednesday. Betty would never realise what was going on, she would simply think Frank wanted to visit his daughter and Joan had the time to plan the perfect scenario. She would dress as a man, complete with a man's suit and tie and a hat pulled down well over her face. She would wear glasses and because she was tall and slim, in the darkness she could easily pass herself off as a man.

Frank's part in this was to take Betty to Oxford but via a route that would take him to the pub. He was to screech to a halt as near the body as he could, where Joan would cry out something like *My God, you've killed him.* The plan was perfect. Betty would be totally confused, she would think Frank had run someone over. Frank would tell her to stay in the car and then rush over the road to help. He would help Joan to load the body into the car, which she would not have been able to do by herself, then come back to his own car to reassure Betty. Obviously Betty would be nervous, but Frank would tell her it was nothing after all. He hadn't hurt the man at all, he was merely grazed and the other driver, who was of course Joan, was taking him to hospital.

Betty would never recognise Joan because it all happened so quickly.

Of course we know where Joan took Charles. Frank told Betty they had better get back to the house as after the accident there was no point in carrying on. He would phone their daughter and make fresh arrangements to visit her. He told Betty not to mention the incident to anyone, But unfortunately in his hurry to get the job done, as Frank swerved across the road in the dark, his car must have clipped his wing mirror on Joan's car. We found tiny fragments of the mirror in the road. There was no time for Frank to start looking for tell-tale evidence on a pitch black night. He could only hope no one had seen what happened and in the course of time any fragments would be washed away by the rain. But he did realise what had happened to the wing mirror and he replaced it himself. He's very good at repairs. So when I went to the cottage and started sniffing around I couldn't charge him with anything. There was no proof.

He had told Joan he would meet her later at Kate's old house. He would have to help her get Charles out of the car and damn quickly."

Frank's mouth dropped.

Lancaster spoke again. "So what Frank did was to get Betty home, have something to eat and then leave the house as Betty retired for the night. He went off as soon as he could to help Joan.

They must have decided to move Charles upstairs where they could be sure he was hidden. But as Sergeant Crown and I had tried those stairs, we knew it was impossible because all the stair rods were poking out at all angles, and it was foolish to try. You certainly couldn't get a dead body up there. They must have just managed to get Charles' body along the hall and into the alcove.

Joan knew all about that house and she knew it was empty. It couldn't have been difficult to find a key to get in and then lock it shut afterwards. What better place to leave a body?"

Frank cried, "You can't prove any of this."

"You know Frank, being a detective is like making an automobile. You just take all the pieces and put them together one by one. Next thing you know, you've got an automobile, or a murderer."

He held out an open hand and in it were some particles of broken glass and metal.

"We found this in the road after the accident."

Crown wrote down *glass* next to *automobile.*

The wind whistled outside. Everything was hushed.

"Of course," Lancaster said, "those of you who are left of the Austin family might think about forgery."

A loud gasp came from Penny and Belinda.

"Just one moment Crown," Lancaster put his finger to his lip.

"There's something else you must know."

Lancaster smiled. "Something that seems to have escaped you all." He gave a chuckle. "I should stay right where you are. We haven't discussed *The Saint.*"

- SOMETHING ELSE -

"You see through all these crimes there was another mystery I couldn't work out. It was all about love."

"Love? What about love? How can you talk about love?" It was Sabina who rose from her chair in anger.

"Those invitations to Clare's party told me about love, simple really."

His voice became quieter now.

"Invitations?" Frank asked.

Belinda looked strained. Lancaster had mentioned *The Saint*. She had told him everything about their affair, she had been honest, why reveal it in front of all these hateful people. but what did it matter now? She hadn't heard from Simon and Charles was dead so he would never find out about Simon.

"What else could there be to tell us?" cried Steven, his voice breaking.

"Ah but it's that old devil called love again, Mr Ross. Love crept into this case on tiptoe. You see someone was so alight with passion and desire that she never realised it would lead to her death." Lancaster continued. "Passion had come to Clare Austin in the guise of a stranger, a man whom I believe is unknown to the arms-around-each-other family."

"A man?" asked Frank. "What man?"

Lancaster looked at his watch. "The passion was for a man, a stranger."

The group before him shifted uneasily. They were listening to intimate secrets now, intimate ones they never suspected.

"Unfortunately so much is expected in marriage and Clare's marriage was on the rocks. I am sorry to say this in front of everyone Mr Austin but you must admit it's true."

"How can you? These things are private," Trevor was red in the face. "You can't tell everyone my personal business. She's dead, God damn you."

"Oh I know that Mr Austin, I was the one who found her shot to death. But I will continue if you don't mind despite your objections. Here was a beautiful woman with a husband like yourself, who to all intents and purposes was no longer her choice. Clare wanted a divorce and you told me so yourself. And she wanted to leave you and East Wood far behind her. So she decided to take a chance. Not something we may have chosen to do ourselves but she was desperate, she wanted to meet another man. And what did she take a chance on?"

They all waited.

"Clare Austin took a chance on love, as the song goes. She decided to answer one of the adverts in the local paper's *Love Lines*. After all she didn't want to pick up anyone in a bar or a local pub, because that would mean all the gossips would have plenty to talk about. There was absolutely nowhere nearby she could meet another man, and for all we know, maybe at the outset she did it for a bit of a lark. Clare, as we remember, was not only beautiful, she was lonely. So she answered one or two very enticing adverts that were placed in *Love Lines*.

Of course the rest is easy to imagine. A beautiful woman answers one or two adverts but doesn't seem to find the man she wants. So what does she do?" Lancaster paused with an enquiring look on his face. "She decides to place an advert in the paper herself. And she must have had dozens of answers. Then by an absolute one-in-a-million chance she finds someone that she falls head over heels in love with. You may wonder who the man was."

He looked around himself eagerly but no one dared to ask. Who would have believed it of Clare?

"The name of the man Clare was in love with was René Valmere."

Lancaster looked around. There was no recognition on any face in the small circle.

"But unbeknown to Clare, René Valmere had made his mind up to meet Clare by hook or by crook, because Clare was part of his carefully worked out plan. Oh yes this René Valmere had a plan alright. He had tried every way to find her and I shall let you know why very soon. In order to find Clare, he began frequenting the local pubs to find out if anyone knew her or her family. Now I'm sure you know what gossip can do locally, and the fellows in the locker room are the first to talk."

"Locker room?" asked Trevor, "what locker room? These are all lies. You are telling lies about my wife. It's slander, I'll kill you." He was standing up now, shouting.

"Please Mr Austin, sit down. You will hear this from me or my sergeant. René Valmere had found out from someone in a pub or a hotel bar that Clare had answered some of the ads, because one of the fellows at the bar had met Clare. In fact a lot of the fellows at the bar had met Clare."

Lancaster carried on. "One of the fellows told us that Clare sometimes put adverts in the paper herself. we have a copy of one of her adverts here. So one day we reckon René Valmere answered one of her adverts because some of the fellows in the bar had told him the score. And short of waylaying her in the street, the advert was his answer. And it worked. There was a lot of luck hanging around for René Valmere. I know how hard it is to trace people, let alone try to talk to them on the corner of the street. That would never have happened with René and Clare. No, he happened to find out what game Clare played, and he joined in the dice game. And it all worked according to plan because Clare was eating out of his hand."

Lancaster cleared his throat and contemplated the dying fire. He held out the advert. No one dared to look at it. Trevor Austin felt tears coming to his eyes. What had Clare done to him? It was shameful.

"However, the odd part in all this is that, at the time, Clare was definitely not on the murder list. No, Clare was murdered because of a terrible coincidence. Oh I don't say she wouldn't have been murdered at some other time, we can't be sure of that, but she was not on Joan's list to be murdered first. A set of circumstances arose that Clare could never have imagined in her wildest dreams.

Clare had arranged to meet her lover René Valmere as soon as the party was over. It was convenient for all concerned because Trevor had told Clare he was popping round to Joan and Steven when all the guests had left, so the coast would be clear. She would meet her lover and they would leave together. You see what had started out as an affair was now becoming something all consuming on Clare's part. She was leaving Trevor and beginning a new life with a new man. So why was Clare the first murder?

It was brought about by a quirk of fate. Clare had just put on a bathrobe to open the door to her lover René Valmere. In order not to be seen she reached up to draw the curtains, when who should stroll up the garden path but Joan Ross."

"No," Joan called out.

"Crown and I think the last person Clare expected to see was Joan Ross. Joan may have popped back to pick up some of her dishes, or decided to have a drink with Clare. That is what we don't know. Whatever her reason Clare never expected to see her. Clare was naked under her robe, and in that brief moment it takes to draw the curtains, Joan sees the man take Clare in his arms."

"You don't know this," Joan cried out.

"No, but I've got a shrewd idea. And I know why she had to die. Suddenly there was Joan approaching the garden room. Clare has to think quickly when she spots Joan, so she leans up, pulls the heavy curtains together and turns off the light switch, leaving the room in darkness so Joan will think she's gone to bed. But it's too late. Joan has already seen Clare in her robe and it was then

293

that she received the shock of her life. In the brief moment that Clare is reaching up to close the curtains she actually sees the man who reaches out and takes Clare in his arms."

"You're a liar, you bastard," Joan whispered.

"Oh believe me I'm not a liar. The man was someone Joan Ross knew immediately. a man she knew by the name of Ricard Le Salle. A man who had Joan as second on his list, the second woman in his scheme of things. He found out about her and that she had a shop It made it easy for him. All he had to do was go to her shop. It didn't take him long with his French charm to make a play for her. He probably bought her flowers, jewellry and all the rest of it. This man would stop at nothing to get what he wanted, and he wanted Joan on his list and by God he would get her."

Lancaster waited. He knew what he was going to say would strike incredulity into the women sitting there.

"He made a huge play for her, and finally she gave in and had an affair with Ricard Le Salle. What woman wouldn't. The attention he lavished on her would be something she had never had in all her life. That is why Joan began an intense affair with him."

Steven began to make little moaning noises.

"Let me continue," Lancaster said. "Now imagine the shock, the earth-shattering discovery Joan made when she toddled up the garden path that night. Who does she spy but the man who was her lover, Ricard Le Salle, holding a near naked Clare in his arms. Joan was utterly distraught. How did Ricard know Clare? What was happening? The man she was in love with was with Clare. She couldn't believe her eyes. It was a betrayal that struck deep into her soul. Imagine how she must have felt."

He glanced toward Joan. She was drained of all colour and emotion.

"Now her other plans, and there were plenty of them, must take a back seat. Her aim was to punish Clare and her lover. She was seething with hatred and her mind was in a turmoil. What was her Ricard doing with Clare? When did he meet Clare? Surely Joan was the only woman in his life? He loved Joan, he told her so day in and day out.

All these thoughts were going round and round in her head. And the first thing that sprang to mind was revenge on Clare and Ricard. She couldn't strangle them with her bare hands and in her torment she remembered Steven had a gun. She rushed back to her car and drove like a banshee all the way home. She found Steven's gun in his desk and made sure it was fully loaded. Then she drove back to Clare's house, all the time fearful her lover could have left by the time she got back to Clare's. She drove in what can only be described as a state of insanity. She wanted to see her lover's face when she shot Clare dead and after that she would shoot him. We know that it was her car because she knocked over Bobby Little's scooter when she drove home and we heard that Bobby's mother phoned the police to report the accident. We compared the scooter with the paintwork on Joan's car and it matched.

While joan was on her way Clare had gone upstairs to get her suitcase and Ricard Le Salle, or as we also know him René Valmere, had gone back to his car. Clare was just going to leave when Joan confronted her. There was no one in the house to hear Clare's screams. You may wonder where Ricard Le Salle, alias René Valmere, was during all this. He has long gone. Clare's lover has other plans. And the reason for this you may wonder? René Valmere is also out for revenge, and this is where the story gets tricky."

Crown remembered *double plot.* He remembered *Vertigo.* He thought of Kim Novak in her grey suit but Joan Ross wasn't wearing a grey suit.

"René Valmere had taken his revenge on Clare. He had turned her into a desperately besotted woman whose one and only aim is to leave her husband and be with him. He has made sure she will never find him again because as soon as he gets into his car he is gone. It is amazing what a man can do when he makes up his mind to get a woman. Of course Clare will never know this because Clare is going to be killed. Joan confronts Clare, who must have been mystified when this banshee, her sister-in-law, rushes in holding a gun. She had no idea Joan knows René Valmere and she never even knew why she was killed. How could she be expected to know that Joan was also a lover of René Valmere. But Joan did not know him as René, she knows him as Ricard. Yes unfortunately for Joan, René Valmere and Ricard Le Salle were one and the same man. Joan told Clare to undress, gets her downstairs and shoots her without hesitation. Clare lifts her arm to ward off the bullets but it's hopeless. She never lived to find out the Frenchman was Joan's lover as well as her own.

To confuse us, Joan throws Clare's underwear in the bin and slices the string of pearls in two with a kitchen knife. And why did she cut the pearls? Joan's lover had also given her pearls, the exact same string of large pearls and clasp that Clare was wearing. In her frenzy of jealousy that was the last straw for Joan. If it wasn't for the pearls we might have thought it was some sort of crazy drug-induced crime committed by a passing opportunist looking for money.

As Joan hadn't planned Clare's murder she is forced to use the clue *Nevermore* for Clare, instead of Penny. So taking the yellow cushion from her car, she places it under Clare's head and twists her body into the position of the painting. The blanket she put under Clare must have been taken from the bed upstairs in the spare room."

Lancaster waited.

"Joan transforms Clare into the Gaugin painting and uses the clue *Nevermore*. She will use *Forger* and *Scream* for the two brothers and she would change her plans on the spot for Penny and Trevor. In her warped thinking, she would work out some words for those two. But there was no time now and she would have to get away."

"You can't imagine what word I had for that bitch Penny," Joan uttered.

"Ah but I can Joan. I can work out exactly what you would use. It would be something to do with materials, possibly a word to do with design or embroidery or even wool. Not daffodils."

"And what would that be?" snarled Joan.

"Oh possibly something to do with dyeing," Lancaster answered with a shrewd look. Joan lashed out at him like a demon. She flew at him with her long nails and managed to scratch him on the chin.

"Joan, for God's sake," Steven cried out.

"I wouldn't do that if I were you," Crown said as he grabbed her hands.

"I think I shall have to take my patient back to the hospital," Doctor Berkowitz said in a concerned voice. "I also suggest we give Mrs Ross something to calm her down. She is clearly very disturbed."

"A good idea Doctor," Lancaster said. "I am only expecting one more visitor. I am sure Mr Ross would like to meet him before he leaves here. By then his wife will be placed in custody. Carry on with your notes Crown, there's a good man." Lancaster clutched Crown's shoulder. Suddenly he pounced on Penny.

"You have met him, haven't you Mrs Austin? The man we're talking about?"

"Met him? What do you mean, met him? Met who? Of course not, how could I?" Penny said, jumping out of the chair. "How could I know this man?"

How could she know René Valmere or Ricard whatever his name was? The only man she had met recently was Raoul Hutton, and how could he have anything to do with either of these other two men? Lancaster was insane, but none the less she felt apprehensive. Why had she suddenly become so tense when she thought of Raoul? She didn't really know where he came from. He had told her he had been out of the country for several years and had no family and lived alone. He had a small flat. That's what he told her but she had never been to his flat. He never invited her there. Surely there was nothing wrong in that. She met him through a phone call. One evening when she was at her lowest ebb the phone had rung and a man had asked if he could speak to Edward. She had to say to the caller that Edward had passed away. She asked if she could help as she was Edward's widow. Yes, the caller said she could help. He would like to speak to her about something important he discussed with Edward last year as he was an old friend. He told her he was very sorry to hear that Edward had died, he had no idea that he had been ill. Would Penny care to join him for dinner while he was in town? Perhaps it might cheer her up a little.

It was tempting to be invited out and she said yes immediately. Stupid really, he could have been a rapist or a killer or a con man. But she was so lonely she didn't care. He came to pick her up the following evening. He arrived in a new car, she couldn't even remember what kind of car it was. She was so happy to be invited out for dinner, it made her feel wanted. When he opened the door to let her in the car, she found a huge bouquet of roses on the front seat. A faint flush appeared on her face when she thought of that evening. Lancaster must know, surely he must know. After that there were so many other wonderful evenings, evenings that she had never known before. So much so that she begged Raoul to give up his flat and move in with her. After all he was single and he wasn't living with anyone. She was lonely and if she lost him to another woman she felt she would die. She would have given him anything, everything. And his name was Raoul. And the other names sounded similar. Oh God, she was on the verge of hysteria thinking about it.

Lancaster looked at her with questioning eyes.

"He was just going to ditch Clare, then ditch Joan. Had you met him." Lancaster looked at her knowingly, "he would have given you a wonderful time Penny. He would be prepared to give you all the passion you could wish for. But as you say you never met him it's a lucky thing he didn't get around to you."

Penny had met his man, Lancaster was sure of that. It showed in her face. There was no use revealing any more about the man now.

Joan Ross had closed her eyes. She let out a racking sob.

Love certainly was a killer.

Suddenly Steven blurted out, "Oh Joan, say none of this is true."

Joan looked across at him with bitterness. "Of course it's true, you fool. Every bit of it is true."

The small group were hushed, not knowing what they might find out next.

"Yes," said Lancaster, "now to the other party." Here he fumbled in his pocket and took out a piece of paper.

"I'm talking about *The Saint.*"

"*The Saint?*" Belinda came forward, she was appealing to him. "Please tell me. What about *The Saint?*" Her hands were shaking.

Lancaster continued. "Belinda you were foolish to answer adverts in the columns of newspapers. It can sometimes be a very dangerous occupation. Compared to Simon the other men you met must have seemed like zombies. For Simon you would have done anything, even leave Charles."

He held the newspaper cutting towards her.

****

"I found this in the library archives.

Looking for a dark beautiful lady to have a good life with,

A life with lots of jewellery, holidays and money.

Of course the whole idea would be tempting to any woman." He would throw out a question about Clare now.

"Did Clare tell you she answered adverts in the paper?"

"Yes," Belinda whispered. "She did. She told me it was the only time she had any fun since she married Trevor."

Trevor's face took on a tortured look. If Clare was here now he would kill her himself.

"And do you know the fascinating thing about all this? *The Saint* wasn't English. No, he had us guessing there for a while. He was French."

"French?" asked Penny. Raoul had an accent but it was well hidden. It only came out occasionally. He told her he was from Ireland. Oh God, who was he? She was meeting him tomorrow night, he was taking her away for the weekend.

"Oh yes, he came from Paris originally," Lancaster drew on

his cigarette. "*The Saint,* as he liked to refer to himself in those interesting little advertisements, was the second biggest problem in this bizarre puzzle. You see I usually deal with murder, I don't deal with love."

He put the piece of paper back into his pocket.

Lancaster felt a pang of sadness for Belinda. He remembered the words of a song the jazz singer used to sing, *You didn't need me, for you had your share of slaves around you to hound you and care.* He'd learnt a lot this week about slaves and caring. Love and passion, no wonder the songwriters made money.

"Yes, it has a lot to do with love.," Lancaster spoke in a hushed voice. Suddenly in the quiet room there came a tap at the front door.

"Unless I'm very much mistaken, our last visitor has arrived," he said anxiously.

"Oh my God, is it Simon?" Belinda had to stop herself rushing to the front door.

As the door opened the first thing she could see was a walking stick, and behind the walking stick appeared an elderly bearded figure wrapped in a thick scarf and overcoat. A black fedora hat was on his head and he was wearing gloves. He wore heavy lace-up shoes which were scuffed with mud. His face, what Crown could see of it, was heavily lined and he had a grey beard. It was hard to see his eyes as they were hidden under thick ridges of eyebrows.

Who could this be? Belinda had prayed it would be Simon, come back by some miracle to find her, found by Inspector Lancaster and brought to this hateful house to take her somewhere far away. But she knew it wasn't Simon. Her heart sank. Could it be the man who was stalking her? Had Lancaster found him?

"Please sit down sir," Crown spoke. He had been warned by Lancaster that there might be a stranger coming here this evening. But Lancaster had refused to say more. Only that the stranger came from Northern France, and there had been a lot of difficulty finding him and convincing him to come to England.

The man removed his overcoat and handed it to Crown. He wore a plain navy polo neck sweater underneath a dark navy suit. To Crown he looked impeccable.

Betty began to worry. Who could this man be? Did he know Frank? She could feel little prickles running up her back and into her arms. Would she be forced to learn more things about her husband, worse than those she already knew?

"And now," Lancaster said, "I must introduce Mr Alexander Austin to you. Some of you will already know him I'm sure. He is here to tell us about the curious story about three unusual names,

René, Ricard and Raoul. It never ceases to amaze me what people will do to avenge injustice."

"Oh no, no, " Belinda cried out. Simon couldn't be involved with these other people, these other names she had never heard of. But then she never knew his real name, did she?

Penny wanted to run away from this house. How could Raoul have three names. What was going on?

Joan stayed hunched up in the corner. To her Ricard was dead.

Lancaster turned towards the man who held his hands out to the fire. After a moment or two the man spoke.

"I am surprised Sabina that you don't recognise me!" His voice was slow and his accent was French.

Sabina answered with shock. "My God, It can't be," Sabina gasped.

"I rather wish it wasn't." The man smiled. "Yes Sabina it is me, Alexander."

"Alexander," she said and her bewildered look made him frown.

"Ah you look surprised. It must be nearly thirty years. I can never remember how long it is since we've met. Time takes its revenge on our looks I must admit.

"Alexander," whispered Sabina in a monotone.

How old could he be, wondered Crown? The beard certainly made him look old.

"Please Mr Austin, do continue with your story." Lancaster patted the man's shoulder.

"It's just not possible," Trevor interrupted. He was standing now. He went over to the man. "It can't be you Alexander. Alexander never looked like this. Alexander was different. It can't be you."

"As you heard the years take their toll," nodded Lancaster. "I assure you it is your beloved brother sitting in the armchair. The brother I am absolutely sure you tried to keep in contact with over the long years. I thought you may enjoy bringing him back into the family fold. That is one of the reasons I brought him here. You must be delighted to know he is alive."

Trevor gasped. But I thought he was dead. I never knew..."

Crown replied. "I don't think you tried very hard to discover if he was alive or dead. He wasn't too difficult to trace."

Trevor looked at Alexander and shook his head.

"I am sure it suited you better this way Trevor," Alexander Austin said, continuing to warm his hands, "leaving me where I was in total ignorance of everything that went on."

Trevor backed away from what he could only imagine was

an apparition.

"Please sir, we are waiting to hear your story," Lancaster said. "I know you must be feeling very unhappy about having to confront these people after so many years have passed, especially your ex-wife."

The man nodded but appeared unperturbed.

"Perhaps you could make our friend a cup of tea, Betty?" Lancaster smiled towards her and took out a cigarette.

Betty desperately needed a valium. She went into the kitchen and reached behind the flour bag before she filled the kettle. How did people live on after things like this happened to them?

"Thank you Inspector," Alexander said. "It is difficult to confront people one hasn't seen in years, especially in these circumstances. But as I promised you I have prepared myself for whatever I may have to tell this evening. Of course I have spoken many times to Inspector Lancaster over the last few days. I learned of the murders of Clare,Charles and Edward."

Betty swallowed two valium then brought in the tea and handed it to Alexander. My God, she had heard about a brother but no one told her he was alive.

Alexander picked up his cup of tea and wrapped his hands around it.

"It may surprise you all to know the reason I am here," he said clearly. "I am here about love."

"Love," said Belinda, crying, "there's no love here."

Alexander leaned forward and clasped his hands together.

"But there is Belinda, it is you isn't it? Alexander Austin enquired, focussing on her face. "You were a young girl when you married Charles. I will begin with the love that Jack, my son, had for his mother. He adored her. When Sabina and I divorced I went to live in France, I've always loved the country and my new partner was French. We married not long afterwards and we were so happy. Her name is Arlette. Then of course we had our first child, Jack. Eventually we could afford to buy a small home, very close to the hotel where I worked. Then when Jack was five years old we had a little girl called Lisette. When jack was in his teens I became rather ill, so Arlette and I decided to leave the hotel and buy a little farm in Provence. We were lucky and we managed to make a living. She had a hard life then, but when I recovered I tried to make it up to her. I insisted she didn't work so hard and I hired a man to help us. We were very happy together."

Alexander smiled thinking about them.

"Neither Jack nor Lisette knew I had family in England but a few letters did arrive in the early years. They ceased after a time."

Alexander sat back. He looked strained.

"I must tell you a little more about Jack. He loved acting. He always had the best part in the school play and he wanted to go on and study drama in Paris. Of course we did everything we could to encourage him. Arlette and I worked hard so he could enjoy his life and if that meant sending him to Paris then we would do it. In fact he became a very well known artist. He lived in Paris for many years working on stage and in cabaret. He had his name in lights all over France. He was reliable and everyone liked him. He even learned to dance and was still young enough to carry on dancing until a few years ago. But acting was his love. He did very well in his profession. And then suddenly one day sadly his life changed."

"This is all a waste of time Inspector," Trevor blurted out. How can this man have anything to do with us?"

"Oh he has lots to do with you Mr Austin. Quite a lot I can assure you. Please continue sir."

"Thank you. You see on the day I am speaking about a certain visitor arrived in Paris, a very old friend of mine. So Jack made arrangements to meet the man and bring him to stay at the farm. He was thrilled to meet someone from England.

So my old friend came to the farm and we had a most enjoyable few days. He decided to stay longer so we could catch up on all the news from England. Arlette prepared her specialities and it was a beautiful weekend. It was during those few days that Jack began to learn something about the family I had left behind in England. Indeed I also learned something I never suspected. I was shocked to learn my mother had died. I also learned my family in England had done quite well for themselves. He unfortunately let me know that my brothers weren't remotely interested in me or my family. Many years ago he had mentioned my name and they had either shrugged their shoulders or just dismissed my name. So much so that they never even let me know my mother had passed away. That was extremely painful for me, as my mother and I always kept in contact. She had even been to France to visit her grandchildren. I felt devastated to hear she had died. I never knew she was ill. I had only spoken to her some weeks before. She told me she was going to the coast for a rest and would write to me.

They should have found a way to let me know. It was heartless. Of course my mother never told them where I lived. She knew them for what they were and she always told me it was best that my life was private. After all I had a good life and was happy with my family. I had no intention of ever returning to England.

When Jack learned his grandmother had died he also learned that I had three brothers. As I told you, I never spoke of them. It was then I discovered that I had been cut out of my mother's will. I was flabbergasted. I couldn't believe that my mother would leave me nothing. I knew she loved me and I loved her. But to receive nothing, nothing to remember her by, not a scarf or even a glove. And what was even more painful was the fact that nothing had been left to her grandchildren. Of course we were all shattered by the news. Jack and Lisette loved their grandmother. My mother would have divided everything between us. I could have sworn to that."

Lancaster could hear the sharp intake of breath from everyone around him.

"After the friend left you can imagine how we felt. What was to have been a few days of memories and pleasure had turned into disbelief and misery. How hard we had worked all our lives, it was incredible such a thing could happen. Then Jack's disbelief turned to anger. He asked me how I could have been cut out of the will when he knew how close we all were.

So Jack decided to make some enquiries for himself. He went to see a solicitor in Paris and asked him to do some investigating for him. The solicitor duly wrote to the old firm of Prince & Prince which I told him were my parents solicitors from the old days. When the reply came back, Jack was horrified to find that my friend had told us the truth, we were left nothing.

Jack was sickened and dispirited. As the weeks passed and he heard nothing more he began to walk about the streets thinking of vengeance. He realised that my brothers had deliberately kept the news from me so that they could be the only inheritors. There was something wrong about this whole thing, Jack was certain. He wanted to do something about it but he wasn't sure what.

I told him not to think of doing anything. There was no point. Even though we had a bitter taste in our mouths we couldn't afford to go to court and contest the will. We had worked all our lives to keep the farm and look after the children. But Jack became a different person. He wanted revenge and he wanted it badly."

Alexander continued. "He knew that somehow or other my brothers had managed to do us out of our share of the family will. and even though he couldn't quite work out how, he swore he would revenge our shabby treatment.

But Jack was not cruel. He would never dream of harming anyone. It was not in his nature. He was and is a good son, a gentle person, who always helped his mother by sending her money every time he was working.

I begged him to forget the whole thing and carry on with his life. Arlette and I didn't mind, it hadn't altered anything for us. A few more pounds would have helped but it wasn't worth torturing ourselves over.

But then I did something very strange. I did something that I couldn't explain to myself. One morning I removed all my mother's photographs from view. I took them and put them in a drawer in my bedroom and they are there to this day. I had been wounded to the core and I was sure these people were the ones who had done that to me. I suffered for a long time, indeed for many years. I had nothing to hold onto that had belonged to her, not a watch, a bracelet or even a piece of china. What they had done had changed my nature psychologically. They had poisoned me.

When Jack saw what had happened to me he was beside himself with fury. How dare these unknown people destroy us? How could they make his mother and father suffer so much by making them feel grandmother cared nothing for them. Jack was positive the will had been forged or tampered with. But as I said he could not afford a court case with accusations, denials and enormous fees for lawyers.

So in his anger he devised a plan which I learned about afterwards. I would have tried to talk him out of it. It was too damaging for himself as well as the others. It would make him an unhappy man. But as I said I knew nothing about it at the time. Jack would exact his revenge on the family in quite another way."

Here Lancaster allowed himself a moment to ask if Alexander wanted to continue.

"Of course. I wish to leave here as soon as I can so I must finish what I came to say. Jack told me it was best if I knew nothing about what he was going to do. To put his plan into action he needed to go to England as soon as possible. And that is exactly what he did."

Belinda cried out, "Oh my God." She knew in her heart what this man was going to say.

"Yes Jack found out that my real name was Austin. Indeed it had been Austin when first came to France. But after I established myself I decided to do a strange thing. Up until now I have been calling my son Jack. You must realise by now that is not his name. France had been good to us and I wanted to change my name altogether, to shake off England forever. So I decided to change my name to Alexander Le Sant. Then Arlette said to me I should think of Jack and change his name also. Then he would really fit in with the country and the people. So I changed his name as well. I changed his name to Jacques. He became Jacques Le Sant."

Belinda knew the rest of the story before Alexander Le Sant

even began to tell it.

"So Jacques rented a car and left for England immediately. He found himself a small place just outside London where no one could possibly know him. He gave himself a different name and put his plan into action.

It was a simple plan when I think about it and it's hard to believe how easily he got away with it. He seemed to have an enormous amount of luck as well. He decided to snare every one of the wives in the family and to put it bluntly, bed the lot of them. Eventually he would tell all the husbands. And every time he managed to bed one of them down, it would be another nail in the coffin of the Austins. You see Jacques didn't realise that the Austins had cut Joan and Frank out of the will as well. He had no idea he may be involved in murder. He told me it was after Clare was found dead that he decided to put an end to the whole business.

But of course it was too late. When he left Clare he had absolutely no idea that she would be murdered and of course it didn't take long before he found out she was dead. It was all over the newspapers and the television news. All he could think about was had he been seen at Clare's house? He knew then he'd been seen by Joan."

He took a sip of water from the glass Betty had left beside him.

"Do you know Inspector," he said, looking into Lancaster's eyes, "this kind of retribution had become like a drug. It was changing his personality. He went for Clare as his first victim. He found out her habits and where she lived and he discovered that she liked answering adverts in the local paper. he must have asked around locally at the pub or somewhere like that. So he decided to place an advert in the local newspaper's *Love Lines*. It was a long shot and if it didn't work there were other ways to snare her. After a few dud replies, she answered. As I said he had a lot of luck. He was so surprised she answered that it took him a few days to work up the courage to phone her, but finally he did. He discovered the woman who answered was no plain Jane. She was a very beautiful looking woman and it wouldn't be difficult to have an affair with her. And that is exactly what he did. Everything he learned in the theatre came into play. He drove her crazy. Jacques was a brilliant actor and he acted with no restraint. Needless to say she fell madly in love with him. He used the name René then. He was as good at changing his name as he was his different personalities.

Clare told him she would leave her husband and they could go away together. She decided to hold a party, which would be a good cover for her to leave. After all who would think the hostess would vanish after a successful evening? They could disappear into the sunset together.

Of course, as the inspector informed me, Clare was shot to death as she was getting ready to meet Jacques. They were both standing in the window of her home when, to Jacques horror, he saw Joan Ross coming up the garden path. And Joan was the other woman on his list. And by his account he had already met her and was carrying on an affair with her. He said the affair was extremely passionate. She would be the next to be left dangling in mid-air."

Alexander looked at Joan. Her face had aged in just that one evening.

"Jacques decided to leave immediately as he knew Joan had recognised him. He would take up with Joan at a later date when he had concocted some sort of explanation. But of course he didn't know Clare would be murdered. So Joan would never see him again.

He had already started his affair with Joan under the name of Ricard Le Salle. He had dispensed with Joan and had to get on with the next woman on his list. The quicker he left England the better. His nerves had got the better of him and there were only two other women to settle the score with.

The affair with Joan had been intense. He bought her all sorts of gifts and she spent a fortune. They were out to dinner every week and stopped in the best hotels whenever they could. I began to think something was terribly wrong with Jacques. When he phoned me his voice had become brittle and hard. Jacques was never like that. He wasn't the same person. I kept asking him what he was doing and why didn't he come home. But he always avoided my questions. I begged him to tell me what was going on but he refused. I told him his mother wanted him to come home and begged him to forget about the Austins. I warned him something would happen that he wouldn't be able to control. But he said he had made up his mind to see it through.

So he decided to put another advert in *Love Lines* and get another Austin wife off his list. He went so upmarket in his next advert in *Love Lines* that he had hundreds of replies. He had never realised there were so many lonely women out there.He had to find another alias quickly so he decided to call himself *The Saint*. The reason for that was simple. As I have already mentioned we had changed our name to Le Sant. What could be easier for Jacques than to call himself *The Saint*."

Lancaster waited.

"You're a wicked liar," Belinda cried out.

Alexander Le Sant ignored her outburst. Lancaster got up

to speak.

"Jacques was very clever. He even had the audacity to follow me about. I realise he needed to keep an eye on me just in case I found out what was going on, but there was another reason. He wanted to know where Belinda was after she had left her house. I saw him standing on the grass in the Rose Garden one summer's day when Crown and I had gone for a walk. I'll say this for him, he was a bloody good actor. He looked like a student."

The bomb is coming, Crown thought.

Alexander Austin continued.

"But Jacques surprised even himself. His advert was a huge success and the letters poured in. Then he finally received one from Belinda. She fell madly in love with this *Saint,* this actor of a hundred parts. And then came the lightening strike. He fell in love with Belinda. When he thought he had lost her he became desperate. He began to follow her about all over the place to make sure she wasn't seeing someone else. He became possessive and jealous.You know what love is like Inspector. He wanted to find a way of getting her to go away with him but he couldn't reveal his true identity. The play-acting had turned real and it would be impossible for them to be together. He might be accused of murder. So all he could do was keep a watch on her and try to figure out what to do next. Unfortunately Belinda got scared. She felt someone was stalking her. She was right of course, that someone was Jacques. Inspector Lancaster told me she called him and asked him to try and find out whoever it was that was following her.

She became so frightened she left her house and stayed in a hotel. Then she left the country, as you know, and went to stay with her Sabina in Venice."

The man hesitated before continuing his story.

"I think when Belinda disappeared he was terrified. I also think he desperately wanted to carry out the rest of his revenge. God only knows if he had begun to enjoy what he was doing. There was another woman on his list. He had started to see Penny Austin."

"No," Penny cried, "oh no, I never knew him."

Alexander Le Sant allowed himself a smile.

"Ah," he said, "but you knew someone called Raoul."

Penny couldn't answer.

"You may well wonder how I know about this. When Jacques returned home he was a changed man . He told me everything that had happened. I found the whole thing distasteful and a tragedy. Tragic for Jacques because he really loved Belinda. But of course he would never return to England. Joan and Frank had their revenge and Jacques had his."

Alexander spoke to Belinda. "Of course Jacques has gone away. He didn't know how long he would be gone. I believe he went to Spain. He promised to let us know when he was ready to return home. He told us he wanted time to think about his life. Of course he changed his name again."

Alexander Austin shrugged and his face dropped.

Lancaster thought it best not to look at the women seated before him just now. They would be remembering this for a long time to come. Joan would always see Clare in the arms of Jacques and Belinda would miss *The Saint*, probably forever.

So he loved me, Belinda thought. Oh why won't he come back? I don't care about the others, just let him come back. I'll find him. I'll get round this man and find him.

Penny Austin looked like a sickly yellow bird. Lancaster knew Jacques had found Penny. Alexander said so even though Penny denied it. Penny was weeping. Something about her touched him. It was probably the first time in her life she had found out about passion. He wondered what new name Jacques had given himself. Perhaps it was best to leave it alone after all.

Belinda was trying to catch her breath. It seemed as if some kind of darkness had descended and she couldn't get a grip on things at all. She felt she was sliding off a cliff. The ground had given way and she would slip down into a crevice. But no one could hear her. She had no voice. It was a nightmare.

Joan closed her eyes. Jacques had murdered her like she had murdered all the others.

Lancaster put out his cigarette and spoke.

"Strange way of getting a bit of revenge, enjoying the wives," he said. "He surely must have heard about the other murders. But he couldn't stop. He carried on just the same. Maybe he even began to enjoy it, that wouldn't be too difficult. After all men were advertising all the time and women were happy to meet them. And they were all looking for love. Jacques might become a French gigolo, or an American one like Richard Gere." He looked sideways at Crown.

American Gigolo Crown remembered. He scribbled it down but he already knew it was bloody *American Gigolo*.

"Anyway," Lancaster said, "we'll probably never know. But as Crown will tell you, we take it all in, sift it and come up with most of the answers. It's like a Greek tragedy really."

Someone scraped a chair along the floor. It screeched like a night owl. Lancaster could hear a slight tapping at the window. A branch of a tree had come down in the wind and was snapping at the pane.

Lancaster carried on. "Yes," he said, "but to a cop the explanation is always simple. There's no mystery in the street, no arch criminal behind it all. If you find a body and you think his brother did it, you're gonna find out you're right."

Crown stopped his pencil.

"Anything wrong Crown?" he heard Lancaster ask.

"No sir, just thinking about when we found the body."

"Get the constable in here Crown."

He turned to Alexander. "I must thank you for coming here sir. And I should be grateful if you would let me know how your son gets on. I'm sure he'll be home soon. I've got a car ready to drop you off."

He shook hands with Alexander.

"Thank you Inspector. I leave for France first thing in the morning."

They watched as Alexander Le Sant found his way out of the small front room.

"To a cop the explanation is simple," Crown said to himself. He never thought it was simple. He tried to remember if Lancaster had used that quote before. He was sure he had.

"Fire's out sir," Crown said.

"I do believe you're right Crown." Lancaster turned his head towards the fireplace.

"Come on Crown. Let's leave the party."

Lancaster picked up his coat and turned towards the door. He watched as the waiting constable went inside accompanied by two other officers. He turned to Betty Gordon.

"I should try and get some sleep Mrs Gordon. I'll get a policewoman to stay overnight."

He wondered if she would ever manage to recover from all the pain. Still she had a daughter and perhaps she would stay with her for a while.

"Funny business, murder," he said.

"And forgery sir."

"Indeed, there won't be many of them sleeping tonight."

"Are you sure we can prove they did it together sir?" Crown asked, knowing he would get one of Lancaster's sarcastic retorts. "I mean Frank and Joan."

"Oh I'm sure of it. As for the will, the women knew all about that. But whether we can pin anything on them, I'm not sure. They'll probably walk."

Crown imagined Lancaster just threw that in for amusement. *Probably walk* was in a million and a half movies.

"It's amazing Joan never got around to killing Trevor."

"I shouldn't worry on that score Crown. Trevor Austin will be dead by morning."

Crown's mouth dropped in amazement.

"What are you talking about? How do you know that?"

"Because Alexander Le Sant will murder him," Lancaster spoke with confidence.

"What? Then why don't we arrest him? How could you let him go back to the hotel without giving him a warning?"

"Crown," Lancaster said in a restrained voice, "how many times do I have to tell you? You can't arrest a man for thinking he wants to kill someone. Sometimes I think I want to kill people. What are we, the Thought Police?"

Lancaster pulled his hat down over his eyes. Little wisps of yellowy white hair poked out of his hat.

"We'll be back here at first light. Better get some sleep when we get back."

"Remember that photograph we found locked away in Belinda's place?" Crown asked. "I think Charles must have locked it away. The photograph wasn't Belinda at all. It was Kate and the Austins when they were children and the little pageboy was Alexander. That's why he locked the photo away. He didn't want anyone to question him about the people in it."

"As to Frank and Joan, Crown," Lancaster spoke absently, "they've committed a murder together and it's not like taking a trolley ride together where they can get off at different stops. They're stuck with each other and they've got to ride al the way to the end of the line. It's a one way trip and the last stop is the cemetery."

Crown might as well have not spoken at all. He had practically invited Lancaster to tell that quote. What puzzled him was how the hell did Lancaster remember all the words so well. He could have placed a bet on Lancaster coming up with *Double Indemnity.* He usually did at the end of a case. Crown closed his eyes and could see Fred McMurray dying on the floor of his office building. They didn't make drama like that anymore. He was beginning to think like Lancaster.

"You do look a bit like Keyes, sir" Crown muttered.

"Thanks Crown. I always admired Edward G."

"It's always money or sex isn't it?"

"Or both."

Neither of them looked back as they left the cottage.

Lancaster got into the car and pulled his hat down over his eyes.

"Amazing story that Crown. Jacques' story I mean. Do you think the old man knows where his son is?"

"I'm sure of it."

"When you think about it, all Jacques Le Sant did was to go to bed with those women. I mean that's not a crime, is it? He didn't try to kill them. He only did what Ingrid Bergman did in *Notorious*."

"So you remembered *Notorious* Crown? Remember where we watched it?"

"In a flea pit in Hull."

"Absolutely! And Ingrid Bergman snared Claude Rains to find out German secrets. She could be excused."

"Well it's the same thing really, isn't it? Le Sant did it for revenge. That's the difference."

"Oh but you forget. Le Sant killed them Crown, he did kill them. He killed them in a different sort of way. All those emotions, all that loving, not to mention passion, and for what? Suddenly Joan was left alone, Belinda was left alone and then Penny. The love of their life had vanished and none of them knew where he was, why he'd gone or how to find him. They must have been frantic. They must have lain awake at night wondering what they'd done to make him disappear. He avenged his parents in spades."

Crown suddenly perked up. He felt hungry. He hadn't eaten anything since Betty's rotten cheese sandwich.

"Care for a drink sir? Get something to eat before we go home? Let's forget about murder for a bit."

Lancaster lifted his hat. His eyes were bloodshot. Tomorrow he would get his eyes tested.

"Damn good idea Sergeant." He felt tired but a drink would wake him up. Besides he fancied some chips. then he began to think about the jazz singer.

He wished like hell he was Robert Mitchum walking into a night club. His eyes would go to the stage and there would be a glorious vision of Jane Russell singing *You'll Know*.

Or Bogart when he first set eyes on Bacall singing near the piano in *To Have and To Have Not*.

He wanted to walk into a night club and see the jazz singer on stage singing *Where or When*. But he knew he wouldn't because there were no night clubs like that anymore, and he certainly knew there were none around here and that all they would find was a crowded pub where the music came out of the ceiling, and no one was singing.

"Find the nearest inn Crown." was all he could say.

Crown drove down the lane and out onto the main road. He didn't want to think of movies or murders or what would happen to Alexander Le Sant. He was thinking of something quite beautiful. He drove slowly along the country road.

"There we are sir. My God, would you believe it? It's the place Charles went on the night he was murdered. There's nowhere else around here so we may as well go in there. Come on sir, I'll buy you a whisky and some dinner, if there's anything left. It's a bloody cold night." He smiled at Lancaster.

"Pull in and park Crown. Mind the daffodils."

They walked through the car park into the bar.

"It took us long enough to solve that one," Lancaster mused as he fiddled with his tie and took out his cigarette pack. "It started with those blasted daffodils. I puzzle about families Crown. They're supposed to be good for kids, but after seeing that lot, I wonder if some of the kids might be better off without 'em."

"Do you think Jacques, or should I say *The Saint* is thinking about Belinda? Maybe we might even get to see him in a play one of these days. We'd never recognise him of course."

Lancaster took off his hat and leaned against the bar. A man in front of him ordered two pints. It was the usual Sunday night crowd laughing and drinking. He took out a cigarette and looked around for an ashtray.

"Shouldn't we try to find Jacques Le Sant? Speak to him? What a time he must have had. Any man would envy what he got up to."

"Do you know Crown, I never thought of it that way, perhaps you're right. Maybe we should put something in *Love Lines* ourselves."

"Good idea, the only trouble is we never get the time. I wonder if Le Sant missed out with Penny Austin?"

"Oh I wouldn't wonder about that Crown. Just think, why would he miss out? No point really. I feel a bit sorry for her. After all those years with Edward she finally found herself a bit of passion. None of it lasts anyway."

Lancaster leaned across the bar, trying to get the barmaid's attention.

Now was the time for Crown to strike back and Crown would seize the opportunity. It was time for him to get a bit of revenge too for all those tortuous inflections, those movie quotes he never really knew, those sharp little digs, those challenging looks and those dreary yellow second columns.

They were being surrounded by more noisy drinkers and thick cigarette smoke. The girl behind the bar was frothing up two beers and tried to make herself heard above the din.

"What can I get you two gents?" she had to shout. "It's always like this on a Sunday night."

"Oh," said Crown. How long had he waited for this moment? He licked his lips around the words as he tried to remember every crazy one of them. Then he spoke.

"Gimme a visky Ginger Ale on the side. And don' be stingy, ba-be."